THEMES IN DRAMA

An annual publication
Edited by James Redmond

3

DRAMA, DANCE
AND MUSIC

CAMBRIDGE UNIVERSITY PRESS

CAMBRIDGE

LONDON · NEW YORK · NEW ROCHELLE

MELBOURNE · SYDNEY

Published by the Press Syndicate of the University of Cambridge
The Pitt Building, Trumpington Street, Cambridge CB2 1RP
32 East 57th Street, New York, NY 10022, USA
296 Beaconsfield Parade, Middle Park, Melbourne 3206, Australia

First published 1981

Set, printed and bound in Great Britain by
Fakenham Press Limited, Fakenham, Norfolk

British Library Cataloguing in Publication Data
Themes in drama.
3: Drama, dance and music
1. Drama – History and criticism – Periodicals
I. Redmond, James, b. 1937
809.2   PN1601   80–40883

ISBN 0 521 22180 3

Contents

REVIEW SECTION

CONTRIBUTORS

Jules Aaron, *Professor of Theatre, California Institute of the Arts*

Jean-Pierre Barricelli, *Professor of Romance Languages, Chairman of the Department of Literatures and Languages, University of California, Riverside*

Laura Brown, *Professor of English, University of California, Riverside*

Geraldine Cousin, *Department of Theatre Studies, University of Warwick*

Alun Davies, *Department of English, Bedford College, University of London*

Warwick Gould, *Department of English, Royal Holloway College, University of London*

Bernard Gredley, *Department of Classics, King's College, University of London*

Wendy Hilton, *Division of Dance, The Juilliard School, New York*

Andrew Kennedy, *Visiting Fellow, Clare Hall, Cambridge*

Frits R. Noske, *Professor of Musicology, Instituut voor Muziekwetenschap, Universiteit van Amsterdam*

P. G. O'Neill, *Professor of Japanese, School of Oriental and African Studies, University of London*

Pierluigi Petrobelli, *Department of Music, King's College, University of London*

S. Gorley Putt, *Fellow, Christ's College, Cambridge*

Christena L. Schlundt, *Professor and Chair of Dance Department, University of California, Riverside*

June Smith, *Division of Theatre, University of West Virginia*

Themes in Drama
future volumes and conferences

The first five volumes in the series *Themes in Drama* are

    1 *Drama and Society* (published 1979)
    2 *Drama and Mimesis* (published 1980)
    3 *Drama, Dance and Music* (published 1981)
    4 *Drama and Symbolism* (forthcoming 1982)
    5 *Drama and Religion* (forthcoming 1983)

Papers are invited for the following volumes, and should be submitted in final form to the Editor before 1 February in the year indicated (potential contributors are asked to correspond with the Editor well in advance of these dates):

    6 *Drama and the Actor* (1982)
    7 *Drama, Sex and Politics* (1983)
    8 *Historical Drama* (1984)
    9 *The Theatrical Space* (1985)
  10 *Farce* (1986)

Themes in Drama conferences, 1982

Annual conferences are held at the University of London and at the University of California. The subject each year is that of the volume in preparation. The 1982 conferences will be on 'Drama and the Actor'. The London conference will take place on 2, 3, and 4 April. Papers should be submitted, by 1 February, to the Editor, from whom application forms for attendance at the conference will be available from 1 November 1981.

James Redmond,
Editor, *Themes in Drama*,
Department of Drama,
Westfield College,
London NW3 7ST

Illustrations

Editor's preface

This is the third volume of *Themes in Drama*, which is published annually. Each volume brings together reviews and articles on the theatrical activity of a wide range of cultures and periods. The papers offer original contributions to their own specialised fields, but they are presented in such a way that their significance may be appreciated readily by non-specialists. The review section is unusually important, since reviewers have much more than customary scope to give detailed critical accounts of drama in performance, and to discuss in depth the most significant contributions to scholarship and criticism. The section entitled 'Forum' provides an opportunity to debate questions of general interest, including those raised in earlier numbers of *Themes in Drama*. Each volume indicates connections between the various national traditions of theatre by bringing together studies of a theme of central and continuing importance.

The present volume considers some of the ways in which text, dance, and music have been related in dramatic performance. Whatever may have been the case in the theatre of fifth-century Athens (and it must have varied considerably in this respect) our ignorance has for centuries encouraged western artists and critics to accept the Athenian theatre as the great exemplar where drama brought together the different art forms in an over-all harmony. We have some of the words of Aeschylus, Sophocles, and Euripides and their best plays have set the highest standards in western theatre for dramatic literary texts to emulate; but we know very little of their music and dance, and our dream has been of dramatic performances where there was a splendid unity of purpose and effect. Similarly in the East, as P. G. O'Neill emphasises with regard to *nō* drama, the ideal of the *Gesamtkunstwerk* has long been cherished: from its medieval origins the ideal of *nō* drama has been to achieve its effects 'by an inseparable blend of music, dance and text' (see p. 113).

The ideal is irresistibly beautiful in its unity, but the reality has been very problematic. Rather than complementary, words and music and dance have usually been in conflict for dominance. Our modern forms – the stage play where music and dance are absent or incidental, opera where language and dance are subservient, ballet where words (spoken or sung) are excluded – demonstrate the mutual antagonisms which have never been avoidable. The dream of total theatre with words of great power, music of intense force, and bodies moving with freedom and elegance, has not commonly been realised. We have been obliged to settle for much less, partly because of our limited ability to respond to theatrical stimuli: our capacities for emotional, sensuous and aesthetic response are themselves limited, and since Socrates it has been recognised that they have a limiting effect on the response of our moral intelligence. In the middle of the eighteenth century, Lord Chesterfield was merely giving an aphoristic turn to a truism when he wrote to his son: 'Whenever I go to an opera, I leave my sense and reason at the door with my half guinea, and deliver myself up to my eyes and my ears.'[1]

Our first paper is on Bertolt Brecht, whose attitudes towards music in drama were contradictory. He felt its enormous power with unusual sensitivity, and he was one of the twentieth century's great lyricists, but what for Chesterfield was material for yet another carefully wrought sentence, and what for W. H. Auden was a fact to be accepted with placidity – 'No good opera plot can be sensible for people do not sing when they are feeling sensible. The theory of "music drama" presupposes a libretto in which there is not one sensible moment or one sensible remark'[2] – was for Brecht a danger to be shunned with violence. Brecht, as a writer of dramatic texts, is forced to speak with fear of the power of music and with intellectual and moral loathing of some of its emotional effects:

> A single glance at the audiences who attend concerts is enough to show how impossible it is to make any political or philosophical use of music that produces such effects. We see entire rows of human beings transported into a peculiar doped state, wholly passive, sunk without trace, seemingly in the grip of a severe poisoning attack. Their tense, congealed gaze shows that these people are the helpless and involuntary victims of the unchecked lurchings of their emotions. Trickles of sweat prove how such excesses exhaust them. The worst gangster film treats its audience more like thinking beings.... Such music has nothing but purely culinary ambitions left. It seduces the listener into an enervating, because unproductive, act of enjoyment. No number of refinements can convince me that its social function is any different from that of the Broadway burlesques.[3]

Brecht's sensitivity to music ensured that he sought and found men of musical genius to collaborate with, but his sense of music's power to turn words into mere noise made him fearful of the collaboration. Joseph Addison's squib 'Nothing is capable of being well set to music that is not nonsense'[4] amusingly suggests the main grounds for Brecht's fear, and Brecht is so very *un*amused in his negative account of the power of music because the conflict had long been waged with extreme earnestness in Germany. Nietzsche is the key figure, and he expressed many contradictory opinions, but one interesting example puts Brecht's outburst in useful context. In the spring of 1871, when he had just finished *Die Geburt der Tragödie aus dem Geiste der Musik* (*The Birth of Tragedy out of the Spirit of Music*), Nietzsche asserted with his customary violence that opera is music and nothing but music, that the singers themselves are musical instruments, that the action in opera is contemptible hocus-pocus, that the composer should not allow himself to be distracted by the words or by the gestures of *his* marionettes, that the music must never serve but must always over-whelm the text.[5]

Auden, in his cool Anglo-American way, makes a very necessary distinc-tion:

> Poetry is in essence an act of reflection, of refusing to be content with the interjections of immediate emotion in order to understand the nature of what is felt. Since music is in essence immediate, it follows that the words of a song cannot be poetry. Here one should draw a distinction between lyric and song proper. A lyric is a poem intended to be chanted. In a chant the music is subordinate to the words which limit the range and tempo of the notes. In song, the notes must be free to be whatever they choose and the words must be able to do what they are told ... There have been several composers, Camp-ion, Hugo Wolf, Benjamin Britten, for example, whose musical imagination has been stimulated by poetry of a high order. The question remains, how-ever, whether the listener hears the sung words as words in a poem, or, as I am inclined to believe, only as sung syllables. A Cambridge psychologist, P. E. Vernon, once performed the experiment of having a Campion song sung with nonsense verses of equivalent syllabic value substituted for the original: only six per cent of his test audience noticed that something was wrong ... in listening to song (as distinct from chant), we hear, not words, but syllables ... In song, poetry is expendable, syllables are not.[6]

The validity of this distinction was emphasised late in 1979 by two contrast-ing productions of the Brecht/Weill *Mahagonny*. In New York John Dexter's production for the Metropolitan Opera was dominated by first-rate musi-cians rendering 'songs' and the evening was one of aesthetic delight; in Jules Aaron's production in Southern California – the subject of our first paper – there was a series of lyrics 'chanted' by actors so that the text was dominant and the moral and political purposes were fulfilled. In this respect neither production was at fault: the contrast, rather, indicates the common awk-wardness that when words and music are combined one or the other may be forced to yield in submission. In the former production we heard Kurt Weill's great music (conducted by James Levine) which has syllables supplied by B. Brecht, and in the latter we heard Bertolt Brecht's poetry of political satire served by the music of Weill. The ideal of mutual support and harmonious balance is in this case not realisable: the director must make bold and ruthless choices between the claims of the music and the claims of the text; if neither dominates, the production will be aimless, and we may hear neither words nor music effectively.

A very different case, to take a comparatively rare example where a composer has responded with complete sympathy to a play already written and performed, is *Pelléas et Mélisande*; Debussy's music is in delicate balance with Maeterlinck's text and in performance there is no sense of strife or of submission; the music and words blend in a common purpose. Paul Claudel strove for a similar closeness of purpose in his collaborations with Darius Milhaud:

> I believe we should look for a means of welding together speech and song. Everything grows from the same root, and one thing gives birth to another – feelings, noises, words, songs, cries, and music – sometimes yielding ground, sometimes claiming it. Don't you think it's a glorious idea? . . . I want music that appears to emanate from the words rather than accompany them, passing imperceptibly from the realm of feeling to that of sound.[7]

In our second paper, Bernard Gredley looks briefly at the controversial roles of music and dance in the origins and development of Greek drama, roles which are all the more exciting to the imagination for being beyond the reach of critical appraisal. And, as Alun Davies recounts in our third paper, some men with very excited imaginations initiated the development of opera in late sixteenth-century Florence when they set out 'to create a new fusion of drama, dance and music after the manner of Greek tragedy' (see p. 31). Before discussing the first great genius of opera, Monteverdi, Alun Davies shows how the central debate about the rival claims of words and music in opera was advanced by the very first men in the field. Jacopo Peri, for example, who composed much of the music for *Dafne* (performed privately in 1597, and the earliest attempt at opera on record), spoke of finding in classical drama his inspiration. He wished to write music which – like Auden's 'chant' music and like Brecht's 'misuc' (see p. 5) – would raise the words of his libretto above the level of conversation, but also restrain itself from rising to the careless, self-preoccupied rapture of the music of what Auden calls 'song'.

The claims of words were in rivalry with those of music from the beginning, but our fourth paper, on Cole Porter, looks in detail at one example of an extraordinarily rare composite art, that of the librettist–composer. Richard Wagner, of course, is the colossus at whose feet the handful of others sit, and Wagner's *Worttondichter* suggests better than any English term the fusion of words and music which is more likely to be achieved when there is one 'poet' of both 'word' and 'tone'. In *Oper und Drama* (1851) Wagner argues that, since the meaning of the words must not be drowned, the musician should normally be at the service of the poet; but the best thing of all is for the same man to combine both functions and achieve a mutual balance.

Cole Porter is the most distinguished practitioner of this composite art yet produced by the American musical theatre, and June Smith places his work in its original context of Broadway musical entertainments before analysing some of his most successful compositions. In Porter's hands the normally very minor form – the song in the modern boulevard music-drama – can be managed to surprisingly subtle effect. His best compositions have a very engaging combination of words and music which together reveal his playful inventiveness and ironic intelligence. Beneath the slight lyric grace there is an incisive referential wit and a good deal of sardonic vulnerability. On the page the words seem thin and flat, for they were never meant for our eyes; but June Smith's analyses demonstrate that Porter was doing what so many successful dramatists have done: he took aspects of the thinking and feeling characteristic of his period, and portrayed them in a variety of 'the bible in pictures' – important experiences were given expression that was arresting and memorable for Broadway audiences. The preoccupation with irony and ambiguity in the communication of personal anguish; the conceits which violently yoke together some contrasting aspects of early twentieth-century experience; the particular use of the past to reflect on the present and of the present to throw peculiar light on the literary past: in these procedures, so familiar in our most distinctive modern poetry, Cole Porter revealed that the American musical had an unexpected potential for intricate sense and complex sensibility.

In our fifth paper Wendy Hilton, a dance historian and professional choreographer, seeks to define what has come to be known as French 'baroque' dance of the seventeenth and eighteenth centuries, to illustrate and discuss contemporary forms of notation, and to encourage us to take an informed, serious interest in recreating and appreciating the earliest stage dances available to us in substantial detail. Christena L. Schlundt, in our sixth paper, surveys the extraordinarily active world of dance in America in the 1970s. The most obvious difference between British and American theatrical performance is that British actors in general have more aptitude and better training in speaking (which is especially apparent, of course, in verse plays and the 'classics'), while American actors are superior in every aspect of stage movement. Professor Schlundt's 'personal view' indicates the enormous interest in America in all forms of theatrical dance, and charts the work done in hundreds of small companies and university departments throughout the nation, as well as honouring the major individual talents and the New York City Ballet, which is the greatest dance jewel in the crown of the western world.

As is the case with Greek tragedy, *nō* drama combines poetic texts of very high literary quality with music and dance. P. G. O'Neill in our seventh paper does for *nō* drama what we would also much desire for any Athenian play. In each instance, in the absence of performances to see and hear, most of us are aware of these plays in the shadowy form of printed literary texts. Professor O'Neill sensitively charts, in the performance of *nō* drama, the constantly changing relationships among the elements of music, dance, and text. There is a familiar distinction between what in this context is called 'strong song', with a limited musical scale and simple, plain melodic patterns, and 'weak song' which employs a wider musical range and a more complicated scale system with much more variety of melody. With respect to dance, too, Professor O'Neill is able to indicate the wide variety in content and style; and his conclusion is perhaps the conclusion that would emerge from a similar detailed analysis of an Athenian tragedy in its original performance: the crucial visual images of movement and dance in magnificent robes supplement the literary text, while music is the element which holds the whole play together. 'It is clear how meagre the text alone must be, as representative of *nō* as a whole. It may be poetry – at least in the original Japanese – but it is not *nō*' (see p. 113).

In 1913 W. B. Yeats was introduced to *nō* drama, and he reacted with great enthusiasm to its combination of speech, song, music, dance and costume. He had for some years been working towards such a form: he had often referred admiringly, for example, to Wagner's use of Germanic legend in his music-dramas; but what he learned of *nō* drama suggested a quieter, more intimate dramatic form which would use ancient national materials in a way more suitable to his temperament. He developed his new form of musical dance-drama in *At the Hawk's Well* and in most of his later plays. What thwarted him, in an enterprise which nevertheless produced some of the finest verse plays in English in our century, was the lack of an appropriate tradition of performance. He could not design the productions, write the music, or create the dances and, although some collaborations were promising – such as those with the Japanese dancer Michio Ito and Edmond Dulac, who designed masks and costumes – he could not regularly overcome the difficulties. What we have are texts still waiting for adequate music, choreography and performance. Towards the end of his life, Yeats wrote:

> I wanted all my poetry to be spoken on a stage or sung and . . . I have spent my life in clearing out of poetry every phrase written for the eye, and bringing all back to syntax that is for the ear alone. Let the eye take delight in the form of the singer and in the panorama of the stage and be content with that.[8]

The sad fact is that, although he hoped to create a continuing tradition where dramatic text would be in harmony with dance and music, his plays have almost no existence for us except on the page: in our review section the piece on Yeats's dramatic imagination (an exulting phrase with a sad undertow) can refer to no adequate realisation of the plays. Like Greek tragedy, they exist in our minds as composite works of art, but they are available only as texts and, to paraphrase P. G. O'Neill's judgement with regard to *no* plays, it is clear how meagre the texts must be as representative of the *imagined* drama.

Our eighth paper, on romantic opera, reacts to a very recent formulation of the argument we have heard from Nietzsche, Brecht, and Auden that music is essentially antagonistic to the verbal text: Jean-Pierre Barricelli follows Peter Conrad in his very wide-ranging discussion of the various art forms relevant to opera – dance and the representational arts as well as the literary forms of drama, epic, romance, allegory, and the novel.

That dance and music have been crucial in most ages of the theatre is clear: but without adequate means of notation or recording, our predecessors could not pass their theatrical arts to us in their complexity. Very few dances were ever given notation and even with respect to music full, intricate notation is comparatively recent. The kinds of musical analysis offered in our two final papers are possible only for modern work. Pierluigi Petrobelli examines the opening of the third act of *Aida*, and offers some general conclusions about the ways in which text and music can sometimes combine to create the finest dramatic effects in grand opera. The collaboration between Verdi and Ghislanzoni in the creation of *Aida* was unusually close and fruitful and, taking it as an especially interesting example, our ninth paper shows how the libretto and the music make their joint contributions to defining the dramatic action.

Frits Noske's elegant comparison of the opening scene of Beaumarchais's *Le mariage de Figaro* with that of Mozart's *Le nozze di Figaro* and his comparison of Shakespeare's *Othello* with Verdi's *Otello* enable him to indicate the great range of dramatic effects that can be achieved through music. In the comic opera's opening scene Mozart takes Beaumarchais's very plain words and uses them as base material to create a moment of music which is rich in emotional content, in character delineation, and in the initial presentation of the opera's feminist theme (see p. 147). The words contribute almost nothing. Of course Beaumarchais as a writer of dramatic texts was as aware as Brecht was to be – but with more quietude and good humour – of the conflict between words and music on stage. In the second scene of *Le barbier de Séville*, for example, the jovial Figaro in the process of composing a song excuses the awkward and banal words that come to him on the grounds that contemporary writers of operas are never expected to use language idiomatically or even meaningfully: in fact, he tells us on behalf of his ironical author 'Aujourdui, ce qui ne vaut pas la peine d'être dit, on le chante.'[9] Figaro is confident that when his verse jingle has musical accompaniment it will pass for profound thinking.

As Professor Noske persuasively argues, Mozart does not 'adapt' *Le mariage de Figaro* or set the play to music. Instead, he takes over Beaumarchais's words (in de Ponte's translation) and, as Nietzsche would say with approval, overwhelms them with his music; the words are reduced to mere syllables.

... Da Ponte's text largely corresponds with that of Beaumarchais. But actually this is misleading, as it concerns two essentially different functions of a single medium. The Frenchman creates a drama through words; on the other hand, the Italian, through words, offers the composer the opportunity to create a drama. (See pp. 147–8.)

Professor Noske's next comparison develops the argument further in that it matches genius with genius. In *Otello* we have not an adaptation of Shakespeare's play but a newly created masterpiece of musical drama. Boito's words 'render the plot' and the drama is in the music. This, the last paper in the main body of the present volume, ends with a complaint that since the Second World War opera has often suffered under the dictatorship of the stage director. Our first paper is by a director who records his attempt to 'create the *Mahagonny* that *Brecht* had in mind' by suppressing the 'operatic' nature of the piece (see p. 24). But our first and last papers are not as contradictory as this opposition suggests. It is true that Frits Noske is a musicologist asking for directors to be less meddling with operas and that Jules Aaron is a director who refused to allow Weill's music to reduce Brecht's words to what Professor Noske calls 'verbal material'. But there is ample scope for such difference in approach for, although the ancient ideal is of perfect harmony, in reality compromise is often necessary. When the collaboration is between Mozart and Da Ponte or between Verdi and Boito the case is not in doubt: the text is sure to be the servant of the music and we would not have that changed. In Greek tragedy perhaps, in *nō* drama, in Gilbert and Sullivan, or Wagner, or Cole Porter there is often a genuine balance. In the Brecht/Weill collaborations there were two artists whose interests in the end were not the same. *Mahagonny* must be performed either for the music or for the words, and in that respect it is representative of the majority of cases.

The theme of the present volume is the very wide range of different ways in which text and movement and music can combine or conflict in drama; the material is extremely voluminous and our ten papers consider a handful of interesting examples where the main issues are raised.

In the review section S. Gorley Putt's article reacts to the studies by Ronald Huebert and Mark Stavig in offering an appraisal of the dramatic art of John Ford. Laura Brown, in responding to the books of Peter Holland and Robert D. Hume, offers an historiographical analysis of the criticism of Restoration drama since the early eighteenth century. Warwick Gould takes Andrew Parkin's book and a new edition of *A Vision* (1925) as starting points in his consideration of Yeats's dramatic imagination.

In the forum section Andrew Kennedy, in his reply to Michael Anderson, takes up and develops the discussion of the mimetic function of dramatic language which was a central aspect of the theme of our second volume; and in her 'Note on mimesis' Geraldine Cousin uses the Stanislavski and Brecht street scenes to emphasise some crucial distinctions made in that volume. Contributions for the forum sections of future volumes will be welcomed.

James Redmond
Editor, *Themes in Drama*

Department of Drama
Westfield College
University of London
London NW3 7ST

NOTES

1. Lord Chesterfield, *Letters to his Son and Others* (London: J. M. Dent & Sons, 1929), p. 252 (23 January 1752).
2. W. H. Auden, *The Dyer's Hand* (New York: Random House, 1962), p. 472.
3. Bertolt Brecht, *Brecht on Theatre: the development of an aesthetic,* edited and translated by John Willet (New York: Hill and Wang, 1964), p. 89.
4. *The Spectator,* 21 March 1711.
5. 'So gewiss auch die Musik nie Mittel, im Dienste des Textes, werden kann, sondern auf jeden Fall den Text überwindet: so wird sie doch sicherlich schlechte Musik, wenn der Componist jede in ihm aufsteigende dionysische Kraft durch einen ängstlichen Blick auf die Worte und Gesten seiner Marionetten bricht ... Die Oper in diesem Sinn ist dann freilich im besten Falle gute Musik und nur Musik: während die dabei abgespielte Gaukelei gleichsam nur eine phantastische Verkleidung des Orchesters, vor allem seiner wichtigsten Instrumente, der Sänger, ist, von der der Einsichtige sich lachend abwendet.' *Nietzsches Gesammelte Werke,* 23 vols (Munich: Musarion Verlag, 1922–9), III, 352.
6. *The Dyer's Hand,* pp. 472–3.
7. Paul Claudel, *Claudel on the Theatre,* ed. Jacques Petit and Jean-Pierre Kempf, trans. Christine Trollope (Coral Gables, Florida: University of Miami Press, 1972), pp. 74, 99.
8. W. B. Yeats, *Essays and Introductions* (London: Macmillan, 1961), p. 529.
9. Pierre Beaumarchais, *Théâtre [sic] Complet de Beaumarchais,* ed. G. D'Heylli and F. de Marescot, 4 vols (Geneva: Slatkine Reprints, 1967), II, 33.

On directing *Mahagonny**

JULES AARON

The opera *Aufstieg und Fall der Stadt Mahagonny* showed the application of the new principles on a fairly large scale. I feel I should point out that in my view Weill's music for the opera is not purely gestic; but many parts of it ... represent a serious threat to the common type of opera, which in its current manifestations we call the purely culinary opera. The theme of the opera *Mahagonny* is the cooking process itself. (Brecht)[1]

Cash alone won't breed passion. (*Mahagonny*)[2]

CONCEPTION

Brecht spoke of the conventional theatre in general, and opera especially, as being 'culinary': plays and operas were dished up for the appetites of the audience, digested easily, then passed through the system. The effect of music on stage was to intensify the irrelevance of the performance: at best, conventional drama was damned by a smothering emotionality, but the superaddition of music meant the exclusion of both reality and sense:

> The irrationality of opera lies in the fact that rational elements are employed, solid reality is aimed at, but at the same time it is all washed out by the music. A dying man is real. If at the same time he sings we are translated to the sphere of the irrational. . . . The more unreal and unclear the music can make the reality . . . the more pleasurable the whole process becomes: the pleasure grows in proportion to the degree of unreality.[3]

His musical collaborations with such unconventional geniuses as Kurt Weill, Paul Dessau and Hanns Eisler tended to subordinate the role of music – the most emotional of the arts – to the philosophical and social purposes of his parables. Brecht spoke of creating *Lehrstücke* which were to be absorbed but not digested: examples of an anti-culinary art which promised to satisfy the appetite and palate, but which would not settle in the stomach.

* Jules Aaron directed *Mahagonny: A Musical Epic* on the Riverside campus of the University of California in November 1979. This is the first of a continuing series of contributions to *Themes in Drama* in which theatre artists will discuss their work in detail.

In the majority of his plays, Brecht used music as a commentary on the
action. The songs were to help create the *Verfremdungseffekt* – loosely translated as 'alienation', but more specifically a distancing of the spectator's
critical intelligence from the emotional sweep of the work.[4] The success of
this intended effect of Brecht's epic style (with its use of placards and
projections, series of short scenes that interrupt the emotional flow, scenery
which comments on the action, abrupt lighting shifts, direct address to the
audience) is debatable. Can these devices neutralize the emotional effect of
Gayly Gay's transformation in *A Man's A Man,* Galileo's decision to send his
masterwork, the *Discorsi,* with André, or the mute Katrin's beating the
drum for help in *Mother Courage?*

All Brecht's plays were to some extent conscious collaborations. Friends
and professional researchers surrounded him continually, and Brecht, like
a cook himself, culled what he needed for the artistic stew. The nature of the
success of these collaborations is also debatable. Lotte Lenya wrote about
the opening of *The Threepenny Opera:*

> Berlin was gripped by *Threepenny Opera* fever. Everywhere even in the streets,
> the tunes were whistled. A Threepenny Opera Bar was opened, where no
> other music was played. Immediately all sorts of scribblers imitated to death
> the 'Brecht Style' and the 'Weill style', or what they understood by these
> words.[5]

The Threepenny Opera was the one great popular success of the team, and
more than any other of their works it came to represent the Brecht/Weill
collaboration in the public's mind. But the irony is that *The Threepenny
Opera,* with all its seedy quality, is decidedly *palatable.* It is charming; it is
developed around characters that are three-dimensional and empathetic.
While they are clearly products of the capitalist society that we are invited
to despise, they nonetheless exude the various charms of the bourgeoisie.
Brecht's *deus ex machina* – Victoria's messenger saving Mac from execution –
is, of course, meant to be ironic. The whores and thieves assure us that
happy endings do not occur in real life. Yet, in *The Threepenny Opera,* as in
Mother Courage, these trappings are not sufficient to distance our feelings
from the mute drummers helplessly caught in the sweep of history.

Of all the Brecht musicals, *The Rise and Fall of the City of Mahagonny* makes
the most effective use of distancing techniques. It is constructed around a
series of Brecht song–poems first published in *Hauspostille* in the early
twenties. The original music was by Brecht in his typical ballad form and
the material was refashioned with Weill in 1927 into six songs for the
Baden-Baden festival. Ultimately, *Das Kleine Mahagonny* (the *Songspiel*) was
expanded into the full-length opera in 1929 and proved to be the controversial end to the Brecht/Weill collaboration (although the men discussed
future projects until Brecht's death). The production was simultaneously

cheered and booed at its première in Leipzig in 1930. The combination of musical styles derived from cabaret, opera, blues, jazz and the ballad makes the score the most striking in the canon. It is a cult favorite of Brecht/Weill enthusiasts, but is not often performed.

The story line of *Mahagonny* is simple. Widow Leocadia Begbick and two cohorts, Fatty the Bookkeeper and Trinity Moses, while heading up an American coast looking for gold, decide to found the city of Mahagonny when they run out of gas. They create a city of nets, an analogue of Berlin in the late twenties and thirties or, for that matter, of a contemporary Las Vegas, Hollywood, New York, or any city where the spirit of capitalism dictates the way of life. The story revolves around the confrontation of Begbick and Jim MacIntyre, who is a European version of an archetypal American, as are his companions. The men are the four musketeers from Alaska, who after seven long years of work have arrived in Mahagonny to spend their money on whisky, women, food and fighting. The geography of the play is intentionally confused. Logically, the locale would have to be California, yet names like Atsena and Pensacola indicate Florida. *Mahagonny* is no more specifically about California than *Happy End*, *Arturo Ui* and *St Joan of the Stockyards* are about Chicago, or *The Threepenny Opera* about London.

Mahagonny is Jim MacIntyre's story, as the Widow announces in the fourth scene of the twenty that comprise the opera. Jim and his friends, as well as the founders of the city and Jenny and the whores (the sharks of Mahagonny), learn about the limitations of total freedom. After a hurricane 'miraculously' bypasses Mahagonny, their motto is 'anything goes'. The inhabitants indulge themselves to the fullest in all the physical pleasures; two of Jim's friends kill themselves, one by overeating, and the other in fighting. Jim himself is executed for committing Mahagonny's one unforgivable sin: he cannot pay his bill. After his execution, 'amid increasing confusion, rising prices, and the hostility of all against all', the people futilely demonstrate for their ideals. But by not leaving the city of pleasure as others have done, they have sealed their own fates: their sin has been participation.

Mahagonny is a modern morality play, a parable of good tempted by evil, and there is a weak innocence behind the capitalistic lust of the inhabitants of Mahagonny. Jim keeps threatening to leave, but because of peer pressure, and his own inability to break away from the city's lure, he stays, continually denouncing what he sees, while still participating. He is a reactionary speechmaker irrevocably tied to the system he denounces. As in some medieval morality plays, hell is always present on stage. And Jim as Everyman is in the end pathetically Christ-like. In the finale of the *Kleine Mahagonny*, the Widow's last words, 'For Mahagonny is just a made-up word' are forcefully ironic: the whole point of the piece is that Mahagonny does indeed exist and is representative rather than extraordinary in its values. The play emerges as more than a Marxist polemic against capitalism; it is a tract against man's surrender to the ideals and the allure of the Mahagonnys of the world.

Of all Brecht's plays, the libretto of the opera is the most cynical, and the most consistently Marxist. In his critical theorizing, Brecht argues that we must resist the emotional sugar of conventional entertainment, the sentimental allure of its theatrical dinners; nevertheless in his other plays he often supplies a feast that is tempting in the traditional way. The Mackies, Peachums, Pollys and Jennys in *The Threepenny Opera* seduce us with their fleshed-out charms, their intricate and warm characterizations and their attractive melodies. Galileo, Mother Courage, Begbick (of *A Man's A Man*), Puntila, Grusha, Shen Te, and Azdak, are either quite conventionally sentimental or they are *disarming* in their cunning duplicity: we may not often condone the actions of Brecht's negative characters, but we frequently admire their endurance and feel for them.

Mahagonny provides no opportunity for these positive emotional reactions. The landscape is intentionally flat, with only enough background to give the characters simple motivations – and definitely not enough to create the textual complexity and vividness of *The Threepenny Opera*. The surface is two-dimensional and the doctrinal strokes are bold in color and execution: there is not one conventionally appealing character in the play, and the rogues are not endearing.

The music, viewed as a series of songs, defies culinary, empathetic connections. The repetitions of the 'Alabama Song', the haunting harmony of 'Benares', and the cabaret/blues of 'Jenny's Song' are hypnotic; yet while their discordant harmonies, unconventionally melodic lines and surprising rhythm changes momentarily engage, they still defy easy retention. We are fascinated and temporarily moved by the music and lyrics, but the individual songs have the allusive darkness of Rothko, the deceptive quality of Ensor's masks, the lingering resonance and horror of Munch.

The music constantly turns on itself. The raging hurricane music parodies grand opera; Jim's distressful lament, 'Deep in Alaska', is a travesty of saloon music; 'Jenny's Song' burlesques cabaret; 'Off to Mahagonny' and 'Five Bucks a Day' flout traditional marches. The quirky rhythms and dissonant harmonies never allow us to relax. Just when we think we are comfortable with the music, it disturbs us with atonal six-part harmonies, accelerates into a tango, begins to wheeze like a harmonium or dwindles off into melancholic nothingness.

The music is like the script: it promises everything but delivers nothing palatable. The range of musical styles is enormous, and yet we never get any one thing substantial enough for us to sink our teeth into. The disparateness in music and book, combined with the bizarre portrayal of a stereotypical

America, keeps us at a crucial distance. Even at the moments of greatest passion, as when Jim expresses his desire to leave Mahagonny, all Brecht lets him whine is 'Oh fellas, I'm sick of being human' ('I Could Eat My Hat').

While *Mahagonny* attempts to attack culinary culture through the use of culinary devices, the overall ironic use of operatic music is not successful. As Brecht wrote in *Mahagonny* in 1931:

> Why is *Mahagonny* an opera? Because its basic attitude is that of an opera: that is to say, culinary.... The opera *Mahagonny* pays conscious tribute to the irrationality of the operatic form.... *Mahagonny* may not taste particularly agreeable; it may even (thanks to guilty conscience) make a point of not doing so. But it is culinary through and through. *Mahagonny* is nothing more or less than an opera.[6]

As Lenya commented in an interview during the telecast of the Metropolitan Opera première on 27 November 1979, Brecht was startled and dissatisfied when he first heard the *Mahagonny* music with an orchestra: 'But Brecht didn't realize that opera is music. It is the most important element.'

Early in his career, Brecht invented the word 'misuc' to describe a non-culinary use of music, one which avoids the emotional complacency of concerts and opera. However, his musical collaborators were not as certain of its justifiability or success. As Hanns Eisler, his collaborator on *The Measures Taken*, wrote:

> For a musician it is difficult to describe misuc. Above all it is not decadent and formalist, but extremely close to the people. It recalls, perhaps, the singing of working women in a back courtyard on Sunday afternoons. Brecht's dislike of music ceremoniously produced in large concert halls by painstaking gentlemen in tails also forms a constituent of misuc. In misuc nobody may wear tails and nothing may be ceremonious. I hope I am interpreting Brecht correctly when I add that misuc aims at being a branch of the arts which avoids something frequently produced by symphony concerts and operas – emotional confusion. Brecht was never ready to hand in his brain at the cloakroom. He regarded the use of reason as one of the best recreations.
> Brecht's strivings for reason in music are a heavy blow for us musicians. For in the case of music, where is reason? I have friends who would not go through fire in the cause of reason in music.
> Writing these lines, I recall that Brecht accused me of having a sceptical and condescending attitude towards misuc, his invention. Unfortunately he was right.[7]

Following Brecht's ideas, Weill envisioned each operatic scene as a separate musical entity: 'The music was not designed to move the story forward; instead, as each step forward was taken, a new musical situation was created. Such was the principle on which the opera was built.'[8] But fully orchestrated and taken as a whole, Weill's ironic, parodic music is indeed culinary, seldom resisting the seductive influences of Wagner, Mozart, or Mahler when they arise.

The Metropolitan Opera production – with its first-rate operatic voices (so unlike those of the singer–actors who played in the Leipzig or Berlin *Mahagonnys* in the thirties) and its powerful orchestra – offered such extreme culinary delight that one's mind was numbed. The director, John Dexter, succumbed to the wonders of Weill's score, which was beautifully played and sung: we were swept away on a flood of startling music. As film critic, Andrew Sarris points out in a discussion of Joseph Losey's film version of *Don Giovanni*, there is tension in the best opera between the ideas and music:

> One finds the same fruitful tension between Brecht and Weill, between Gilbert and Sullivan, between Lerner and Loewe. Time and again, bitter, acerbic, cynical words are lifted aloft by winged melodies as men's cerebral and emotional sides struggle for domination. Literature comments ironically on music, but in opera it is music that is invariably triumphant . . .[9]

For a production of *Mahagonny* to fulfill Brecht's intentions, the director must make choices more radical than when to use the half-curtain, project backdrops, or make scene divisions. Brecht, above all, was pragmatic. He and Weill reset the *Mahagonny* music for Lenya, who was more an actress than singer. Brecht would often rework characters, scenes and indeed entire plays. (*He Who Says Yes* became *He Who Says No* in deference to the feelings of the student cast who performed the work in 1930.) For a man who borrowed from such disparate sources and who in such a cavalier fashion 'adapted' Shakespeare, Marlowe and Gay, no holds were barred; and the director of *Mahagonny* must find a theatrical correlative for Brecht/Weill's operatic artifices, indulgences, parodies and flights of fancy.

The theatre is, of course, all artifice. Behind the most realistic decor is a stage hand pulling a fly, reading a newspaper, or waiting to go home. The essential quality of the theatre is its unreality. And that precisely is the lesson of *Mahagonny*. The city does exist, but it does not exist as it appears. The thinness of the libretto is an asset to the director, and *Mahagonny* is a Brechtian masterpiece precisely because of its flat, two-dimensional quality. Like Brecht, we must promise the audience something which we never intend to deliver. The meaningless excesses of Mahagonny are to be paralleled by the meaningless excesses of the theatre.

PREPARATIONS

The *Mahagonny* at the University of California, Riverside, was based on the six songs of the *Kleine Mahagonny* – 'Alabama Song', 'Off to Mahagonny', 'Five Bucks a Day', 'Benares Song', 'God in Mahagonny', 'Finale' – together with the transition music. Dialogue and additional music from the opera were also used and the production was given the title *Mahagonny*: *A Musical Epic*.

Of all the *Mahagonny* translations Michael Feingold's was chosen as a basis, since it is the most theatrical, most decidedly American and most forcefully ironic. The cast numbered eighteen (for musical balance I added a fifth 'musketeer', Goodtime Charlie, to lend a strong bass line to the lumberjacks' songs). The orchestrations were based on the *Kleine Mahagonny*. There were thirteen pieces in the orchestra with heavy emphasis on woodwinds and brass – clarinet, saxophone, trombone and trumpets.

The large theatre of the university has an excellent 500-seat auditorium, a computer lighting board, good fly space and a large scene shop behind the stage with motorized central doors. Four physical spaces were used in the production: an area in front of the theatre and a conventional proscenium and auditorium for the first act; arena seating on stage for most of the second act; the trial and final scenes were set in the scene shop. This use of the theatre parallelled the rise and fall of the city within the play. The audience comes to the theatre expecting to be entertained by 'theatrical reality', and as the nature of Mahagonny becomes more apparent, so does the physical working of the theatre itself. The audience comes to see, but is led to see through, the subject of the play and the means of presentation.

The overall look of the sets, as designed by Christopher Andrews, suggested Southern California – or more more specifically, Palm Springs, the notoriously 'glamorous' resort which is close to Riverside. The first act sets were alluring in an operatic way: the supports, however, were quite visible. The second act used wagons backed by murals, even more evident in their operation. The final scenes, in the shop, employed scaffolding and risers, the most makeshift and theatrically-undisguised of all the settings.

The time period was late gold-rush (around 1910), a time for a wide range of fashions: the costumes, as designed by Marc Langois, caught the women's tailored elegance and the dapper quality of the men's three-piece suits; a potpourri, exotic look for the whores; a frontier look (buckskin, flannel, vests) for the lumberjacks from Alaska.

As Brecht suggests, the acting in his plays must have a basis in reality and yet in effect be distanced, simultaneously representing and commenting on the action: 'every gesture signifies a decision; the character remains under observation and is tested'.[10] It is a difficult style to create or sustain. While there are realistic objectives at stake, the actor/character is nevertheless always aware of the audience/clients in the theatre/city. The actors should suggest other options of behavior, yet they must temporarily commit themselves to their immediate goals and decisions.

A graduate seminar, 'The World of the Play', and special acting projects in playing Brecht, were offered simultaneously with the production. The seminar student who played Fatty wrote about the role:

The key came when the director commented that Fatty and Begbick were too likeable, were having too much fun with each other. From that point on, Fatty's attitude needed to change toward Begbick. Fatty and Begbick's use of each other is without affection and functions solely on a business basis. Their physical relationship is only one aspect of this arrangement. If at any time it stopped being mutually beneficial, their association would end.

I'm not sure that I succeeded in making a personal commentary come through. My feelings as an actor were in direct opposition to the desires of the character. How does one communicate such conflicting attitudes? Jules suggested I look at the role in the specific context of each scene, and decide how to focus on the attitudes and simultaneously, to step out of the frame and comment, as an actor, through physical gesture, tone of voice or body line.

Acting in Brecht depends on the details which help both to focus the choices and to suggest the paradoxes. Fatty always wore his hat and vest, and always had his cigar, even when making love or boxing. Trinity was never without his elegant flask and cane. In Brecht's poem, 'The Old Hat', the young actor playing Filch in *The Threepenny Opera* puts a great deal of thought into selecting the right hat to convey the nuances of the 'professional Beggar'. He is torn between two hats and finally chooses one: it is the right hat, but still he is not satisfied. Brecht speaks with admiration of how the actor selects his props with extreme care. An old toothbrush peeping out of his pocket makes Brecht react with delight, since it is a sure sign of the actor's powers of observation and deduction – the main powers of the natural scientist.

This 'actor of the age of science' is what is required for playing Brecht. In *Mahagonny*, the overall style of playing was zestful in movement, yet world-weary in spirit. While the characters tried to make the best of every situation, everyone had a suitcase or carpetbag ready. They were an expedient group, ready to move on at a moment's notice.

PRODUCTION

Scene 1: The founding of the city of Mahagonny
The members of the audience are told that the first scene will take place outside and that no one will be allowed in the theatre. They wander around casually, buying their tickets, meeting friends and so on. On sold-out nights, when people wait for names to be called for returned tickets, a sense of hawking arises before the show starts. The front of an old battered pick-up truck can be seen around the corner from the theatre. Some of the crowd examine it. Expectation of some kind of theatrical event begins to grow.

At 8.15 a scoop light is turned on, flooding a central area in front of the theatre. People move outside from the comfortable lobby, uncertain where to stand. The effect of the truck's being an actual truck in an actual street is undercut by its starting up next to the theatre and being treated 'as if' it had been driven a long way. As the headlights go on, the truck, driven by Fatty, moves away from the theatre, around a group of trees, then lurches uncertainly towards the audience and jerks to a stop: the motor appears to have died. 'Goddamn it. Anytime anything happens, it's always my responsibility', says Trinity, as he climbs out of the truck. He opens the hood to investigate and burns his hand on the dead motor.

Fatty pokes his head out of the open window; he and Trinity consider the difficulties of going on. The audience gathers around, amused by their Absurdist banter. The opening exchange in the play could very well be from *Waiting for Godot*. In this version the plaintive tones we have come to associate with Gogo and Didi are heavily Americanized, but Brecht's gangsters, who pre-date Beckett's tramps by three decades, are in the same bind. The same geographical stalemate metaphors the same moral and spiritual slough:

> *Fatty the Bookkeeper.* Hey, we gotta keep going!
> *Trinity Moses.* But the motor's had it.
> *Fatty the Bookkeeper.* Yeah, then we can't keep going.
> 　[*Pause*]
> *Trinity Moses.* But we gotta keep going.
> *Fatty the Bookkeeper.* But there's only desert up ahead.
> *Trinity Moses.* Yeah, then we can't keep going.
> 　[*Pause*]
> *Fatty the Bookkeeper.* In that case we gotta turn back.
> *Trinity Moses.* But the constables are after us, and they know our faces from one pore to the next.
> *Fatty the Bookkeeper.* Yeah, then we can't turn back.
> 　[*They sit down on the running board and smoke*]
> *Trinity Moses.* You know they've found gold up on the coast.
> *Fatty the Bookkeeper.* Yeah, that's one long coast.
> *Trinity Moses.* Yeah, then we can't head up that way.
> *Fatty the Bookkeeper.* But they have found gold up there.
> *Trinity Moses.* Yeah, but the coast is too long.
> *Mrs Leocadia Begbick.* Can't we keep going?
> *Trinity Moses.* No.

A blanket in the back of the truck moves. Elegantly-dressed, Widow Begbick stands, adjusts herself and evaluates the situation. She decides to make the best of it: 'Okay, then we'll stay right here. I've got an idea. If we can't make it up there, let's stay down here.' She takes an electronic sports megaphone from her bag – like the truck, a blatant anachronism – and announces in a flat voice: 'Scene 1 – The founding of the city of Mahagonny'. She signals Trinity to give her a note from the pitchpipe and sings *a cappella:* 'Then we might as well build a city here / And we'll call it Mahagonny / Which means Spiderweb' – the only singing in the first

1 *Mahagonny*, scene 1. Fatty the Bookkeeper, Widow Begbick, and Trinity
Moses

scene. Fatty and Trinity are tortured by her 'aria'. She retaliates by
becoming overtly physical in her approach to Fatty (see plate 1). Through
this use of sexual 'business' between Widow and Fatty, we are made to
understand that they are unimpassioned, expedient lovers. In their operation, Begbick is the brains and Fatty keeps the books; Trinity pimps the
girls.

As the Widow speculates on the nature of an 'ideal' Mahagonny, Fatty
and Trinity begin to box. Fatty grabs a pole to strike Trinity, but Begbick
deflects the blow, seizes the stick and hooks an old-fashioned corset to the
top of it – a flag fashioned by the founder of the city of Mahagonny. They
look at the theatre before them. The Widow picks up the megaphone and
invites the audience to follow them into the theatre, promising everyone a
good time. Fatty carries her off the truck over his shoulder.

Once inside the theatre, the audience faces a stark, black asbestos fire-
curtain within the proscenium arch. While the audience is being seated, the
orchestra plays the 'Kleine March' from the *Songspiel*. Latecomers are
harassed by the Widow. Begbick orders the orchestra leader to stop play-

ing. The scene ends when the three 'founders' are lit in a 'freeze' before the
fire-curtain, stage left. The Widow breaks and walks to the proscenium
wall, where a followspot lights her face, as it will for each scene announcement. The house lights are still on.

Scene 2: *The discontented of all the continents headed for Mahagonny, city of gold*

The Widow announces the scene then hangs the megaphone on a coat rack.
The lumberjacks, Jim MacIntyre, Bank Account Bill, Jack O'Brien, Alaska
Wolf Joe and Goodtime Charlie, burst into the auditorium through the left
audience door; they are picked up by a spotlight (the convention for all the
songs). As they make their way onto the stage, they sing 'Off to
Mahagonny'. The Widow, also in a followspot, encourages and harasses
them. Their movements are stylized – in effect choreographed – as is the
blocking for all the songs. This convention emphasizes the songs' commentary on the action. The men settle in a freeze stage right, as does Begbick,
with the founders, stage left.

Scene 3: *The city grew quickly in the weeks that followed and the first 'sharks' drifted into town*

Jenny and five whores come hustling through the opposite audience door.
(Both the lumberjacks and whores initially seem startled to see the
audience/clients.) Jenny, a 'real pro', immediately sings the 'Alabama
Song'; the other whores adjust themselves haphazardly, then join her for
the chorus, at the same time off-handedly propositioning individuals in the
audience. Their effect as whores is built on contrasting actions: the six
women drape themselves across the end seats of the rows, parade through
the aisles with parasols, position themselves across the front of the audience
and finally freeze alluringly center stage. As they talk–sing the three
choruses – 'And must have whisky/boys/money / Oh you know why' – we
are attracted by their seductive semi-nude bodies, while at the same time
held at a distance by their business-like expressions and tough, calculated
manner.

Scene 4: *Among the many who came to Mahagonny at that time was Jim MacIntyre, and it is his story we want to tell you*

With the three groups frozen on stage, the fire-curtain rises, accompanied
by a drum roll to elicit audience applause for the, implicitly promised,
spectacular set. Andrews' first act settings, however, are two-dimensional
profile pieces (combining greens, lavenders, turquoises, and cream, against
black) of palm trees and Southern Californian architecture, suggesting
Palm Springs. The spectacle of the elaborate scene painting and
opera-height sets framed by a profile piece portola, is undercut by rods

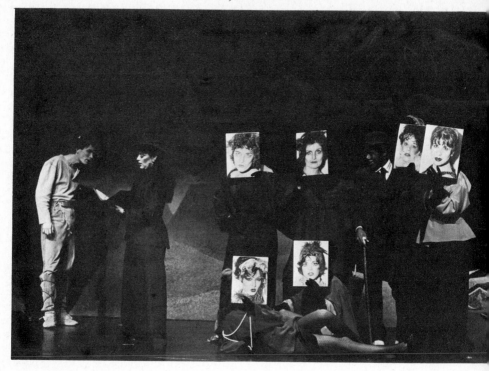

2   *Mahagonny*, scene 4. Jim would like to see more than pictures

obtrusively holding together the set pieces. A row of exposed lighting
instruments hangs overhead; there is no masking of the offstage area.
Behind the rear black scrim, rows of chairs can dimly be seen. A huge
golden moon hangs behind the profile pieces during the first act, lighting
each scene change. The mechanics are never hidden from the audience.

At the beginning of scene 4, the whores prepare themselves for business
by covering their faces with 11 × 14-inch glossy photographs of their faces, a
theatrical cliché which comments on their business veneer as well as Jim's
comment that he needs to see more than pictures before he is willing to pay
cash (see plate 2). Jenny's 'Havana Song', where she tries to get a higher
price from Jack O'Brien, becomes a broad music-hall tango (in a
followspot), with Jenny leading and mechanically manipulating an unimpressed Jack. He offers her ten dollars less. Jim, however, is intrigued by
'Jenny Smith from Oklahoma'. The scene ends harshly. Jim's firm 'I'll take
you' is undercut by Jenny's cool 'Chin up, Jimmy', while she grabs his
crotch.

Scene 5: Instruction

The 'instruction' scene becomes an ironic musical counterpoint to the last gesture of scene 4. In a followspot with the moon glowing behind them, Jim and Jenny mime-walk in place, skilfully giving the illusion of movement: the Brecht actor is called upon for a wide range of theatrical expertise. The delivery of the words is lyrical, mocked by their salacious content:

> *Jenny.* Then there's the matter of my lingerie, Jim. Should it be fancy under-
> wear or should I just skip the undies?
> *Jim:* Skip the undies?

While continuing the duet, Jenny obligingly leaves the spotlight and takes off her underpants in the semi-darkness, returning for the last musical exchange. She passively presents the lace underwear to Jim and the spot-light blacks out.

Scene 6: All great enterprises have their crises

The scene takes place in the moonlit bar, The Sign of the Rich Man. The new profile piece flies in while the first one flies out. (During all scene changes, the actors carry in the minimal pieces of furniture needed.) Begbick announces the scene in a followspot. Because business is failing, the Widow initially decides to leave Mahagonny, but changes her mind when Fatty shows her a newspaper article about the constables' search for her in Pensacola. The scene's overall irony is sharpened by its location between two musical scenes. A sense of expediency dominates the scene, and the tension is heightened by the actors' preoccupation with commonplace activities.

When the scene opens, Fatty and Trinity are playing gin: finishing the game is their objective. The Widow enters in her bathrobe, epitomizing the city's salacious vulgarity which is quite empty of any real sexuality. Begbick tries unsuccessfully to get Fatty's attention by placing her carpetbag on the table, then settles for getting dressed while loudly bemoaning her fate to the audience: 'The struggle for existence has turned me into an empty shell.' Her anguish is a travesty: she stands muttering in black bloomers while her partners play cards. Finally dressed, she tries to drag Fatty off with her. He shows her the newspaper article, slaps her on the behind and returns to his card game. Undaunted, Begbick, to regain her hold on business activity in Mahagonny, invents the fact that two suckers have arrived who may have money. Only then do Fatty and Trinity show any interest. Fatty silently extends his hand, pulls Begbick onto his lap, spits out his cigar and kisses her. Trinity takes a drink.

Scene 7: All true seekers shall be disappointed

Jim, bored and disillusioned, attempts to escape Mahagonny. The action takes place in the same bar, a musical counterpoint to the previous scene. Jim's four friends await him. Two of them are playing cards. Like Begbick,

Jim enters with a suitcase, on his way out of town. The actors' actions are again paradoxical. The opening of the song, 'I Could Eat My Hat', is a barber-shop quartet, sung by Jim's friends, praising the peace and contentment of Mahagonny. It is staged with stylized gestures, sung *a cappella*: the four men attentively watching the conductor for musical cues. Jim's reaction of 'There's something wrong', refers both to the inappropriateness of the style of music, and to the lumberjacks' advice which ignores Jim's heartfelt disenchantment. They push him into a chair while seductively outlining the glories of Mahagonny.

Jim's subsequent song reinforces his desire to leave ('I think I just might drive to Georgia'). It is staged mockingly to play against the engaging rhythm of the chorus ('The ABC's of drinking now are yours') and the fact that his friends are physically preventing him from leaving. A large chair which swivels on castors is used, and Jim's friends literally 'take him for a ride' – not away from Mahagonny but back and forth across the stage, menacingly brandishing a hangman's rope ('We're beating you black and blue, Jim / Till you decide that you Jim / Are human'). Jim's repeated 'Oh fellas I'm sick of being human' punctuated by his standing and snarling out the high note on 'fellas', becomes painfully comic. At the end of the song, the chair and Jim are – absurdly – exactly where they started. His friends crowd around the chair and in unison deliver the scene's last words, 'Come back to Mahagonny like a good boy.'

Scene 8: 'Kindly be careful with my chairs.' 'No rough stuff.' 'Avoid
          offensive songs.'

The scene changes to the street, accompanied by a bar-room-style cadenza on the piano. Trinity serves drinks to Jim, Jenny and the lumberjacks. Jim argues with the pianist in the orchestra pit, urging him to play something else. He drags Jenny away from flirting with Joe then begins 'Deep in Alaska', an angry lament about the hardships endured there. In the sentimental arrangement of the music, as well as in the reaction of Jim's four friends, the song is parodic. They react as if the song were a *shared* validation of their friendship: during each verse the lumberjacks attempt to hum along. Jim's anger builds and he begins to abuse them physically; they are nonplussed, until he takes out a gun. The music continues after the song, threatening to do so for ever, and Jim vents his anger by shooting the piano player. The old, clichéd joke is contrasted by the convincing noise and smoke of the gun. He fires again, which brings Begbick out. She enters grudgingly, half-dressed, followed by Fatty, who is himself trying to get dressed. The Widow is unimpressed by Jim's complaint that 'there is too much a man can depend on in Mahagonny'. The others freeze during Jim and Begbick's confrontation – to undermine the sentiment and emphasize Jim's immobility.

Scene 9:   A hurricane is moving toward Mahagonny
Scene 10: On this night of horrors a simple lumberjack named Jim
MacIntyre discovers the laws of human happiness

The moon profile piece is flown out, and the last three scenes of the first act are played against a 'rain curtain' (layered strips of transparent plastic which create a 'wall' of cool blue, shimmering light). The build in the fugue-like hurricane music is travestied by the cast entering in various stages of undress, forming a striking group picture just in time to sing the first notes of the most operatically scored music in the work – 'How frightful! A disaster! / The town of pleasure will be doomed!' The group assumes 'horrified' freezes while a three-part contrapuntal interlude is sung. The cast finally moves into a tight formation in stylized *commedia* manner, holding a terrified freeze in an expanding spotlight until the end of the song.

The next scene begins with Jenny plaintively reprising the 'Alabama Song' chorus *a cappella*. Jim's desperate energy contrasts with the others' lethargy and fear. The only moment of excitement is when the Widow rejoices at the news that everyone, including the constables, has been killed in Pensacola. An acting problem presents itself in the scene when Jenny subsequently joins Jim in urging the others to sing – something which has been forbidden in Mahagonny. The actress must deliver the lines ironically, *indulging* Jim. (They are all going to be killed anyway.) The song's key lyric – 'If there's got to be kicks, then I'll give them / And the kicked one, believe me, will be you' – refocuses the debate about singing forbidden songs. Defiantly singing, the entire cast moves to the edge of the stage, and pointing at the audience, freezes.

A profile piece of a large world globe, with the cities printed in large letters, is lowered. The cast separates into two groups to frame the map. A stage hand walks behind it to operate the lights. It is the first time that we openly see a stage hand. The Widow announces the progress of the hurricane. As usual, the blank, amplified delivery of announcements by Begbick contrasts with the melodramatic action on stage (and has become progressively more comic, underlining Brecht's point).

The cast watches the hurricane's progress out over the audience, rather than on the map, and reacts with stylized, frantic gestures, taking freezes during each of Begbick's announcements. White lights trace the path of the hurricane and a red light indicates when a city is hit. When the hurricane bypasses Mahagonny, the crowd is momentarily overjoyed; the map flies out and the stage hand exits. With the delicate opening of the 'Rescue Song', however, the cast turns angelically to the audience, undercutting their relief with the complex, soaring chorale, 'O Glory, what a rescue'. But as the song builds, like a Bach cantata, their calculated innocence builds to sensuality, as they *share* their relief. By the song's last notes, they have moved into an undulating group stage center, enclosed by Trinity's out-stretched arms, his back to the audience. He turns slyly and winks at us on the last note.

The Widow pushes her way out of the mass of people, and looking back longingly at the group, she staggers to the proscenium arch to announce dryly 'From then on the motto of the people of Mahagonny was, "Anything goes!" ' The motto has economic and ideological force but its immediate expression is in physical terms. Dehumanized, a mass of tightly-packed bodies, the actors begin to touch each other while moaning erotically. Slowly the remaining profile pieces fly out. This catches the attention of the cast, and the group begins to break up. They smile knowingly at the audience and move off stage in small 'intimate' groups. The house lights come up. We see the rows of seats on stage facing a raised platform upstage against the closed shop wall. Begbick walks stage center and tells us, 'Okay, folks, you've got fifteen minutes to do . . . whatever. Then I want you to get your asses back on stage.' The stage lights come up. The Widow walks off stage, and stage hands begin to clear the props and furniture left in the wings and put up more seats. The orchestra – the pit is on an elevator – is brought up to stage level. There is a fifteen-minute intermission.

Intermission

The audience seats itself on stage, arena style, facing the twelve-foot-square playing area. The Assistant Stage Manager checks last-minute details. The musicians move into place in the raised pit (which is now behind the audience). The audience's perspective is changed. They are now in close proximity to the action. The make-up is the same as in the first act, but it looks heavier up close; all the lighting instruments are visible; we can see the seams in the costumes, and exactly how each piece of scenery is changed. Stage artifice has been replaced by uncomfortable immediacy. The acting seems broader, more stylized. We see the crew in headphones in the doorways in the scene shop wall. The play becomes more transparent, pointedly about the mechanics of Mahagonny and the theatre. Each scene ends with a harsh moment of 'reality' to jar with the theatricality. As Peachum says in *The Threepenny Opera*, 'Since this is opera, not life, you'll see / Justice give way before humanity.'[11]

The Widow enters through a side door behind the audience. She is dressed opulently. A successful year has passed in Mahagonny. She banters with the audience: 'Did you have a good time? Ready for more?' She stands center stage on the platform, signals to the Stage Manager in the light-booth, and the shop wall rolls open fourteen feet revealing a hanging black backdrop masking the shop. Two whores stand ready. 'Okay, girls', says Begbick, and they set up a 'lip', which will connect the second act wagons to the platform. The Widow tells the audience, 'We're going to have lots to eat, plenty of loving, a nasty fight and plenty to drink.' (This synopsis seems to emphasize Brecht's abandonment of traditional plot suspense, but the Widow's promises will again prove empty.) Begbick walks up stage next to the platform to a step unit with a stool (and the same coat tree from act 1) and announces the scene in a followspot.

Scene 11: *Hectic activity in Mahagonny about a year after the great hurricane*

From the side proscenium doors behind the audience the men come up the aisles singing what we will call the 'Men's Vamp', which outlines the four activities in Mahagonny – eating, fornicating, fighting, drinking – with the tag line, 'But mainly get it through your head / That nothing is prohibited'. They form a line across the back of the platform. Blackout. The four morality scenes which follow are the heart of the play.

The Widow intones 'Eating' into the megaphone, and we see the crew and cast push out the 'Eating' wagon. (Each of the four morality wagons is backed by a large mural depicting the activity involved. The style of the painting is glamorous compared to the actions played on the stage.) To the strains of the 'Eating Song' (like a Viennese waltz, played on the chord organ and mandolin), Jack O'Brien begins eating voraciously, gorging himself on (undisguisedly plastic) meats and fruits. The men urge him on, sharing his 'performance', until he eats himself to death. As they sing the barbershop-quartet coda, 'Brother Jack has departed / See his look of sheer ecstasy!', Charlie lifts Jack's head. A realistic green film of food covers his tranquil face – realistic detail over artifice. Tobby Higgins, the undertaker, measures the body (which will become a repeated, progressively nastier piece of business). Undaunted, the men complete the dirge. Biblical tableau. Blackout.

Scene 12: *Loving*

As in the 'Eating' segment, Weill's music in this 'Loving' scene provides an ironical counterpoint to the action. These two scenes have no spoken lines. 'Loving' builds through the seductive tango rhythms of the 'Mandalay Song', a sly piece of music that pointedly comments on Brecht's lyrics: 'Spit out your chewing gum first / Then give your hands a good washing', is spoken/sung by the Widow, then repeated by the men. The men stand in a line along one side of the platform; the downstage man sits in a chair. An elegant settee, a whore lying across it, graces the wagon. The Widow sits on a stool across from the men. During the opening music, the whores parade around the perimeter of the platform, leaning out over the audience. The men grab lustily for the women as they pass by, though the men themselves appear detached: the whores and clients are going through a ritual. Their

3   *Mahagonny*, scene 12. Their bodies tell us one thing, while the clinical lyrics
and singing tell us another

bodies tell us one thing, while the clinical lyrics and singing tell us another
(see plate 3).

   Appropriately, the rhythm of the song is tortuously slow and the men
ironically repeat the impossible instructions *ostinato*: 'Fellas move faster'.
The men's repetitions of Begbick's lines are accompanied by a march step
which creates diagonal formations, a chorus line commenting on the intensity of the words. The Widow does an impassive tango with Fatty and when
he chooses a whore she pointedly detains him until he pays. Each chorus of
'Will the moon shine every night over you, Mandalay?' is sung in a repeated
barber-shop-quartet formation, while another whore and client leave. A
new customer sits in the chair and another whore occupies the couch.
During the final chorus five couples stand around the periphery of the
platform, the whores perfunctorily moving as the men impassively sing the
romantic lyrics. The lights begin to fall and with the last notes, two spots
pick up Jim and Jenny sitting and waiting – like any whore and client –
thereby hardening the scene's 'lesson'.

Scene 13: Fighting

As the boxing ring is set up, the men repeat the 'Vamp', and the whores and men gather to watch Alaska Wolf Joe foolhardily fight Fatty. 'Anything goes' in Mahagonny. Jim bets on Joe, but Bill refuses ('when it comes to cash . . .'). Again, my direction of the scene places the sentimental relationship between Joe and Jim in contrast to the horrible indignities of a fight which is murderously one-sided. The black irony is emphasized by the men fighting in their symbolic costumes: Alaska Wolf Joe in his ever-present fur hat and Fatty in shorts (pulled over long underwear), vest, hat and cigar. Trinity impassively watches the fight, openly holding a crowbar; Fatty ultimately grabs it and smashes Joe's head. Jim and Bill help Charlie to lift Joe onto his shoulders. (The undertaker measures Joe's body.) Fatty stops the men, looks at Joe's face (trick blood streams across his forehead): 'Sorry about that', he says, through his cigar. The scene ends on an overly-sentimental note, as Jim and Bill, in two spots, sing the 'Vamp' as a dirge, with Joe's hat held mournfully by Jim.

Scene 14: Drinking

Scene 15: In those days Mahagonny was already full of people in search of another, better city: Benares. But Benares was visited by an earthquake

Scene 16: 'If there's got to be kicks, then I'll give them. And the kicked one, believe me, will be you.'

The 'Drinking' wagon is pushed in. Jim's disgust at Joe's senseless death sets up the men singing 'If you had five bucks a day/You could live in Mahagonny.' The march tempo of the music is emphasized by the over-choreographed, vaudeville group-movements of the men. The *a cappella*, mournful humming at the end is mitigated by a 'barber-shop' tableau, again suggesting a comradeship which does not exist. The Widow untangles herself from a loveless, 'passionate' embrace with Fatty to stop the humming. 'Pay up, gentlemen' is directed to Jim. Jim implores the unresponsive Bill and Jenny to give him money; he'll head back up to Alaska because he doesn't like this town. Freeze.

The lights dim halfway, and the 'Benares Song' begins scene 15. A distanced version of Jim's personal story is presented. Jim remains frozen during the song, but the Widow, Jenny, Bill, Charlie and Trinity drag stools and chairs down stage to sing the haunting three-chorus song of a town bereft of whisky, phones and life: 'There is not much fun on this star.' The languid musical movement here complements the inactivity. 'Johnny' is changed to 'Jimmy' in the repeated, 'Let's go to Benares /To Benares Jimmy let us go.' With Jim sitting frozen in the background, as the others sing of the impossibility of escape, the song is a nightmarish, slow-motion enactment of Jim's despair. During the last notes of the song, the

others resume their original positions, the freeze at the end of the drinking
scene.

With the Widow's announcement, the action of the drinking scene
resumes. The 'Benares Song' has served as a 'lesson', a counterpoint to the
action: there is no escape by leaving Mahagonny. Jim is trapped. Neither
Bill nor Jenny will give him money. ('The things they ask us girls to do.')
Everyone, except Jenny, exits to take Jim to trial. The wagon is moved off,
and Jenny starts to leave the platform, then reconsiders. She snaps her
fingers for a spot light, drops her shawl provocatively and begins to sing the
'Kick' song herself.

The song, with its blues tempo and *Sprechstimme* introduction, is ironically
the same 'forbidden song' of scene 10. The song is now about getting back to
business: Jim is a lost cause. As Jenny sings defiantly about who will be
'kicked', she wanders through the audience, passing out pictures of herself
with her name and phone number. She sits on men's laps, sexually provok-
ing them, rewarding them with a sneer. During the last chorus, she adjusts
her makeup and hair in a hand mirror which reflects the audience as well.
With her last line, 'And the kicked one will be you!' she signals the spotlight
off with a snap of her fingers and exits into the black.

Scene 17: The courts in Mahagonny were no worse than anywhere else
With the trial, Mahagonny is stripped of its last veneer: Justice is strictly
business. The shop wall opens fully, and the black backdrop opens simultaneously to reveal the entire scene shop. The Widow, Trinity and Fatty are
seated in the middle section of a scaffold that is twenty-four feet high. The
others sit in bleachers facing the audience. The paint frame at the rear of the
shop electrically brings a series of irregularly-placed white flats to form a
backdrop. The wagons, lights and stage hands are undisguised. The Widow
is putting on her judge's robe (her bathrobe turned inside out), and for the
first time is caught unawares by a scene change. She impatiently signals for
the spot and announces the scene.

Trinity opens the scene by re-establishing the audience's role as custom-
ers at a theatrical *Mahagonny*. He moves about the platform in front of the
shop hawking tickets to the trials. There are never any takers: we also sense
the empty ritual of 'justice'. He gives us 'the finger', and the trial begins.
Except for the last three lines of the scene, there is no music. Again, the cold,
unemotional action of the scene is calculated to prevent or at least mitigate
involvement with Jim's fate.

The activities of the court and spectators are self-centered. Some read,
some flirt, others embroider. Fatty meticulously paints the Widow's
toenails and Trinity files his fingernails: metaphorically it is a scene about
personal hygiene. The health of the perverse city itself is in critical condition. Tobby Higgins, the Undertaker, during his trial, barters with the

Widow (by holding up fingers to signal the amount of the bribe), but making the deal is an empty ritual. The others do not even pay attention. Tobby is acquitted of murder because the injured party will not come forth to testify: 'The dead don't tell no tales', comment the spectators wearily, in unison. Stylization of the sentimental and self-conscious melodrama is used consistently in the scene to underline Brecht's derision of 'capitalistic justice'.

There is a murmur of interest, especially from the women, when Jim is brought forward to be tried: Jenny has obviously not been the only one admired by Jim. Like Tobby, Jim is placed on the stage platform, his back to the audience. The charges and bartering go on, but Jimmy cannot bargain without money. Although Jim and Bill repeatedly rhapsodize about the 'seven years in Alaska', Bill is still practical 'when it comes to money'. By the third and last time they repeat the refrain, everyone, including the orchestra members, chants in unison about those wonderful times in Alaska. Also, Jenny's entrance as the injured party – 'compelled with cash to commit a carnal act' – dramatically hushes the crowd. She walks across the shop dressed in an iridescent black dress and veil, stops before Jim, throws off her veil, and says in a hushed voice, 'I'm the one'. With a pointed glance, she forces another whore to move so she can sit next to Bill. By the end of the next scene it is clear who her current client is.

When the Widow unrolls a floor-length sheet of charges against Jim, the spectators' reactions are stylized in rhythm, yet convey mixed feelings to both the charges and punishment. Only Jenny coolly faces the audience without displaying emotion. The punishment is light for Jim's major offenses, but for drinking three bottles of whisky without paying, the verdict is death. This is underscored by Begbick, Fatty and Trinity singing the last three lines *a cappella*: 'In the whole human race / There is no greater criminal / Than a man without money.'

> *Scene 18: Execution and death of Jimmy MacIntyre. Many people may prefer not to witness the execution of Jimmy MacIntyre here following, but in our opinion even they would not want to pay his bill. So great is the respect for money in our times.*

For the first time, the spotlight remains on Jim during the blackout between scenes, while the Widow makes her announcement in another spotlight. The ritualistic goodbyes between Jenny and Jim are accompanied by the 'Instruction' music played on the piano. The sentiment is undercut by having Jim and Jenny's two farewell kisses accomplished by Jim lifting his handcuffed hands over Jenny's body in order to kiss her. The cast freezes as they attempt to overhear the farewells.

Jim's long climb to the top of the scaffolding, where the electric chair awaits him, is accompanied by the 'Vamp' softly sung by the entire cast staggered across the length of the shop, their backs to the audience. Jim clears his throat and waits until he has everyone's attention. His last speech literally outlines the culinary disappointments of Mahagonny – 'I ate and was still hungry. I drank and was still thirsty.' It is delivered as a self-conscious 'speech', underscoring the emptiness of words in Mahagonny. In response to his last pathetic request, 'Could somebody give me a glass of water?' Trinity places the helmet on him and he is electrocuted in a burst of stylized light accompanied by a dissonant chord from the orchestra.

Scene 19: God in Mahagonny

'God in Mahagonny' is played as a separate scene, a strong, typically Brechtian statement used here as a transition between Jim's execution and the finale. Like 'Benares', it offers a general comment on the action of the play. Musically, the song shows an Eastern influence in its dissonant narrative of God's response to life in Mahagonny. The Widow tells the audience that the 'God in Mahagonny' play is for their edification. Begbick, Jenny, Fatty, Trinity, Bill, Charlie and Tobby perform it as an Oriental puppet show, wearing plastic half-masks which distort their features.

During the repeated choruses, the tight formation of actors slowly moves down stage toward the audience, rhythmically paralleling the build in the music. Two men carry a rolled-up banner which they slowly unfurl, revealing the words, 'God in Mahagonny'. Actors appear and disappear from behind the sign. The attempted Eastern stylization – through body movement, freezes and vocalization – is gradually dropped in the course of the four-verse song. By the time Fatty, who plays God with hat and cigar, tells the inhabitants of Mahagonny that they are going to hell, the oriental veneer of the play is completely gone: they are no longer playacting. They shout to God, 'You can't drag us down to hell / Cause we've been in hell for years already.' Jenny breaks from the group, rips off her mask, crosses the platform into the audience: 'No, they said, the people of Mahagonny!' The others rip off their masks and angrily repeat the line. During the musical transition to the 'Finale' they defiantly confront the audience unmasked. As they walk back to the shop, black-and-white slides, depicting the poverty and desperation of city life, flash across the back panels.

Scene 20: Amid increasing confusion, rising prices and the hostility of all against all, those not yet killed demonstrated during the last weeks of Spiderweb City for their ideals — they had learned nothing.

The finale of the *Kleine Mahagonny* musically conveys the emptiness of Spiderweb City. The cast is divided into two intersecting groups, resignedly moving back and forth across the shop. After the music begins, Jim climbs down from the top of the scaffolding and from the middle level he and

Trinity (both in followspots) sing the lead lines: 'People only dream of Mahagonny.' The moving group freezes and faces the audience each time they echo the words of the lead lines. By the last chorus, Jim and Trinity have joined the strikers.

During the last chorus, Begbick, in a spotlight, walks onto the platform to speak–sing: 'But Mahagonny does not exist / Mahagonny is just absurd/ Mahagonny is only a made up word.' The spot goes out and she joins the others. As the music unwinds to a hauntingly dissonant conclusion, the actors begin to take off their costumes, and the stage hands start to strike the set. The shop wall slowly closes. Simultaneously, the proscenium fire-curtain *behind* the audience is lowered, closing off the orchestra with the last notes. The audience is isolated, trapped in darkness. They applaud; then, the onstage work lights come up suddenly. Nothing happens. Thirty seconds later the side stage doors are opened and they are ushered into the parking lot. Like the inhabitants of Mahagonny, they have paid their money, and have received nothing tangible in return: 'Mahagonny is just a made-up word.' They have been enticed into, through, and out of the theatre.

IN RETROSPECT

Brecht specifically intended Mahagonny to suggest Berlin of the late twenties and early thirties, but the metaphor is general in its application. The 'city' also represents Southern California in the eighties: a land of plenty with everything promised, but where earthquakes, gas shortages and energy crises lurk behind a sunny veneer. Though the rebalancing of the music and text for this Southern Californian *Mahagonny* changes the 'landscape', the commentary is focused where it should be, on the ideas. Brecht's theatre remains anti-culinary.

As Brecht wrote, *Mahagonny* requires innovation:

> Perhaps Mahagonny is as culinary as ever – just as culinary as an opera ought to be – but one of its functions is to change society; it brings the culinary principle under discussion, it attacks the society that needs operas of such a sort; it still perches happily on the old bough, perhaps, but at least it has started (out of absent-mindedness or bad conscience) to saw it through ... and here you have the effect of the innovations and the song they sing.

Real innovations attack the roots.[12]

Mahagonny: A Musical Epic willfully attacked the roots of conventional 'culinary' musical drama; it emphasized, as Brecht vowed to do in subsequent works, 'the didactic more and more at the expense of the culinary element. And so to develop the means of pleasure into an object of instruction, and to convert certain institutions from places of entertainment into organs of mass communication.'[13] The production attempted to create the *Mahagonny* that Brecht had in mind.

NOTES

1. 'On the Use of Music in an Epic Theatre', *Brecht on Theatre*, trans. John Willett (New York: Hill and Wang, 1964), p. 87.
2. Bertolt Brecht, *Collected Plays*, vol. 2, ed. Ralph Manheim and John Willett (New York: Vintage Books, 1957), p. 117. The translation of *Mahagonny* is by Michael Feingold.
3. 'The Modern Theatre is the Epic Theatre', *Brecht on Theatre*, pp. 35, 36.
4. See 'Alienation Effects in Chinese Acting', *Brecht on Theatre*, pp. 91–9.
5. Lotte Lenya-Weill, 'Threepenny Opera', *Brecht As They Knew Him*, ed. Hubert Witt (New York: International Publishers, 1974), p. 62.
6. 'The Modern Theatre is the Epic Theatre', *Brecht on Theatre*, pp. 35–6.
7. 'Bertolt Brecht and Music', *Brecht As They Knew Him*, p. 95.
8. 'Notes & Variants: On Texts by Weill', *Collected Plays*, vol. 2, p. 285.
9. Andrew Sarris, 'Films in Focus', *The Village Voice*, 19 Nov. 1979, p. 57.
10. 'Short Description of a New Technique of Acting Which Produces an Alienation Effect', *Brecht on Theatre*, p. 137.
11. *The Threepenny Opera*, *Collected Plays*, vol. 2, p. 225.
12. 'The Modern Theatre is the Epic Theatre', *Brecht on Theatre*, p. 41.
13. *Ibid.*, p. 42.

Dance and Greek drama

A review article by BERNARD GREDLEY

The importance of music, song and dance in the communities of ancient Greece is beyond question. As an influence shaping classical Greek drama their roles were decisive. Tragedy, comedy and the satyr-play, whether performed by actors or chorus, all show the same characteristic blend of spoken word and song and dance. But the texts of Greek plays preserve only the words of the songs; they tell us nothing of the movement and music which accompanied them. How can such skeletal remains be clothed in flesh and blood? Metrical study of the songs does not by itself provide many clues to the musical score or the choreography and isolated remarks by ancient writers assume that the reader can hear the music and see the dances referred to. The sound of fifth-century music is probably lost forever. Indeed we have only one tiny fragment of what is likely to be a classical score (for six lines of Euripides's *Orestes*) and, because of evidently fundamental differences between ancient Greek and modern western music, little can be made of it.

If, then, we will probably never know what the choruses of Greek drama sounded like, can we discover what they looked like and how they moved? Here, Greek vase paintings provide silent but vivid evidence which is often far more illuminating than the rather opaque descriptions of ancient writers. Furthermore, many vase paintings are much earlier than the earliest possible dates for the beginning of organised dramatic performances at Athens and may therefore provide testimony to the character of the pre-dramatic activities which were to grow into fifth-century tragedy and comedy.

Mme Ghiron-Bistagne's book is, as its title suggests, concerned mainly with actors;[1] but in a long and lavishly illustrated appendix she turns her attention to a time before the actor and spoken dialogue had achieved their later importance and argues, from the evidence of vase paintings, that classical Greek tragedy and comedy both originated in performances known as *komoi*.

What is a *komos*? Mme Ghiron-Bistagne isolates three main senses of the word. First, a procession, part solemn, part burlesque; second, a 'chorus' of singers and dancers (evidently those who take part in the procession); and third, a banquet which participants in the *komos* (the komasts) are going to or from. These meanings she describes as 'une realité mouvante', three faces, as it were, of a single prism. A prism still evident in the characteristic behaviour of Greek dramatic choruses who, at the beginning of a play, enter the circular dancing area via a passageway and sing an 'entry-song', remain *in situ* throughout the performance singing and dancing intermittently, and at the end move out of the dancing area, often to enjoy a celebratory banquet. The *komos*, Mme Ghiron-Bistagne believes, provides the essential musical and orchestic nucleus of Greek drama and as such is much older than drama itself.

For the komasts and their dances our earliest evidence comes from Corinthian vases belonging to the end of the seventh century: they show men dancing with legs bent, backs sharply concave so as to accentuate heavily padded bellies and buttocks, arms in a variety of angular positions. The movements of these padded figures correspond to a dance called the *kordax*, a solo performance which we know later from Aristophanic comedy. The dance is vigorously acrobatic and evidently relies more on leg move-ments than on the use of the arms and torso (which was, of course, almost immobilised by the padding). Mme Ghiron-Bistagne rather quaintly suggests that it may have originated in the movements of peasants treading grapes. Almost certainly the padding points to what was originally a fertility ritual.

Many vases indicate that musical accompaniment for the *komos* was provided by the flute (the instrument used *de rigueur* in drama). Was it also accompanied by singing and, in particular, by songs that told a story? If so, did the dancers represent only themselves or might they also impersonate figures in the story? Mme Ghiron-Bistagne has a piece of evidence which strongly suggests that they might. A Corinthian wine jar (see plate 4), dated to the period 600–570 BC, shows two padded figures one of whom dances the *kordax* while the other accompanies him on the flute. Next to them is another figure who is hitting two men trying to steal wine. All these figures have been given names by the vase painter. On the other face of the base, the thieves are being punished in the stocks. If we believe, as we reasonably may, that the two faces of the base tell a continuous story and add that the figures are wearing masks, it becomes almost certain that this vase depicts an early theatrical performance in which music and dance accompany a mimed representation of the story. And the story, Mme Ghiron-Bistagne might have added, is a cautionary tale entirely appro-priate to an occasion involving Dionysus, the patron god of wine and drama.

But the *kordax* is evidently an individual performance. How are we to account for the fact that in fifth-century Athenian drama dancing and

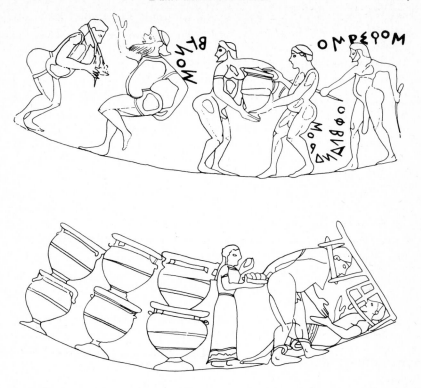

4   Drawing taken from the Corinthian wine jar. From L. Breitholz, *Die Dorische Farce im Griechischen Mutterland*, Studia graeca et latina Gothoburgensia 10 (Stockholm: Almqvist & Wiksell, 1960)

music are associated above all with the chorus, a group who regularly engaged in strictly disciplined and uniform movement? Part of the answer lies in a series of Attic vases, belonging to the years 550–475 BC, which show choruses of animals – more often than not men dressed as animals – performing similar movements to music provided by the flute. These are the predecessors of the animal choruses of Aristophanes's plays and, on one vase, their dance is led by a masked dwarf. If, as Mme Ghiron-Bistagne suggests, this dwarf is the successor to the padded dancers of Corinth but is here attached to a quite different tradition (the zoomorphic cults of Mycene and Ionia), several fundamental questions arise. Is the Athenian comic actor a descendant of padded komasts? Is Athenian comedy a mixture of originally quite separate traditions of song and dance? If so, how did such a mixture come into existence?

Mme Ghiron-Bistagne prefers not to answer such questions because she believes that the origin of comedy should not be discussed in isolation from that of tragedy in which, she claims, the activities of padded dancers were also influential. At this point her argument becomes more controversial, for Aristotle, at least, seems to have thought of the two genres as always separate from each other, as the products of quite different practices. Mme Ghiron-Bistagne, relying on archaeological evidence, begs to differ. She points to a series of sixth-century vases in which komasts are associated with 'serious' scenes from mythology and observes that in some cases the dancers are men dressed as women – a significant point as men always impersonated female roles on the Athenian stage. She further points out that these dancers often seem to assume a mythological identity, posing as satyrs or maenads. She concludes that these vases depict theatrical *komoi* on mythological themes in which the dancers play the part of the chorus and further, that the *kordax*, always described in literary sources as vulgar and comic, had not in the sixth century acquired such a connotation. In short, until the closing years of the sixth century there was a common core of komastic activity, variable in its association with 'comic' and 'serious' themes, which did not diversify into what we know as comedy and tragedy until much later than had previously been thought. To this view there is a serious objection. Given that vase painters were not photographers, are we compelled to believe that the appearance of padded dancers in association with mythological scenes was intended to suggest an organic relationship between the two? Do such vase paintings depict a single event? Mme Ghiron-Bistagne sees the difficulty and admits that in many instances the association is purely decorative but believes that the vase surfaces in question do display cohesive composition. But if her argument is not to be circular, the relationship must be proved independently of the assumed probability of this particular association. No such independent proof is offered.

From her survey of the evidence Mme Ghiron-Bistagne concludes that the separation between tragedy and comedy was not complete until the time of Aeschylus – that is, until the early years of the fifth century. To Aeschylus and his predecessor Phrynichus belongs the credit for the invention of a musical and orchestic tradition which elevated tragedy beyond its popular origins and gave it a success with which comedy, adhering to the more archaic form of the *komos*, could not compete for several decades.

In short, Mme Ghiron-Bistagne's argument is that the sharp distinction between the seriousness of tragedy and the frivolity of comedy is not of great antiquity, that the music and dancing fundamental to them both had no inherent generic associations. Such associations were, on the contrary, due to the activities of early fifth-century poets.

One is left with strong misgivings. Her view makes the apparently sudden but rigid differentiation between tragedy and comedy a mystifying process. And why, it may be asked, did Aristotle have no inkling of this obvious and simple explanation? Without doubt, Mme Ghiron-Bistagne's argument raises questions of fundamental importance. If her answers often lack conviction it is perhaps because she fails to give sufficient weight to such imperfect literary evidence as there is. But her survey certainly has its uses – not the least being that her copious and excellent photographs, which are accurately observed and often imaginatively discussed, will provide a valuable addition to discussions of the origins and nature of dancing in Greek drama.

NOTE

1. P. Ghiron-Bistagne, *Recherches sur les acteurs dans la Grèce antique* (Paris: Les Belles Lettres, 1976). *Appendice*: 'Komos et Komoi. Recherches sur l'origine des acteurs et des genres scéniques', pp. 207–97.

The hellenism of
early Italian opera

ALUN DAVIES

Opera began as an attempt to create a new fusion of drama, dance and music after the manner of Greek tragedy. In late sixteenth-century Florence the Camerata of Giovanni de' Bardi – an informal academy of men with intellectual and aesthetic interests – was concerned to reform music by replacing the excesses of counterpoint with a new style of monody. For all the achievements of ecclesiastical and secular music, there was widespread dissatisfaction with the way in which the many voices and melismatic ornaments of polyphony smothered the meaning of the words. The members of this Camerata, believing that ancient Greek drama had been performed to music of one kind or another throughout – the sections in iambic verse for the main characters as well as the sections in lyric metres for the chorus and sometimes other characters too – looked to it for an ideal of monody which, by melody, harmony and rhythm, would allow the words to predominate in all their clarity and force. Music should aim not simply to give pleasure but to edify and exalt as part of a theatrical experience. In this way the excellence of Greek tragedy would be revived.

In fact, of course, there is no clear evidence to suggest that there was any musical accompaniment of Greek tragedy, except that of the flute to some or all of the speech and movement of the chorus. But various kinds of lyre were used to accompany non-dramatic verse, and sometimes other instruments too, and in general poetry and music were strongly associated. The rhythms of Greek music were closely linked with the metres of Greek poetry, which were themselves controlled by the pitch accent of speech and the quantity (long or short) of vowels, and were often elaborate when they were also choreographic. In sixteenth-century Italy even less was known about Greek music than is known today, but some excitement was caused by the identification in a manuscript in Rome of a few Greek melodies, authentic though post-classical hymns by the Cretan Mesomedes, to the Muse, to Helios and to Nemesis. One of the members of the Camerata, Vincenzo Galilei, referred to them in his *Dialogo della musica antica e della moderna*, and is said to have been influenced by them in compositions of his own, now lost; it is difficult to guess what this influence could have been.

The understanding of Greek tragedy by members of the Camerata must have been partial and their perception of it refracted, but the printed texts of the three tragedians were available, and had been for nearly a century, to those who knew Greek (admittedly few) and several plays had been translated into Latin or Italian. Even if, by modern standards, the line between history and myth was somewhat blurred, as in other ways it had been for the Athenians themselves, at least some of the differences between the nature and circumstances of Greek tragedy on the one hand and the various kinds of Italian musical drama on the other must have been apparent. Yet always there was this blinding radiance that surrounded the achievements of classical Greece, not least when they had to be taken on trust. So that Galilei, for example, could write: 'For all the height of excellence of the practical music of the moderns, there is not heard or seen today the slightest sign of its accomplishing what ancient music accomplished.'[1]

It may be helpful at this stage to offer a brief reminder of some of the relevant aspects of Greek tragedy in order to clarify the differences and similarities between that form and those that led to early Italian opera. The thirty-three plays and many fragments that have survived from the work of Aeschylus, Sophocles and Euripides (and it should be remembered that the poets were also composers of the music) are works in verse of between 1000 and 1800 lines. The form developed from choral hymns and satyric drama. The plays were performed at Athens, taking about one and a half to two hours each, in groups of three followed by a satyr play, in a competition lasting several days, at the expense of a few rich individuals, as part of a religious festival in honour of Dionysus attended by a mass audience. They were a *dramatic fusion* of poetry, music and dancing (the three elements were also found in works that were not dramatic). Music and dancing were probably confined to those parts of the play which were entirely or partly choric. ('Choric' means 'a dance' or 'a group of dancers', and they danced in a circular space called the 'orchestra'.) The role of the chorus, and the proportion of the play it occupied, changed considerably in the course of the fifth century BC, during which all the extant Greek tragedies were written, tending to diminish in relevance and length. But throughout the development of the form, from *The Persae* at its beginning to *The Bacchae* at its end, a clear structure was maintained of dramatic episode followed and preceded by choric songs and dances with varying amounts of interfusion.

The stories were taken from traditional epic or mythical material, rarely from history, and treated of the actions and sufferings, thought and emotions, of heroes and heroines in relation to one another, to society and to the gods. The principal themes were those of love, duty, honour, war and revenge. The tone was high and serious; suggestions of humour were rare. The characters were distanced, and presented as ideal, though credible, types (becoming gradually more naturalistic as the form developed). Masks of various sorts were worn by the actors (there were no actresses) to dramatise emotions and make them visible in a large open-air theatre. Wearing thick-soled boots, they did not move much; expression of voice and significant gesture were of first importance. Use was occasionally made of stage machinery, notably for the intervention of gods and goddesses and the presentation of tableaux. The scenery was simple, but the costumes could be grand and elaborate. The spectacle could be deeply impressive. In his analysis of the elements of tragedy, however, Aristotle put spectacle last, even after music: he regarded both of them as 'pleasurable additions'; less important than the ordering of the incidents (which was primary), the revelation of characters in action, the quality of thought, and the expressive use of words. Tragedy for him was the representation of a serious action bringing about by means of pity and fear the catharsis of such emotions.

This tragic form was part of a vision of classical antiquity that haunted the imagination of many who contributed to the slow growth of what finally became opera, though this is our perspective not theirs. The vision included Greek and Roman literature, mythology, philosophy and history, art and architecture. But although important it was not always dominant, and classical influences on the development of opera must be set against or related to a host of other elements. These would include: the religious services and liturgical plays of the medieval Catholic church; the performances that developed from them, known in Italy as *sacre rappresentazioni*; the secular pageants and festive entertainments of city and court, rich in spectacle and movement; many kinds of song – the *canzonetta*, the *ballata*, the *frottola*, the *strambotto*, the *canto carnascialesco*, and the madrigal, especially the madrigal cycles; and the pastoral play. Opera's formal and thematic links with classical antiquity should be related to this context.

A good place to begin is with Poliziano's *Orfeo*, performed for a festivity in the late fifteenth century at the court of Mantua, appropriately the birthplace of Vergil, then the most revered of ancient poets. The ruling family, the Gonzagas, had long been patrons of the art and culture of the Renaissance, persuaded of the high values of Roman civilisation, which Mantegna represented for them in painting. Poliziano's work may be considered a lyric drama, though in its reliance on dialogue rather than action it is more of an eclogue: a poem for performance with occasional music by solo and chorus (a lament, serenade, finale) with ballet and spectacle. The music is lost. Originally of 434 lines, mostly in *ottava rima* but partly in *terza rima*, it was later revised and amplified and divided into five acts (*pastorale*, *ninfale*, *eroico*, *negromantico* and *baccanale*). The Italian text has occasional lines in Latin given to Orpheus. Poliziano used the story of Orpheus and Euridice as related by Ovid in the *Metamorphoses*, but although he kept the tragic ending (unlike some later versions of the myth) with a disconsolate

Orpheus beheaded by Bacchantes, he made little of his grief over her loss. The legend is given a setting appropriate to a *favola pastorale*. This reincarnation of Greek myth had a symbolic force as glorifying the musician whose songs woke all nature to life and had the power to overcome death. Its significance for the art of the Renaissance and as a precursor of opera is obvious.

In following years several other musical dramas made use of the classical heritage. Giampietro della Viola's *Rappresentazione di Dafne* (Mantua, 1486) and Nicolo Corregio's *Cefalo* (Florence, 1487) had mythological subjects that were to recur a century later. Castiglione, together with Francesco Gonzaga, produced at Urbino in 1508 an eclogue, *Tirsi*, in which *canzonette* were interspersed with passages of declamation. Agostino Beccari's *Il Sacrificio* (Ferrara, 1554), with music by Alfonso dalla Viola, contained a scene where the priest of Pan and a chorus exchanged responses with one another in what is perhaps the earliest surviving example of music integrated with drama: the composer's brother, singing to the lyre and later to a vocal quartet, was the monodist. The same composer also harmonised Alberto Lulli's *Aretusa* and Agostino Argenti's *Sfortunato*, two idylls that attest the continuing appeal of pastoral.

Tragedy did not occur at this stage of musical history, although there were revivals, translations and imitations of ancient classical dramas. Cornelio Frangipani's *Tragedia all'antica* (1574), to music, now lost, by Claudio Merulo, was probably so called because its personages were gods and goddesses. Its speeches, songs and choruses were not dramatic: they made up a homage performed at Venice in honour of the King of France. Such musical festivities, of a more or less dramatic kind, were frequent at Venice in the late sixteenth century. This one may well have been a model for the *Balet comique de la Royne,* or *Circé* (1581) a crucial work in the development of French opera, in which dancing has always played a significant part. Then in 1585 an Italian version of Sophocles's *Oedipus Rex* was performed at the opening of the Teatro Olimpico in Vicenza, designed by Palladio and Scamozzi after Serlio's interpretations of the ancient stage designs of Vitruvius. For this performance Andrea Gabrieli, the Venetian madrigalist, composed music for the chorus, who were fifteen in number as they probably were at one stage of Greek tragedy. The music, mostly sonorous and grave but with a fair amount of dynamic variety, for singing without accompaniment, was in a simple homophonic style which kept the beat of the verse and made the words clear.

An interesting contrast, and a reminder of other, more popular traditions that were also leading the way to opera, was offered by Orazio Vecchi's *Amfiparnaso* (Venice, 1579), a comedy of masks set to music in a series of fourteen madrigals. A brilliant *commedia armonica*, intended for the ears and not the eyes, to be sung by participants and not heard by an audience, it is perhaps the earliest extant text of a *commedia dell'arte* play. Its title indicates only the lower slopes of Parnassus, but Vecchi shows a feeling for pitch and rhythm in the inflections of conversation and an ability to balance melodic interest with lively characterisation that point towards the achievement of fully developed opera. In arguing in the preface that it is not a violation of good taste to mix the serious with the light in music he makes nice, if fanciful, use of ancient authority: 'Aristotle vouches for it; and Homer and Vergil prove it.'

The central tradition in the growth of opera was that of the *intermedio*, and a classical thread ran right through them. The *intermedi* began as incidental music with words for various kinds of festival and entertainment, usually to do with a court, and for plays. They developed into *entr'actes* that became more elaborate than the play itself. They usually involved *tableaux vivants*, dances, sumptuous costumes, and amazing scenes of transformation. Whether the music was vocal or instrumental or both, the musicians often remained out of sight. Classical motifs and mythological figures were frequent, mostly taken from Ovid's *Metamorphoses*, with its rich supply of transformations. *Intermedi* at Florence for the wedding of Cosimo de' Medici to Eleanora da Toledo in 1539 sported solos by Aurora and Silenus, and choruses of nymphs, sirens, satyrs and Bacchantes; those for the wedding of Francesco de' Medici to Johanna of Austria in 1565 a playful treatment of the tribulations of Cupid and Psyche. There were many other such occasions at Italian courts in the sixteenth century, of growing complexity and length.

Perhaps the most magnificent, and certainly the most significant for the birth of opera, were the *intermedi* at the wedding of Ferdinando de' Medici and Cristina of Lorraine in Florence in 1589. There were six, framing the five acts of Bargagli's spoken comedy, *La Pellegrina*, and they must have taken nearly two hours. The music, by several composers, most of whom belonged to Bardi's Camerata, was printed and is extant, though it is not complete. It is of great interest and variety, moving towards opera in its sense of dramatic contrast, its strophic methods of setting and its ornamented solo singing (the melismas are printed), though there is more choral music than was to be usual in early opera. The spectacle, with its vistas and transformations, its infernos and seascapes, its gods and monsters, was a wonder to behold.

The titles of the *intermedi* suggest the scope of the celebration: *The Harmony of the Spheres, The Singing Contest of the Muses and the Pierides, Apollo Slays the Python at Delphi, The Prophecy of the Golden Age and the Terrors of Hell, Arion is saved by the Dolphin, Rhythm and Harmony descend to Earth.* They were familiar themes, mostly from Ovid, but the fifth and sixth from Plato. They were combined to proclaim the power of music and dance. At the end the gods descended from heaven to present these gifts to twenty pairs of mortals on this happy day of marriage which would consolidate the glories of Medici and Lorraine and bring back the beauty and goodness of the golden age.

For the future of opera the most important episode was the third, *Apollo Slays the Python at Delphi*, with music by Marenzio and poetry by Rinuccini. was a reminiscence of the ancient Greek *nomos* or hymn on that subject by the legendary Olympos, described in detail by ancient commentators, and a forerunner of later victories by Apollo in early operas. In particular, Rinuccini made use of it in 1594 for the text of a pastoral drama which, as altered and amplified in 1597 became the libretto of the earliest recorded opera, *Dafne*, with music – almost all lost – mostly by Jacopo Peri. Peri belonged to a later, less speculative, more practical Camerata than Bardi's, under the aegis of Jacopo Corsi, that was more interested in music for the stage, and the first performance took place at the Palazzo Corsi in Florence. It was on a modest scale, but the select audience is said to have been enchanted by the whole occasion: music, singing, dancing, story and spectacle. The testimony comes from Marco da Gagliano, who was present and was himself to compose a superior setting of the same libretto (performed at Mantua in 1608 and at Florence in 1610). Rinuccini's elegant high-flown text owed more to the poetry of Italian pastoral dramas by Tasso and Guarini than to Greek tragedy, but Peri was concerned to set it in the new style that he took to be classical.

He declared his aims in the preface to his later opera *Euridice*:

> I judged that the ancient Greeks and Romans (who in the opinion of many sang their tragedies throughout in representing them upon the stage) had used a harmony surpassing that of ordinary speech but falling so far below the melody of song as to take an intermediate form. And I considered that the kind of speech that the ancients assigned to singing and that they called 'diastemica' (that is, sustained or suspended) could in part be hastened and made to take an intermediate course, lying between the slow and suspended movements of song and the swift and rapid movements of speech and that it could be adapted to my purpose.[2]

It was a justification of monody as the way to sustain a dramatic poem in music: the method of recitative. Music was to imitate speech so that the language of drama and the gamut of human emotions should be reflected in the accents of the singer. It was a part of the whole movement in the late sixteenth and early seventeenth centuries towards a new style of musical expression, sacred and secular, in which a single voice, accompanied by the *basso continuo* on a stringed or keyboard instrument, would express in a clear and melodious line the meaning of the words. It was in accord more especially with the theories of both the earlier and the later Camerata. Bardi in his *Discorso sopra la musica antica e 'l cantar bene*, written about 1585, advised Giulio Caccini, the composer and singer, to arrange the verse well and to declaim the words intelligibly, arguing that 'just as the soul is nobler than the body, so the words are nobler than the counterpoint'.[3] Caccini himself, in his preface to *Le Nuove Musiche* (Florence 1602), a volume of madrigals and arias, spoke for a new manner of composing and singing solo songs which 'had more power to delight and move than the greatest number of voices singing together'.[4] He invoked the preference of Plato and other philosophers for a music of words and rhythm rather than pure sound ('a kind of music by which man might, as it were, talk in harmony, using in that kind of singing ... a certain noble neglect of the song').[5] In fact, however, he varied his accompaniment and embellished his vocal line in the interests of expression to create an arioso midway between melody and recitative.

Peri's setting of Rinuccini's poem *Euridice* is the first extant opera, although for the first performance in October 1600 use was also made of a few arias by Caccini composed for his own setting of the opera. (Caccini's setting is the first printed opera, but it was not performed until 1602.) There is a general similarity between the two settings. They are mostly recitative, of a syllabic kind, not lacking in variety and sometimes affecting, especially in cadences, but they include a few strophic arias and some choruses in unison for dancing as well as singing. There is no overture; simply a fanfare of trumpets, and little incidental music. They are mostly in common time, though triple time is occasionally used. They survive as vocal scores with a figured bass for continuo accompaniment. These would have been embellished by the singers in performance. The players of the (concealed) orchestra would have had their own parts. It is difficult to imagine how the performance would have sounded, but it made a distinct impression on what must have been a great occasion. Peri himself sang the role of Orfeo when his work was first given, as part of the celebrations in Florence of the wedding of Marie de' Medici to Henry IV of France, and it has been conjectured that Monteverdi and Rubens were in the audience.

The libretto was that of a drama rather than an opera. The requirements of music with regard to arias, ensembles and choruses had not yet begun to dominate the structure and texture of a libretto. The framework is clear – a first part on earth, a second in Hades, a third again on earth – and the literary finish is high. As in a Greek tragedy, short scenes are separated by choruses, and messengers are brought on to announce the important events: the death of Euridice, the grieving of Orfeo and his consolation by Venus, and the reunion of Orfeo and Euridice. (Soon there would be a tendency to choose for opera those subjects of classical mythology that allowed for the maximum of spectacle, but this was not so in the early Florentine works.) Orfeo lives among shepherds whose simple life is in accord with the simplicity of characters and plot. The tone is serious. The prologue is given to the tragic muse, and death is shown to be as strong a power as love, but the opera ends happily (as befitted the occasion of its first performance) in a divine union, and the reserved style gives way to jubilation at the close. The sad fable had been transformed into a serene pastoral.

The celebrations in 1600 also included *Il Rapimento di Cefalo*, with music by Caccini and others to words by Chiabrera, an *intermedio* that was more of a ballet than an opera, with stagecraft so lavish that a prose description of it took on poetic qualities that were not to be found in the libretto itself. The other major piece was *Il Dialogo di Giunone e Minerva*, with music by Emilio de' Cavalieri to words by Guarini, perhaps best described as an early kind of cantata. As a member of Bardi's Camerata, Cavalieri had contributed to the *intermedi* of 1589, and had written music for two lost semi-dramatic pastorals, *Il Satiro* and *La Disperazione di Fileno*. In 1600 he composed for the Oratorio della Vallicella in Rome his most famous work, *La Rappresentazione di Anima e di Corpo*. An allegorical drama in three acts, more of a devotion than an opera, related to the earlier *laudi spirituali* and the later oratorios (named after the building where they were performed), it was set to simple music for singing in recitative, *stile rappresentativo*, in dialogue, and for singing in hymns by a chorus between the episodes, with dances, and acted with costumes and scenery of an impressive kind. The instruments varied 'to accord with the affection expressed by the singer' who was enjoined 'to pronounce the words clearly so that they be understood and accompany them with gestures and movements not only of the hand but also of the feet', so that his actions would 'contribute to the affection'.[6] Cavalieri specified that ideally the work should always be given in an auditorium not too large for the words to be heard (and therefore seating a thousand at most) and indoors on a raised stage. He was in favour of a compact piece of theatre not exceeding two hours, or 700 verses of from five to eight syllables. Its phraseology should be simple, its tempo rapid, its style concise. Variety of musical means – solo, chorus, harmony and orchestral interludes – is as important as that of costumes, miming and sets. The occasion was intended to be an intense experience in which, according to the doctrines of the Counter-Reformation, aesthetic sensations would reinforce religious beliefs. The publisher, Alessandro Guidotti, declared boldly: 'Cavalieri reproduces the dramatic manner of the Greeks and Romans. In some tunes the resemblance is perfect. He endorses singing and playing ... to the accompaniment of two flutes. He has rejuvenated classical art.'[7] With reference to the last sentence it is interesting to consider how the performance of *La Rappresentazione* must have differed from that of *Dafne*, and how different both must have been from that of a Greek tragedy.

The performances of all these early works are difficult to imagine, and yet without an awareness of them something essential is lacking to our appreciation of the different elements in the evolution of opera. In this context it is worth remembering that there was a significant change in methods of singing during the period. Pietro della Valle was to write in his *Discorso della musica dell'età nostra* in 1640:

> However, all those singers of the previous century had hardly any other techniques of singing apart from trills and florid passages and a good voice production. As to *piano* and *forte*, gradual *crescendo* and graceful *diminuendo*, expression of feelings, judicious bringing out of the sense of the words, of making the voice sound cheerful or melancholy, tender or courageous, and of other similar *galanterie* which modern singers do supremely well – all such things were never so much as talked about in those days.[8]

There may be some exaggeration here, but it seems to be clear that a more dramatic style of singing had been established. It is hardly too much to say that the foundations were being laid of the whole Italian system of singing.

The composer of genius who was to realise the possibilities of these early works into the form of the first great operas and to foreshadow the idea of opera as *Gesamtkunstwerk*, a fusion of all the arts, was Monteverdi. According to definitions given by himself in the preface to his Fifth Book of Madrigals (1605) and by his brother in his *Dichiaratione* (1607), he followed not the *prima prattica*, in which the word is the servant of the music, but the *seconda prattica*, in which the word is the mistress of the harmony. There is a sense in which the music may be said to have been in fact dominant in his work from the beginning, but he never lost a respect for the words, and achieved a new kind of dramatic union between them. Together they were blended to express profound and varied emotions – passions of every kind but especially those of love, anger and suffering – in his search for the truthful representation of human nature, with which his comments always show a concern. In the preface to his Eighth Book of Madrigals (1638) he declared: 'I was aware that it is contraries which greatly move our mind, and that this is the purpose which all good music should have – as Boethius asserts, saying "Music is related to us, and either ennobles or corrupts the character".' In the same preface he distinguished three main 'affections': the soft, moderate and agitated, and described his style of music (*concitato*) for the last of the three. In a famous letter about the setting to music of a *favola marittima* in 1616, he asked:

> How, dear sir, shall I be able to imitate the speech of the winds since they do not speak? And how shall I be able to move the passions by their means? Ariadne moved the audience because she was a woman and equally Orpheus because he was a man and not a wind. This tale, taken all in all, does not move my feelings in the least, due perhaps to my no little ignorance, and I find it difficult to understand, nor does it inspire me to a moving climax.[9]

Several points here are significant: the stress on the human, indeed moral, qualities of music; the interest in dramatic shape and contrast; the desire to move the affections; the concern with imitation. This last question was much discussed with regard to interpretation of words in music. Earlier

techniques of detailed word-painting (which represented certain words,
e.g. 'rejoice' or 'arise' by what were thought to be appropriate notes) or
eye-music (in which a word such as 'death' would be given a black note)
were rejected by such members of the early Camerata as Girolamo Mei and
Vincenzo Galilei on the grounds that such imitative artifice of detail was
self-contradictory and at odds with making the whole work a structure of
ideal beauty. They argued for a kind of imitation that would represent the
words by a musical texture that might be less pleasing but would be more
expressive as a whole. A moderate use of the various techniques of the
maniera madrigalesca should be allowed but not so as to unbalance the new
relationship, thought to be truly antique, of form to content. This was to be
achieved by Monteverdi, himself, of course, a great madrigalist, who moved
beyond the ideals and accomplishments of the Camerata composers to
create for the first time ample and complex operas in which music and
drama were finally wedded: the complete *dramma per musica*.

It is important, however, to distinguish between his first and later operas.
The first was *Orfeo*, performed in 1607 at the court of Mantua, with a
libretto by the duke's secretary, Alessandro Striggio, a poet and translator
of classical tragedies. It is interesting, though hardly surprising in view of its
significance and popularity, that Monteverdi and Striggio used the same
Greek myth for their *favola in musica* as had Poliziano for his lyric drama at
the same court over a hundred years before. Striggio had kept to the original
fable in which, after the final loss of Euridice, the Bacchantes claimed
Orpheus as their victim, but Monteverdi, in the version of the opera that we
have (although not in an earlier one) made Apollo take pity on Orpheus and
lead him up to a heavenly Parnassus. So pastoral moved through tragedy to
the transcendent ending of an *intermedio*.

Striggio produced an admirable libretto, shaping his few scenes into a
satisfying structure of change and contrast. All five acts have a similar
scheme, in which a situation is broken by an action to which Orpheus reacts
before a choral conclusion. A chorus of nymphs and shepherds changes to
one of infernal spirits in Hades (its entrance bears Dante's warning – one of
several Christian touches) and then back again. The chorus dance as well as
sing. Their praises of man in act III are reminiscent of the well-known
stasimon in Sophocle's *Antigone* and if their comment at the end of act IV is of a
kind more general in Greek literature ('Orpheus overcame Hell and was
overcome by his passions; eternal fame is deserved only by him who
overcomes himself') their concluding words of blessing to Orfeo, now a god,
again put us in mind of Sophocles, this time of *Oedipus at Colonus*, though the
promise of happiness with a transfigured Euridice does not. Individual
members of the chorus are given lines from time to time.

The characterisation is slight, a suggestion of moods and feelings appropriate to the swift conduct of the fable. A prologue is sung by Musica; the

happiness of Orfeo is shattered by a messenger who announces the death of Euridice; Speranza leads him to the underworld; he displays all the charms of his singing but Charon has no pity and goes to sleep; Proserpine persuades Pluto to release Euridice, but Orfeo on his return journey yields to Cupid, looks back and loses Euridice again; he sings a heart-rending lament; and is finally given life and fame in heaven by Apollo. The diction, spare but telling, achieves a high poetic quality in its intense simplicity (not excluding the use of silence) which leaves to the composer and the singers possibilities of amplification and colour. The key themes are: the power of music; the overriding force of love; the beauty of the universe; the fame of the artist; the pathos of death; the presence of the gods; the transcendence of the world. Not all of them are characteristic of Greek tragedy but the seriousness and delicacy of Striggio's handling combined with the clarity and elegance of his form justify *Orfeo* as a lyrical drama in that tradition.

Monteverdi, for his part, did justice to both the structure and the texture of Striggio's libretto, using a whole gamut of musical forms and drawing on a wide range of instruments. The often dry and monotonous, if sometimes tuneful and expressive, recitative of the Florentine composers blossomed into a more supple and varying arioso that yet always allowed the words to be clear. It was sung, mostly one note to one syllable, to a *basso continuo* of varying plucked instruments. In the orchestral music (the orchestra was concealed), whether heard on its own or to accompany singing or dancing, Monteverdi showed his mastery of old and new techniques to compose music that would be theatrically effective. Contrasts of every kind – of pace, dynamics and tone, of solo and chorus, of singing and music; dissonance and syncopation; association of instruments and themes with characters; repetition of words – all were deployed in the cause of expressing drama in music. The opera was received with acclamation.

Monteverdi's second opera was *Arianna*, performed in 1608 for the wedding at Mantua of Francesco Gonzaga to Margherita of Savoy (as also was Marco da Gagliano's new setting of Rinuccini's *Dafne*). The score is lost, except for the famous lament 'Lasciatemi morire', but the libretto by Rinuccini survives. It treats of the story of Dionysus and Ariadne in which after several human vicissitudes she becomes a goddess. The lament was originally a solo interrupted by a chorus of fishermen: what we have is her arioso recitative. (It was the first of many such laments, perhaps the best known being that of Dido in Purcell's *Dido and Aeneas*.) A five-part arrangement of it was published in Monteverdi's Sixth Book of Madrigals (1614), a reminder of the influence that monody and madrigal still had on each other. The music is said to have been notably sensitive to the text.

The music of Monteverdi's other dramatic works, written before and after his move to Venice in 1613, has survived only in part. Whether extant or lost, they offered a range of entertainments in which the blending of word, song and dance – and, of course, spectacle – varied. If the *Ballo delle Ingrate* (of the French court style which had begun to influence Italy) may be called a ballet, it differs from the less dramatic dance-songs of *Tirsi e Clori*, as presumably did the *intermedio Gli Amori di Diana e di Endimione* from the pageant *Mercurio e Marte*. Such classical themes were doubtless more seriously treated in the lost operas *Proserpina Rapita* and *Le Nozze di Enea con Lavinia*. He may also have composed a (lost) *Adone*; a scheme for an *Andromeda* was cancelled; and he did not like a libretto that he was sent for an *Andromeda*. But in the two surviving operas of his old age Monteverdi again created works of a new kind.

He was now writing for a different sort of audience. The first public opera house had opened in Venice in 1637 and other theatres were soon built. The city was ruled by a rich oligarchy, not a monarch, and the audiences were larger, more mixed socially, and if less cultivated probably more lively. They wished to see and hear characters who were recognisably human in the range and intensity of their emotions. There was an even stronger taste than before for spectacle, but there was less money available for instrumentalists and chorus. They wanted music that was beautiful and passionate but they were not so concerned with the clarity and meaning of words. It should be remembered that the libretto was available and could be read in the theatre by the light of little wax candles.

For *Il Ritorno d'Ulisse* (1641) Monteverdi and Badoaro, his librettist, went to Homer and dramatised the last half of the *Odyssey*. (There are some differences between score and libretto but both are faithful to Homer in most details, partly because the text was familiar to many in the audience – in fact which also allowed certain features of the story to be taken for granted.) The opera begins with an allegorical prologue sung by Human Frailty, Fortune and Love. Odysseus, after his years of wandering, is brought to the shore of his own island and, slowly and cunningly, moves to reveal and assert himself against the suitors of his faithful wife, Penelope, who finally recognises and accepts him. A concluding duet of happiness is sung by the reunited husband and wife. The human story of love, suffering and anger, with its series of divine interventions, offered Monteverdi a satisfying subject for a Venetian opera. The simple form in which the score survives (like all scores of the period) is more than sufficient to show its quality: it is for strings and continuo instruments. The orchestra in Venice now sat in front of the stage and included female players. (Female singers had, of course, always been acceptable everywhere except in Rome, where *castrati* were used.) Monteverdi's variety of musical forms, the expressive dramatic texture and the feeling for continuity are all remarkable; the flow of recitative into arioso and aria (although that term raises questions of definition) has become even more flexible and assured; characters sing alone or to one another or in groups, as psychology and action dictate. It seems appropriate that it should be one of the earliest and most influential Greek stories that was thus reborn as musical drama.

For his last opera in 1642 Monteverdi and his librettist, Busenello, moved from myth to history – the first time this had been done, though the distinction between the two was not then felt so sharply – and chose a subject from imperial Rome: *L'Incoronazione di Poppea*. It is the story, taken from Book XIV of the *Annals* of Tacitus, of how Nero and Poppea got rid of their spouses and married one another, a story of love and ambition. The libretto is swift and concise, tighter than that of *Il Ritorno d'Ulisse*, with a fuller presentation of characters as they move through passion and intrigue to a variety of ends. Monteverdi, in turn, drawing on a mature knowledge of human nature in all its aspects and using every resource of music, formal and expressive (as he had, though they were then less developed, for *Orfeo*), produced his operatic masterpiece.

L'Incoronazione di Poppea is a glorification of love, as foreshadowed in the prologue, and love of an unedifying kind. Monteverdi and Busenello took advantage of their freedom in Venice to create a disturbing representation of some facts of life. They were able to portray an emperor unflatteringly as they were not writing for a ducal court, and to draw a full-length portrait of a courtesan. None of the characters is altogether admirable; not even Seneca the philosopher, although he, when sentenced to death by Nero at Poppea's instigation, does show himself a true Stoic in the calm and resolution with which he bids farewell to his friends before he goes off to commit suicide. He does at least provide some kind of contrast .to the pervading egotism and sensuality of the other characters. Contrasts of another kind are offered by a love duet between a page and a maid, and by a drinking scene, at once hilarious and sinister, where Nero and some male friends rejoice in Poppea's beauty and Seneca's death. It recalls the mock-heroic treatment of the cowardly gourmand, Iro, in *Il Ritorno d'Ulisse*, and is an indication of how far opera had already moved from the austere elegance of a courtly pastoral to the realistic tragi-comedy of the public theatre.

The music for *L'Incoronazione di Poppea*, like that of its predecessor, was scored for strings and continuo alone. The interplay and fusion of aria, arioso and recitative had become even more dramatic, and the expression of character by musical means – both as a consistent structure and in details of feeling and action – had been developed to a high point. Perhaps the most striking example is the way in which the instrumental *stile concitato*, for imaging anger and warfare and other sorts of agitation, now sometimes appears in the vocal line. Monteverdi marks the change in the relationship of Nero and Poppea and points the reversal at the heart of the plot by his wonderful contrast between the opening and the closing duet: the broken shape and frequent dissonances of the first transformed into the harmony and melody of the final *chaconne*. Indeed melody, sometimes highly voluptuous, often invades the score, and the rhythm is constantly varied, on occasion suggesting dances. There was no chorus: the characters themselves sang such concerted music as there was.

This last fact may be taken as a symbol of the truth that with Monteverdi the hellenism of opera came to an end. The idea persisted until the eighteenth century that in some respects opera was a reincarnation of classical drama; Berlioz and Wagner were only two examples of nineteenth-century composers influenced by their knowledge of the Greek and Roman classics; and in our own century – apart from several works by Richard Strauss, and Hans Werner Henze's version of *The Bassarids* – there has been Stravinsky's brilliant setting of *Oedipus Rex* to a libretto in Latin by Cocteau. It is interesting to consider the changing relationships in the different national traditions of opera between the elements of music, singing, dance and spectacle, and especially the ways in which the Greek chorus has had its various roles reflected not only by groups of singers and dancers (sometimes by both in the same opera), but also by soloists in arias. Calzabigi made the point that some arias in Italian operas of the seventeenth and eighteenth centuries were, as lyrical meditations of universal significance, comparable to Greek choruses. There is also the fascinating history of the use, and changes in use, of historical and mythical themes and of ethical values from the ancient world. This present enquiry has been limited to the beginnings of Italian opera in the hope of elucidating on the one hand those aspects which may be related to classical antiquity and on the other those which from the beginning belonged to a new form of musical drama: a form which, as it came to full being in the hands of Monteverdi, showed itself as no longer, if it ever was, neo-classical, but as the quintessential art of the baroque.[10]

NOTES

1. Oliver Strunk *Source Readings in Music History* (New York: Norton & Co., 1950; London: Faber & Faber, 1952), p. 306.
2. *Ibid.*, p. 347.
3. *Ibid.*, p. 295.
4. *Ibid.*, p. 379.
5. *Ibid.*, p. 378.
6. A. Solerti, *Le Origini del melodramma* (Milan: Remo Sandron, 1903), p. 6. Cited and translated by M. F. Robinson, *Opera before Mozart* (London: Hutchinson, 1966) p. 51.
7. Cited and translated by S. Towneley in *The New Oxford History of Music*, 11 vols. (London: Oxford University Press, 1954–), vol. IV, ch. 15, p. 837.
8. *Ibid.*, pp. 784–5.

9. Cited by G. F. Malipiero, *Claudio Monteverdi* (Milan: Fratelli Treves, 1929), p. 166. Translated and quoted by D. Arnold, *Monteverdi* (London: Dent, 1963), p. 116.

10. Valuable bibliographies are to be found in volumes IV and V of *The New Oxford History of Music* and in Gerald Abraham, *The Concise Oxford History of Music* (London: Oxford University Press, 1979). Angelo Solerti, *Gli Albori del melo-dramma*, 3 vols. (Milan–Palermo–Naples, 1904–5) is a historical survey which discusses the various texts. Nino Pirotta, *Li Due Orfei, da Poliziano a Monteverdi* (Turin: Einaudi, 1975, 2nd edn; in English as *Music and Theatre from Poliziano to Monteverdi*, Cambridge University Press, forthcoming) is an account of the two treatments of the myth and of the changes in musical drama between them. *The New Golden Age* ed. Iain Fenlon (London: British Broadcasting Corporation, 1979) was published to coincide with a broadcast performance of the Florentine *intermedi* of 1589; contributors discuss some problems treated in this paper.

Cole Porter in the
American musical theatre

JUNE SMITH

It is a curious fact that despite his great artistic success in the American musical theatre, working with variations on a genre which is part of our 'mass culture', Cole Porter seldom achieved mass acceptance. In 1916, when *See America First* was withdrawn after only fifteen performances – a painful beginning for his professional career – Elsa Maxwell's judgement was that he need only wait for general audiences to mature to his level of sophistication. But as late as 1927 the Broadway producer Vinton Freedley refused some of his songs because the lyrics were too unusual and esoteric, and in 1929, after he had achieved a measure of success in both New York and London, Porter's songs were being vilified by the moral watchdogs of the press and censored by the commercial managements. Even in the 1930s at the peak of his success 'Love for Sale' (*The New Yorkers*, 1930) was banned from the radio, 'My Heart Belongs to Daddy' (*Leave It to Me*, 1938) was expurgated, and the White House found his lyrics for 'You're the Top' (*Anything Goes*, 1934) too disrespectful for performance at Mrs Roosevelt's New Year's Eve Ball. When he finally found a huge international audience, in the Hollywood film adaptations of such great musicals as *Kiss Me Kate*, the lyrics were much cut by the film industry's censorship, the effect being at best blandness and at worst emasculation.

In the years following his death in 1964, however, Porter's lyrics have been much more adequately appreciated. There have been revivals of the musicals themselves, and even more successful have been productions which brought some of his songs together in the form of the musical revue. Ben Bagley's *The Decline and Fall of the Entire World as Seen Through the Eyes of Cole Porter* opened in New York in 1965, the Mermaid Theatre's *Cole* in London in 1974, and towards the end of the decade Cole Porter, who as a student at Harvard and Yale began his career as one of the very brightest of American University Wits, was once again acclaimed in major universities: in 1977, for example, *At Long Last Cole* was produced at the Los Angeles campus of the University of California, and *An Affair With Cole Porter* was produced at Berkeley in 1979 (written and directed by the present writer). So, while much of his work has not received the general approbation lavished on the comparatively pastoral works of Rodgers and Hammerstein, Porter's most characteristic songs continue to appeal to that discriminating minority whose numbers, as Elsa Maxwell predicted at the start of his career, increase with the years.

Cole Porter's words and music have been written about mainly in journalistic reviews, where they have been easily labelled with the tired words 'urbane', 'genteel', 'sophisticated'. In this paper I shall look closely at some representative examples of his songs and indicate his unique position in the American musical theatre.

See America First was his first show to be produced professionally. The songs were outstanding in the American theatre of 1916, and they already had some of the main characteristics of his mature work. A truly Gilbertian dexterity runs through the lyrics, and some of the complicated rhyme schemes reveal in their adroit management a direct indebtedness to Robert Browning. By the standards of the others at work in the same field, he was ridiculously over-educated, and by any standards his ironical wit was quick and incisive. The causes of the failure of this first play are problematic; the production history is obscured by differences in opinion on casting, directing, collaboration, and by the recriminations which accompany such differences. But even under the best of conditions it is unlikely that Cole Porter could have succeeded on the commercial Broadway stage of 1916.

Theatre in the United States before World War I was dominated by the same mentality that today controls its commercial television. Sentimental romance, melodrama, and simple-minded farce were ordered by monopolistic producers and enthusiastically accepted by undiscriminating audiences. Although an advance guard of intellectuals and artists had already begun to engage the enemy in battle, the effects of these skirmishes were not significantly experienced until long after World War I. Meanwhile, commercial values dominated both the musical and the non-musical theatre.

In musical theatre, sentimental melodrama was translated into American versions of Viennese operetta, farce was made into the simple-minded musical entertainments of George M. Cohan, and love of spectacle created its own genre in the lavish musical revues. There was no ready-made demand for Cole Porter's esoteric and subtle wit, which would have been especially out of place in sentimental operetta.

Although the comic form of operetta played in New York before and during the war, by far the most popular was the sentimentally romantic form of which Victor Herbert's *Naughty Marietta* (1910) and Sigmund Romberg's *Maytime* (1917) are representative. Oddly, the more famous *Naughty Marietta* was not as successful as *Maytime* in its original production; however, its 'romantic' eighteenth-century New Orleans setting and melodramatic situations – a quadroon girl hopelessly in love with a white man, a virtuous captain spurned by the love of his life, and a French pirate masquerading as a member of the governor's family – ensured a run profitable for producer Oscar Hammerstein (the grandfather of the lyricist). *Maytime*, on the other hand, was the most popular play in what has been called the worst season in American theatre.[1] The focus of this 'typically Shuberty'[2] play is a frustrated love affair that spans a tearful sixty years of separation: the lovers from each other, and the would-be husband from the family mansion. Eventually, the story ends happily, albeit still tearfully, when the children of the original lovers (from their separate marriages) are united in matrimony and ensconced in the retrieved family mansion. *Maytime*'s popularity may have been due in part to its use of American characters in an American setting, but there was very little that was genuinely American in what was still a Viennese concoction.

The book musicals of George M. Cohan were American through and through. Vaudeville was the figurative birthplace of Cohan, and his plays always carry the spirit of a vaudeville scene. But whatever the inspiration, his plays, written, directed, produced, and danced and sung by Cohan himself, dominated Broadway in the first twenty years of this century. For the most part the plays were set in the world that Cohan knew best, New York City and its environs, and they followed a formula of three-chord music with spots for specialty dances, recitations, and the infamous flag numbers. One of the later and most popular of these shows was *Hello Broadway!* (1914), an almost plotless script in which Cohan and a sidekick tour New York City as a weak excuse for presenting the standard formula numbers. Cohan appealed exclusively to the folksy and commonplace, and no show of his could have accepted any Cole Porter song.

In the tradition of the Paris *Folies Bergère*, Florenz Ziegfeld opened his first *Follies* in 1907, featuring beautiful women with sex appeal and elaborate costumes in even more elaborate settings. In 1915 Joseph Urban became his designer, and productions attained new heights of spectacle replete with an underwater ballet and sets adorned with elephants spouting water from their trunks. Meanwhile, not to be outdone by Flo Ziegfeld, Jake Shubert had opened his own revue, *The Passing Show* (1912), and in 1913 appropriated for his chorus girls the runway that he had seen in Max Reinhardt's visiting production of *Sumurun*. In later years these extravaganzas were joined by others, and Cole Porter found a modicum of success after the war in a revue with a difference, *The Greenwich Village Follies*, whose format both evoked and satirized the Bohemian culture of the Village.

In the ten years after World War I, momentous changes on and off the stage took place in America. On the stage the advance guard of intellectuals and artists appeared in New York theatre. Eugene O'Neill arrived, and the American theatre grew up as he was followed by Sidney Howard, George S. Kaufman, Philip Barry, S. N. Behrman and many others. Melodrama gave way to tragedy, farce to comedy of manners, extravaganza to intimate, sophisticated revues, and sentimentality yielded some ground to satire and irony. There would always be a place for the former values, but more and more that place would be in the cinema and later in television. After the advent of *The Jazz Singer* in 1927 and the subsequent popularity of the 'talkies', Broadway began to gear itself to a more sophisticated and wealthy audience. This change was abetted by the Crash and the Depression, when the mass audiences who had previously filled the theatres could no longer afford such luxuries. Major changes, of course, did not stop with the theatre and economics; in the years after the war came a revolution in manners and morals as the more sophisticated standards of Europe infiltrated the American consciousness. The horror of the war itself had engendered a disillusionment with the romantic and sentimental world most Americans had been taught to believe in, and the popular image of Freud had introduced sex as the force to fill the void. The stage was set for Cole Porter to return from Europe where he too had changed, having developed the essentials of his mature style. By 1928 when *Paris* opened at the Music Box Theatre in New York, Porter had a unique style with roots in two primary sources; first, his association with the elite of international society and, secondly, a psychological disposition towards a dualistic mode of perception. These are the fundamental causes of the 'sophisticated' quality of the lyrics, their subtlety and complexity, and they invite a close inspection.

Born in 1891 the son of a doting, protective mother, and the grandson of a tyrannical millionaire, Cole Porter was groomed from infancy for the kind of social life that his mother Kate had never had for herself, but wanted for her son. At the age of six he was taking private French lessons and piano lessons; soon afterwards Kate enrolled him in violin and dancing lessons. In 1906 when the time came for him to go to high school, his mother sent him to a very prestigious eastern school, the Worcester Academy in Massachusetts. When, after the obligatory European tour, he went to Yale in 1909, he joined an exclusive set which included campus leaders Monty Woolley and Gerald Murphy as well as the upper-crust scions, Robert Lehman, Leonard Hanna, and Vanderbilt Webb. From his Yale and Harvard coterie it was a small step to the drawing rooms of Mrs Astor's 'four hundred' and then on to the salons of Europe where he met divorcée, Linda Thomas, a millionairess, a leader of Parisian society, and considered one of the most beautiful women in the world. Cole, a homosexual, followed the pattern of the times and married Linda; they were devoted friends and hobnobbed throughout Europe with what Porter called 'the rich rich'. Bored with Paris, he sought refuge in Venice where he and Linda rented the Palazzo Rezzonico, once occupied by Robert Browning. There they gave a ball for two thousand people, supplying costumes for everyone and entertainment by Diaghilev and company. By the time they came back to New York for Cole to take up his career in musical theatre, he was internationally famous as a millionaire playboy and virtually ignored as a composer.

But he had not neglected his music. Long before he came back to New York, he had found in his own friends an enthusiastic audience for his songs. As he played and sang for them, he amused himself by incorporating little bits of gossip and name-dropping, framing the whole with his distinctively satiric wit. When he began to write for Broadway again, he used the same technique with the same sense of intimacy and immediacy.

'The Tale of an Oyster', first heard by Broadway audiences when Helen Broderick sang it in *Fifty Million Frenchmen* in 1929, had been heard in its original version, 'The Scampi', by a group of Italian and British aristocrats, American heiresses, and his other friends in Venice in 1926. Written as part of the entertainment for a charity ball staged by the Principessa di San Faustino, 'The Scampi' made specific references to Elsa Maxwell, Lady Cunard, and the Principessa herself, all of whom were in the audience that night in Venice. When Porter adapted the song for the stage, the plot remained the same, but the names and places were changed to accommodate the New York audience. In the final version, a lonesome oyster is adopted by the Park Casino's chef and served on a silver platter at a luncheon of millionaire's wives. This little oyster is thrilled to be in the company of such illustrious society ladies, even when he becomes their first course.

> See that bivalve social climber,
> Feeding the rich Mrs Hoggenheimer,
> Think of his joy as he gaily glides,
> Down to the middle of her gilded insides.
> Proud little oyster.

But his pride is short-lived, as Mrs Hoggenheimer becomes ill and returns on her yacht to her home in Oyster Bay.

> Off they go through the troubled tide,
> The yacht rolling madly from side to side,
> They're tossed about 'til that poor young oyster,
> Finds that it's time he should quit his cloister,
> Up comes the oyster.

> Back once more where he started from,
> He murmured 'I haven't a single qualm,
> For I've had a taste of society,
> And society has had a taste of me.'
> Wise little oyster.

The satirical bite is curiously sharp in the words and music of this song where he ironically deflates both the 'real' members of the 'upper set' and their imitators. The form of the song contributes importantly to the complex effect: a parody of a German *Lied* using a modified strophical form, dramatized piano accompaniment, and a pointed return to the beginning stanza at the end of the song.

The Park Casino was the most expensive, and the most pretentious, dining and dancing establishment in Manhattan. Its advertisements in the contemporary magazines call attention to the facts that its interior design was by Joseph Urban, that its menu was in French, that its music was subdued and in elegant taste. In 1929 millionaires were being created overnight by the vagaries of margin buying, and the Park Casino advertisements appealed crudely to Mrs Hoggenheimer as a representative of the nouveaux riches who were determined to do some very quick social climbing.

In the years before World War I, the Hoggenheimers had become such familiar and popular characters on the New York stage that for many years the mere mention of the name was sufficient to evoke the image of the newly rich social-climbing Jew. In 1903 Charles Frohman imported *The Girl From Kay's* from London with Sam Bernard in the role of Mr Hoggenheimer. Since the character and show were popular (223 performances), Frohman engaged Harry Bache Smith to write the book and lyrics for a sequel in 1906, *The Rich Mr Hoggenheimer*, and the Shuberts attempted an update of *The Girl From Kay's* in 1914, *Belle of Bond Street*, still featuring the Hoggenheimers. And even if the character were not known to the audience, the name itself suggests Porter's meaning, characterizing the nouveaux riches as at home with the hogs.

When Mrs Hoggenheimer leaves the Park Casino and her sister millionairesses, it is to return on her private yacht to her home in Oyster Bay, Long Island's elite community of country estates of the yacht-and-stables social set. This locale was consistently featured in the society section of the Sunday *New York Times*, and Porter was assured of his audience's familiarity with the place and its connotations.

'The Tale of an Oyster' is one of those Porter songs that was considered disgusting by some members of the audience and of the press, and it was ultimately dropped from the original production in response to social pressure. Only in the 1960s did the song begin to be appreciated by a wide audience, no doubt because of the continuing changes in manners and morals but more importantly because of the growing number of people who shared Porter's dualistic perspective.

Permeating the Porter lyrics, there is a characteristic dualism which is the source of the most potent effects in his style, and is best approached through analysis of one of those effects: the ubiquitous irony. He employs three distinct forms of irony: traditional, classical, and romantic.

Traditional irony is at work when a situation turns out to be the opposite of what was expected, i.e. when one expected circumstance is supplanted by a second, opposite circumstance. Porter uses this form least of the three varieties, employing it for simple humour, especially in the ballads and character sketches where the details of the narrative set up an expectation and then work against it. 'The Tale of an Oyster' uses this form as does 'The Cocotte' (*Nymph Errant*, 1933). This prostitute discovers, to her dismay, that she has become too respectable for her clients, because they have been spoiled by their society wives, who stole all the prostitute's techniques. In addition to its use in the ballad and character sketches, this irony is the controlling mechanism in many individual humorous lines. For instance, in these lines from 'I Happen to Like New York' (*The New Yorkers*, 1930),

> I like the city air, I like to drink of it,
> The more I know New York the more I think of it,
> I like the sight and the sound and even the stink of it,
> I happen to like New York,

the list of desirable qualities leads an audience to expect more of the same, but instead a definitely undesirable quality is substituted and, in an interesting ironic twist to the basic irony, is presented as being desirable.

More pervasive in the lyrics than traditional irony, classical irony occurs when knowledge is withheld for effect, i.e. when one circumstance is disclosed and another is concealed. The word 'irony' is derived from the Greek *eiron*, one who dissembles, and it is this connotation of the term which informs almost all of Porter's lighter material. He knew classical Greek, having studied with Dr Daniel Webster Abercrombie at the Worcester Academy, and since classical irony begins to appear in the lyrics almost immediately after his leaving Worcester, it is likely that this study taught him the value of dissembling – of withholding information and deliberately misleading his audience, and of maintaining an ironic detachment from his material. For example, Herodotus in *The Histories* ironically insists that he writes only according to hearsay. The same ironic tone informs the following lyric written in 1913 while Porter was still at Yale.

Oh What a Pretty Pair of Lovers

Verse
Let's live once more the day
Of warriors' surging fable.
When no one ran away,
And King Arthur ran a table.
I love you so my dear,
I swear I'll never doubt you.
Alas, I greatly fear
I'm incomplete without you.
My heart is out of key
It yearns for you to tune it.
How happy we shall be
When once a perfect unit.
Like lovers of the Moyen Age are we
Singing silly persiflage are we:

Refrain
Oh what a pretty pair of lovers
We two shall be.
Side by side and always tied
In a true blue lover's knot we.
We don't care what the thoughts of the rabble are
I'll be Eloise. I'll be Abélard.
Words of love with hints interlinear,
I'll be Paul, and I'll be Virginia.
Climb the balcony by the trellis and
I'll be Pelleas. I'll be Melisande.
We don't care if the round table talks a lot,
I'll be Guinevere. I'll be Launcelot.
So cemented, quite unprecedented,
Oh! What a pretty pair of lovers
We two shall be.

This lyric purports to list 'pretty pairs of lovers' singing 'silly persiflage', but any examination of the stories of the lovers would make it clear that the narrative is functioning on two contrasting levels. Far from the light banter described in the verse, all of these lovers actually sang a tale of woe. Abélard's reward, for impregnating Eloise and marrying her after she had his child, was castration and imprisonment. The famous letters were exchanged after Abélard was in prison and Eloise in a cloister. The less famous Paul and Virginia appeared in a romance by Bernardin de Saint-Pierre, *Paul et Virginie*, published first in 1787. These incestuous siblings meet obligatory and poetically just early deaths: she in a shipwreck from which she could have been saved had she been willing to jump into the arms of a lowly sailor, and he from a broken heart brought on by his sister's departure to the deep. Melisande, too, dies of a broken heart after Pelleas is killed by his older brother, her husband. Finally, the myriad of legends surrounding Launcelot and Guinevere agree in placing Guinevere in a convent for atonement, but vary as to whether Launcelot suffered in expiation or dissipation. Tennyson, whom Porter had studied extensively at Yale, portrays them as symbols of the corruption of Camelot. All four of these couples are presented in a sentimentally romantic setting by the verse; only when the specific names are heard and their stories are evoked in the refrain does the duality in the song become clear. And even then, of course, the ironic mechanism functions only when one knows the full story behind the allusions. The real 'pretty pair' of the lyric is the pair of juxtaposed opposites – the romantic cliché of the true blue lover's knot and the sardonic evocation of the ill-fated romance.

The third form, romantic irony, recognizes fullness of knowledge; there is no dissembling either with others or with the self. The term 'romantic irony' was first used by the German Romantics and has been adopted and adapted by students of the modern theatre. It is perhaps best understood in comparison with the two foregoing forms of irony. The first, traditional irony, occurs when one expected circumstance is supplanted with its opposite. Whereas traditional irony would separate the two circumstances, suggesting the expected one only through a theoretical implication but admitting only the second circumstance to reality, romantic irony would accept both circumstances in juxtaposition and eschew the manipulation of information inherent in traditional irony. This manipulation is even more immediately evident in classical irony where the dissembler discloses one circumstance but conceals another. Romantic irony recognizes that in modern society there is a surfeit of knowledge which prevents a categorical, fixed perspective. In the perspective of the romantic ironist, there is no reality that may not be a dream, and no dream that may not become a nightmare: nothing is pure or constant, everything is alloyed and mutable.

In the lyrics of Cole Porter the perspective effects an ironic detachment from the subject and he dwells, in a pervasive motif, on the evanescence of love. Both these characteristics of the mature style emerge for the first time in *Wake Up and Dream*, a revue produced by Charles Cochran at the London Pavilion, 27 March 1929, with 'I Loved Him, But He Didn't Love Me' particularly revealing the Porter perspective in the first verse:

> The gods who nurse this universe
> Think little of mortals' cares.
> They sit in crowds on exclusive clouds
> And laugh at our love affairs.
> I might have had a real romance,
> If they'd given me a chance.

To introduce 'the gods' into a 1929 song is to induce a distancing effect and provide the first step in the process of ironic detachment. The second step is the vagary of blaming the vicissitudes of the love affair on the whim of these gods, and the third step is the ironic judgement solicited by the disavowal of human responsibility at the end of the verse.

The imagery in the verses lightens the effect of irony by providing a textured tone in the narrative. The image in the first verse of a universe nursed by fashionable gods implies that the universe and the mortals who inhabit it are but infants in desire of instant gratification – infants who might be expected to flit from one breast to another without need of celestial prompting. Such an image reinforces the detachment from subject matter while setting the refrain in more accurate perspective. Against the background presented by the verse, it is virtually impossible to take seriously the refrain's 'weary wail' of 'I loved him, but he didn't love me', and its ironic reversal in the last lines:

> Now he loves me,
> But I don't love him.

The effect of the irony and detachment is so strong that it tends to obscure the theme of evanescent love which makes its appearance here also. To perceive, as in this lyric, that love can disappear in one moment on a mere whim, is to let go the myth of love-that-lasts-forever and to short-circuit the emotional commitment of love with an intellectual, dispassionate impulse. Later in more serious portrayals of the theme, Porter will describe a love that can inflict pain in spite of the relative safety provided by ironic detachment, but here he seems to 'think little of mortals' cares' as he laughs at their loves.

This descriptive background of Porter's varied uses of irony provides a frame of reference for understanding the function and importance of the concept of duality in the lyrics. It is important to remember at this point that all three forms of irony depend upon a dualistic perception, i.e. the juxtaposition or implied juxtaposition of at least two circumstances: in traditional irony the expected circumstance is supplanted with its opposite; in the classical form one circumstance is revealed while another is hidden; and in romantic irony the surfeit of knowledge prevents a purity of position and requires recognition of at least two circumstantial possibilities. But the importance of the dualistic perspective does not end with these basic forms of irony, for they in turn comprise the foundation for other characteristic devices of the Porter style. And there are still other stylistic elements that grow directly out of the dualistic perspective itself, thus bypassing the ironic structure. The devices supported by traditional and romantic irony have already been described; I shall look now at the classical progeny – satire, mask of boredom, and various configurations of pun and innuendo.

The dualistic perspective operating through classical irony juxtaposes the satirical artistic construct (the circumstance revealed) with the real object of the satire (the hidden circumstance). Sly allusions are made to the real object, but in classical satire there is always the 'fact withheld' which the dissembler uses both to lure the audience into participation and to protect himself from libel. Cole Porter's satire is most often aimed at the social upper crust of which he was a member (his ambivalent attitude towards this group being another obvious manifestation of the dualistic perspective), but he also made frequent sallies against such favourite subjects as fundamentalist religions, music, theatre, and politics.

He wore his mask of boredom with flair, as Byron had worn his mask of brooding, and both used the mask to whet the interests of their publics. At Yale he had already begun to experiment with the mask, but it was while entertaining in the salons of Europe that he perfected its use. He would pretend to be bored with whatever was fashionable, donning the mask while concealing the cause of his boredom. This device led to Porter's early reputation as a jaded dilettante.

His dualistic attitude to life was expressed through innuendo, the pun and the double entendre. 'Let's Do It, Let's Fall in Love' which relies on double meanings for its effect, was first sung by Irene Bordoni in *Paris* (1928) and then incorporated into other plays and films, most agreeably, the Hollywood version of *Can-Can* (1960). No doubt its implied improprieties have contributed to its endurance, as this selection from one of five refrains indicates:

> The dragonflies, in the reeds, do it,
> Sentimental centipedes do it,
> Let's do it, let's fall in love.
> Mosquitos, heaven forbid, do it,
> So does ev'ry katydid do it.
> Let's do it, let's fall in love.
> The most refined ladybugs do it,
> When a gentleman calls,
> Moths in your rugs do it,
> What's the use of moth balls?

Although in 1928 some critics remarked on Porter's propensity for chronicling the mating habits of animals, no one seems to have been offended by anatomical specifics.

'Let's Do It, Let's Fall in Love' also provides examples of a more straightforward effect of duality: antithetical syntax, i.e. the arrangement of words, phrases, and clauses into a balance between two contrasted elements. In the title, those elements are the two clauses. Ostensibly, the first clause, 'Let's do it', means exactly the same as the second. But as the lyric develops, it becomes clear that the mere act of falling in love produces neither Siamese Twins nor caviar, and one is forced to look beneath the first level to recognize a balance of contrasts, the sexual versus the sentimental.

The lyrics are as saturated with antithetical structures as they are with irony. Three other songs also written for *Paris* illustrate the extent to which antithesis pervades the lyrics, and also provide a description of theatre and audience in 1928.

'Dizzy Baby' is written in the fast 4/4 time of the Charleston which still held sway in 1928:

> You go so fast, I can't keep up with you,
> I'm tired of op'ning plays, and closing cabarets,
> I'd rather breakfast, dear, than sup with you.
> Why don't you let me make a bride of you,
> And stop that dynamo inside of you?

The syntactical antithesis occurs first in the gerundive phrases 'op'ning plays' and 'closing cabarets', and secondly in the compound verbs in the following line. The specifics of contrasts tend to be actual opposites and reflect the theatrical and social climate of 1928. As the twenties raced towards the disaster of 1929, Broadway kept pace, with 255 new productions in eighty theatres in 1928. In the legitimate theatrical season of September to May, it would have been possible to attend an opening on every night of the season, and Cole's 'Dizzy Baby' seems to have done just that, ending in the morning at one of the many cabaret superclubs fostered by prohibition.

The contrast between the fast-paced social nights and less frantic day-time activities, begun in 'Dizzy Baby' is amplified in 'Which'.

> Which is the right life,
> The simple or the night life?
> When, pray, should one rise,
> At sunset or at sunrise?
> Which should be upper,
> My breakfast or my supper?
> Which is the right life,
> Which?
> If the wood nymph left the park,
> Would Park Avenue excite her?
> Would the glow-worm trade her spark
> For the latest Dunhill lighter?
> Here's a question I would pose,
> Tell me which the sweeter smell makes,
> The aroma of the rose
> Or the perfume that Chanel makes?

Whereas in 'Dizzy Baby', the antithetical syntax was only a fragment of the whole lyric, here the song is structurally antithetical, and the antithesis is extended from the merely syntactic level to the thematic level. The theme introduced is the same as in 'Dizzy Baby', the simple versus the night life. Then Porter extends the contrast to the issue of nature versus art when he contrasts a wooded park with Park Avenue, a glow-worm with a Dunhill lighter, and Mother Nature's rose with Madame Chanel's perfume. In further verses of this song he extends the contrast to compare the pastoral delights of Arcadia with the urban desires of Bohemia.

In another song from *Paris*, 'Don't Look at Me That Way', the feminine singer tries to resist the temptations of her companion, protesting,

> My will is strong, But my won't is weak,
> So don't look at me that way.

The phrase is quintessential Porter, employing as it does, antithesis, pun, and sexual innuendo. The pun on the word 'will' operates with an interest-ing mechanism: it registers first as my 'determination', its second meaning being suggested only by contrast with 'won't' in the next clause. This meaning indicates the real feelings of the character, who actually wants to say 'yes' but must conceal that desire in the social context.

Nowhere is Porter's style more marked and accomplished than in *Any-thing Goes* and *Jubilee*. Both written at the height of his career in the mid-thirties, every aspect of these plays demonstrates his preoccupation with contrast and duality, from the smallest elements of style to the grandest production concept.

The title *Anything Goes* aptly describes what is Porter's most popular show with the general public. To be sure, Porter's references to international society, his irony and his satire are abundant in the lyrics, but in this tale of a small-time hoodlum who wants to be Public Enemy Number One, a stowaway who is following his former fiancée, and a nightclub singer who leads a revival aboard ship and captures the heart of an English Lord, Porter demonstrates that he can write for the masses while not sacrificing his own standards.

In the 1930s, only three musical productions had longer Broadway runs. The only legitimate book musical to run longer than *Anything Goes* was George and Ira Gershwin's *Of Thee I Sing*, which ran for twenty-one performances more. The other two productions to run longer than *Anything Goes* were revues: Harold Rome's political *Pins and Needles*, which ran for three years in the small Labor Stage Theatre, and Olsen and Johnson's infantile *Hellzapoppin'*. *Anything Goes* was one of the two most popular book musicals of the decade, but it had scarcely opened when Porter began work on the score for a very different kind of show. When *Jubilee* opened in 1935 it was praised for being aristocratic, suggesting both its excellence and its portrayal of the privileged class. Inspired by the recent Silver Jubilee of King George V, *Jubilee* is predominantly English in tone. Musically there is barely a trace of the American hot jazz vernacular; the score is subtle and complex with great variation: 'Kling-Kling Bird in the Divi-Divi Tree' is pure Gilbert and Sullivan; 'Me and Marie' recalls the music-hall tradition; 'When Love Comes Your Way' salutes Noël Coward; and 'Just One of Those Things' and 'Begin the Beguine' are vintage Porter. The mythical royal family of the book is obviously drawn from a knowledge of British aristocracy. When they try to elude royal responsibility by disguising themselves, they meet another kind of aristocracy, characters who are satirical portrayals of two of Porter's best friends, Noël Coward and Elsa Maxwell.

Almost the only thing that *Anything Goes* and *Jubilee* had in common is that they were the work of Cole Porter. One was written for brass, the other, for strings. One dealt with low-life, the other with aristocracy. One depended on low comedy, the other on wit and satire. Both were highly acclaimed, but only one achieved either monetary or popular success; however, taken together they represent Porter at the height of his form.

I shall discuss just two songs from the rich score of *Anything Goes* that includes 'All Through the Night' with its innovative descending chromaticisms and romantic irony, 'Blow, Gabriel, Blow', whose satire of fundamentalist revivals upset the New York religious community, the title song itself,

'Anything Goes', which, with its description of the topsy-turvy conditions of
the 1930s,

> The world has gone mad today,
> And good's bad today,

became the theme-song for the decade, and the two songs selected for
discussion here, 'You're the Top' and 'I Get a Kick out of You'.

'You're the Top' was unquestionably the most popular song from *Anything Goes* when the show first opened. In the midst of the furor over the
novelty of the lyrics there was some indecision: should it be called a
catalogue-song or a laundry-list-song? An eclectic list of rhyming superla-
tives, the song at the height of its popularity inspired hundreds of parodies.
The excerpt printed here is the original first verse with a partial refrain
(there are seven in the original) made up primarily of theatre references.

> *You're the Top*
> At words poetic, I'm so pathetic,
> That I always have found it best,
> Instead of getting 'em off my chest,
> To let 'em rest, unexpressed.
> I hate parading my serenading,
> As I'll probably miss a bar,
> But if this ditty is not so pretty,
> At least it'll tell you how great you are.
>
> *Refrain*
> You're the top. You're a Waldorf salad,
> You're the top. You're a Berlin Ballad.
> You're the nimble tread of the feet of Fred
>   Astaire,
> You're an O'Neill drama,
> You're Whistler's mama,
> You're Camembert.
> You're a prize,
> You're a night at Coney,
> You're the eyes
> Of Irene Bordoni.

The verse of 'You're the Top' is paradigmatic of the mature Porter style.
One purpose of the verse is to serve as an antithetical introduction to the
refrain, the contrast being set up by the individual internal antitheses, the
ironic expectation, and the manner in which the expectation is established,
self-deprecating and theatrical. The self-deprecation in 'At words poetic,
I'm so pathetic', and 'But if this ditty is not so pretty', originally sung by
Willam Gaxton in the role of stowaway Billy Crocker, reflects not so much
on the character as on Porter himself. He sheds his Byronic pose for the
other Byronic pose of comically feigned incompetence. The freedom of the
musical in the thirties allowed for this sort of communication with the

audience, and Porter encouraged the breaking of the fourth wall with his own sense of the theatrical. He often uses the verse to call attention to the fact that the words are indeed being sung, that the audience is indeed in the theatre sharing an experience with the performers. And in any Cole Porter production, a major part of that experience must be enjoyment of the intricate rhyme. This verse with its 'pathetic words poetic' contains fifty-three words of which fifteen are rhyming.

It is obvious that Porter garnishes his lyrics with the names of famous people, friends and others. But exactly how specific and timely his references are is not so apparent. The four theatrical references in the refrain, when examined against the background of theatre in the thirties, bear witness to the care with which he used allusion. The 'Berlin ballad' refers to Irving Berlin, perhaps the only friend that Porter could count among the Broadway composers and lyricists of the 1930s. Berlin had lost his entire fortune in the crash, and, in addition, had undergone a professionally unproductive period of several years during which time he was unable to write a successful score. However, in 1933 *As Thousands Cheer*, a musical revue with sketches written by Moss Hart, opened successfully and played for 400 performances (almost equalling *Anything Goes*). This revue contained two Berlin ballads, the classic 'Easter Parade' and the less famous 'Supper Time' sung by Ethel Waters. The reference to Fred Astaire is even more pertinent. He had made his first solo Broadway appearance, without his sister Adele, in Cole Porter's *The Gay Divorce* (1932). When with Adele, Astaire's style had a bouncy, uptempo delivery; however, the most important dance number in *The Gay Divorce* was 'Night and Day', for which Astaire began to develop the smooth style that he made famous in films. When *The Gay Divorce* was adapted for film, it became *The Gay Divorcée*, the first of the many films in which Fred Astaire and Ginger Rogers were dancing partners. It was released on 12 October 1934, a little over one month before *Anything Goes* opened on 21 November.

The last two references, to Eugene O'Neill and Irene Bordoni, lack the chronological immediacy of the two previous allusions, but have nonetheless a special significance. Eugene O'Neill had long been recognized as the prime revitalizing force for American theatre in the 1920s. In the 1930s he continued to dominate the legitimate theatre. *Mourning Becomes Electra* was performed in 1931, *Ah, Wilderness!* in 1933, and *Days Without End* in 1934. Not as famous as Eugene O'Neill, and by 1934 a fading star on the musical comedy horizon, Irene Bordoni was a personal favourite of Cole Porter. Their history together went back to 1915, when Cole was still a student at Harvard. Literary Agent Elizabeth Marbury had managed to get one of Cole's songs, 'Two Big Eyes', placed in Jerome Kern's *Miss Information*, where it was sung by Miss Bordoni. Furthermore, when, in 1928, the Porters returned to New York, it was for Cole to supply the

music for *Paris* produced by E. Ray Goetz as a vehicle for his wife, Irene
Bordoni.

Of the many other theatrical and personal allusions in 'You're the Top',
two are particularly interesting for their reflections on American theatre. In
the second verse, Ethel Merman sang

> Now gifted humans like Vincent Youmans
> Might think that your song is bad.

Vincent Youmans had written his last songs for the theatre in 1932 when
Ethel Merman sang 'Rise 'n' Shine' in *Take a Chance*. In 1933 Youmans had
moved to Hollywood to join the many composers who were working in
films. He composed the score for one film, *Flying Down to Rio*, and then was
stricken with tuberculosis. In 1934, the year of *Anything Goes*, he retired from
his long and successful career. A shorter and less successful career in
Broadway musical theatre was also evoked by Porter. In the second section
of the second refrain, the musical line ascends through the lyric,

> You're the purple light of a summer night in Spain,
> You're the National Gall'ry,
> You're Garbo's sal'ry,

and climaxes on the final word of the section,

> You're cellophane.

The product cellophane was an oddity in 1934, still sufficiently new to
warrant full-page advertisements in major magazines. However, for theatre
audiences, the product had made a more specific claim to fame on 20
February 1934, when the Gertrude Stein and Virgil Thomson opera *4 Saints
in 3 Acts* (naturally, it had four acts) opened on Broadway. The production
was the subject of much publicity and notoriety – not least because of its sets
which were made entirely of cellophane.

While 'You're the Top' immediately became the most popular song from
the *Anything Goes* score, the path of 'I Get a Kick out of You' was long and
circuitous, and in its original form it was subject to the distortion of
censorship.

The title 'I Get a Kick out of You' appeared first in a score prepared for
Stardust, an unproduced musical with book by Herbert Fields which E. Ray
Goetz had tried to produce in 1931. At this time, the last 'A' section[3] of the
song contained this lyric:

> I shouldn't care
> For those nights in the air
> That the fair
> Mrs Lindbergh goes through.

But when the Lindbergh baby was kidnapped on 1 March 1932, Porter
withdrew this lyric, and the song disappeared until 1933 when it emerged as

background music in *Nymph Errant*, an English musical produced by Charles B. Cochran and starring Gertrude Lawrence. *Nymph Errant* had a successful run in London, but never crossed the Atlantic, primarily because of the economic depression, but probably also because of the subject matter of the play: a young girl's struggle to unburden herself of her virginity, a struggle ably highlighted with some of Porter's most risqué lyrics. When next Porter wrote for an American audience, it was for *Anything Goes*. He had still not abandoned 'I Get a Kick out of You' and asked producer Vinton Freedley to obtain the rights from Cochran so that he might use the song in *Anything Goes*. In what must have been one of the better investments of 1934, the rights to the song were obtained for $5,000, and Cole's final version was included in the score.

I Get a Kick out of You
My story is much too sad to be told,
But practically ev'rything leaves me totally cold.
The only exception I know is the case,
When I'm out on a quiet spree,
Fighting vainly the old ennui,
And I suddenly turn and see,
Your fabulous face.

Refrain

I get no kick from champagne.	a
Mere alcohol doesn't thrill me at all	bb
So tell me why should it be true	c
That I get a kick out of you.	c
Some get a kick from cocaine.	a
I'm sure that if I took even one sniff,	dd
That would bore me terrific'ly too	dc
Yet I get a kick out of you.	c
I get a kick ev'rytime I see	e
You're standing there before me.	fe
I get a kick though it's clear to me,	e
You obviously don't adore me.	fe
I get no kick in a plane.	a
Flying too high with some guy in the sky	gggg
Is my idea of nothing to do.	gc
Yet I get a kick out of you.	c

Porter's dual perception is everywhere apparent in this lyric. The mechanism for classical irony, to reveal one circumstance while concealing another, underlies the mask of boredom which Porter raises in the first two lines. He reveals that he suffers from a jaded satiety, but conceals the whole story, or at least pretends that there is a story to be concealed. This contrast, set up in the first two lines, gradually yields in the remaining lines of the verse to a more obvious antithetical structure, the contrast between 'practically everything' and that 'fabulous face'. In the refrain the generality of the introductory verse is replaced with carefully chosen examples.

The governing principle underlying the choice of specifics in the refrain is to flaunt conventional attitudes and to mix his subjects satirically. Champagne, cocaine, and airplanes are all items about which the general public had strong, definite feelings. Champagne and airplanes aroused, in 1934, very positive responses. Champagne had always been considered the drink of the wealthy and aristocratic, and as such had a snob appeal for the socially conscious. After the lifting of Prohibition, however, the appeal was made stronger by a concentrated advertising campaign touting the virtues of champagne over its more potent rivals in the whisky family. The airplane needed no advertising to enhance its image. Ever since Lindbergh flew to Paris in 1927, he had been a hero to the American public, and the airplane a symbol of that esteem and affection. The seven years since the Paris non-stop flight had also seen a growth in aviation – so that one could indeed speak of 'the industry'. It was a growth that continued unabated into World War II when its romantic image would once more be enhanced by military pilots. When Porter used these two symbols as specifics with which he was bored, he invited a bifurcate response, i.e. one response is to regard the device as amusing hyperbole, and the other is simply to accept the statement as part of the story 'too sad to be told'. This duality of response is the logical concomitant to the posture of irony which posits the opposite of what is expected, in this case, boredom or lack of response being substituted for an enthusiastic positive response. But in the case of cocaine, it is a negative response which is expected by most of the audience. When the response is, instead, casual boredom, the reaction of all but the most liberated in the audience was to be shocked and to wonder at what evils were lurking behind the mask that Porter had raised.

Duality, antithesis, irony, the mask of boredom, and the (sometimes very radical) defying of convention are Porter trademarks. So also is complexity of rhyme.

The rhyme scheme of 'I Get a Kick out of You' is remarkably complex for a lyric born in the Broadway theatre, and it requires special notation. Customary practice calls for an indication of the basic scheme of end rhymes using small letters of the alphabet, the same letter being used for all lines rhyming with each other. This practice has been followed in the lyric printed here, with the special addition that when the letter is repeated on the same line or in the following line, each repetition indicates an internal rhyme the same as the end rhyme of the line where the letter first appears. The first characteristic to note is that all three 'A' section stanzas are linked by the same rhyme in their first lines, a repetition which reinforces the musical repetition of the first line (the only such musical repetition except for the burden at the end of the first two stanzas). This linkage of the stanzas supports the meaning of the song as well as the form, saving as it does this particular rhyme for the introduction of each new specific in the list of examples. It is with the second line of each of the 'A' section stanzas that the more intricate effects of Porter's rhyming are seen. The first stanza has only a double internal rhyme, 'alco*hol*' with 'me at *all*', and the rhyme does not extend into the final two lines of the stanza. After this first stanza, however, the number of rhymes begins to grow, spreading out into the third and fourth lines of the stanza. Note the second stanza's second and third lines,

> I'm sure that *if* I took even one *sniff*,   dd
> That would bore me te*rrif*ic'ly too,   dc

and the same lines in the fourth stanza (third and final 'A' section):

> *Fl*y*ing* too *high* with some *guy* in the *sky*   gggg
> Is my *i*dea of nothing to do.   gc

So, by the fourth stanza, Porter has built up to four pure internal rhymes, 'pure' here meaning a rhyme on an accented syllable and an accented musical note, and distinct from internal light rhyme, in which words that actually rhyme with end-stopped, accented rhymes are found on musically unaccented beats. If one considers this light rhyme, the lines quoted in the fourth stanza yield an additional rhyme in the word 'my'. And if one continues on to the burden beginning 'Yet I get', there is one more rhyme, hidden, as it were, between a different set of internal rhymes not even mentioned in the schema. The total of rhymes with 'sky' including all four lines in the fourth stanza is eight, an example unmatched in American musical theatre.

This final stanza requires further notice because of the amazing mergence of sense with the form of the musical line. Looking once more at the second and third lines printed in this manner:

> Flying too high with some guy in the sky is
> My idea of nothing to do

should help to make clear this mergence. The first line ascends naturally in a graceful arc that reaches its zenith on the word 'is', and the second line takes over at that height, arcing downward in a flowing, unhurried line. This is also the pattern followed by the music. The first line ascends in an unbroken scale going four notes beyond the octave, and the second line, rather than descending in a direct line, comes down gently, backing up one step and advancing two in studied casualness. The form of the line, then, as well as the meaning of the words themselves, builds towards an anticipated climax, only to drop off in disappointment just before fulfilment. In this manner the musical line also functions ironically in the traditional manner setting up one expectation and then delivering its opposite.

'I Get a Kick out of You' has endured in spite of its detractors and friends. It was many years before the American public as a whole actually heard the original lyrics to this song. In 1934 radio censorship bowdlerized the lyric, forcing a substitution of 'champagne' for 'cocaine' in the second stanza. As late as the 1970s, Chappell and Company and Random House published a collection of Porter songs including 'I Get a Kick out of You' with this substitution for the 'cocaine' reference:

> Some like a bop type refrain.
> I'm sure that if I heard even one riff
> That would bore me terrific'ly too.

But in spite of such accommodations to public taste either real or imagined, this song, with its champagne, cocaine and planes, has not only survived for almost fifty years; it has prospered.

So has 'Begin the Beguine'. First sung in *Jubilee* by June Knight playing nightclub singer Karen O'Kane, the song was showcased in a performance setting – an elaborate Jo Mielziner creation – that received more attention than the song. 'Begin the Beguine' was clearly ahead of its time, for it is a masterpiece of popular theatre music.

Begin the Beguine

When they begin the beguine,
It brings back the sound of music so tender,
It brings back a night of tropical splendor,
It brings back a memory ever green.
I'm with you once more under the stars,
And down by the shore an orchestra's playing,
And even the palms seem to be swaying,
When they begin the beguine.
To live it again is past all endeavor
Except when that tune clutches my heart,
And there we are swearing to love forever,
And promising never,
Never to part.
What moments divine, what rapture serene,
Till clouds came along to disperse the joys
    we had tasted.
And now when I hear people curse the chance
    that was wasted,
I know but too well what they mean;
So don't let them begin the beguine!
Let the love that was once a fire remain an ember.
Let it sleep like the dead desire I only remember
When they begin the beguine.
Oh yes, let them begin the beguine, make them play
Till the stars that were there before return above you,
Till you whisper to me once more 'darling, I love you'.
And we suddenly know, what heaven we're in,
When they begin the beguine,
When they begin the beguine.

Of Cole Porter's serious songs, 'Begin the Beguine' is the most effective. It is a dramatic monologue set to music; the music evokes the character's memory of a past love affair, transmuting the memory into the reality of the present. Then, with this duality of past and present, of memory and reality already established, the body of the song can explore the living memory by means of primary immediate experience as well as through the more controlled retrospect. Such complexity of content demands equal complexity of form. The mergence of content, form, meaning, music, and emotion is so complete that the evocation of the first few lines of the song brings back not only the immediate dream of the singer, but also the atmosphere and ambience of Cole Porter.

'Begin the Beguine' effects a radical transformation of the conventional thirty-two-bar popular song form, as a complex frame for the monologue. The song's great length – 108 bars – allows for six four-line stanzas of sixteen bars each and a twelve-bar coda. The form can be simply notated 'A A¹ B A² C C¹' plus the coda. Stanzas one to four are thus a greatly extended traditional song form; but in the addition of stanzas five and six (C C¹), along with the coda, the song declares its independence of the limits hitherto accepted for such songs. The musical juxtaposition of similar sections in the first four stanzas (the third, though different, bears distorted echoes of the first two) is analogous to the verbal and emotional juxtaposition of past and present, experience and reflection in the lyric, and serves as the first example of the complex mergence of components in the song.

The first stanza begins to present expositional detail, setting the stage for the narrative of the memory evoked in the last line. The beguine that has started in the present calls forth the memory of other similar music heard on a special night of 'tropical splendor'. This sensuous appeal to sound and sight summons the whole memory, 'a memory ever green', that is, a memory which is vivid and alive in the present, unaffected by the passing of time. Although this meaning is undoubtedly the most important in the last line, the contribution of the primary meaning of 'green' should also not be overlooked, since it reinforces the visual image of the lush tropical forest. The last three lines of this first stanza all repeat the words, 'It brings back', which gain power each time they are spoken, to insist upon recognition. And so, when the memory is brought back, it is young and alive and defies the confines of narration.

The second stanza joins the memory in a dream in which the past has become present. There is no narration here, but an immediate experience:

> I'm with you once more under the stars.

This one line not only establishes the move into the present reality of the memory, but also emphasizes that this is a repetition of a previous experience, a repetition to be triggered whenever a beguine is heard. More details are added. It is a clear night 'under the stars', and an orchestra is playing near the beach. A breeze, ruffling the fronds of nearby palms, makes them appear to sway with the rhythm of the beguine as the orchestra begins. With the fourth line of this stanza, 'When they begin the beguine', two things happen. First, these two sections are brought full-circle in completion of the first juxtaposition of sections, that is, the first line of the first stanza recalls the singer from her actual surroundings, while the last line of the second stanza restores her to those surroundings. Secondly, in this latter function of restoration, the line becomes a fulcrum, facilitating the change of position that begins the next stanza.

The first two lines of the third stanza are antithetical to the preceding stanza and to the third and fourth lines of this third stanza, for they at first deny the power to live again what has just been relived. Then the explanation is given, that it is impossible without the impetus of the music, and suddenly the dream re-establishes itself as the music soars to the first of several crescendos on the words, 'And there we are', asserting its power and evoking the dream once more. But this time the dream is not immediately experienced; it is rather viewed with an objective theatricality. The difference is stated in specific terms: 'I'm with you', versus 'There we are'. It is an important difference, for it is this objectification which allows for emotional detachment and the resultant assertion of romantic irony. It is the ironic perspective which, knowing the outcome of the affair, focuses on the empty vows and promises of the affair and exaggerates them for effect. 'Swearing to love forever' is balanced with 'And promising, never, never, to part' and the very bareness of the juxtaposition weakens the strength of both phrases, jeopardizing their efficacy on the level of ironic perception. Simultaneous with this intellectual perception, however, there is an emotional change as 'never' is first spoken and then repeated. Porter's musical direction calls for diminuendo here, a gradual lessening in volume, the opposite of the crescendo called for in the first phrase. The effect of words and music is to allow the dream to slip away in a mist; the music returns, meanwhile, to the keynote and, in the next stanza, the reality of the present.

Melodically, the material of this third stanza distorts fragments from the previous stanzas, as if repeating that tune, like reliving the moment, were 'past all endeavor'. And when the words of the fourth stanza move on to introspection – to actually thinking about the situation, not just bathing in the memory – the music exploits the formal convention (return of the 'A' theme) by crucially extending the musical vocabulary. Introspection brings tension and pain in the third line, so the music sharpens dissonance and strains the melody (augmented chords, whole-tone scale): it is as if the melody, mocking the lyrical rise of the first two stanzas, laments the wasted chance remembered in those stanzas.

The fourth stanza also contains several stylistic devices worth mentioning because of their contribution to the whole. Three of these are in the second line. The choice of clouds as a metaphor for the troubles that beset the affair is superior because of the unifying effect it produces with the previous stanzas' description of the shoreline setting with its tropical evening. This metaphor of clouds acts upon the 'joys' to lend an air of personification, as though the clouds gathered over a picnic and dispersed the crowd. And finally in this line there is the choice of the word 'tasted' which suggests physicality, sensuousness, indeed sensuality. In the last line, referring to 'the chance that was wasted', the singer says that she knows 'but too well' what it means. By so doing she lifts the Byronic mask, hinting at greater pain than she has acknowledged, and leading to rejection of the dream in the following stanza.

The fifth stanza begins by establishing a causal relationship with the fourth, i.e. because the memory of the affair brings pain, don't let them bring it back. The imagery of the stanza is sexual: 'love that was once a fire' but that burned itself down to 'an ember' and is now only 'dead desire'. The plea of this stanza is desperate, and the music supports the sense of it by suddenly jumping up an octave and repeating the same note in throbbing intensity throughout the first two lines, falling off only at 'remain an ember' after using the same note for fourteen out of the twenty-two syllables in those lines.

The last stanza, while it stands in antithetical contrast to the fifth, utilizes the same devices for supporting the emotional climax. Like the fifth stanza, it operates causally off the preceding, but more subtly. The motivation for this reversal of wishes is contained in the last two lines:

> Let it sleep like the dead desire I only remember
> When they begin the beguine.

They have begun the beguine and wakened the 'dead desire' from its sleep, and the first line reinforces the conclusion with the first words, 'Oh, yes, let them begin the beguine, make them play.' The commanding quality of 'make' signifies how far the lyric has developed from the gentle memories of the first stanza, and this emotional climax of yearning is reflected in the same throbbing, repeated note that was used in the fifth stanza, only here it is used for fifteen out of twenty-five syllables.

The last stanza, as with all of Cole Porter's finest work, is characterized by duality, an effect of that romantic irony which prevents a purity of position. Undoubtedly there is an earnestness about this last stanza, a painfully vulnerable, unmasked pleading for what has been lost to time and now lives only in memory and dreams. But there is also a trace of irony in the last lines. The beguine cannot bring back the stars any more than it can bring back the lover to whisper 'I love you'. It can only continue to bring back the 'memory ever green' each time 'they begin the beguine'.

Even the coda appears to have an ironic function. Ordinarily, the purpose of a musical coda is to bring a musical composition or movement to a complete, formal close; this one, on the other hand, appears to suggest a cyclical pattern. The coda itself is composed of the repeated clause 'When they begin the beguine' sustained over the final twelve measures of music. The first time the clause is sung the work is brought to the expected musical close, in repose with the keynote in both the treble and bass. When the repetition of the clause takes up the minor mode again, it is as though a new movement has started on the heels of the other. And this is the intention. Porter has suggested a purgatory of memory in which the lover must continually repeat the dream of the lost affair, continually 'curse the chance that was wasted'.

In 1935, when Cole Porter wrote the score for *Jubilee*, it had been twenty years since his first songs were heard on Broadway; he would continue to write for the Broadway theatre for another twenty years, his final score for the theatre being *Silk Stockings* which opened at the Imperial Theatre in New York on 24 February 1955 and ran for 477 performances. And throughout this forty-year period, his work was marked by that peculiar idiosyncratic perspective which, in spite of all the topical relevance, made him belong as much to the future as to his own time.

NOTES

1. Sheldon Cheney, founder of *Theatre Arts Monthly*, in conversation.
2. 'Like a show that's typically Shuberty', *Kiss Me Kate*, 1948.
3. The standard form of the American popular song was 'A A B A' – one 'A' section of eight measures, followed by a second, identical 'A' section, with that followed by a 'B' section, a different theme often called the 'bridge' or 'release', and finally a return to another 'A' section of eight measures for a total length of thirty-two measures.

French baroque dances
in the serious or noble style:
their notation and performance

WENDY HILTON

While music from the Middle Ages onward has been preserved in various forms of notation, the art of dance lacked any real equivalent until the first system of notation was devised in France during the last two decades of the seventeenth century, and ballroom and theatrical dances began to be published in 1700. During the preceding two hundred and fifty years, treatises relying on verbal descriptions of steps and dances appeared in clusters, with decades of silent years separating them. The first cluster belongs to the latter half of the fifteenth century and deals primarily with the lively and beautiful school of Domenico of Ferrara, and with the dance which predominated in Western Europe, the *basse danse* or *bassa danza*. The second cluster, published between 1580 and 1620, is concerned with *pavanes*, *branles*, and the intricate steps and technique of *gaillardes* and some Italian *balli*.

The foundations of a new style, which for want of a better term has been labelled 'baroque', are indicated in a book published in 1623, fifteen years before the birth of Louis XIV. The outstanding differences between the new technique and those of previous centuries were to be an outward rotation of the legs (to an angle of approximately forty-five degrees), and the use of the arms in a stylized opposition to the forward foot. Otherwise, the central social dances were still performed by one couple at a time, and the basic ingredients of dance remained the same: architectural spatial figures and an eloquent rhythmic wit. Because of Louis's active interest in dancing, the new style became highly developed artistically, technically, and scientifically during his lifetime (1638–1715). With theoretical principles established, and a notation devised, the art became more readily transmitted.

The book which inspired many others is a textbook explaining the notation, *Chorégraphie ou l'art de décrire la danse, par caractères, figures, et signes démonstratifs*, Paris 1700, by a Parisian dancing master, Raoul Auger Feuillet (see plate 5). The notation, however, is almost certainly the invention of another master, Pierre Beauchamp(s) (1631–*c.* 1719), previously dancing master to Louis XIV, and director of dance at the Paris Opéra (then the

5   A page from Feuillet's *Chorégraphie*: the first of eight pages showing the various ways of performing and notating one step-unit, the *pas de bourrée*

Académie Royale de Musique) during Jean Baptiste Lully's régime from 1672 until his death in 1687.

Feuillet was granted the exclusive right to publish in notation for six years, and he labored hard. By 1705 he had produced three large dance collections, fulfilled orders for ballets from foreign courts, and established an annual publication of the three or four new ballroom *danses à deux* (those designed for one couple to dance alone), composed each year for the court and high society. Feuillet published some of his own dances, but otherwise concentrated on ballroom and theatrical pieces by Louis Pécour (1660–1729), Beauchamp's successor at the Opéra. The majority of Pécour's dances were choreographed to music by Lully or André Campra (1660–1744), the most successful composer at the Opéra to follow Lully. Dances by Pécour are also extant to music by other composers such as Marin Marais, Cardinale Destouches, Theobaldo de Gatti, Louis de Lully and La Coste (see plate 6). The composer is rarely identified in dance scores but in theatre dances the name of the work is usually given. Among those of Lully are: *Amadis*, *Atys*, *Cadmus*, *Thesée*, and scenes from others which comprised the entertainment *Fragments de Mr de Lully* presented in 1702. The Campra pieces are largely from *L'Europe galante* (1697), *Carnaval de Venise* (1699), *Tancredi* (1702) and *Les Fêtes Vénitiennes* (1710).

When Feuillet's exclusive *privelège* expired in 1706, other masters hastened into the lucrative and prestigious market, and translations and paraphrases of *Chorégraphie* began to appear. Outside of France, the largest numbers of original dances were published in England, while elsewhere the most popular ballroom *danses à deux* from Paris were usually reprinted. In 1712, a few ballroom and many theatrical dances by Pécour were published in a beautiful book notated by the dancing master Le Sieur Gaudrau.[1] In addition to the printed sources, there are several large collections in manuscripts containing ballroom and theatrical dances by Pécour, Feuillet, and other French masters.

In England, a highly-respected court dancing master, Monsieur Isaac, composed a new dance every year in honor of Queen Anne's birthday. His later dances were notated and published by Mr Pemberton, who continued the series with Anthony L'Abbé, Isaac's successor at the court of George I. Anthony L'Abbé (*c.*1680–*c.*1737) came to London about 1699. He quickly became renowned as a dancer and choreographer and a good deal of his work is preserved in an undated collection notated, engraved, and published by F. le Roussau.[2] The first dance in this book had been 'performed before his Majesty King William ye 3rd by Mons. Ballon and Mr. L'Abbé'. Jean Ballon, star of the Paris Opéra, made his first visit to London in 1699. In 1707, L'Abbé was appointed 'Master to Compose and Teach at the Queen's Theatre', and later he was dancing master at the courts of George I and George II. While some of the music of L'Abbé's dances can be

6 A sarabande from *Issé* by Destouches. Pécour's dance is contained in a manuscript collection notated by F. le Roussau

identified as French, two have music by George Frederic Handel: 'The Prince of Wales, A New Dance for The Year 1727' is danced to part of an aria from *Julius Caesar*, and the 'Queen Caroline, A new Dance For her Majesties Birth Day 1728' to a march from *Scipione*.[3] Further associations of L'Abbé and Handel await the interested researcher.

As a result of all this activity some two hundred and fifty *danses à deux* and two hundred theatrical dances have survived. The latter are primarily solos (for a man or a woman) and duets (for a man and a woman, two men or two women). The ballroom *danses à deux* are virtually indistinguishable from many of the theatrical dances for one couple. Early eighteenth-century ballet had developed out of seventeenth-century ballroom dance and *ballet de cour* in which many of the performers were members of the court headed, in his younger years, by Louis XIV. With the establishment of L'Académie Royale de Musique in 1672, a purely professional company began to be built, but the same dance technique was to be shared by amateurs and professionals for some years to come. Stylistically the professionals emulated the noble and cultivated bearing of the amateurs, but ballet technique, especially for the male stars, soon became virtuosic.

It might be said that three levels of technical accomplishment are illustrated in the dances. There are many which would have been within the scope of almost all amateurs (bearing in mind that dancing lessons began in early childhood), others which were first performed by professionals and then taken over by the best amateurs, and there were dances for professionals which would have been well beyond the scope of all but the most exceptional amateur. The French notators usually indicate which dances were designed for the ballroom or the theatre, but Mr Pemberton is not so explicit. It is unclear, therefore, whether the Isaac and L'Abbé dances were performed by professionals as part of a royal entertainment or by members of the court in the ballroom.

The published theatrical dances by Pécour were selected from his compositions for stars of the Opéra, the most acclaimed of whom were Messieurs Ballon, Marcel, Blondy, and Doumoulin, and Mesdemoiselles Subligny, Prévost, Menèse, and Guiot. Roussau lists the combination of visiting male and resident female dancers who performed the L'Abbé dances in London:

Mons' L'Abbé	Mrs, Elford
Mons' La Garde	Mrs, Santlow
Mons' Dupré	Mrs, Bullock
Mons' Desnoyer	Mrs, Younger

The dances preserved in notation must have been considered to be the best contemporary dances and would have been composed for the abilities of the professional and most gifted amateur dancers. At least half are the work of the formost choreographer, Louis Pécour, and must be taken as representing the highest achievements in early eighteenth-century ballet and court dance – achievements which followed those of Beauchamp and Lully, himself an outstanding dancer and mime as well as composer, in their collaborations in the seventeenth-century *ballets de cour* and *tragédies-lyriques*, and with Molière in his *comédies-ballets*. Pécour had been a leading dancer at the Opéra under Beauchamp, and was highly praised for his ability 'to take all kinds of parts with grace, precision, and lightness'. The same writer describes Pécour's success as a choreographer: 'He had need to put forth all his powers in order to fill worthily the place of the master who preceded him; this he accomplished by the new turns and additional graces he gave to the ballets already composed by Beauchamp.'[4]

Pécour was basically choreographing with the step-vocabulary developed and systematized by Beauchamp and other masters during the silent years between 1623 and 1700, when no book on the 'serious' style of dance is known to have been written. The publications between 1700 and 1735 (after this date authors mainly repeated the same information and only a few new dances were notated) provide material which may be applied with discretion to the works of Lully and Molière because their dance forms, many of which were introduced by Lully, were retained into the eighteenth century. Moving forward in time, the same principle applies to much of the dance music of Jean Philippe Rameau.

The current dance types were almost all employed in both the ballroom and the theatre, although (with the exception of the *courante* which was almost totally abandoned by 1700) the slowest types were generally used in the theatre. These were the *sarabande, chaconne,* and *passacaille,* all in triple meter, the duple *entrée grave* (similar to the opening section of a French overture), and the *gigue lente* or *loure.* The *canarie,* by contrast one of the liveliest dances, also belonged primarily to the realm of the theatre as did the hornpipe in 3/2 time, a wonderfully happy and exciting dance found in English sources. The ballroom and theatre dances were the more moderate triple-meter *menuet* and its faster version the *passepied,* the duple *gavotte, bourrée, rigaudon,* and *allemande* (although only one example is extant), and the *gigue* and *forlane,* a new dance introduced at the end of the seventeenth century. The *loure* appeared occasionally as a triple-meter dance, as opposed to the compound-duple *gigue lente* or *loure,* the most famous *loure* of all being the air and dance *Aimable Vainqueur.*

Only the *menuet* and the *passepied* had their own step-units (step-units were combinations of steps, springs or other actions, one unit usually equalling one measure of music). Some of these were comprised of non-springing steps, others contained some springs, while yet others were comprised entirely of springs. The more lively the type of dance, the more sprung step-units it contained. Only the minuet, however, was danced without any springs at all, and then only in its simplest form.

Of the twenty or so basic step-units, about two-thirds had several variations or became elaborated in various ways. In addition to these units, which were used both in the ballroom and in the theatre dances, there were the more elaborate units developed only for the theatre. Theatrical dances also contained many of the technical feats which were often thought to have been developed in nineteenth-century ballet; *tour en l'air, pirouettes à la seconde,* and *entrechat six.* A dance in Roussau's L'Abbé collection calls even for a lady to perform one-and-a-half *pirouettes* on one foot, the other lifted sideways off the floor; and the combination of a *tour en l'air* and *entrechat six* is common in L'Abbé's dances for men. These technical elaborations are slipped into the rhythmic flow of the dance and are consequently harder to perform than in nineteenth-century ballet where *pirouettes*, for instance, are usually preceded and concluded in a position with the weight firmly placed over both feet. With a knowledgeable audience, almost all of whom would have at least struggled with the minuet, such technical accomplishments did not need to be emphasized by an obvious preparation or concluded with a flourish. The experienced audience could appreciate the ease with which the dancer overcame the difficulties without disturbing the complicated rhythmic pattern he was phrasing.

For the dancer today, even the simplest baroque dance is taxing technically and intellectually. The rhythmic content, often with long phrases and teasing musical interplay, is an unfamiliar idiom requiring musical sensitivity and a relish for intellectual exercise. Above all, today's performer must aspire towards the carriage and the style of motion of his ancestors, the air of the nobleman, the man of high birth and good breeding, qualities which most professional performers could only do their best to emulate. Here today's actor can join the dancer for a while, because the simplest baroque social dance, the minuet, may be required of him in period productions or the increasing number of television features concerned with historical personalities.

The most comprehensive instructions on carriage, bows and courtesies, ballroom etiquette, and the basic step-units of the dance, are found in eighteenth-century dance manuals, the most useful of which are *Le Maître à danser* by P. Rameau, Paris 1725, and *The Art of Dancing* by Kellom Tomlinson, completed in 1724 and published in London in 1735. Rameau in particular stresses above all the need for an assured ease of manner, an avoidance of all affectations, an open, relaxed, and pleasant countenance. The professional dancer would have to convey these qualities from the stage and as the famous English master John Weaver observed, '*Common-Dancing* [ballroom dancing] has a peculiar Softness, which would hardly be perceivable on the Stage; so Stage-Dancing would have a rough and ridiculous Air in a Room'.[5]

The simplest *danse à deux* was the *menuet ordinaire* which was in vogue from about 1664 until the disturbances of the French revolution (see plate 7). But simplicity poses great problems as Kellom Tomlinson observed: 'The Minuet is one of the most graceful as well as difficult Dances to arrive at a Mastery of, through the Plainess of the Step and the Air and Address of the Body that are requisite to its Embellishment.'[6]

The two dancers winding their way through the confines of the minuet were exposed to the critical gaze of their peers. With nothing of an elaborate nature to serve as camouflage, defects in breeding and character were

7   A moment in the standard ballroom minuet as given by Kellom Tomlinson in
The Art of Dancing (London, 1735)

mercilessly revealed. As Sarah, Duchess of Marlborough observed, 'I think
Sir S. Garth is the most honest and compassionate, but after the minuets
which I have seen him dance, and his late tour into Italy, I can't help
thinking that hee may sometimes bee in the wrong.'[7]

Dances other than the minuet use the stylized arm motions in which one
arm is raised in 'natural' opposition to the forward foot. The difficult
coordinations involved in this apparently simple action (see plate 8) put the
other ballroom dances beyond the scope of present-day actors, primarily
because so little time is given to studying any dance thoroughly in drama
schools. How many actors can waltz, for instance, beyond a shaky, basic
down-up-up?

The ballroom *danses à deux* are best performed today by those who have
studied both modern dance and ballet to a reasonable level of competency,
and who have an instinctive rapport with the period. The dancers must

8   A figure from *Le Maître à danser* by Pierre Rameau (Paris, 1725) showing the
use of the arms in opposition to the forward foot

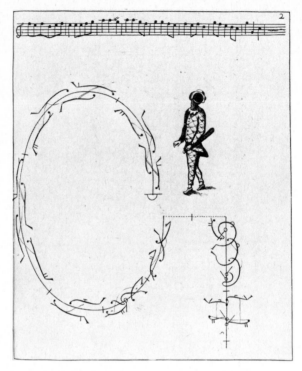

9   A page from *Chacoon for a Harlequin* by F. le Roussau

appear believable as persons schooled in the ideals of eighteenth-century deportment, and approximate those courtiers who won the praise of their peers for being fine dancers. Because the *danses à deux* are so similar to theatre dances they also furnish modern choreographers with valuable models for their work in baroque opera. The theatre dances in the noble or serious style (dances which employ the basic steps and elaborations with only the orthodox arm motions) offer examples of pieces for such diverse personifications as Greek gods, French and Spanish ladies and gentlemen, less formal French, Spanish and Venetian personalities, nymphs, graces, shepherds and shepherdesses, and *peasants héroiques*. Other dances in which the same step-vocabulary is utilized have arm gestures expressive of the character represented. Such a dance is F. le Roussau's *Chacoon for a Harlequin*. The notated score is augmented with drawings showing typical situations of the body and head, and arm gestures, hat in hand, for Harlequin's bows (see plate 9). Other scores show specific places where peasants make use of their own particular brand of hat.

Another aspect of eighteenth-century dance which has attracted considerable attention, especially in America, is the experimentation with dramatic gesture directly expressive of the passions, notably the work of John Weaver and Marie Salle in London, and the performances at the residence of the Duchesse du Maine at Sceaux. This type of dance is not documented in a notation and the interpreter must rely on verbal description and pictorial evidence. That this aspect of dance remained outside the continental mainstream is indicated by Jean-Georges Noverre's need to rail in violent terms against the continuing lack of direct dramatic expression in dance during the mid-eighteenth century.[8]

The time is auspicious for a serious revival of interest in baroque dance, which should also make a crucial contribution to the performance of baroque opera. In the course of the 1970s notable inroads were made at the Stockholm Opera, Drottningholm, the Royal Opera House, Covent Garden, and in New York at the Juilliard Theatre; but no choreographer can call on a sufficiently large number of dancers trained in baroque style (as the style is conceived by those who try to reconstruct it). Choreographers must usually do what they can with dancers trained only in nineteenth-century ballet, in a short rehearsal period allowing inadequate time to teach style. In fact it takes two years for an already accomplished dancer to mature in baroque dance and to do it justice stylistically, rhythmically, expressively and technically through the whole gamut of its range from the so-called 'simple' minuet to the most complex theatre dance. Only with an extraordinary natural talent like that of Eileen Cropley, who is the most noble performer of baroque dance today, could a dancer appear mature in the idiom without many months of earnest application.

Because of its demands, baroque dance must be earnestly undertaken if the performer is to meet his responsibility to the material and to his (almost entirely) unknowledgeable audience. A central problem is that these demands are often obscured under a heap of superficialities. First, there is the feeble style falsely labelled 'baroque' conjured up for presentation in the nineteenth century and further corrupted by twentieth-century choreographers. There is also the misleading notion that baroque deportment was flamboyantly 'affected'. Nothing could be further from the truth. The ideal of baroque deportment as described in the numerous contemporary treatises was a very intricately studied *simplicity*. As was noted in *The Spectator*, 'Good breeding shows itself most ... where it appears the least.'[9]

The baroque dancer must maintain a strong center line in the body, even when the shoulders are shaded in conjunction with the opposition of the arms. The arm motions, although primarily actions of the lower arms, must begin from the back and centre of the body. And more than any other grace, it is the carriage of the head which distinguishes the nobility of the fine dancer in the noble style (see plate 10). Those who failed to achieve an impressive formal presence through simple means were regarded as weak or

J. Berin del.

10 A professional dancer. Dance collection, New York Public Library at
Lincoln Center, Astor, Lenox and Tilden Foundations

at least suspect characters, lacking in breeding or education. Dancing was studied for its own sake, of course, as an enjoyable social activity, but primarily it was studied as the means of achieving the ideal realization and presentation of oneself in public. We must be constantly aware of this seriousness of purpose in our attempts, as historians, to understand baroque dance and, as practitioners, to recreate the movements and emulate the tone of the original dancers in the serious, noble style.

NOTES

1. Gaudrau, *Nouveau recüeil de danse ... de la composition de Mr Pécour* (Paris, 1712). For a comprehensive bibliography of early eighteenth-century sources, see Wendy Hilton, *Dance of Court and Theater: The French Noble Style 1690–1725* (Princeton: Princeton Book Company, 1980).
2. F. le Roussau, *A New Collection of Dances ... by Monsieur L'Abbé* (London, early eighteenth century).
3. These identifications were made by Carol Marsh Rowan.
4. Pierre Rameau, *Le Maître à danser* (Paris, 1725). Preface, translated in Cyril W. Beaumont, *The Dancing Master* (London: privately published, 1931).
5. Quoted by Joan Wildebloode in the preface to her translation of *Apologie de la danse*, by F. de Lauze, 1623 (London: Frederick Muller, 1952).
6. Kellom Tomlinson, *The Art of Dancing* (London, 1735) p. 105.
7. David Green, *Sarah, Duchess of Marlborough* (New York: Charles Scribner's Sons, 1967) p. 200.
8. Jean-Georges Noverre, 1727–1810. His letters were published in 1760.
9. *The Spectator*, 17 July 1711.

Dance in America in the 1970s:
a personal view from Los Angeles

CHRISTENA L. SCHLUNDT

In the course of the 1970s dance came to occupy the attention of more Americans than in any previous decade. First of all, it was supported by the government as never before: in 1960, the annual budget of the National Endowment for the Arts (NEA) was $2·5 million; by 1979 this had risen to $150 million in the form of matching grants (that require local groups to raise equal amounts in their own communities). Secondly, dance activity is no longer centered so exclusively in New York: when the endowment started, thirty-seven permanent companies, classic and modern, existed in the country; by 1979 there were more than two hundred. The NEA support has greatly increased the amount of dance and has spread it throughout the nation: in 1970 80 per cent of the audiences for dance performance in the United States were in New York City; by 1979 that figure was 20 per cent.[1] So the fact that this report comes from the westernmost edge of this vast country is not inappropriate, as such a report on any previous decade *would* have been. There are now a good number of American cities that produce dance of national importance. New York has not dwindled, but the rest of the country has flourished and the premier city no longer dominates American dance as it did. As a result, those of us who have been part of this decentralizing trend have a new opportunity to speak as participants rather than as observers.

Of course no other American city has the equivalent of George Balanchine and his unique New York City Ballet, but nor does any European city. That company remains preeminent, and there are recent signs that it is not going to remain a monolith forever. True, as dancers report,[2] all the decisions are still made by Balanchine and, except for the contributions of Jerome Robbins, the choreography shown by the company remains that of Balanchine. The sign of a break in this practice is the nurturing of the choreography of Peter Martins, the Danish-trained and Balanchine-honed dancer. Most recent to be seen was his *Sonate di Scarlatti*, a dance for an ensemble of ten, broken into several couple-dances with opening and closing group work. Deborah Jowitt of *The Village Voice* reports that, whereas in Martins's first ballet, *Calcium Light Night*, there were 'assertions on the spiky dissonant aspect of Balanchine's style', the Scarlatti piece, while reflecting both the Danish background and the Balanchine training of Martins, is more truly Bournonville in its 'subtly cordial interplay between dancers'.[3] Whatever the sources of either of these works by Peter Martins, the significance for us is that a choreographer who makes good dances with his own personal stamp is emerging at a crucial time in the history of the New York City Ballet. Even Balanchine will not live forever, we all keep telling ourselves, and what then for the New York City Ballet? Robbins is erratic and he is no longer a young man; for such a major company to have just one choreographer would not have been satisfactory, but now with Martins, who is very young, a fresh, continuing supply of aesthetic integrity is promised.

The spread of dance activity has fostered dancers of high quality in areas very remote from New York. Southern California, for example, is fortunate to have a person of such integrity as Bella Lewitzky. Born and raised in this desert, Bella has many admirable qualities which remain unspoiled by the belatedness of her recognition. Her achievement is now being given nationwide exposure and it promotes a positive image across the country. That other native-born California dancer, Isadora Duncan, scandalized the world as she danced. Bella is similarly extreme about the elemental truths in her art, but as a leader in her country, her community, and her company, she is a solid, thoughtful dance citizen. She was the existential, holistic Californian long before people began to make money selling that as a commodity. A piercing intellect shines forth in both her choreography and her teaching. No other dancer's technique respects the physical qualities of the human body to such a degree as hers. Not female in a limited way as Graham's or aesthetically surgical as Cunningham's, her technique articulates the body as a whole and, respecting its operations, lets the body speak. Her recent choreographies have carried this orientation to the extreme: *Recesses*, for example, is a series of solos which take for their subject matter the personalities and performance styles of the dancers themselves.

The grants she receives from the most prestigious foundations are pittances in relation to her needs. And what does she spend her money on? Her dancers. She requests money for a touring van elaborately equipped to service those fragile frames which are extensions of herself now that she no longer performs. Dancers for this great lady have always been artists worthy of support and care. Bella Lewitzky raises the level of the art in every appearance her company makes, in America and Europe alike. Wherever regional dance has representatives of such thorough integrity as Bella, dance will be in healthy condition.

But I must also report the less admirable aspects of dance in Southern California. For example, Harry Kipper (of *The Kipper Kids*, identified as practising 'Neanderthal commedia dell'arte'[4]) is reported by Kay Larson to have engaged in certain 'art' activities in Los Angeles and Santa Monica: 'an all-night Nietzschean/Dionysian immersion in crucifixions, blood and gutted animal carcasses, accompanied by the wail of trumpets'. On a similar level are Chris Burden's crawl over broken glass on a Los Angeles street, and his entombment in a locker at the University of California for seven days, which Hoberman claims to have 'grown into art-world legends'. These incidents apparently do occur; and I have personally accepted the invitation to share in the achieving of new psychic, racial, and sexual relations through art with Ann Halprin of San Francisco, and also in the processing of old cosmic myths through happenings with Allan Kaprow of San Diego. The term 'dance' sometimes becomes confused with a multitude of activities.

The impact of recent technological advances on the art is extremely significant. In addition to the efforts of NEA, the dispersion of dance across the land has been carried on through the medium of television. And now this has been greatly extended by the video cassette recorder, which makes it easily possible to record dance performances, in the way musicians have for decades been able to store music on discs and tapes.

The programmes available on television will largely determine the nation's tastes in dance. In fact, public television (PBS), the major presenter of theatrical dance on television, will be the determining force if present trends continue. Though supported ostensibly through citizen subscriptions, public television depends a great deal on grants for the funding of such expensive productions as ornate operas and panoramic dances. These grants come from various places, chiefly government and corporate, the latter supporting almost half of PBS programmes.

As is true in other areas of programming, the kind of art these corporate sponsors choose to support is established and safely non-controversial. The 'Dance in America' series, for example, is of consistently high quality even if the list of companies presented is predictable and is predictably led by the New York City Ballet. Most of us jump for joy that the treasures of the established national companies are being recorded for repeated viewing. Balanchine creations can now be studied in great detail, Merce Cunningham constructs can be dissected, Alvin Ailey block-busters can be savored. The last 1979 programme in this series was an analysis of the workings of the Eliot Feld Ballet, with appearances by cooperating musicians Aaron Copland and Morton Gould. The variety of this prolific young choreographer can only be suggested in a single hour, but his beautiful *Intermezzo* (to music of Johannes Brahms), a series of *pas de deux*, is wonderfully thrilling. Other dances by Feld included in this show are *Danzon Cubano* and *La Vida*, both to music by Copland, *The Real McCoy* (Gershwin music), and *Sante Fe Saga* and *Half Time*, both to Morton Gould music.

Besides PBS productions, the commercial television stations have let us see some dance events when they have been spectacular enough. Again sponsored by corporations, those selected have been established companies doing the established dances – *Giselle* by the Bolshoi, *Nutcracker* by the American Ballet Theatre, *Sleeping Beauty* by both American Ballet Theatre and the British Royal Ballet. Just as independent film makers seldom have their new and different talents presented on television, so the idiosyncratic dance company is seldom given a viewing. No controversial companies are ever seen nationally.

Modern dance and ballet have about equal time on television. Martha Graham had good exposure in the mid-seventies and in 1979 she adapted her evening-length *Clytemnestra* to fit a television time slot. In the past, Graham shocked small-town America with the emphasis on sex in her choreography. She is still having trouble playing in small-town Peoria – no longer because her central focus is shocking, but now because it seems dated and irrelevant. In *Clytemnestra*, the queen as dancer, shown on her platform brooding, remembering, while her memories are represented by dancers cavorting around her feet, seemed to be demented over nothing. The America that has lived through some bad wars has come to regard her preoccupations as superficial and cannot now take her personal pain so seriously. The nature of the Graham Company's protracted existence puzzles not only the television audience but the dance world in general; and Fonteyn selling leotards on television talk-shows causes us to turn away in confusion and shame. Television dissemination of dance and dancers across the land has its virtues and limitations. The ability to select the excellent over the shoddy is always necessary.

Live dance, of course, remains the essence of the art form, and a number of those two hundred dance companies are at work on the West Coast – some in Los Angeles, more out of San Francisco, a few in San Diego – they are all companies which flourish because their members so desperately want to dance. This drive to dance, a drive honoured at length in the musical *Chorus Line*, is combined in these small companies with the desire to choreograph, to make dances. Not just to dance someone else's choreography, but to make one's own statement – that is what is behind the plethora of dance companies (those led by Martha Graham, Merce Cunningham, Jose Limon, Rudy Perez, and Alvin Ailey are only a few of the best known) which cover the United States. The desire to make one's own dances is essential to modern dance, and is unrelated to ballet. At the beginning of the century, Isadora Duncan and Ruth St Denis both made their own dances as expressions of their personal philosophies. They insisted that dances could make serious statements, and need not be beautifully empty. Martha Graham, Doris Humphrey, Charles Weidman, Helen Tamiris, Hanya Holm also expressed themselves in the 1930s through their own choreography based on their own technique. Choreography out of technique out of message – this way of making dances was disseminated in the schools by John Dewey's work at Columbia Teachers' College. His slogan 'learn by doing' helped to send dance into the schools and universities, where it still flourishes with a crucial influence on the whole national scene.

The West Coast, for example, is interlaced with a network of educational institutions which foster this philosophy of expression through movement. In the Los Angeles area alone, prestigious schools based on this philosophy include CalArts, which presents it most purely without any academic 'load'. The University of California at Los Angeles and California State University at Long Beach are the largest of the more than twenty institutions which turn out dancers who make their own dances. These institutions support the myriad small companies by using the company members as teachers and choreographers, sometimes importing the entire companies as artists-in-residence; and in reciprocation they send their dancers out to the companies as performers. No one surveying any urban scene in the United States can ignore this interlocking support of dance between the small companies and the university departments.

Let us look at just one of these college departments. A fluctuating but persistent part of the Los Angeles dance mix has been the new educational institution, endowed with Walt Disney money, the California Institute of the Arts in Valencia, on the northern periphery of greater Los Angeles. At one time Bella Lewitzky determined its educational philosophy in dance; other dance teachers have followed with their own emphases and creativity. In 1979, the Paul Taylor dancer Nicholas Gunn was in town; he was invited to join the faculty, and he reconstructed his roles in two of his mentor's works, *Aureole* and *Duet*, and performed them along with the students at Cal Arts.[5]

One of the Los Angeles companies, the Eyes Wide Open company, was composed of five young artists nurtured by Bella Lewitzky, the University of California, and CalArts. During the seventies, these dancers and designers set up a representative modern dance company, though it was run cooperatively rather than monarchically. Eyes Wide Open began, small and earnest, by presenting the usual program with four or five works, each dance choreographed by one of its members, some mounted with money from the National Endowment for the Arts. Infrequent performances at a supporting church, a summer arts colony, various friendly colleges, random enterprising shopping malls, and at the arty 'Rug Concerts' of the Los Angeles Music Center kept the group going for two or three years. It then combined with another dance company to set up the Pacific Motion Dance Studio in Venice, on the western coastal periphery of greater Los Angeles. There all members of both companies taught their specialties, gradually adapting their offerings as the preference of their Los Angeles clientele told them what classes were in demand. Jazz and tap, it turned out, sold more than modern dance.

These old skills, learned by the artists when they were children, found new expression. Soon the Eyes Wide Open company broke up into various new groupings. One member with a short skit based on Betty Boop teamed up with another who had perfected an Olive Oyl creation, and they left for Las Vegas. Three dancers, Fred Strickler and Lynn Dally (out of Ohio studios) and Camden Richman, came to work together then teamed up with a percussion group under the name Jazz Tap Percussion Ensemble, and performed in Los Angeles, San Francisco and New York, where they were very well received. In *The Village Voice* Sally R. Sommer argued that this group is in the forefront in new directions being taken by dance in the country. In a review covering two months of performances in the New York area, she wrote: 'The exploration of rhythm and intonation possible when tapping, uniquely combined with a modern dance sensibility, gives the Jazz Tap Percussion Ensemble, visiting from Los Angeles, an amazing distinction. By far the most accomplished of all the groups, their technique is impeccably enunciated, and their play with tap *sounds* is sophisticated as musical composition.'[6] She sees the use of tap in concerts as more than a nostalgic revival, rather an encompassing of traditions of the past in new explorations in the choreography of sound and movement.

Two favorite choreographers working today are Meredith Monk and David Gordon, both of whom are based in New York and tour the country infrequently. Their ability to set up a reverberation of memories, tensions, references, in non-related roughhewn material, causes thrills of recognition both while their works parade before us and after they recede into our minds. Monk was on two stages of the University of California at Los Angeles this spring, one large for her dance *Paris/Milan*, the other small for *The Plains*. In the former, all of Italy tumbled before our eyes as the out-sized Lee Nagrin cartwheeled across the stage. In the latter, the inevitability and loneliness of dying on the prairie splayed out to encompass us all, as the plainswoman character took the dark figure of death to her bosom. Such choreographic invention in the handling of disparate images makes the workings of a Tai Takai seem simple in comparison. Cerebral performances, when they are once understood – a giant jig-saw puzzle gradually takes up the space and obliterates the few people posturing there, or a shower of rocks litters the space of the ritualists pounding both cold rocks and vulnerable feet – bring only an intellectual nihilism, which is powerful for some people but completely foreign to the rich, reverberating human feeling of a Monk or a Gordon. Both performed in New York in the fall of 79. Gordon played variations on an old work in *The Matter (plus and minus)*,[7] Monk explored new territory in *Recent Ruins*.[8] Each has a unique co-worker who rings her own reverberations in the audience's mind – pensive heavy-lidded Velda Satterfeld for Gordon, puckish monumental Lee Nagrin for Monk. Nagrin presented her own work in the spring, a piece simplistically categorized as environmental (she is a painter, among other things), but it was richly reverberatory as theatre.

Tired terms such as 'opera' are used to describe these works, but they do not adequately describe the experience. Super intelligences are working here, with no limitation either of movement or theatrical means. Each element selected and used – objects from daily life juxtaposed with artfully made articles, dancers' techniques combined with everyday movements, elemental dirt dropped on silver Mylar, alien sounds blended with Muzak – carries a load of reference for both mind and heart.

But not all of the two hundred companies which dot the States are composed of modern dancers. Ballet is supported in this country by studios in every urban center. Quality varies, of course, according to the individual instructor. Dance studios dating from the turn of the century and earlier, have courses of instruction which follow Cecchetti, some variation of the British Royal Academic series, or a mixture of the training brought in by immigrant teachers. San Francisco has fared excellently with its ballet, solidly based in the Christianson Brothers' work, and recently boosted by innovations from American Ballet Theatre's Michael Smuin. Dance in San Diego flounders among internecine squabbles and discontent caused by the importation of international stars. All these ballet companies produce some female dancers who are skilled enough to do a crowd-pleasing *pas de quatre* from *Swan Lake*. But once trained (that is, once they have been introduced to the addiction), these women normally do not stay at the home studio. Eagerly, they are off to New York or San Francisco or Washington to disappear into the corps of the large United States companies. Or some get to dance in the crowd scenes when the international companies come to visit.

As part of the spread of Balanchine ballet over the land, New York City Ballet dancer John Clifford moved to Los Angeles in 1973. Clifford has stuck longer than the many others who have tried to create a permanent ballet company in Los Angeles. The *Los Angeles Times* will not accept the Clifford product, whether or not its repertoire is glossed over with Balanchine influences. The *Times* music and dance critic, Martin Bernheimer, and his staff are not eager to beat chauvinistic drums just to say Los Angeles has a first-rate ballet company. Instead, they beat Clifford productions unmercifully for what they take to be pretentiousness. For example, the Clifford production for Christmas 1979, a lavish mounting at the Los Angeles Music Center of *The Nutcracker*, was to emulate the stunning and lucrative winter production of that ballet put on every year in New York by Balanchine's company. In a long review in the *Times*, Lewis Segal challenged the claim, made in both announcements and programs by the company music director, Clyde Allen, that this LAB *Nutcracker* was unique because of historical research restoring the ballet's 'musico-dramatic synchrony'.

> This research reportedly included obtaining from Soviet sources (but un-available to the *Times* upon request) a copy of the original scenario that choreographer Marius Petipa sent to Tchaikovsky and then commissioning a translation of it from Russian into English. According to Allen, using this detailed scenario enabled LAB choreographer John Clifford to avoid the trivialization of many previous productions. This choreography will be in sync with the music.[9]

Segal proceeded, then, to demolish the claim by pointing out the specific passages in which the choreography did not 'sync' with the music. He dismissed LAB's *Nutcracker* as being no more professional than any small-town production.

> ... it is artistically faceless – the same type of traditional children's ballet production every regional company mounts each Christmas using troops of local kids, platoons of aspiring ballet students and a handful of professional dancers. Its best ideas are borrowed and its failings are those endemic to sub-professional companies: mediocre choreography, uneven dancing, in-adequate conducting.[10]

The production was well mounted, with unusually opulent sets and cos-tumes by Robert O'Hearn, but the stand-off continues: John Clifford tries doggedly and the local paper will not applaud.

The *Los Angeles Times* itself still shows signs of provincial attitudes. It clamours for a Los Angeles Ballet; it insists that Los Angeles should have one, since it is a big city now. But the *Times* is unwilling to accept the fact that Los Angeles has had its dance company for years in the line established by Lester Horton and continued by Bella Lewitzky. At every chance, the newspaper acknowledges the excellence of Lewitzky's work, but as modern, the 'other' dance, not as ballet, the primary dance. Indeed, the *Times* continues the provincial practice of combining the roles of dance critic and music critic. The newspaper itself has not yet grown up to the 'big-city' maturity of separating the two and giving dance primary rather than secondary distinction among the arts. The *Times* fulminations at the inade-quacies of the Los Angeles Ballet would be taken more seriously if in its own house dance were more than a step-sister of music. One clear indication of the *Times* attitude to dance is the fact that the report on the December 1979 Bournonville Centenary festival in Denmark was farmed out. If dance had full status, its own critic would not have missed such an important occasion in western dance.

When we consider some over-all characteristics of the dance scene, whether ballet or modern, musical comedy or movie, we see that the so-called 'revival' is everywhere. From Los Angeles to New York, the practice of presenting a dance choreographed for some previous performance has become the dominant mode of presentation. Brendan Gill of *The New Yorker* finds nothing wrong with this practice.

> It occurs to me that the word 'revival' ought to be forcibly retired from our theatrical vocabularies. Increasingly to contemporary audiences, it appears to carry the stigma of something diminished from the original – of being second-hand and therefore necessarily second-rate, bearing the tarnish of age rather than a patina. Most plays worthy of being revived are, after all, classics, and we need say of them no more than that they are being given new productions, the quality of which we are free to praise or damn solely on their merits, without prejudice or apology.[11]

Gill was here discussing not only revivals of such plays as Turgenev's *A Month in the Country*, but also the latest re-staging of Rogers and Hammerstein's *Oklahoma!* Both are 'classics' for him; the latter, first produced in 1943, is now acknowledged as a pioneering musical comedy. Quickly we look to see who has done the choreography in this revival; it was originally done by Agnes de Mille and it was an important aspect of the 'pioneering' quality of the first production. The credits list tells us 'choreography by Agnes de Mille (re-created by Gemze de Lappe)'.

Now 'revivals' in dance cause quite different problems from those in drama, mostly because the record has been vague and general in the former and in accurately printed texts in the latter. To reproduce dances from another period is extremely problematic. Steps used in dance 'classics' vary enormously: lines from dramatic classics do not. To a considerable extent, almost every dance described as a revival is in fact a new dance, because there is no objective record, only fallible human memory. (Dances notated in systems such as Labanotation number so few as to be insignificant considering the great number of dances which exist.) Yet 1979 saw a great deal of a kind of re-cycling of dances. Fewer and fewer new dances were made; more and more dances of the past were danced again. For example, a whole enterprise for reviving dances, the American Dance Machine, was founded and directed by Lee Theodore, specifically focusing on dances from Broadway shows.[12] Similar activity has occurred in modern dance. The elaborate process of reviving dances (finding original performers, perhaps the original choreographer, checking photographs, rare movies, etc.) has been carried on during this decade by Klarna Pinska and Joyce Trisler for Denishawn, and Maria Teresa and Annabelle Gamson for Isadora Duncan.

Ballet, of course, has always passed its dances on from one generation to the next, so that classics from the nineteenth century still exist, but that is also the reason why so *few* ballet classics exist. Electronic means ensure that dances will continue to exist from now on, and in very large numbers, but whether as they age they will develop a patina, as Gill of *The New Yorker* suggests, or just slowly tarnish with the years is open to doubt. What is not in doubt is that fewer and fewer dances will be made, as more and more dances are copied. The repertory of dances seems to be entering a new phase, in which dances will grow old in an unprecedented way.

In addition, its greatest choreographers – George Balanchine, Martha Graham, Agnes de Mille – never give up. They, too, are part of the aging process. They continue to dominate American dance by playing endless variations on their original inspirations. Never have so many of the old been in power so long in dance. And, most stultifying for the art, they are abetted by young artists who should be doing their own work and supporting their own contemporaries. These great choreographers in their last periods do not nurture the growth of young choreographers. Today, the art of dance, like all America, is caught in a much prolonged veneration of the venerable. The average age of the population of America is rising quickly and nowhere more lamentably than in this art where the breath, muscles and bones must be young to be vital. A dancer is old at thirty; a choreographer at fifty is already out of touch with the genuinely new impulses. George Balanchine, Martha Graham, Agnes de Mille, Hanya Holm, Merce Cunningham, Bella Lewitzky, Alwin Nikolais – never have so many sexagenarians and septuagenarians been in power in dance. Does their work show patina or tarnish?

'Is Broadway drowning in revivals?' asks Martin Gottfried, taking a different tack from Brendan Gill.[13] He sees an exclusion of new work from the theatre as revival after revival is mounted: *The King and I, Man of La Mancha, Peter Pan.* 'Yesterday is being celebrated as if there were no tomorrow. . . . Producers once instigated projects, sought out new material, molded it and staked their reputation on it. The producer played an initiator's role. Today, producers are functioning as packagers putting together recycled material they are all but certain can be marketed.'[14] And, as in dance, the old stars of the American musical are re-creating their old roles: Rex Harrison as Henry Higgins in *My Fair Lady*, Richard Burton as King Arthur in *Camelot*, Richard Kiley in *Man of La Mancha*, Yul Brynner in *The King and I*, Carol Channing in *Hello Dolly*.

Walter Kerr discusses this same phenomenon, seeing it as setting up a nostalgic confusion in Americans. In a review of *Sugar Babies*, a recapitulation of the burlesque circuits that flourished before the Great Depression, he records the mix-up of memories (Aristophanic plays, situation comedies, Mickey Rooney's childhood and youthful antics) brought forth by that historically unstable revival.[15] Ann Miller, the star of the movie extravaganzas of the forties and fifties and the re-born star of *Sugar Babies*, came right out and admitted she was dancing again at fifty-six just for the money. Though married twice to oil millionaires, her standard of living could not be afforded even by them. 'I have to earn $9,000 a month just for expenses, and that doesn't include food or even my chauffeur.'[16] So she dances in *Sugar Babies*, and recycles her old image, preventing some young dancer from creating a new image through innovative dancing.

The *Times* tells us that, credit or no credit, Agnes de Mille, that legendary iconoclast, made sure no one else's innovations in choreography appeared in the revival of *Oklahoma!* She is quoted as saying, 'I redid one dance for the new cast. It has originally been built around Joan McCracken – now deceased. Irreplacable. So I did a new dance, more or less. It works. I can't get out on the floor, you know. Also, I don't really remember the dances, but I make a point of not remembering. Then my mind's clear. I can do new things.'[17] Did this septuagenarian make the new dances, and de Lappe just follow her directions? What is important is the fact that no new dances emerged from a young choreographer; the old dances and the old choreographer were dominant as the decade closed.

Nureyev, of course, led in the revivalism in 1979 in his work with the Joffrey Ballet and their production *Homage to Diaghilev*. The Joffrey, in accordance with its purpose to present a mixture of revivals and contemporary pieces, had revived the dance *Parade*, under Massine's direction. Marking the fiftieth anniversary of Diaghilev's death, Nureyev and members of the Joffrey Company revived three ballets in which the Ballets Russes Nijinsky had starred: *Petrushka* (Fokine/Stravinsky), *Le Spectre de la Rose* (Fokine/Weber) and *L'Après-midi d'un Faune* (Nijinsky/Debussy). Critics disagreed as to the effectiveness of Nureyev's portrayal of the great Russian dancer, but no one faulted the productions or decried the motive. But, again, no one did any 'pioneering' as de Mille had done in the 1940s and Nijinsky in the 1910s.

Similarly, the Bournonville revivals were brought over to the States. Los Angeles was one of the first cities to see the Danish dancers, who toured in anticipation of the festival in Copenhagen in honor of the Bournonville centenary. A mere handful of dancers, the men as young and fresh-faced as the women, were lost on the Pasadena Civic Center stage but, for those few of us who sought them out, they were enchanting. Especially, as a dance historian, I reveled in seeing the fleeting academic pieces, apparently revived only for this trip, which demanded a soft flexible shoe, the point of which was used only to pass through, not to posture on as though it were a nail or turn on as though it were a screw. Gone was the clatter of blocked shoes; landings were taken with a cushioned technique that respected the human ankle, knee and frame. The whole Danish contemporary training and style seemed to have resisted the 'Russian' influence. How we longed to go to Copenhagen to step back a century in attending the Bournonville festival. But Arlene Croce disenchanted us about the purity of even these revivals. Reporting on the Centenary Festival, she writes of how contaminated the supposedly pure Danish Bournonville repertory is. She quotes the historian Allan Fridericia:

> None of Bournonville's own dances to the second act [of *Napoli*] are preserved. They are all the work of later productions. Drastic and frequent cutting of the score during the period from 1900 to 1971 has resulted in so gaping a monotony that audiences begin to call 'The Blue Grotto' the 'Brønnun Act' because ballet lovers preferred a refreshment pause at the well-known Copenhagen restaurant nearby. Just as the music has been cut, so has the act lost its underlying conflict.[18]

So much for revivalism in dance. As usual, Balanchine is right. He never revives a dance. He always re-choreographs.

One result of the increased interest in dance in America is the helter-skelter outpouring of publications on the subject. Almost anything that promises quick appeal to this new public has found a publisher. Picture books of the super-stars were inevitable – *The Nureyev Image* by Alexander Bland and *Baryshnikoff at Work*, photos by Martha Swape, edited and introduced by Charles Engell France. Quick glosses on some of the cult stars came next – *Merce Cunningham*, edited with photographs and an introduction by James Klosty; *The Alvin Ailey American Dance Theatre*, photography by Susan Cook, commentary by Joseph H. Mazo. Old publications were quickly reissued – *Balletomania Then and Now* by Arnold Haskell. Established writers had new impetus to reissue old material – *I Was There: Selected Dance Reviews and Articles, 1936–1976* by Walter Terry. How-to-do-it books in dance had immediate commercial success. *The Dancer's Book of Health* by Dr L. M. Vincent, published in 1978, had sold 45,000 copies by the end of 1979 and was in its fourth printing; a modest paperback volume, Vera Kostrovitskaya's *101 Classic Lessons*, translated and published privately by John Barer, sold 500 copies at $24.40 during its first month in stock at The Ballet Shop in New York.[19] These figures are even more revealing, and more startling, than those from the National Endowment.

The plethora of publications to be reviewed also brought out old critics to explain and promote their favorite iconoclasts. Richard Kostelanetz, for decades the beater of drums for the 'avant garde' in dance, was of course ideal to review the new publications of John Cage. Not able to categorize Cage's work with any identifiable art form, Kostelanetz invented a new genre, that of 'language works that cohere primarily in terms of sound, rather than syntax or semantics'.[20] Then he declared Cage, the 'literary musician', the master of that new art. This legerdemain still left Cage outside any main stream in either music or literature. Undaunted, Kostelanetz, knowing there is no place for Cage in the main stream of music (Cage has started his own stream there), ingeniously put Cage in an American stream of poetry, because of his new works. He explains,

... since both *Empty Words* and *Writings Through Finnegans Wake* are language-based, they belong to the great American tradition of poetry that incorporates an eccentric innovation in the machinery of the art – a radical change not in meaning or in sensibility but in the materials indigenous to poetry: language, line, syntax and meter. (In this sense, Cage's principal poetic precursors are Whitman, Cummings and Gertrude Stein.) Considered in this way, Cage is not a literary curiosity but an exemplary American poet whose work, once we understand it, is less peculiar than it may seem at first.[21]

Who else but Kostelanetz would put Cage into such company? Who else but John Cage would try to out-Joyce James Joyce?

But scholars in other fields do not always passively accept such presumptuous intrusions by dance writers into their territory. When a major figure in dance is also important in some other area, a knowledgeable critic in the other field will occasionally review the dance criticism and lament its shortcomings, rather than rhapsodize in the Kostelanetz fashion. One case was exemplary. Simon Karlinsky, author of distinguished studies of Gogol, Chekhov, and Nabokov and widely informed about modern Russian cultural history, reviewed two recent books by dance critics.[22] Richard Buckle is an authority on Diaghilev and his associates in the world of dance, and his biography *Diaghilev* (New York: Atheneum, 1979) was well received by dance specialists. John Percival's *The World of Diaghilev* (New York: Harmony Books, 1979) very ably documents the international period of Les Ballets Russes. In his review in *The New York Times Book Review*, Karlinsky reprimands both dance critics for knowing too little about Diaghilev's general cultural context: and the reprimand is not restricted to the two books under review – 'Mr Percival's limited purview is typical of Western dance historians who write about Diaghilev and who tend to consult only the sources in their own field.'[23] Buckle's book is also reprimanded for qualities which are representative

> ... he has disregarded (or was not aware of) the important recent publications in the Soviet Union that are based on archival materials not available in the West ... nor has Mr Buckle consulted the books by Western historians of Russian painting ... Richard Buckle has only a vague idea of the social and cultural realities that shaped Diaghilev.[24]

Professor Karlinsky closes his review with a statement that indicates ideal standards that dance criticism must try to meet if it is to achieve general rather than limited cultural stature.

> As a chronicle of Diaghilev's works and days, Mr Buckle's *Diaghilev* possesses considerable value: as a biography, it is a headless torso, as any biography of Diaghilev is bound to be that restricts his significance to ballet alone. More than a great ballet impresario, more than an influential taste-maker, Diaghilev was a cultural educator of genius. His heritage and his artistic principles live on in the works of three Russian artists who epitomize the synthesis of the best in Russian and Western art of this century. Two of them,

Igor Stravinsky and George Balanchine, were formed by their personal contacts with Diaghilev. The third one, Vladimir Nabokov, had little to do with Diaghilev personally. Yet, when Nabokov wrote of the brilliance of Russian cultural life in the years 1905–1917 and added 'I am a product of that period, I was bred in its atmosphere', he was speaking of the period best defined by the name of Sergei Diaghilev.[24]

That very good books on Diaghilev as a giant of ballet should be so sternly rebuked is salutary for us all. Dance is international, and geographical parochialism is easily recognized as stultifying laziness. But dance is also enmeshed in *general* international culture, and we should strive to understand and teach dance in its broad cultural context, avoiding intellectual provincialism.

During the first part of 1979 a barrage of mailings hit the country, fliers which announced the publication of a new magazine devoted to dance. Being, in one capacity or another, on most of the lists used by its publicity department, I must have received fifty copies of the advertising leaflet for the new magazine, *Ballet News*. Now that I have six issues in front of me, I can begin to assess its character. The term 'ballet' is used, surprisingly, to cover all kinds of theatrical dance. In America 'dance' has always been the generic term, and 'ballet' a sub-division. The first issue of the magazine gives National Endowment for the Arts figures. There was a 600 per cent increase in dance attendance in the United States during the years 1970–5, a rate rise more than for baseball or the movies. At the same time, as the editor-in-chief Robert Jacobson notes, the number of periodicals on the subject of dance has not grown proportionately. *Ballet News*, therefore will 'blend words and pictures so as to reach out to that burgeoning new dance audience'.[25] Modeled on *Opera News*, *Ballet News* is intended to appeal to the same audience. Bella Lewitzky has commented trenchantly on this trend: 'The American ballet audience is starting to take on the dreariest qualities of the opera audience. And because this audience is seldom challenged, when it does encounter something new it feels inadequate to it and therefore turns hostile. But what will happen should high society adopt some other art as its pet? Our ballet boom may contain its own built-in bust.'[26]

And what of the magazine itself? Words and pictures. Will it be an equivalent of *Sports Illustrated* for dance? Jacobson's opening editorial, entitled 'Viewpoint', suggests that it will. In an answer to his own question, 'Why a new dance magazine?' posed in the first issue, he sums up the appeal intended: 'Excitement, exhilaration, physical participation, escapism, entertainment ... dance is all this, and more people are experiencing it every day.'[27] Dance will be captured by his magazine, 'in a way never done before'.[28] Admittedly, at least, not dance as art.

The six issues already released of volume 1 have the following format.

Jacobson's editorial 'Viewpoint' is immediately followed by what can only be called a gossip column, a condensed *People's Magazine* of the dance world entitled 'Footnotes'. In it, Danilova puts down Vaganova or de Mille casts out *Swan Lake*. Two or three feature articles follow, based on the subject of the month – Balanchine, Ashton, Bournonville, Nureyev – the all-time great coaches and athletes, all of whom are selling at the moment. In the latter part of the magazine are the reports from critics around the Western world, following the lead of *Dance Magazine* which has had a team of such correspondents for years. Mixed with these are infrequent obituaries, book reviews, and record listings, the inevitable haphazard 'Calendar', and Britain's transplanted Clive Barnes. His last-page column, 'Barnes on . . .', dwells on the boggling statistics quoted above, and attempts to explain them. He knows the athletes by their first names: Margot, Rudi, Misha, Maya, Natasha, Peter, Cynthia, and the sports writers like 'Bucky', have been his friends ever since they sat in the last balcony together as students.

Although Barnes does not quite say that the media caused this dance renaissance alone, *Ballet News* brings together most of the established writers for the media. Walter Terry writes again on Ruth St Denis,[29] James Monahan on Fonteyn,[30] B. H. Haggin on Balanchine,[31] Richard Buckle on Diaghilev,[32] Don McDonagh on the American Dance Festival,[33] Dale Harris on Anthony Dowell,[34] Svend Kragh-Jacobsen on Bournonville,[35] David Vaughan on Ashton.[36] Impressive, and matched by the list of establishment correspondents who write from Houston and Boston and San Francisco: Horst Koegler from central Europe, Clive Barnes from Monte Carlo, Sali Ann Kriegsman from Washington, D.C., and Lewis Segal, one of the reviewers of the *Los Angeles Times*, which dominates opinion throughout Southern California. There are no maverick critics, and no minor players. Establishment dance – the major league – is what *Ballet News* wishes to reflect through established critics.

But this is not entirely a sports magazine. Dance has a glamour which makes it more like the movies than the baseball leagues, the two entertainments dance is leading in increased attendance. For sheer panache, *Ballet News* is stunning. Page after page of color photographs, with a few black and white documentaries, live up to Robert Jacobson's promise. Inevitable, then, for the poster-buying dance public, was the inclusion of centerfolds in issues 3 and 6: Dance Star poster 1 pictures Nureyev; number 2 is Peter Martins.

But the most important innovation of the decade did not come from the great company leaders, choreographers, or star dancers; not from the university departments of dance or from critics, or journalists or publicists. A handful of working dancers made the most significant contribution towards the end of 1979. The intricate details of the strife between the management and dancers of the American Ballet Theatre are not clear. What is clear is that the dancers in the corps have long felt themselves to be exploited in a company dominated by an extreme form of the star system. For centuries, dancers have put up with poverty and hardship because they have been addicted to their art – not just ballet dancers, but dancers of all kinds. Of her years with Lester Horton, for example, during which the Horton dancers appeared in second-rate movies to support themselves, Bella Lewitsky has given the simple explanation: 'That was the only way we could afford our "habit"; we were modern dance junkies hooked on art.'[37]

The life of a dancer which revolves around this addiction had a successful showing in the movie *The Turning Point*. The worldly-wise Herbert Ross (who made *California Suite*, for example), aided by his one-time ballerina wife Nora Kay, gave the world a picture that rang true, uniquely balancing soap opera and art in its depiction of dance junkies. There were the stars – Baryshnikoff, Danilova, Shirley MacLaine, Anne Bancroft – but mostly it was Martha Scott as Lucia Chase who dominated the picture. The ruthless manipulation of dancers for the good of the company was effectively portrayed with new clarity in this movie, though all of us in dance knew of it. We knew the depicted Chase character was only one representative of a practice which has existed from eighteenth-century slave ballets, through nineteenth-century jockey club harems to twentieth-century stables of long-legged female 'racehorses'. Dancers have always been sacrificed to the art of dance.

And American Ballet Theatre, whose dancers had constantly bargained for money, roles and recognition at both ends of the scale (did Godonov, the latest Russian defector, really sell himself for that outrageous sum?) was the one which was finally brought down by its dancers. Who knows the truth of what goes on inside this world which trades on human flesh in order to produce commodity art? Was Lucia Chase as black as she had been painted, or was she too a victim of the system? We record here only that the 'drug addicts' at the bottom of American Ballet Theatre finally said that their 'habit' had to be supported on a living wage. Lucia Chase's grand opening in December at the Kennedy Center in Washington, D.C., with super-star Godonov, was scuttled when the supporting dancers refused any longer to keep afloat a company top heavy with stars. No other event of the decade will have such far-reaching reverberations in the United States. The 1970s ended with some ballet dancers asserting their human rights with unprecedented force. American Ballet Theatre – and the ballet world – will never be the same. A contract involving a doubling of pay for beginning dancers in three years is very significant for the future of the art form. 'How did they exist with such wages as long as they did?' people now ask, and 'What will Baryshnikoff be able to accomplish when he takes over next fall?' Power in that company has irreversibly shifted toward those who, blessed with the 'habit', have been dancing for much bigger audiences in the seventies than in any other decade.

NOTES

1. Mike Silverman, 'The 70's: Looking Back', *The Press* (Riverside California) 27 Dec. 1979, Section B, p. 10.
2. Lee Edward Stern, 'How it Really Is, in the Dance World', *New York Times*, 18 Nov. 1979, Section D, p. 14.
3. Deborah Jowitt, 'Profusion within Tidy Limits', *The Village Voice*, 3 Dec. 1979, p. 91.
4. J. Hoberman, 'Approaching Las Vegas', *The Village Voice*, 18 Nov. 1979, p. 93.
5. Lewis Segal, 'CalArts Dance Ensemble on Campus', *Los Angeles Times*, 10 Dec. 1979. IV, 22.
6. Sally R. Sommer, 'Ms. Tappers Take Over', *The Village Voice*, 24 Dec. 1979, p. 87.
7. Deborah Jowitt, 'Carry Me Back to Act IV', *The Village Voice*, 24 Dec. 1979, p. 85.
8. Sally R. Sommer, 'Moving through the Debris', *The Village Voice*, 26 Nov. 1979, p. 105.
9. Lewis Segal, 'L. A. Ballet introduces *Nutcracker*,' *Los Angeles Times*, 29 Dec. 1979, II, 4, 11.
10. *Ibid.*
11. Brendan Gill, 'The Theatre: Two Classics', *The New Yorker*, 24 Dec. 1979, p. 70.
12. Glenn Loney, 'American Dance Machine', *Ballet News*, Jan.–Feb. 1980, vol. 1, no. 8, pp. 22–5.
13. *New York Times*, 25 Nov. 1979, Section D, p. 3.
14. *Ibid.*
15. Walter Kerr, 'Waxing Nostalgic, but Why?' *New York Times*, 21 Oct. 1979, Section D, p. 5.
16. Moira Hodgson, 'An Old-Fashioned Movie Star Scores on Broadway', *New York Times*, 28 Oct. 1979, Section D, p. 5.
17. Jay Carr, 'Agnes de Mille Steps out with an Old Friend – *Oklahoma*', *New York Times*, 9 Dec. 1979, Section D, pp. 3, 53.
18. Arlene Croce, 'The Romantic Ballet in Copenhagen', *The New Yorker*, 24 Dec. 1979, p. 91.
19. Terry Trucco, 'Paging the Dance', *Ballet News*, Dec. 1979, vol. 1, no. 7, pp. 7, 13.
20. Richard Kostelanetz, 'Master of Several Arts', *New York Times Book Review*, 2 Dec. 1979, pp. 48–9.
21. *Ibid.*, p. 49.
22. Simon Karlinsky, 'Transformer of the Arts', *New York Times Book Review*, 7 Oct. 1979, p. 22.
23. *Ibid.*
24. *Ibid.*, p. 24.
25. 'Viewpoint', *Ballet News*, May 1979, vol. 1, no. 1, p. 4.
26. Jack Anderson, 'Bella Lewitzky's Dances are about People', *New York Times*, 28 Oct. 1979, section D, p. 14.

27. Jacobson, 'Viewpoint', p. 4.
28. *Ibid.*
29. 'Prophet/Pioneer', *Ballet News*, July–Aug. 1979, vol. 1, no. 3, pp. 14–16.
30. 'Salut d'Amour', *Ballet News*, Oct. 1979, vol. 1, no. 5, pp. 16–19.
31. 'A Lifetime of Discovery', *Ballet News*, June 1979, vol. 1, no. 2, pp. 8–14.
32. 'Diaghilev Comes to America', *Ballet News*, May 1979, vol. 1, no. 1, pp. 15–21, 24.
33. 'Cross Currents', *Ballet News*, July–Aug. 1979, vol. 1, no. 3, pp. 8–12.
34. 'Spreading his Wings', *Ballet News*, Sep. 1979, vol. 1, no. 4, pp. 8–14.
35. 'A Dream Come True', *Ballet News*, Nov. 1979, vol. 1, no. 6, pp. 8–10.
36. 'Birthday Offering', *Ballet News*, Oct. 1979, vol. 1, no. 5, pp. 10–14.
37. Anderson, 'Bella Lewitzky', p. 14.

Music, dance and text in *nō* drama

P. G. O'NEILL

Like western opera, ballet and the modern musical, *nō* is a combination of artistic elements which, ideally, produce an effect greater than the sum of the parts. In the case of *nō*, the elements are those of music, dance and language, but there is even now only a limited understanding of their relationship in the west. For nearly a hundred years our knowledge of *nō* was based on translations of some of the texts, and although there have been occasional opportunities since the 1950s to see stage performances outside Japan, the undoubted literary quality of most of the plays in the modern repertoire has maintained the general impression that *nō* is primarily a literary form. The following account is, therefore, an attempt to present its three main constituents in a truer balance.

In spite of the apparent inflexibility of form arising from the recommendations of Zeami Motokiyo (?1363–?1443), when he codified virtually the whole of *nō* theory and practice in a series of writings on the subject, the plays show a surprising variety of structure; but, for purposes of illustration, the most typical form, known as 'spirit *nō*' or 'dream *nō*' (*mugen nō*), is assumed below. This kind of play begins with a travelling priest, the *waki* (secondary actor), arriving at a place with historical or literary associations and meeting a local person, the *shite* (main actor), often a woman, who then appears there. This person relates to the priest the incident for which the place is known and then, just before leaving the stage at the interval between the two acts of the play, makes the account so personal that it is clear that he or she is possessed by the spirit of its main character. In the second act, the *shite* reappears, this time in the form of the main character as he or she was in life, and re-enacts the incident forming the central theme of the play. The *shite* then disappears with the coming of dawn, and the priest wakes from what seems to have been a dream. This second act thus reverts to a time earlier than that of the piece as a whole, and is a form of the flashback technique familiar to us in the modern cinema.

Ever since the time of Zeami, the standard structure of a *nō* play has been based on three sections called *jo-ha-kyū* (introduction, development and climax), comprising five parts in all. The structure of the typical 'spirit *nō*' outlined above falls into the following five parts:

> *Act I*
> *Jo* (Introduction): entry of secondary actor
> *Ha* (Development) (i): entry of main actor
>   (ii): dialogue between the two
>   (iii): account of incident or story on which the play is
>   based, given by the main actor or chorus
>
>   *Interval*
>
> *Act II*
> *Kyū* (Climax): re-enactment of the source incident in the form of a dance by
>   the main actor

It is the progression through these parts that determines the changing relationship among the elements of music, dance and text.

The music in *nō* is provided by the singing of the actors or chorus, all of whom are men, and by four or five instruments: a flute, two small hand-drums (the *ko-tsuzumi* (small drum), held on the right shoulder, and the *ō-tsuzumi* (large drum), held on the left hip) and, in certain plays, a larger drum (*taiko*) mounted on a low stand and played with sticks. There are different types of singing, flute melodies, rhythms and drummers' calls, and the various combinations of these elements creates very complex patterns, but an account of their main characteristics can show something of how the musical effects in *nō* are achieved.

The texts of *nō* consist of parts without any fixed melodic pattern known as *kotoba* (words), and others which are in a poetic metre of alternating groups of generally seven and five syllables, making a twelve-syllable unit, and are sung to a fixed melodic progression. Thus, although *kotoba* are given a special chant-like intonation, which differs according to the particular character, it can be said that the texts consist basically of spoken and poetic sung parts. The lines of individual actors will include both types, but the chorus has only the latter.

Nō singing is of two kinds, 'strong song' (*tsuyo-gin*) and 'weak song' (*yowa-gin*). Having a limited musical scale and simple, plain melodic patterns, strong singing is masculine in character and predominates in solemn, majestic pieces such as the god plays which traditionally open a programme. Weak singing, on the other hand, has a wider musical range and a more complicated scale system, and these give much more variety of melody. It is thus well suited to the subtle expression of emotion and elegance, and occurs most often in plays of the third and fourth of the traditional five groups of plays, in which the main character is a woman. Both types of singing are found in nearly all plays, but some pieces are so typical of the characteristics of the one or the other that they use only one: the god play *Takasago*, for example, has nothing but strong singing, while

Matsukaze and *Izutsu*, gentle and romantic plays centring on female characters, have only the weak type.

The scales employed in these two types of singing have changed over the
years since the last quarter of the sixteenth century, when they were first
differentiated, but at least from 1870 they have had a fixed structure.
According to this, the weak style has had three basic tones (*jō, chū* and *ge*,
respectively 'upper', 'middle' and 'lower') at intervals of a fourth, with
three secondary tones (two higher than the main ones and one lower than
them) and two other intermediate tones; and the strong style has had two
main and three secondary tones spanning a much narrower scale:[1]

Half-steps	Weak singing (*Yowa-gin*)	Strong singing (*Tsuyo-gin*)
1	*kōguri* —————	
5	*kuri* ————	
6	*jō-no-uki* · · · · · · · · · ·	————————*kōguri*
8	*jō* —————	
11	*chū-no-uki* · · · · · · · · · ·	———————— *kuri*
12		——————————*jō* (or *chū*)
13	*chū* —————	
15		——————————*ge-no-chū* (or *ge*)
18	*ge* —————	—————————*ryo*
24	*ryo* ————	

It is the use of these different styles, according to the general character of a
play and the situation and roles within it, which provides *nō* with much of its
variety and atmosphere.

Even if the various flute tunes are not forgotten, however, it is in its
rhythms rather than its melodies that *nō* music is most subtle and
developed, and it is in the combinations of melody and rhythm that it shows
the greatest variety.

In the first place, the singing may fit into the basic eight-beat rhythm of *nō*
music in one of three ways, or it may not fit into it at all. In the latter case of a

non-congruent, or free rhythm, the lines may be given a rhythmic pattern similar to that in which Chinese and Japanese poems have been traditionally recited in Japan or, like operatic recitative, they may approximate to speech forms.

When, instead, a sung passage is fitted into the eight-beat rhythm, it is most often in the pattern known as *hira-nori* (level beat), in which the twelve syllables of the common seven and five couplet are fitted into the eight beats by allowing basically two syllables to a beat and lengthening four of the twelve syllables to make the equivalent of sixteen, as in the following line from *Takasago*:

	1		2		3		4		5		6		7		8
Hira-nori:	I	–	ma	o	ha	–	ji	me	no	–	ta	bi	go	ro	mo

where the first, fourth and seventh syllables are straightforwardly lengthened and the final syllable ended before the final beat. The standard practice is for the first four beats of an eight-beat sequence to come mainly from the hip-drum, and the second four from the smaller shoulder-drum.

Variant congruent rhythm patterns are called *chū-nori* (centre beat) and *ō-nori* (major/great beat). In the former, there are simply two syllables to each beat, with an emphasis on each alternate syllable, with the beat:

	1		2		3		4		5		6		7		8
O-nori:	ka	ta	ki	to	mi	e	shi	wa	mu	re	i	ru	ka	mo	me
															(Yashima)

This type of pattern is most suited to producing an active, tense feeling, as in the depiction of a battle scene, for example, and being often used in the final part of warrior plays (*shura mono*), the second of the five main groups, it is also known as the *shura-nori* (warrior beat).

The *ō-nori*, in contrast, gives a regular, calm and relaxed feeling by allowing at least one beat per syllable:

	1	2		3		4		5		6		7		8
Ō-nori:			A	–	–	zu	–	ma	–	a	–	so	–	bi
	–	no	–	–	ka	–	–	zu	–	ka	–	–	zu	–	–	ni
															(Hagoromo)

Since this is virtually the only pattern that is accompanied by the stick-drum (*taiko*), it is sometimes called the *taiko* beat, and it occurs most often in the very last part of a play, as an accompaniment to the dance.

These basic rhythmic structures do not necessarily result, however, in a regular-sounding series of eight-beat phrases: longer or shorter phrases often arise from a varying number of syllables in a line – six or eight instead of seven, for example, or four instead of five – or from artistic variations in the length of the hold on a syllable. Further variety in the music comes from the very different characteristic sounds produced by the three types of drum

– soft, 'feminine' beats from the laxer, moistened skins of the small shoulder-drum; hard, 'masculine' cracks from the taut, dried skins of the hip-drum; and rich, dominant beats from the stick-drum, when it is used – and from the various calls and range of instrument sounds produced by each of the drummers. The player of the shoulder-drum, for example, uses a variety of calls – *ya, ha, yaa, haa, iyaa, yaahan*, etc. – and three basic drum-tones referred to as *ta, chi* and *po*, which result from varying the tension on the cords linking the two skins of the drum and striking different parts of the face of the drum with various degrees of force; and the other drummers produce similar varied calls and instrument tones.

The dances in *nō*, the main ones of which occur in the second acts of two-act plays, show a similar wealth of content, style and atmosphere. Individual movements known as *kata* are put together to form sequences of movement and, as with the individual *kata*, it is usual to categorise these sequences according to whether they are non-descriptive or representative of meaningful actions and, thus, to classify them on balance as either pure dances (*mai*) or dance-like actions (*hataraki*). The other co-ordinate by which they can be classified is their musical accompaniment – instrumental, or vocal (sometimes with instruments too) – and, given that there are exceptions with either categorisation, this is the one that is followed below as being more appropriate to our present purpose.

Pure-dance sequences performed only to an instrumental accompaniment are danced primarily to the flute, playing in time with the beat, with the two (or sometimes three) drums providing merely a background rhythm. There are no fewer than nineteen standard types of dance within this group, ranging from the majestic *shin no jo-no-mai* (true introductory dance) and the graceful and more frequent *jo-no-mai* (introductory dance) and *chū-no-mai* (intermediate dance), through rather special ones like *gaku* (an entertainment), derived from the Bugaku court dances, and *shishi* (lion), a form of the originally Chinese lion dance, to unique pieces such as the *ranbyōshi* (wild beat), now found only in the play *Dōjōji*, and those which go to make up the set of songs and dances known as *Okina* (Old man). Although the movements themselves generally have no identifiable meaning, each dance plays an important part in conveying the character of the particular role and in developing the general atmosphere of the play as a whole. Indeed, the common practice is to subdivide the five groups of play according to the main dance within the piece. All but two of the thirty-eight woman plays in the modern repertoire, for example, contain pure-dance sequences, and since these plays typify the side of *nō* which seeks to portray the ultimate level of elegant beauty, nearly all of these dances are the appropriate *jo-no-mai* or *chū-no-mai*, rounded off in some cases by a short and somewhat quicker *ha-no-mai* (development dance).

Dance-like action sequences known as *hataraki* (actions), which are similarly performed only to an instrumental accompaniment but are shorter than *mai*, comprise some six distinct types. Most of them have the two smallest drums leading the accompaniment, with the flute playing in a subsidiary way, in free rhythm; but exceptionally the stick-drum is also found and, in the sequence known as *mai-bataraki* (dance actions), the flute plays in time to the beat, as in the pure-dance pieces.

The distinction between *mai* with only musical accompaniment and *hataraki* is not an exact one and largely depends, in fact, on a traditional categorisation. It can be said generally, however, that they are distinguished by the role of the flute and by the fact that, while *mai* are non-descriptive and not closely related to the particular character in the play, *hataraki* contain a number of descriptive actions and mimicry elements indicative of the role being portrayed by the actor. The content of *hataraki* sequences is very varied, but representative examples are *iroe* (colouration), short pieces usually performed by an elegant female character and conveying a calm, gentle atmosphere; *kakeri* (literally 'soaring'), more active pieces found in warrior and mad-woman plays, for example, where they represent respectively the suffering in the hell of warriors and derangement through the loss of a loved one; and *kiri-kumi* (sword fights), in which stylised fighting is enacted.

Dances which go with singing, with or without the addition of musical accompaniment, are very common in *nō*. Just as dances done only to a musical accompaniment can be divided into pure-dance *mai* and to some extent meaningful *hataraki*, as described above, so these *mai* in some cases indicate only the general style and mood of the character and play and, in others, are connected with the meaning of the text. A dance in a *kuse* section, which is located in the third part of the development section (*Ha* (iii) in the structural outline above) and is the textual heart of a play, is generally of the first type; and one in a finale (*kiri*; last part of the climax section) is generally of the descriptive kind. Once again, a dance is often not exclusively of one type or the other, but even descriptive movements have been fined away to a point so far from simple realism that there is no discord in a mixture of different elements within a single sequence. For example, the fan is used in many ways in *nō* – to represent such things as a sword, wine-jar, pillow or flying arrow, held aloft to indicate that the character is gazing into the distance, or simply as a property in the dance – and even the easily recognisable action of weeping is shown by raising one hand (or, to show violent grief, both hands) before the eyes in a very stylised way.

Having seen something of the wide range of music and dance elements available in *nō*, we must now look at the part these aspects of performance play in the total scheme of things, and this means, in particular, their relationship with the text.

Virtually all the *nō* plays in the modern repertoire date from the fifteenth

or sixteenth centuries, and the authors of their texts, as well as the composers of the music to the plays, were in nearly all cases professional *nō*
performers. Since few of these were well educated in any formal sense, the
textual quality of the plays comes largely from the peculiar circumstances of
their composition.

In the first place, the content of *nō* performances was much more diverse,
and the texts, music and style of performance of the plays much more fluid
in the medieval period than would seem possible from the reverence for
tradition which has been the very basis of *nō*'s existence in modern times. In
the period of Zeami and his father Kan'ami (1333–84) at least, *nō* was still
at the stage of using popular song and dance forms and other styles of drama
to increase its appeal, and these provided a good deal of ready-made
material. One of Kan'ami's greatest achievements, for example, was the
adoption into *nō* of a song entertainment called *kusemai*. Immensely popular
at the time, its very rhythmic music made a striking and attractive contrast
to the softer, melodic *ko-uta* musical style traditional in Kan'ami's type of *nō*,
and its texts provided the subject-matter for complete new plays. *Kusemai*
left its mark on the standard structure of *nō* plays in the form of the *kuse*
section, which has already been mentioned as being the literary core of a
play, and Zeami laid down that any famous poems or phrases associated
with the site of the play should be written in there, in the third part of the
development section.[2]

Then, too, the rage among all classes for making linked verse (*renga*)
meant that a facility for producing adequate verse did not necessarily
depend on a high level of literacy or wide reading, and Zeami recognised an
interest in poetry as the only outside activity to be encouraged in anyone
dedicated to the pursuit of *nō*.[3] With the quotation of earlier poetry and
other literary material also being regarded as an entirely respectable and
expected practice, the whole environment surrounding the writers of *nō* was
helpful to them in their work, for this was more to organise and link together
literary material already to hand than to create completely original texts.

Zeami describes the composition of a *nō* play in the following way in his
writings:

> In general, [the making of a *nō* play] comes from the three-stage process of
> subject, structure and writing. First, you discover your main character;
> second, you structure the *nō*; and third, you write it out [with words and
> music]. Having obtained the main character from an original source after a
> thorough examination of it, you build up the three forms of introduction,
> development and climax into five parts and then, gathering together the
> words and adding the music, write the piece out.[4]

This makes the operation sound much simpler than it must have been in
practice, but Zeami clearly expected a writer to take as his subject, which he
saw in terms of the main character of the play, someone who would provide

a wealth of poems and quotations on which the author could draw. Apart
from earlier dramatic pieces of various kinds, the main sources for such
characters were the romantic novels of the court period, and the later war
tales from the period of military rule which had begun some hundred and
thirty years before Zeami was writing. The subject had to be selected with
care, Zeami tells us:

> By subject is meant a character from the original source for the play, who does
> what will be [required] in it, and it must be realised how very relevant this is to
> song and dance – for this entertainment form of ours *is* song and dance. If the
> subject is a person unconnected with these two arts, the entertainment will
> hold no attraction for the audience, no matter what kind of historic figure or
> outstanding personage he may be. You must well and truly grasp this truth.[5]

After describing various types of persons – divine beings, priestesses,
court nobles, poets and poetesses, and famous courtesans – whose associations would allow songs and dances to arise naturally within a play, Zeami
adds a note and a caution about another type of *nō*:

> There is also something known as a made-up *nō* which, being a new composi-
> tion with no original source at all, captivates its audiences by being composed
> in connection with some famous place or historic site. This [, however,] is a
> task for one who is supremely accomplished and learned.[6]

In his teachings on the 'making' or structuring of a play, Zeami took the
three-section, five-part system of introduction, development and climax,
and applied it both to a single *nō* play and to an entire programme containing a number of plays, traditionally five. This system indicates primarily
different musical moods, and the change in tempo from one play to the next
follows, on this larger scale, the development within a single play. The *jo*,
being the first part, is the most simple and straightforward. The *ha* section,
with three parts, introduces variations and is the most rich and colourful,
besides being the most sustained. It leads on to the final section, *kyū*, again
of one part, in which the tempo is markedly quickened to bring the piece, or
the programme, to a climax. In the case of an individual play, Zeami took
his structuring down to the level of the main components in each of the five
parts:

> Having decided on a five-part structure, you construct a piece by thinking
> how much song there will be in the introduction, how much 'three-coloured'
> song in the three parts of the development section, and how much there will be
> of a musical style suitable to the climax, and thus you decide on the number of
> lines in the various songs. This is what I mean by structuring a *nō*.[7]

The constraints imposed on a writer by the framework set up by Zeami
would seem to be very great, and when strictly followed it did allow only one
isolated incident to be treated in a fairly fixed way. But *nō* is not designed
for, or concerned with, intricacies of plot, and the plan could be varied in a

number of ways without destroying its basic simplicity. In the first place, the structure itself could be changed:

> Alternatively, there will be cases where there are six parts, depending on the nature of the original source. Also, depending on the type [of play], there will be nō which are one part short and have only four, for example. Generally [, however,] five parts are what have been set as the basic form.[8]

Then, too, the structure was equally applicable to both one-act and two-act plays, but it should be noted that, in the latter case, the asymmetry was always the same: the interval always came at the end of the long development section, leaving a short second half consisting of the climax alone. Zeami lays down no principles for determining whether a play should be in one act or two and, practical man of the theatre as he was, it is likely that he assumed the choice would be based on which form was better suited to the material in hand. Both types are mentioned in his writings and found among his own plays; but those in two acts are much more numerous, and since they usually have the advantage of a dramatic change in character and costume in the second act to regain the attention of the audience, Zeami considered them comparatively easy to write.[9] The interest of the audience would not normally be quickened in the same way in a one-act play, but Zeami pointed out that, even within a single act, a distinct change of scene could be introduced to prevent the piece from dragging.[10]

Turning from the structuring of a play to the writing of the words and music, Zeami makes it clear that, although the climax in the performance of the play as a whole comes at the end, in the *kyū* section, from the literary point of view the third part of the development section, which is based on the *kuse*, is the most important. He recommends not only that famous poems and lines should be worked into the text at this point, as we have seen, but mentions elsewhere that poetic quotations familiar to the audience should be put in here and that such important parts of the text should not be used where they are unconnected with the words or actions of the main actor.[11] This third part of the *ha* section usually gives a coherent account of the subject matter of the whole play, and any well-known lines added here embellish the most important sung part of the play – and it is the sung parts which are important. All actors, whether playing main or secondary roles, have spoken lines to say at various points in the play, but these serve only to intrduce or link the verse parts which are sung by the actors or, in certain places, by the chorus.

The quotation from earlier works has always been looked on with favour in Japan, as in China, but nō has probably drawn on earlier works more than any other form in Japanese literature, for there cannot be a play which has not taken from outside either the incident on which it is based or quotations with which to enrich its language; and in some plays almost all

the worthwhile literary parts are quotations. There was also widespread
rewriting of *nō* plays themselves, especially in the formative period of the
fifteenth century. A writer of *nō* could use an existing play in one of two
ways: he could either extract from it certain songs which, being in keeping
with the subject of his own play, could be fitted into the new text without
difficulty; or he could set out to modify the existing play by making
alterations to one or more of the elements of text, music and dance which,
together with the actual performance of the players, form the amalgam of
nō. A new writer might leave the piece largely unchanged, or he might carry
the alterations to such lengths that the work could in all fairness be
described thereafter as his own.

Thus, the text of a *nō* play consists of unimportant spoken lines and of
poetic, sung passages composed largely, but not entirely, of poems, parts of
poems, and beautiful phrases taken from earlier literature. In these sung
passages are to be found all the embellishments and intricacies of traditional Japanese poetry: the time-honoured symbols, associations of ideas,
and the puns, conventional epithets and associated words. The result is
clearly not poetry of great originality, and the delight in word-play leads to
a plethora of references to the names of plants, flowers, birds, placenames
and so on which strike no immediate response in the experience of the
westerner nor, indeed, of the modern Japanese. But when viewed within its
own conventions and within those of Japanese poetry as a whole, the texts of
nō plays are seen to occupy a unique place in Japanese literature. Based as
the plays are on incidents depicted in earlier writing of all kinds, and
drawing much of their poetry from the best of what had already been
written in Japanese and in Chinese, they stand as a focal point of earlier
Japanese literature. Much of the material they used, both stories and
language, would have been familiar to both writers and audiences in the
fifteenth century from their use by the many popular chanters and singers
who were such a feature of the period, but this does not detract from the
qualities of the material itself. What *nō* does, and all that its writers sought
to do, is to bring together the best available material, both earlier poetry
and original writing, in order to create the particular mood or moods which
formed its sole aim.

In doing this, it nullifies to some extent the criticism often made of
Japanese poetry that, once it discarded the long-verse form after the eighth
century, its remaining poetic forms were too short for a powerful and
effective expression of emotion or ideas. When a *nō* writer gathered together
and supplemented a body of literary material appropriate to his purpose, he
was creating a sustained and unified poetic expression of a type which stood
virtually alone in Japan during the twelve centuries between the *Man'yōshū*
anthology and modern times. The only other poetic form of any length
during this time was the *renga* (linked verse), but in these each of the poets

taking part had only to ensure that his verse had some connection with the one immediately preceding. The progression was thus quite aimless, and the whole sequence lacked any kind of unity. With a nō play, however, all the poetry was chosen and shaped to fit into a predetermined pattern, in order best to achieve a conscious artistic effect.

The elements of performance itself were analysed by Zeami as the *nikyoku santai* (the two arts and the three forms), which he stressed as the basis of any true achievement in nō. The 'three forms' were the basic roles of old man, woman and warrior, from which the portrayal of all other roles derived; and the three together can be taken as representing the element of *monomane* or mimicry in general. *Monomane* had been the element in the type of performance which led eventually to nō ever since the comic mimicry of the tenth and eleventh centuries, and its importance was emphasised by Zeami. The ideal state in mimicry, he tells us, was such an identification with the character being represented that the actor no longer felt that he was giving an imitation. This element of mimicry was the constant, under-lying one in a nō performance, on the basis of which 'the two arts' of song and dance were presented.

Zeami saw song as the very source of this level of nō,[12] and it was the duty of the author to provide the main sung parts with rich and beautiful words and music 'in order to open the ears' of the audience.[13] It was then the function of the main actor to perform the dance towards the end of the play in order 'to open their eyes'.[14] Plays which were unbalanced by undue emphasis on either song or dance were not difficult to write, he tells us, but what was an achievement was for the writer to produce a play in which both were so blended that they were as one.[15]

The words were thus of importance in the sung parts of the play, but were at least matched there by the music; and the element of song itself was rivalled in the performance as a whole by the dance. Also, the custom of having a player give an account of the subject matter of the piece during the interval in a two-act play suggests very strongly that the texts must have meant very little to some sections of the medieval audience. Even in Zeami's time, therefore, the words alone formed a very minor part of the whole performance.

In other words, in a nō play, the main visual element in the form of a dance by the magnificently-robed main actor makes a major contribution to the artistic effect of the piece as a whole, and the text itself is also important in this; but both are of less moment than the music which, combining as it does with both the dance and the poetry, must be seen as the element which holds the whole play together. Since nō is a composite art and, ideally, achieves its effect by an inseparable blend of music, dance and text, it is clear how meagre the text alone must be, as representative of nō as a whole. It may be poetry – at least in the original Japanese – but it is not nō. With that emphasis repeated, I offer an English version of the *nō* play *Higaki* (The Cypress-wood Fence).

Few *nō* are perfectly regular in all their features and *Higaki*, an important and highly regarded play by Zeami, is no exception. Although its general structure is standard enough to serve as an illustration, its unique aspects give a good idea of the variety possible within this framework.

  Higaki is a two-act woman play of the 'spirit' kind, but the main character being an old woman throughout, it has none of the dramatic contrast between the two acts usually found in this kind of play. Based on a poem found in tenth-century literary works, it centres on a poverty-stricken old woman who had once been a beautiful and popular dancing-girl. A nobleman passing by the old woman's hut one day asks for water and then, to her distress and humiliation, insists that she dance for him. After death, her unhappy spirit broods obsessively on this and, finding no peace, comes back to earth to seek salvation from a priest.

  With such a subject, *Higaki* has no place for 'strong singing' and uses 'weak singing' throughout. Structurally, it differs from the norm in having the interval between acts after the second part of the *ha* section, instead of after the third. As a result, both the *kuse*, the main sung passage, and the main dance, a gentle and elegant *jo-no-mai*, come in the second act of the play.

Characters

Waki (secondary actor)	a priest
Shite (main actor)	in act I: an old village woman, the spirit of the old woman who was once a dancing-girl
	in act II: the ghost of the old woman as she was in life
Entr'acte player	a local person

ACT I

  Stage assistants bring onto the stage a simple covered framework representing a hut, and set it down at the back of the stage.
  The priest slowly enters to the accompaniment of the flute and comes to the centre of the stage.   *JO* SECTION

Priest. I am a priest who lives here at this mountain called   (*Nanori:*
  Iwado, in the province of Higo. I have shut myself away here   'naming'
  because Kannon, the goddess of Mount Iwado, is said to be   passage)
  wondrous in the miracles she works; and as I look at the
  scene before me

> South and west stretch into one,   (In free rhythm)
> Giving me an awareness of eternity.
> With so few people and so much solace,
> With such a scene far from the dwellings of men,[1]
> I feel this is a truly inspiring place to stay,
> And so have spent three years here.

Every day, an old woman I feel must be a hundred years old
has come to draw water here. If she comes again today, I
shall ask her name and what manner of person she is.
He then moves to the far front corner of the stage and sits down.

To a quiet musical accompaniment, an old woman moves slowly   HA SECTION,
along the gallery from the dressing-room and onto the stage. She   PART 1
leans on a cane and carries a pail in the other hand.

Woman.　　　When I draw water from the shining White[3]   (*Narai no shidai*;
　　　　　　River,   in time)[2]
　　　　　　When I draw water from the shining White
　　　　　　River,
　　　　　　Both moon and water wet my sleeves.

　　　　　　The caged bird longs for the clouds;   (*Sashi*; free)
　　　　　　The goose returning north misses those it leaves
　　　　　　behind.[4]
　　　　　　It is the same with man, yet
　　　　　　A poor home has few callers
　　　　　　And misfortune sees old friends grow cold.[5]
　　　　　　No one spares me a glance now
　　　　　　In the decrepitude of my old age,
　　　　　　And my dewdrop[6] life comes to an end
　　　　　　Life a frost[6]-seared leaf.

　　　　　　From this sad world,   (*Sage-uta*; in
　　　　　　Transient as the foam[7] on flowing water,[8]   time)
　　　　　　I now draw[8] my knowledge of this truth.

　　　　　　This place itself is the White River of   (*Age-uta*)
　　　　　　knowledge,[9]
　　　　　　This place itself is the White River of
　　　　　　knowledge,
　　　　　　And though my sins are as deep as its waters,[10]
　　　　　　In the hope of having them washed[10] away
　　　　　　By one who has forsaken the world,
　　　　　　I have dragged my weary steps[11] here
　　　　　　For a meeting with the priest,
　　　　　　And arrive now at his hut below the mountain,
　　　　　　And arrive now at his hut below the mountain.

The old woman goes towards the priest.   HA SECTION,
Woman.　　　I have come today as usual to offer up this holy   PART 2 (*Mondō*:
　　　　　　water.   'dialogue')
She sits in the middle of the stage and puts down the pail.
Priest.　　　How hard it must be for you, old lady, to come
　　　　　　here continually day after day.
Woman.　　　Such a thing might spare me at least   (Free)
　　　　　　A small part of my sins.
Joining her hands in supplication
　　　　　　Pray for my soul, I beg you, when I am gone. I
　　　　　　shall come again tomorrow, but take my leave of
　　　　　　you now.

As the old woman gets to her feet with the aid of her cane.

Priest.　　One moment – do please tell me your name.

Woman.　　What is that? Tell you my name, do you say?

Priest.　　Yes, indeed.

The old woman sits again and puts down her cane.

Woman.　　What an unexpected thing for you to ask me. In
　　　　　the *Gosenshū*[12] is a poem which says
　　　　　'So many years have passed that my once-black
　　　　　hair
　　　　　Is as white as the White[13] River,

And I am now so old and bent / That I can do nothing but
draw water[14]; and I am the one who composed it. Long ago,
as Dazaifu in the province of Chikuzen, a dancing-girl lived
in a hut surrounded by a fence of woven cypress-wood, but
later, as age took its toll, she came to live beside the White
River.

Priest.　　In truth, I have heard something of the sort:
　　　　　How, when Fujiwara no Okinori
　　　　　Was passing her hut on the White River,

Woman.　　He asked her for some water,
　　　　　And as she drew it from the river
　　　　　To give to him,

Priest.　　'I am now so old and bent
　　　　　That I can do nothing but draw water'

Woman.　　Was the poem she composed.

During the following passage an entr'acte player (ai) *enters unob-
trusively and sits down at the back of the stage.*

Chorus.　　These lines of the poem, then;　　　　　(Age-uta; in time)
　　　　　These lines of the poem, then,
　　　　　Tell not only of her drawing water
　　　　　From the White River,
　　　　　But also of her being old and bent.[15]

As the old woman takes up her cane and rises to her feet
　　　　　'If you would see the proof of all this,
　　　　　Pray for my soul, I beg you,
　　　　　Beside the White River' –
　　　　　And with these words
　　　　　She fades into the evening gloom;
　　　　　She fades into the evening gloom.

*The woman moves backwards with short, quick steps, throws down
her cane, and disappears into the covered framework representing her
hut.*

INTERVAL

*The entr'acte player, in the role of a local person, comes to the centre
of the stage and talks to the priest about the poem and its meaning
and then, realising that the local woman who had been there was the
spirit of the author of the poem, urges the priest to pray for her before
retiring again to the back of the stage.*

ACT II

Priest.　　It was, then, that woman from long ago　　*HA* SECTION,
who appeared before me for a while and spoke with me.　　PART 3

Telling myself that this may perhaps have been a miracle,
even in this degenerate age, I go now to seek her out. As I do
so,

Strange to say, the sun here has set all too early;   (*Age-uta*)
Strange to say, the sun here has set all too early,
But beyond the deep enveloping mist
From the river, a light in the hut
Can be dimly and strangely seen.

He joins his hands in prayer.

Oh, you spirit from another world,   (Free)
May you achieve enlightenment,
Shake off the toils of life and death
And reach the state of Buddhahood forthwith!

*A quiet musical introduction signifies the presence of the main
character, who at first sings unseen from within the hut.*

Woman.   How grateful I am for the prayers;
        How grateful I am for the prayers.

The wind drops over the green land,   (*Sashi*)
And willow boughs hang straight.
The clouds lie still on the mountain top,
And the moon is round.[16]

Morning sees a red-cheeked enjoyment   (*Kuri*)
Of all the bustle of life.

Chorus.   But evening brings whitening bones
        Rotting in a far-off place.[17]
Woman.   Each and every living thing
Chorus.   Illustrates the truth of impermanence.
Woman.   Who, in the midst of life and death,
Chorus.   Can fail to give thought to their rule?
        No one knows when his time will come,
        For it is always thus.
        Young and old are as one
        In having change bring their time to an end.
        Who does not foresee his own mortality?
        Who does not foresee this for himself?
Priest.   How strange! The voice I hear   (*Kake-ai*)
        Is that of the woman I met before.
        Rather should she show herself to me,
        For I shall then pray for her.
Woman. I shall show myself to you, then, and receive your holy
    prayers.
        Speak not of me, though, to others.   (Free)
Priest.   Indeed, I shall say nothing.
        Show yourself to me now, without delay.
    *Stage assistants remove the cloth enclosing the framework of the hut,
    revealing the old woman seated inside.*
Woman.   With tear-lined face
        And changed so by the ravages of time,
        Who would know[18] me now
        Beside the waters of the White River?

	My appearance in this bent[19] old age
	Fills me with shame.
Priest.	What a pitiful sight,
	To see you returned to this life
	And drawing water as before,
	Because of your attachment to this world.
	Quickly cast away such feelings and find your
	peace.

Woman. In former times I was famous as a dancer, but because of the sinfulness of this, I must suffer even now. Beside Hell's River of the Three[20] Rapids, I am laden with buckets of red-hot iron and carry fiercely flaming pails, and when I draw water with these, it boils up and scalds my body. I know no rest from this, but now that I have met you, priest, though the pails remain, the fierce flames will be no more.

Priest.	Draw water, then, as your fate decrees,
	And cast off obsession with this world
	To find more swiftly the peace of Buddha.

Woman. If I draw off all the water with this pail to wash away my obsession, then, with your help, priest,

	Perhaps my sins will grow shallow too.
Priest.	With this deep hope, deep[21] into the night,
	With tied-back sleeves bejewelled[22] with dew,
Woman.	While the moon shows white[22] in the White River,
Priest.	Even the clear water in its very depths
Woman.	Shall I draw off.

The old woman emerges to stand in front of the hut.

Chorus.	The fallen moon, caught in the pail,	(*Shidai*; in time)
	Seems to climb her sleeve
	As she draws it in.

	Under the morning stars, fill the cauldron	(*Kuri*; free)
	With water drawn from the valley to the north;
	In the small hours light the fire
	With brushwood cut from the peak to the south.[23]
Woman.	Ice comes from water, but is colder;	(*Sashi*)
Chorus.	Blue comes from indigo, but is richer in hue.[24]
	Thus, if this is retribution for my former life,
	My present suffering will never disappear
Woman.	But will only grow and grow.
	At this thought, the fire of my feelings[25]
	And my burning tears consume me utterly.

During the next passage, the old woman performs actions illustrative of the text.

Chorus.	Repeatedly I draw in the rope on my pail,	(*Kuse*; in time)
	As repeatedly I grieved in days gone by.
	But even they, like a spring morning
	Filled with red-tinged cherry blossom
	And an autumn evening of red maple leaves,
	Have become no more than the dream
	Of a single day.
	Fair of face and form, a special fame

                    I won as a dancer.
                    But the bloom has gone from the raven-black hair
                    Which set off such beauty of face,
                    And frost has settled on eyebrows
                    Once shaped like crescent moons.
                    The face I now see in the water
                    Is sunken and racked with age,
                    And the green-sheened blackness of my hair
                    Is like the muddy brown of water-weed.
                    How wretched I am when I see myself!
                    Truly, when I recall the days that once were mine,
                    How I long for them again!
                    Here beside the waves[26] of the White River,
Woman.   Fujiwara[26] no Okinori
Chorus.   Asked me to dance a dance of my youth,
                    But the flowered robe and long, hanging sleeves
                    Were now a faded hempen[27] wrap with narrow
                    sleeves,
                    And in my distress[28] at the ill-fitting thing
                    Made from narrow strips of cloth,
                    I replied that, try as I might,
                    There could not even be the shadow
                    Of the dancer[29] there once had been.
The old woman stands still at the back of the stage.

                    'Even so, since you once danced all the time,   *KYU* SECTION
                    You must dance for me',
Woman.   Okinori persisted, and so
Chorus.   With a heavy[30] heart and hempen[30] sleeves
                    She wiped away her tears
                    And began to dance.
Woman.   The woman who lived within the cypress fence   (Free)
Chorus.   Shows where life has brought her ...
          She performs a very quiet and slow jo-no-mai, *falteringly but with
          an inherent elegance which tells of her former skill.*
Woman.   As time and again I draw in   (*Waka*)
                    The rope with its pails of water,
                    The rope with its pails of water,
Chorus.   Let me bring back the past just once   (In time)
                    Beside the waves of the White River,
                    Beside the waves of the White River,
                    Beside the White River.

Woman.   Yet knowing the grief of a world   (Free)
                    As uncertain as foam[31] on the water
                    Has brought me here now.

Chorus.   With weary steps,[32]   (*Uta*; in time)
                    Like a rootless,[33] drifting reed,
                    I hear the plaintive cry of a crane[34]
                    As I bring water for a holy offering
                    Wash away my sins, I pray you;
                    Wash away my sins.

NOTES

1. The table is adapted from two main sources: W. Malm, 'The musical characteristics and practice of the Japanese Noh drama in an East Asian context', in J.
   Crump and W. Malm (eds.), *Chinese and Japanese music-dramas*, Michigan Papers
   in Chinese Studies no. 19 (Ann Arbor, 1975), p. 101; and Kobayashi Shizuo,
   'Nō no ongaku', *Nōgaku zensho* (Tokyo, 1943), IV, 82–3.
2. 'Sandō', in Omote Akira (ed.), *Zeami Zenchiku* (hereafter ZZ), Nihon Shisō
   Taikei (Tokyo: Iwanami, 1974), pp. 35–6.
3. 'Fūshikaden', ZZ, p. 14.
4. 'Sandō', ZZ, p. 134.
5. *Ibid.*
6. *Ibid.*
7. 'Sandō', ZZ, p. 135
8. *Ibid.*
9. 'Sarugaku dangi', ZZ, p. 288.
10. *Ibid.*
11. 'Fūshikaden', ZZ, p. 47.
12. 'Sarugaku dangi', ZZ, p. 274.
13. 'Sandō', ZZ, p. 141.
14. *Ibid.*
15. 'Fūshikaden', ZZ, pp. 49–50.

Notes to the translation of *Higaki*

1. It is likely that the above lines are quoted, but no source is now known.
2. Since the singing is of the weak type throughout, no special mention is made of
   this; but the references within parentheses are to the name of the particular
   passage (here, '*shidai*') and to how the passage is sung: either 'in time (to the
   beat)' or '(in) free (rhythm)'. The latter reference should be understood as
   applying also to the following sung parts until a change is noted.
3. An important feature of traditional Japanese poetry is the use of the same word
   or part of a word in different contexts, often in quite different meanings (here,
   e.g. 'shining-white' and 'White River'), with the object of leading one image
   smoothly into another. Such words will be shown hereafter by capital letters
   (e.g. *kage* SHIRA*kawa* in this instance) without further comment.
4. These lines are derived from the early thirteenth-century *Heike monogatari*, and
   similar ones occur in the play *Atsumori*, also by Zeami.
5. Lines from a Chinese-style poem in the eleventh-century *Honchō monzui* anthology.
6. Associated words, another traditional embellishment of Japanese poetry.
7. *mizu no* AWA*re-yo*.
8. Associated words.
9. *tokoro no* SHIRA*kawa*.
10. Associated words.
11. *hakobu* ASHI*biki no; ashibiki no* (lit. 'foot-dragging') is a conventional epithet
    used to introduce the word *yama* (mountain).

12. A poetic anthology compiled at imperial command in 951. The introduction to the poem says that it was composed by an old woman when a nobleman passing by her house beside the Shirakawa (White River) asked her to bring him water. The poem is also found in other works of the same period.

13. *kurogami mo* SHIRA*kawa*.

14. MITSU-WAGUMU (=MIZU WA KUMU).

15. The phrase in question (see note 14) covers both meanings.

16. The above four lines seem to be quoted, probably from a Chinese-style poem, but no source is known.

17. The above four lines are quoted from a Chinese-style song in the early eleventh-century *Wakan rōeishū*.

18. *tare* SHIRA*kawa*.

19. *Shirakawa no* MIZU/MITSU-*wagumu oi*.

20. *kurushimi o* MI*tsusegawa*. What follows is a description of the Hell of Burning Heat, as found in Buddhist scriptures.

21. *omoi no* FUKAKI *sayo*.

22. *tsuyu no* TAMA*dasuki* KAKE/KAGE SHIRA*kawa*.

23. These lines clearly seem to be a quotation, but the source is not known.

24. A proverb deriving from the Chinese philosopher Hsün-tzu.

25. *omo*HI *no iro*.

26. Associated words (*fuji* (wistaria) was conventionally described as growing in 'waves').

27. *iro mo* ASA*goromo*.

28. *tsuraki* MI*chinoku*.

29. *nani to ka* SHIRABYŌ*shi*.

30. Assonance: ASA*mashinagara* ASA *no sode*.

31. *mizu no* AWA*re*.

32. *hakobu* ASHI*tazu*.

33. *ashitazu no* NE *o koso tayure*.

34. The previous two lines are based on a poem by Ono no Komachi in the *Kokinshū* anthology, compiled in 905.

Enriching contradictions: romantic opera

A review article by JEAN-PIERRE BARRICELLI

Not infrequently, an amazing display of insights shapes a book which, in final analysis, turns out to be as ingenious and provocative as it is glib and inconclusive. Such is the case with Peter Conrad's *Romantic Opera and Literary Form*,[1] with its engaging generalizations about the much discussed interrelationship between literature and musical opera, which keep unfolding equally engaging perspectives on works, literary and musical, popular and esoteric, we all had placed into comfortable and convenient niches in our private museum of intellectual experience. For, as is the case with attractive associations and ingenious analogies, we are often left with starry-eyed conceptualizations which resist paraphrase or close analysis. Part of the problem is in the format laid down by the publisher, the University of California Press, which defines the 'Quantum Book', in which series Mr Conrad's work is published, as a short study of one hundred or so pages, rich in detail and insight, and 'short enough to be read in an evening and significant enough to be a book'. I found the book rich in insight but not in detail (in fact, quite wanting in this category – but perhaps inevitably so given the Quantum specifications of brevity), and I found it impossible to read in an evening (not because of time but because of its undetailed richness) for the very reason that it should have been a book.

Conrad's thesis (simply put on the book's jacket as well as it might be anywhere) is that Wagner's notion that opera should become music-drama is erroneous. On the surface it might seem acceptable, but intimately it is impossible, since a) other literary forms (epic, romance, allegory, the novel) and wordless art forms such as dance and painting have shaped operatic realizations for some time, and b) romantic opera in particular ultimately discards the activism (front-line action, situation consciousness) of drama, which has to be condensed into the brief time of an evening and the brief space of a stage, and favors instead the introversion of the novel (the whole nexus of spacious context and intimate, psychic consciousness), whose very nature renounces dramatic externality and prefers to adopt a psycho-aesthetic relationship with its apparent opposite, the symphonic poem. 'My argument', declares Conrad, 'is that music and drama are dubious, even antagonistic, partners and that opera's actual literary analogue is the novel' (p. 1).

To demonstrate this, in Quantum-like brevity, Conrad journeys quickly through five topics: operatic form and romance, operatic Shakespeare, operatic allegory, the operatic novel, and dance and painting in relation to opera. He is not always easy to follow, since he constructs unusual intellectual bridges between not unusual ways of perceiving works, and buttresses these bridges with ingenious verbal associations. We are made to reckon with his manipulation of facts because we are invited to respond to his manipulation of language, and then by extension required to react to the ideas generated by the manipulations. This kind of game-playing corresponds quite intimately with the game of modern practice in the arts, as Robbe-Grillet and Picasso would have it: the game of taking what is, or what is accepted, and shaping it into what might not be, and of converting what might not be into what could be, or indeed ought to be. The *Ludus Tonalis* of Hindemith is the 'l'art c'est jeu' of Robbe-Grillet is the 'pourquoi me prend-on au sérieux?' of Picasso is the 'la parola è affascinante, ma dormici sopra' of my wise Italian friends. This is not to say that Conrad's words may be slept off and forgotten, for they leave an echo which keeps telling you that while it is just an echo it springs from a sound source which says that the *ludus* has significance, perhaps because it is a game, but also perhaps because the game is to be taken seriously.

In describing the operatic meanings of epic and romance, Conrad ranges from ambiguously stated differences between personal and social virtues (i.e. epic versus romance) to completed actions (epic) as opposed to constant, non-concluding experiencing (romance). The skip is brief to Byron's *Don Juan* who rescues Mozart's *Don Giovanni* from the throes of being a hero of romance. He insists that the inconclusion of romance remains inherent in the factor of experiencing, which characterizes romance, and then proceeds to engage in a comparison of Wagner and Dante, Wagner's chivalric operas midway between Dante's diagram of the spirit and Balzac's (a logical guest in the party) secular and mercantile society. No sooner is this stated than we dip into a Rossini–Meyerbeer comparison, during which we are made to leap imaginatively to Heine and Meyerbeer's 'institutional models of democratic parliament and the army' (compared with Wagner and Berlioz), institutions which find parallels in the aesthetically logical creations of the factory and the conservatively processed organizations of the museum. What does all this mean? It becomes a moot point to continue to read the chapter, since the author has manipulated ideas, partially through language, to put us on our guard for the rest of the journey.

Still in the first chapter, we continue the ingenious experience: for the sake of contrast – the contrast between History and Myth – we plunge into a discussion of Berlioz (*Les Troyens*) and Wagner (the *Ring*), whose works 'face

one another as epics of the two contrasted kingdoms of romantic imagination, the lyricism and lucidity of the Mediterranean and the visionary
dreariness of the dark, fearful North' (p. 19). The instinctive question is just
how 'Mediterranean' is Hector Berlioz? And, in developing critically the
Wagnerian line, is it really so bad that the *Ring* demands total immersion on
our part (Conrad sees Bayreuth as an attempt to remove us from our private
lives in our home towns), since the composer aims for a total experience? A
novelist does not care to be read piecemeal either. But Conrad is out to show
that the host of Bayreuth leans more toward northern romance than southern epic. He describes convincingly how Wagner's music, in contrast with
Berlioz's which reflects a historical consciousness (the vision of Rome
atoning for the casualties of Troy and Carthage), is finally self-destructive
in the mythic return to its origin, whereby all possibility of change is
aborted by necessary accidents. The conclusion that such drama as the *Ring*
looks backward and is therefore pessimistic (Berlioz's is optimistic, given its
historical thrust) is intellectually rich, particularly when the discussion
bears on the leitmotif, the score's memory device denoting 'an introverted
psychological dependence on the past'. The backward direction is clear
when we get to *Götterdämmerung*, the epic installment in an otherwise non-
epical tetralogy, which extends – backwards – from this drama of force to a
juvenile hero's quest for self-knowledge (the romance), to a guilty society's
search for redemption through its hero (the novel), to the story's ideological
prologue (the morality play). According to Conrad, this is not music
drama, as Wagner would have it; this is more a novel's examination of
private conscience, and since music by nature transcribes affection and
complicity rather than active externality, the dramatic development of the
tetralogy is impaired.

To advance the argument, in the second chapter Conrad delves into
Shakespeare, whose 'plays are treated either as lyrical monologues, in
which case the corresponding form is the symphonic poem, or else as
frustrated novels, which is the implication of Verdi's use of them. The
alternative musical forms are related: the symphonic poem is a species of
musical novel, since in its submergence of plot in atmosphere it snubs the
drama and prefers to record, like the novel, the meditative life of motive and
self-examination' (p. 43). Through the monodrama, *Lélio*, attached to the
Symphonie fantastique, Berlioz appears the introspective composer very much
at home with this kind of self-interrogatory soliloquy we find in *Hamlet*, thus
suggesting that Shakespeare is fundamentally a musical novelist, or, to
refine things further in Conrad's language, that since the monologues *are*
the plays for all intents and purposes the introverted poetry finds its
analogue in the symphonic poem, that is, undramatized opera. All of this is
quite intriguing, of course, except that it would need to be more specific to
be fully convincing. I am not convinced that Conrad's private definitions of

drama, musical novel, and the like would withstand rigorous analysis. But it is provocative to think that monologue reflects a desire to avoid drama (meaning action), just as a tone poem avoids the declamatory outwardness of opera: Hamlet and Falstaff, who aspire to dreamy passivity, retire into the safety of the monologue. The music of Berlioz's Hamlet (Lélio) and of Verdi's Falstaff allows them this lyrical privacy.

Falstaff, in fact, is redeemed by music: a degraded creature, by the time we pass from the *Henrys* to *The Merry Wives*, he is saved in the opera through singing. 'Music pardons all faults', writes Conrad. However, instead of leaving this good thought at that, it might have been helpful if Conrad had addressed more the question of why this should be so. For without such an approach we have the feeling that Conrad is again spinning his web of incantation. The nature of music makes ugliness impossible; are not the hell tones at the end of Mozart's *Don Giovanni* beautiful? Grétry's notion of realism notwithstanding, it took Wagner's and Berlioz's and Boito's and particularly Liszt's (in the *Dante Symphony*) reversal of harmonic practices and conventional composition to begin to approach the ugly – though never with total success. Music is aesthetically one notch above literature, so that Liszt's Inferno is not quite as ugly as Dante's and Violetta comes off more appealingly than Marguerite.

Yet, if Iago acquires some fascination in *Otello*, for Conrad the fact remains that, unlike *Falstaff* where Shakespeare is improved, *Othello* is diminished in Verdi/Boito. Romantic music and tragedy are incompatible, it would seem – and here again Conrad plays with concepts a bit too glibly – 'because melody is always consoling and uplifting, and the final bars of *Otello*, like the end of *Tristan*, transmute possible tragedy into divine comedy. The symphonic poem ... not only romantically releases Shakespeare's characters from drama, but releases them from tragedy, because the symphonic poem is their justification ... Music's ambition is to render drama obsolete: hence the reduction of Shakespeare's complicated dramatic amplitude to the lyrical monologue of the symphonic poem' (p. 69). (Conrad uses Liszt's *Hamlet*, Tchaikovsky's, and Strauss's *Macbeth* as examples – hardly what one might wish to prove the point.)

I have dwelled in some detail on the first two chapters of *Romantic Opera and Literary Form* in order to communicate some of the joys and some of the frustrations in store for the reader of this book. On balance, the joys win out, if only because they tend to set our mind in motion along trails that may depart considerably from the direction of Conrad's itinerary. There is, after all, just so much we can do with: 'In Shakespeare's case, drama surrenders to music, which claims to grant Hamlet's wish in dismissing the trappings and suits of verbal representation to probe the inarticulate life of feeling', and there is not much we can do with: '[Goethe's] *Faust* rejects the operatic form because it is already an opera' or with its designation as a 'scientific opera' by becoming 'allegorical science fiction' as distinguished from Wagner's 'critical science fiction', after which Shelley's *Prometheus Unbound*, which makes nature sing, emerges as a 'symphony of science'! But when Conrad introduces operatic allegory with *Die Zauberflöte* and *Die Frau ohne Schatten*, connected across the length of the romantic period, we ponder in our own minds the nature of allegory; we think of how it aims beyond the text and is therefore conducive to its opposite: to stressing the text, therefore, in order to understand better what it is that it points to beyond itself. Unwittingly, Conrad can make us delight in our own thoughts, though they may not always be terribly original.

This exercise, which in time takes us through *Fidelio*, Goethe's alterations of Mozart, Kierkegaard, more Hofmannsthal, and Auden, prepares us for a very rewarding appreciation of the opposition between drama and the novel, of the operatic novel (as opposed to the mistaken notion of musical drama), and of the inalienable enmity between words and music, each claiming privileges which are mutually exclusive. To quote but one passage:

> Music tends to subdue and inundate its text, and this confirms opera's adherence to the novel. For as music invades a text, it re-enacts the process Schopenhauer discerned in the creation of a novel. He made it a rule that a novel would be the finer the more it concentrated on inner life to the exclusion of that outer life which belonged to the dramatist, and even proposed that the ratio between internal and external might be a means of computing a novel's excellence ... From the first, opera has conceded that music can probe states of mind but not advance actions. The formal balance of eighteenth-century opera virtually institutionalizes this conflict between drama and the novel: plot is dealt with in the brisk gabble of recitative, while in the arias music intervenes to describe a static condition of spirit. (p. 113)

It is in this manner that Conrad's book must be taken, except for its Quantum brevity, as something like a Wagner opera: questionable unclarities which tax our patience, all redeemed by moments of real beauty and power. D'Annunzio, Balzac, Hofmannsthal, Forster ... Strauss, Mozart, Verdi, Berlioz ... all and more enter Conrad's whirl of ideas at different times or overlapping or together, and in the end even the worlds of dance and painting are brought in. Paradoxical combinations and definite virtuosity: there is a definite excitement generated on every page one can accept, or understand. The *Ring*, supposedly a history of literary form, runs backwards; Shakespeare's plays are lyrical poems, reduced to symphonic monologues; drama is turned into its opposite, the novel, when music invades it; and 'the operatic union of the arts is hardly the industrial merger it seems, for it involves a virtual extinction of each art in turn ... Opera does more than suffer conflicts like these: it foments them. Its genius lies in the potentiality for an enriching contradiction between its elements' (p. 177). This is an author who has thought a lot, and gets carried away a lot. But this is also an author who thoroughly enjoys his own provocative richness. The Quantum book must be read in shorter doses than imagined, and over several evenings.

NOTES

1. Peter Conrad, *Romantic Opera and Literary Form* (Berkeley, Los Angeles, London: University of California Press, 1977).

Music in the theatre
(à propos of *Aida*, act III)

PIERLUIGI PETROBELLI

To Nicola LeFanu

In opera, various 'systems' work together, each according to its own nature and laws, and the result of the combination is much greater than the sum of the individual forces. In this essay I wish to discuss the interaction of the three main systems – dramatic action, verbal organisation and music. The dramatic action unfolds the events of the plot, the verbal organisation, structured most of the time in lines and verses, offers support and definition to the action, and the music interprets and transforms, in its own terms, both action and text; I may add that by 'music' I do not only mean the musical declamation of the text, but also the orchestral part(s) along with it. Musical theatre involves the interaction of these three systems. But how does the chemical compounding take place? And what is the nature of the bonding?

Rather than expound abstract theories, I prefer to allow the basic principles to emerge from a specific example, and shall consider the first part of the third act of *Aida*; only at the end of this essay I shall suggest some conclusions – which I shall offer for discussion and development.

Let me start by summarising the situation at that point in the opera.[1] It is night time on a bank of the Nile. Amneris, daughter of the Pharaoh, and the high priest Ramfis enter on a barge. Amneris is betrothed to Radamès, a young but already victorious Egyptian captain, and she has come to pray at the temple on the eve of her wedding. Aida is an Ethiopian princess held in slavery by the Egyptians; she is in love with Radamès and is afraid of being abandoned by him. She dreams of Ethiopia, but fears that she will never see it again. Her father King Amonasro is, in disguise, also a prisoner of the Egyptians: he is planning revenge and wants Aida to obtain from Radamès the secret of the Egyptian plan to attack Ethiopia. Aida is forced to yield by the psychological violence inflicted on her by her father, who then hides himself so that he may spy on the lovers.

This part of the plot is articulated in three distinct episodes: the entrance of Amneris and Ramfis, Aida's monologue, and the exchange between Aida and her father. These episodes, however, do not have equal importance. Underlying the entire opera there are some basic conflicts: one between the feelings and the aspirations of the individuals, and the interests of the state and religious establishment; the other within each of the two protagonists (Aida and Radamès) between their mutual love and the love for their own country. Because of these conflicts, not only are Aida and Radamès in the end crushed, but Amneris as well. These conflicts explain why, in the scenes we are analysing, Aida weeps over her country rather than her lover; and the reason why Amneris and Ramfis do not take part in the action here, but are absorbed in the Nile landscape until the end of the act: none of the conflicts concerns them at this point of the dramatic action. Aida is in a totally different situation; she is alone and motionless, but her inner conflict and especially her desperate longing for her homeland will set this part of the tragedy in motion.

All this is clearly discernible in the structure of the lines created by Ghislanzoni, the author of the libretto, under Verdi's watchful eye.[2] While the dialogue between Amneris and Ramfis is in plain, traditional recitative metre – eleven- and seven-syllable lines freely alternated – the episode in which Aida expresses the basic 'affect' of the situation consists of two quatrains of eleven-syllable lines alternately *piani* and *tronchi*[3] and with alternate rhymes:

> O cieli azzurri ... o dolci aure native
> Dove sereno il mio mattin brillò ...
> O verdi colli ... o profumate rive ...
> O patria mia, mai più ti rivedrò!
>
> O fresche valli ... o queto asil beato
> Che un dì promesso dall'amor mi fu ...
> Ahimè! d'amore il sogno è dileguato ...
> O patria mia, non ti vedrò mai più!   (lines 21–8)

The dialogue between Amonasro and Aida, on the other hand, is articulated in various sections; each of them is a well-calculated step forward in the crescendo of dramatic tension, and the verbal structure is clearly differentiated with respect to metre and rhyme; it can be summarised as follows:

a) Amonasro informs Aida that he knows all her feelings, and he lists them: love for Radamès, rivalry with Amneris, pride in her royal origin, longing to return to their country (lines 29–38).
Eleven- and seven-syllable lines are freely alternated in recitative style and concluded with a *rima baciata* (lines 37–8), the usual device in the libretto technique to indicate the closing of a section. After this recitative the duet proper begins.

b) Amonasro: 'Aida will be able to see her country again' (lines 39–46).
There are two quatrains of eleven-syllable lines with alternate rhymes

piane and *tronche*, each of them stemming from a couple of lines to Amonasro, immediately echoed by a couple to Aida:

Amonasro	Rivedrai le foreste imbalsamate ...
	Le nostre valli ... i nostri templi d'òr! ...
Aida	Rivedrò le foreste imbalsamate ...
	Le nostre valli ... i nostri templi d'òr! ...
Amonasro	Sposa felice a lui che amasti tanto,
	Tripudi immensi ivi potrai gioir ...
Aida	Un giorno solo di sì dolce incanto ...
	Un'ora di tal gaudio[4] ... e poi morir!

c) 'The cruel Egyptians have invaded and soiled their beloved country' (lines 47–54).

Again, there are two quatrains of eleven-syllable lines, with the same structure as the two previous ones, a quatrain to Amonasro (47–50) and a quatrain to Aida (51–4), which echoes that of Amonasro:

Amonasro	Pur rammenti che a noi l'Egizio immite
	Le case, i templi e l'are profanò ...
	Trasse in ceppi le vergini rapite ...
	Madri ... vecchi e fanciulli ei trucidò.
Aida	Ah! ben rammento quegli infausti giorni!
	Rammento i lutti che il mio cor soffrì ...
	Deh! fate o Numi che per noi ritorni
	L'alba invocata dei sereni dì.

d) 'The time of revenge has come; everything is ready, but for the discovery of the military secret' (lines 55–8).

There is a quatrain of eleven-syllable lines to Amonasro, alternately *piani* and *tronchi*:

Amonasro	Non fia che tardi – In armi ora si desta
	Il popol nostro – tutto pronto è già ...
	Vittoria avrem ... Solo a saper mi resta
	Qual sentiero il nemico seguirà ...

Sections *b*), *c*) and *d*) form a unity in themselves since they all stem from quatrains of eleven-syllable lines, each line being alternately *piano* and *tronco* with alternating rhymes. It is the very same structure of metre and rhyme scheme as Aida's monologue (lines 21–8). The 'affect' expressed there, the longing for her country, is structurally brought forward and the dramatic function is developed to a maximum.

e) Amonsaro finally reveals his scheme: it is up to Aida to get from Radamès the military secret; Aida refuses violently (lines 59–62). These are four eleven-syllable lines of recitative, *liberi*.

f) Amonsaro: 'Let then the Egyptians come to destroy our country'; Aida is terrified (lines 63–72). There are two quatrains of six-syllable lines (*intrecciate* thus: a *rima piana* at the second and sixth lines, and a *rima tronca* at the fourth and eighth lines), plus a couplet of six-syllable lines, the second rhyming with the previous *rima tronca*:

Amonasro	Su, dunque! sorgete
	Egizie coorti!
	Col fuoco struggete
	Le nostre città ...
	Spargete il terrore,
	Le stragi, le morti ...
	Al vostro furore
	Più freno non v'ha.
Aida	Ah padre! ...
Amonasro	Mia figlia
	Ti chiami! ...
Aida	Pietà!

g) 'The Egyptians will raid Ethiopia' (lines 73–8).

A sestet of seven-syllable lines, alternately *sdruccioli* without rhyme and *piani* with rhyme, is concluded by a *verso tronco*:

Amonasro	Flutti di sangue scorrono
	Sulle città dei vinti ...
	Vedi? ... dai negri vortici
	Si levano gli estinti ...
	Ti additan essi e gridano:
	Per te la patria muor!

h) 'The ghost of Aida's mother will come to curse her' (lines 79–84).

Again a sestet of seven-syllable lines, but with the second and third lines rhyming a *rima baciata* ('affaccia' / 'braccia') and the fourth and sixth lines connected by assonance to the *rima tronca* of the previous sestet ('muòr' / 'levò' / 'Ah! nò'):

Aida	Pietà! ...
Amonasro	Una larva orribile
	Fra l'ombre a noi s'affaccia ...
	Trema! Le scarne braccia
	Sul capo tuo levò ...
	Tua madre ell'è ... ravvisala ...
	Ti maledice ...
Aida	Ah! no! ...

i) 'You are just the Pharaohs' slave!' (lines 85–6).

Two *quinari doppi* without rhyme for the *parola scenica*:[5]

Aida	Padre ...
Amonasro	Va indegna! non sei mia prole[6] ...
	Dei Faraoni tu sei la schiava!

j) Aida is doomed; she will do what her father requests, in order to rescue their country. Amonasro hides himself (lines 87–94).

Two quatrains of *quinari doppi*, with the rhyme scheme ABBC DCEC (the rhyme C being a *rima tronca*):

Aida	Padre, a costoro schiava io non sono ...
	Non maledirmi ... non imprecarmi ...
	Tua figlia ancora potrai chiamarmi ...
	Della mia patria degna sarò!
Amonasro	Pensa che un popolo, vinto, straziato,
	Per te soltanto risorger può ...
Aida	O patria! o patria ... quanto mi costi!
Amonasro	Corraggio! ei giunge ... là tutto udrò ...

As a whole, then, the duet is articulated in three distinct parts, each of them characterised by its metre and rhyme scheme, in turn determined by their dramatic content and function. The two 'bridges' in recitative style between the three parts do not function as links; they serve to emphasise the *parola scenica* and isolate it from the symmetry of the musical discourse. In any case, for dramatic purposes Verdi rejects in this duet the conventional organisation in four parts which had been customary in Italian opera from the time of Rossini: *allegro, cantabile, allegro* and *cabaletta*.[7] He does not hesitate to return to it, for instance, when the drama requires it in the scene immediately following, the Aida–Radamès duet.

The verbal structure, therefore, implies the musical structure in its points of articulation. The position of the set pieces, and their internal organisation, are results of the overall conception of the musical drama; in giving binding instructions to Ghislanzoni, Verdi refuses or accepts, according to the needs of the drama, the conventions of nineteenth-century Italian opera. The duet has the form of an arch, whose culminating point coincides with the *parola scenica*: 'Dei Faraoni tu sei la schiava!'; but its articulation can be understood only if considered in the economy of the entire act, and of the opera as a whole. All this becomes even clearer if we compare the text of the libretto with the *programme*, or scenario written by Mariette Bey, which has only recently been published. The main difference between the two texts lies in the dramatic coherence (and resulting tension) given by Verdi to that succession of events, logically understandable but rather ineffective and poorly organised from a dramatic point of view:

The set represents a garden of the palace. On the left the oblique façade of a pavilion, or tent. At the back of the stage runs the Nile. On the horizon the Libyan mountains, vividly illuminated by the sunset. Statues, palm trees, tropical bushes. As the curtain rises, Aida is alone on stage. Radamès is in her thoughts and heart more than ever. The trees, the sacred river which runs at her feet, those distant hills – where the ancestors of her beloved rest – all this is witness of her constancy and fidelity. She is waiting for him. May Isis,

protector of love, lead him to her, who wants to be only his. But it is not
Radamès who comes, it is Amonasro. [Here follows a description of
Amonasro's appearance.] He informs his daughter that Ethiopia has again
lifted the flag of revolt, and that Radamès will again march against it. In a
moving speech he reminds her of the land where she was born, of her
desolated mother, of the sacred images of their ancestors' gods. But the love
inspired by Aida in Radamès has not escaped his fatherly intuition (or
premonition). She should take advantage of this love to seize from Radamès
the secret plan for the Egyptian troops' march. Radamès will be taken during
the battle, and led as a slave to Ethiopia, where eternal bonds will ensure
forever their happiness. Won by her father's supplications, by the remem-
brance of her childhood, by the joy at the idea of being united to her beloved –
away from a land where she has suffered all too long the tortures of slavery –
Aida promises.[8]

If the dramatic structure and the verbal organisation already contain the
essence of the episode, what then is the function of music? In my opinion, it
is twofold: not only does it characterise in its own terms the elements of the
dramatic discourse, but – and this is its crucial function – it determines its
temporal dimension, its duration. These durations should not therefore be
valued in abstract and absolute terms (indeed the same is true for the
characterising musical elements); on the contrary, they should be related to
the other durations which determine episodes, scenes, acts, the entire
opera.

By shifting from the purple light of the sunset, as in the *programme*, to the
dark night of the libretto, Verdi created the possibility of characterising the
entire opening scene with the simplest of all 'musico-dramatic signs' – to use
the terminology of Frits Noske[9] – a simple note, G.[10] This pitch repeated at
different octaves by the violins, and around which unfolds also the 'exotic'
melody entrusted to the flute, is further defined by the particular colour the
composer gives it by using the overtones in the divided cellos; the sonority of
G is – so to speak – 'wrapped' with these overtones, which give it an
unmistakable character. This G is sustained in the orchestra throughout
the chorus – off stage – of priests and priestesses, thirty-four bars altogether
andante mosso;[11] it is interrupted at the beginning of the dialogue between
Amneris and Ramfis, and it starts again on the last sentence of the high
priest, continuing further for fourteen bars, during which the material of the
introductory chorus is repeated 'telescoped' both in its components and
with the melody entrusted to the flute.[12] Through this dove-tailing of the
sonority of G onto the recitative, and with the recapitulation of the opening
material, the dramatic point is perfectly established, and Amneris and
Ramfis are 'absorbed' into the night, cold and impassive as is the chanting
of the priests. All this is realised dramatically by Verdi not with musical
gestures, but with the very absence of them: the dramatic situation is
defined by the static persistence of just one pitch.

Both the stage direction in the score and the *disposizione scenica* ask at this point for an 'empty stage for a few moments',[13] but Aida's arrival is announced by the motif which characterises her throughout the opera, and her few sentences of recitative lead directly into the two-verse *romanza*.[14] In contrast with Mariette Bey's *programme*, in which Aida, like a Metastasio heroine, calls on surrounding nature as witness of her fidelity to her beloved, the libretto emphasises just one 'affect', a desperate longing for her home country; and in the score all this is carried to the extreme. Verdi takes the last line of the first quatrain, 'Oh patria mia, mai più ti rivedrò', and transforms it into a true leitmotif of the *romanza*. The melodically passionate declamation of this line is preceded by an instrumental 'figure', entrusted to two oboes, two clarinets in C and a flute, modally articulated, which concludes first on F (four bars) and then on E (six bars).[15] This modal contour and this instrumental colour have an important structural function in the economy of the act; they return later, during the Aida–Radamès duet, when Aida mentions the 'novella patria' to her beloved, her own country where they will take refuge.[16] The *romanza* is articulated in two verses which are parallel also from a musical point of view; the second verse opens with the repetition of the *second* phrase (six bars long)[17] of the instrumental 'figure', and it is varied, in comparison with the first verse, only in the figurations of the accompaniment and in its scoring, and it is three bars shorter; a small coda, a sort of cadenza, repeats the leitmotif – both instrumental 'figure' and melodic line[18] – thus sealing the dramatic function of the *romanza*: it is only because of this longing for her home country that Amonasro can bend Aida to his will. The musical articulation of all the 'signs' which characterise Aida's 'affect', especially their duration, is determined by their dramatic function. It was necessary first to state them, and then to prolong them for sixty bars *Andantino mosso*. Only by being given a pertinent temporal dimension can they acquire the necessary weight in the economy of the drama.

The duet between Aida and Amonasro opens with a quick recitative, given almost exclusively to 'that proud and cunning king', as Verdi puts it:[19] twenty-eight measures *Allegro vivo*, just to sketch the ancillary events, and then back *in medias res*.[20] The three stages through which Amonasro pushes his daughter into the trap prepared for her have in common the same metrical structure (eleven-syllable lines alternately *piani* and *tronchi*), as well as the same rhyme scheme. This tripartite articulation unified by common elements is perfectly matched at the musical level.[21] The musical metre is the same, 4/4, in the three sections, as is the key signature, five flats; but the relationship between these sections is a dynamic one, since the tension is gradually increased through the modification of common 'signs':

a) a semiquaver ostinato in the violas

moves to the cellos in the second section and becomes

and finally, in the third section, is entrusted to the first violins:

b) the melodic phrase given to Amonasro, at the beginning relaxed and *cantabile*,

becomes

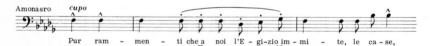

where the rhythm remains the same, but the melodic shape becomes tense and moves to the relative minor; in the third section the vocal part becomes a sort of declamation, dissociated from the movement in the orchestra:

c) the first section is in D flat major, the second in the relative minor, B flat minor, moving to B flat major at the intervention of Aida; the third section again in B flat minor;

d) the crescendo concerns the agogic as well, from *Allegro giusto* (MM. 100 at the crotchet) in the first two sections to *Poco più animato* (MM. 116 at the crotchet) in the third section. Furthermore, the first section is seventeen bars long, the second twenty, the third only eight.

The musical crescendo is the direct result of the dramatic situation, the cruel trap into which Aida is led without her realising it. It is important also to notice that each of these sections, from the point of view of the harmonic rhythm,[22] is very static at the beginning, while their second part is richer in changes of harmony. In other words, Verdi first states and then develops the 'signs' of his dramatic language, and clearly distinguishes between static and dynamic durations.[23] The last section, as we have seen, is by far the shortest and it is dove-tailed with the recitative. Notice how the figuration

becomes

punctuating the crescendo of Amonasro's insinuating questions. The gradual thinning of the texture in the orchestra points in the same direction, as does the sequence of the cellos' motif:

Aida finally understands, refuses horrified, and Amonasro explodes.

The central part of the duet is subdivided, as is the first part, into three sections, both at the verbal and at the musical level. As in the first part, each section is linked to the following by common musical features.[24] The metre, 6/8, is the same, and the three sections are connected by a harmonic relationship, though by no means a 'classical' one: C minor, A flat major, E minor. Actually, these keys are neither established nor developed through cadential or even tonal movements; rather than keys, they are better regarded as tonal levels, and indeed one follows the other without clear-cut cadential caesurae, and they are more and more unstable as the dramatic tension grows. Each of these sections is subdivided, as are the previous sections of the duet, into two parts: one part, in which the main musical 'sign' is asserted,[25] is harmonically static; in the other the 'sign' is elaborated and developed in musical terms.

The *parola scenica* central to the duet, 'Non sei mia figlia! Dei Faraoni tu sei la schiava!', exploits the highest register of the baritone voice and, at the same time, almost completely dispenses with the orchestra. The contrast between elements of dynamics and of texture, on which the crescendo in dramatic tension is built up from the previous pages, reaches at this culminating point its extreme and most elementary form. The dramatic climax coincides with the barest use of language.

The third part of the duet, *Andante assai sostenuto* (MM. 76 at the crotchet), lasts thirty-one bars and is identified and unified, as are the previous parts, by common musical 'signs': first of all by the rhythmic pedal in the violins

which is extended through its entire duration, a musical transfiguration of Aida's inner sighing. This part is also in one key only, D flat major, the key of the opening section of the duet. Here also a first section, characterised by the repetition of the rhythmic pedal on the dominant – A flat – and corresponding to Aida's broken utterances *molto sotto voce e cupo*,[26] is followed by its dynamic counterpart, in which the syncopated pedal moves, always in the violins, upwards stepwise for the span of no less than two octaves, and where the harmonic rhythm undergoes different subtle fluctuations. Considering the first bar as introductory, the border-line between the two sections of this part of the duet is placed exactly half-way through, that is at the sixteenth bar, in correspondence with the beginning of the second quatrain of *quinari doppi* and, dramatically, with Amonasro's hypocritical 'consoling' intervention.

A more detailed and thorough analysis would certainly reveal other symmetries and relationships between the various components of the musico-dramatic language of this episode. On the basis of what has been said about this one example, I would like now to identify some of the general principles which govern the unfolding of the dramatic 'language' of opera. They can be summarised as follows:

1) The articulation of the musical language is already present in the organisation of the libretto. In other words, the verbal structure is determined by the musical structure, and is governed by dramatic principles. From this it follows that every analysis on the purely musical level of an opera score is bound to be incomplete and in the end to fail in its essential purpose; such an analysis grasps only one aspect of the musico-dramatic language, and constantly risks missing the essential point.

2) All the elements of the musical language can be used as 'signs'; they may be articulated as 'themes', and have a complex organisation defined by key, rhythm, melodic shape, harmony, timbre. They may, however, be just sonorities, or simple pitches used *per se*, without articulation, and yet be by no means less effective dramatically. Indeed, the simpler the musical 'sign', the more complex and articulated its dramatic function.

3) The articulation of these musical 'signs' is directly related to their duration, i.e. to their temporal dimension. A 'sign' which is not characterised by an appropriate duration, becomes unrecognisable, and ceases to be a 'sign'.

4) The articulation of a musical 'sign' can be static; the 'sign' is sustained, or repeated without modification throughout its duration. But it can also have a dynamic temporal dimension, during which it is developed, modified, and related to other 'signs', albeit always recognisable in its identity. One can find also both static and dynamic articulations of the same 'sign' – static articulations to assert it, dynamic articulations to qualify its function during its temporal dimension.

5) The value and the function of a musico-dramatic 'sign' can in no way be evaluated in abstract, by taking the 'sign' in isolation as an absolute musical element. Instead, one must always take into consideration its position, its articulation through well-defined durations, not only within the episode in which it appears, but also – and especially – as a part of a larger dramatic structure, as a structural factor in a scene, in an act, as a constituent element of the entire opera.

NOTES

1. The original Italian text of the libretto is available, besides the current Ricordi edition, in L. Baldacci (ed.), *Tutti i libretti di Verdi* (Milan: Garzanti, 1975), pp. 449–71. For the present study, however, I follow the libretto printed for the first Italian performance: *Aida*. Opera in quattro atti. Versi di A. Ghislanzoni. Musica di G. Verdi. R. Teatro alla Scala. Carnevale-Quaresima 1871–72 (Milan, Naples, Rome, 1872). The layout of the print in this edition clearly

reveals the poetic structure. The edition also contains some very interesting variants from the text as it appears in the score. I will indicate these variants in the corresponding places. For an English translation of the Italian libretto, see W. Weaver, *Seven Verdi Librettos ... with the original Italian* (New York: Norton, 1975), pp. 343–415.

2. The known Verdi–Ghislanzoni correspondence is published in G. Cesari and A. Luzio (eds.), *I copialettere di Giuseppe Verdi* (Milan, 1913), pp. 635–75. A few of the letters have been published in English translation in E. Istel, 'A genetic study of the *Aida* libretto', *The Musical Quarterly*, 3 (1917), 34–52, and in Charles Osborne (ed.), *Letters of Giuseppe Verdi* (London: Gollancz, 1972), pp. 155–67. The most comprehensive collection of documents concerning the birth of *Aida* and its early years is H. Bush (ed.), *Verdi's 'Aida' – The history of an opera in letters and documents* (Minneapolis: University of Minnesota Press, 1978). It is, however, absolutely essential to consult also Philip Gossett, 'Verdi, Ghislanzoni and *Aida*: The uses of conventions', *Critical Enquiry*, 1 (1974), 291–334: in this important essay not only is a correct chronology of the extant correspondence established, but also basic compositional conventions – especially for the duets – are identified; these conventions determine the overall as well as the detailed structure of the libretto, and they are typical of nineteenth-century Italian opera. For Aida's *romanza*, see the letter of Verdi to Ghislanzoni of 5 August 1871 (Cesari and Luzio, *I copialettere*, pp. 674–5: Bush, *Verdi's 'Aida'*, pp. 196–7; Istel, 'A genetic study', p. 47).

3. For the English-speaking reader a brief outline of the peculiarities of the Italian accent and verse system is perhaps in order here. Italian words are *tronche* (truncated) when the accent falls on the last syllable; they are *piane* (plain) – most of them – when the accent falls on the penultimate syllable; they are *sdrucciole* (slippery) when it falls on the syllable before the penultimate. A line takes its name from the position of the accent in its last word: thus, we have a *verso tronco*, a *verso piano*, and a *verso sdrucciolo*. Furthermore, the number of syllables in a line is calculated taking the *verso piano* as a standard measure: thus, 'O cieli azzurri ... o dolci aure natìve', an eleven-syllable line ending with a 'plain' word, is an *endecasillabo piano*, while 'Fiumi di sangue scòrrono' is a *settenario sdrucciolo*. A line or a group of lines can also take its name from the rhyme scheme adopted; consecutive rhymes are called *rime baciate* (AA BB CC DD ...); alternate rhymes are called *rime alterne* or *alternate* (AB AB CD CD ...); recurring rhymes are *rime incatenate*. *Verso libero* is a line without matching rhyme. For a detailed analysis of the Italian metrical organisation as applied to opera, see R. A. Moreen, *Integration of Text Forms and Musical Forms in Verdi's Early Operas* (Ann Arbor, Michigan, and London: University Microfilms International, 1979), and J. Budden, *The Operas of Verdi 2: From 'Il Trovatore' to 'La Forza del destino'* (London: Cassell, 1978), pp. 17 ff.

4. In the score: 'gioia'.

5. With this term Verdi indicates 'the word which cuts (*scolpisce*) the dramatic situation and makes it clear and evident': letter to Ghislanzoni of 17 August 1870; see Cesari and Luzio, *I copialettere*, p. 641; Osborne, *Letters of Verdi*, p. 159 (a pale and imprecise translation). Bush, *Verdi's 'Aida'*, p. 50, gives another translation. The above is mine.

6. In the score, Verdi destroys the metrical structure by changing the line into a much more direct and effective: 'Non sei mia figlia!' (You are not my daughter).

7. See Gossett, 'Verdi, Ghislanzoni', pp. 300–6.

8. J. Humbert, 'A propos de l'égyptomanie dans l'oeuvre de Verdi: attribution: à Auguste Mariette d'un scénerio anonyme de l'opéra *Aida*', *Revue de Musicologie*, 62 (1976), 229–56. The passage quoted here is on pp. 250–1 (text in French and in Italian; the translation is mine).

9. Frits Noske, *The Signifier and the Signified – Studies in the operas of Mozart and Verdi* (The Hague: Nijhoff, 1977); this book is a landmark in research on musical drama; it is the first attempt to apply systematically the principles of semiotics to the problems of opera, seen as the meeting point of different systems of communication. Particularly important, from a methodological point of view, is Appendix 1, 'Semiotic devices in musical drama', pp. 309–21, from which I take the following definition: '*Musico-dramatic sign* [...] – A musical unit which stresses, clarifies, invalidates, contradicts or supplies an element of the libretto. The sign is semantically interpretable and discloses dramatic truth' (p. 316).

10. On the dramatic function of single sonorities in Verdi's operas, see my essays 'Osservazioni sul processo compositivo in Verdi', *Acta Musicologica*, 43 (1971), 125–42, especially pp. 140–2, and 'Per un'esegesi della struttura drammatica del *Trovatore*', *Atti del 3° Congresso Internazionale di Studi Verdiani* (Parma, 1974), pp. 387–400, especially pp. 392–5.

11. G. Verdi, *Aida*. Opera in quattro atti. Libretto di A. Ghislanzoni. Partitura d'orchestra [Milan], G. Ricordi, s.a., n. ed.le P.R. 153, pp. 265–7. The reader is kindly urged to consult the orchestral score while reading the following pages.

12. Orchestral score, pp. 269–70.

13. Orchestral score, p. 271; G. Ricordi, *Disposizione scenica per l'opera 'Aida'*. Versi di A. Ghislanzoni. Musica di G. Verdi, compilata e regolata secondo la messa in scena del Teatro alla Scala da G. R. [Milan, Naples, Rome], G. Ricordi, s.a., n. ed.le 43504, p. 40.

14. Verdi calls Aida's solo a *romanza* (and not an *aria*), no doubt because of the basically strophic nature of the piece, as opposed to the structure of a regular *aria*, where a *cantabile* is followed by a *cabaletta*. On the use of the term *romanza* in Verdi's operas, see M. Chusid, 'The organization of Scenes with Arias: Verdi's Cavatinas and Romanzas', *Atti del I° Congresso Internazionale di Studi Verdiani* (Parma, 1969), pp. 59–66, especially pp. 61–2 and 66.

15. Orchestral score, p. 273.

16. Orchestral score, pp. 316–17.

17. Orchestral score, p. 275, last system.

18. Orchestral score, p. 278, second system.

19. Letter to Ghislanzoni of 7 October [1870]. See Cesari and Luzio, *I copialettere*, p. 650; Bush, *Verdi's 'Aida'* ..., p. 75.

20. Orchestral score, pp. 279–80.

21. In the orchestral score the first section (*Allegro giusto*, MM. 100 at the crotchet, rehearsal letter I) spans from the beginning of p. 281 to the penultimate bar of the second system, p. 283; the second section, starting from this bar, ends on the first chord of p. 288 (rehearsal letter J); finally, the third section (*Poco più*

animato, MM. 116 at the crotchet) runs up to the third bar in the first system of p. 289, but the musical flow continues without break in the ensuing recitative.

22. This term commonly signifies the rhythm created in a musical composition by changes in the harmony.

23. For instance, the static dimension is created by the absence of harmonic rhythm, emphasised by an A flat pedal distributed between three instruments: oboe (top A flat held for seven and half bars), violas, which repeat the figuration of the first music example on p. 136 above, and the basses (cellos and double basses), which repeat the pitch (at different octave levels) on the rhythm

24. The first section (*Allegro*, dotted crotchet 96, rehearsal letter K) goes from p. 292 to the first bar of p. 296; the second from this bar to the first bar of p. 298 (rehearsal letter L); the third section from this bar to the last bar of p. 300; as in the first part of the duet, there is no break with the following recitative.

25. Here again the static dimension is realised above all by the absence of harmonic rhythm: in the first section, by the persistence (six bars) of the C minor chord; in the third, by the pedal on top B in the first violins (ten bars).

26. The extraordinary expressive power of this page, one of the highest and most moving moments in Verdi's music, derives from the contrast between the *ostinato* pedal in the violins and the melody entrusted to the violas, cellos and one bassoon, playing in unison *ppp con espressione*. This melody is articulated, both in detail and at the overall level, following the principles of the poetic quatrain in nineteenth-century Italian opera, in consequence of which the first and second lines have the function of asserting a situation, the third of developing the tension to its maximum, and the fourth of concluding the episode (see L. Dallapiccola, 'Parole e musica nel melodramma', *Quaderni della Rassegna Musicale*, 2 (Turin, 1965), pp. 117–39, definitive version in *Appunti, incontri, meditazioni* (Milan: Suvini Zerboni, 1970), pp. 5–28; English version: *Words and Music in Italian XIX Century Opera* (Dublin: The Italian Institute, 1964)). In the melody we are considering, the poetic line has its equivalent in a melodic fragment one bar long, the quatrain in a four-bar phrase. Significantly, Aida sings in unison with this melody only from the beginning of the third quatrain ('Ancor tua figlia ...'), and the climax of the episode – corresponding with the highest pitch of the melodic line – lies in the second 'line' of the fourth 'quatrain', at the words 'della *mia* patria'.

Verbal to musical drama: adaptation or creation?

FRITS R. NOSKE

The comedy *Le mariage de Figaro* by Beaumarchais, first performed in 1784, starts with the following dialogue:[1]

Figaro. Dix-neuf pieds sur vingt-six.
Suzanne. Tiens Figaro, voilà mon petit chapeau: le trouves-tu mieux ainsi?
Figaro [*lui prend les mains*]. Sans comparaison, ma charmante. Oh! que ce joli bouquet virginal, élevé sur la tête d'une belle fille, est doux, le matin des noces, à l'oeil amoureux d'un époux!

In English:

Figaro. Nineteen feet by twenty-six.
Suzanne. Look Figaro – my bonnet. Do you like it better now?
Figaro [*taking both her hands in his*]. Infinitely better, my sweet. My, what that bunch of flowers – so pretty, so virginal, so suited to the head of my lovely girl – does to a lover on the morning of his wedding!

Two years later, Lorenzo da Ponte writes the libretto of *Le nozze di Figaro*, to be set to music by Mozart.[2] The corresponding fragment reads:

Figaro. Cinque ... dieci ... venti ... trenta
... trentasei ... quarantatre ...
Susanna. Ora sì, ch'io son contenta,
sembra fatto in ver per me.
Guarda un po', mio caro Figaro,
guarda adesso il mio capello.
Figaro. Sì, mio core, or è più bello,
sembra fatto in ver per te.
Figaro. ⎱ Ah, il mattino alle nozze vicino,
Susanna. ⎰ quanto e dolce al mio tenero sposo
questo bel capellino vezzoso,
che Susanna ella stessa si fè.

A translation is hardly necessary, since the two fragments differ only in minor points. From the almost identical stage directions it appears that the action starts on the morning of the wedding. At the raising of the curtain we see Figaro busy measuring something on the floor of a half-furnished room, while Susanna standing or seated in front of a mirror tries on a little hat. Moreover, the Italian Susanna tells that she has made the hat herself, a piece of information that is lacking in the French text. But this detail is insignificant; the Paris spectators were well aware of the fact that a servant was supposed to manufacture her own bridal outfit.

The quoted lines from the spoken play take up no more than ten seconds; the sung fragment, on the other hand, lasts little less than three minutes, that is, seventeen or eighteen times as much. This disproportion cannot be explained by the mere fact that sung words take more time than spoken words. Even when singing in an excessively slow tempo, Figaro and Susanna would have needed not more than one minute. Moreover Mozart's tempo prescription is not *largo* or *adagio*, but *allegro*. Therefore something else must be the matter here, and in order to discover this, it is necessary to examine the score (see pp. 146–7).

Because of the informative character of the words one would expect the dialogue to be set in the manner of a recitative. However, not only the fact that Da Ponte wrote verses instead of prose, but also the synchronic singing at the end of the fragment contradicts this assumption. Despite the unlyrical text these characteristics point to a little duet, and so the piece is called by Mozart. It is obvious that Da Ponte took the composer's intention to write a *duettino* into account.

The orchestra commences with a theme, the first half of which, played by strings, has a rhythmically sharp profiled character and ends on a half-cadence, that is, on the dominant. The second subphrase forms a contrast with the first; it is a *cantabile* melody in which the woodwinds predominate and which ends on the tonic of the key (G major). Then the curtain rises and we see Figaro measuring the floor, while Susanna fits her bonnet. The theme is almost exactly repeated, this time however with the sung text, the first four lines. Now the significance of the two contrasting subphrases becomes perfectly clear; the first belongs to Figaro, who picks up only a few of its notes, sufficient for his series of numbers, while the second is completely sung by Susanna. Until this moment there has been hardly any difference between the play and the opera, but from now on the parallelism will be disturbed. Instead of answering Susanna's implicit question (as in Beaumarchais) Figaro once again starts to measure: 'cinque' etc. Being absorbed in his occupation he obviously didn't hear Susanna's words. The orchestra faithfully follows Figaro and for the third time starts to play the first subphrase. Susanna, however, reacts unhesitatingly with her ensuing lines: 'Look, my dear Figaro, look at my hat'. Naturally she sings these words on Figaro's music. At first she does not succeed in drawing Figaro's attention and therefore she repeats the word 'guarda' no less than seven times, continually interrupted by Figaro:

Guarda un po', mio caro Figaro (dieci), guarda un po', mio caro Figaro (venti), guarda un po' (trenta), guarda un po', guarda adesso il mio capello (trentasei), guarda adesso il mio capello (quarantatre), guardo un po', mio caro Figaro, guarda adesso il mio capello, il mio capello, il mio capello.

The textual repetitions result in a remarkable extension of the first subphrase. Even more important is the fact that the gradually rising tension is clearly reflected in the music. While in the previous instances the subphrase was kept within the framework of G major, now it modulates to D and even seems to exceed the limits of the latter key. This however does not happen, since the threefold mention of 'il mio capello' produces at last its effect: Figaro reacts with the words 'Sì, mio core, or è più bello/ Sembra fatto in ver per te.' As the first subphrase must be logically followed by the second, Figaro sings these words on Susanna's melody. Susanna, however, is as yet anything but sure about Figaro's lasting attention. Hence her insistence at the end of the phrase:

Susanna.	Guarda un po'
Figaro.	Sì, mio core ...
Susanna.	Guarda un po'
Figaro.	Or è più bello.

These repetitions are not only important from a dramatic point of view, they also serve the musical balance: the extended first subphrase is followed by an equally extended second subphrase.

The rest of the duet principally consists of the concluding lines which are sung homophonically by both characters ('Ah, il mattino alle nozze vicino ...'). The detente is again reflected in the music, namely by the return to the key of G major. Conspicuously Figaro's music vanishes from the score, and what we hear is Susanna's subphrase. In this way Mozart makes it clear that Susanna is the winner.

What conclusion can we draw from our analysis of this little fragment? Like the French dialogue in prose, the Italian verses principally function as indirect information to the audience. However, by creating a little conflict the music adds to this a new dramatic dimension. While it is true that the conflict is soon resolved, nevertheless this procedure gives the opera an advantage over the play, an advantage which amply compensates for the loss of time. At the moment that the conflict starts, that is, where Figaro, deaf to Susanna's words, resumes measuring the floor, a curious paradox manifests itself between text and music on the one hand, and the drama proper on the other. Precisely because words and music hark back to something old, they create a new dramatic situation. In other words, the literal repetition of a signifier generates a new signification. Beaumarchais's dialogue is changed by Mozart into a double monologue, and this is done with purely musical tools. The manner in which Susanna handles the situation – not only does she gain Figaro's attention but she also succeeds in

Duettino

Figaro, Susanna.

getting him to sing on her music – is equally Mozart's achievement. He did
not change the text, nor did he add a single word to it.

Far from being a gratuitous episode for the audience's entertainment, the
little conflict contained in this duet has a clear structural significance for the
drama as a whole. At the end of the scene we know a lot more about bride
and bridegroom than after the corresponding fragment in the French play.
The clever Figaro, known from *Le barbier de Seville,* appears to be strongly
self-centred in a social situation. As for Susanna, she certainly will not
become a submissive wife: alert and very intelligent, she knows how to
manage her *promesso sposo.* Therefore the germ of the feministic tendency in
this opera – the female will carry the day – is already contained in this initial
duet.

In the case of *Le nozze di Figaro* one usually speaks of the adaptation of a
verbal drama. Nevertheless we may raise the question: exactly what was
adapted here? Was it really the drama, that is, the theatrical intergenera-
tion of action and emotion? Or was it merely the fable, the pre-dramatic
datum, which in principle could equally well have been realized in an epic
form? I am convinced that the latter answer is the correct one. It even seems
doubtful whether the musical adaptation of a verbal *drama* is possible at all.
We have seen that Da Ponte's text largely corresponds with that of

Beaumarchais. But actually this is misleading, as it concerns two essentially different functions of a single medium. The Frenchman creates a drama through words; on the other hand, the Italian, through words, offers the composer the opportunity to create a drama. The fragments discussed most clearly demonstrate this fundamental difference.

What holds for a separate scene also holds for an entire drama. On the level of the fable and that of its textual elaboration – the plot – the opera *Otello* of Giuseppe Verdi does not essentially differ from Shakespeare's *Othello*. It is true that for practical reasons the composer and his librettist Arrigo Boito discarded the Venetian act – in point of fact a prologue – and incorporated the relevant information contained in this act in various dialogues and the love duet. For the rest, however, the intrigue takes a parallel course in both works. But this parallelism does not hold for the level of the drama proper: here we find essential differences. If one might speak of a certain affinity between the characters of Otello and Othello, this is certainly not the case with Jago and Iago, or Desdèmona and Desdemòna.

Admittedly Shakespeare's Iago is a villain, yet a human villain. He acts from real motives: the military promotion denied to him, the animosity of the professional soldier against the aristocrat Cassio, the unfounded but nevertheless sincere conviction that his wife Emilia has had an adulterous relationship with Othello, and finally his thirst for power, or rather the gratification of sentiments of power.[3] Of all these motives only the first is mentioned by Verdi's Jago and even this one loses its value, when shortly after the beginning of the second act the ensign sings his demonic *Credo*; here Jago shows himself explicitly as a villain who professes his villainy on absolutely gratuitous grounds:

> Credo in un Dio crudel
> che m'ha creato simile a sè,
> e che nell'ira io nomo.
> Dalla viltà d'un germe
> o d'un atomo vile son nato.
> Son scellerato perchè son uomo,
> e sento il fango originario in me.

> I believe in a cruel God
> who in his image has fashioned me
> and whom in wrath I worship.
> From some vile germ or from
> a paltry atom I took mine issue.
> I am vile, because I am human
> and I feel the primal mud-flow of my breed.

Jago's perfection as a villain is matched by that of Desdemona as a saint. Otello's spouse is completely unattainable for Jago's machinations, not because she is almost an ingenuous child as in Shakespeare, but because she lacks as a mature female any affinity for evil. Her repeated plea for Cassio's rehabilitation is the compelling consequence of her innate goodness. Therefore a scene like the dialogue of Desdemona and Iago in the play's second act would be absolutely unthinkable in the opera. At the moment of her husband's great danger, Verdi's Desdemona would be incapable of displaying the superficial and even coquettish prattle which Shakespeare puts in her mouth. On the contrary, despite the fact that this opera is virtually enacted by no more than three characters two of them never speak with each other. The reason for this is very apparent: by keeping Desdemona strictly apart from Jago, Verdi and Boito succeed in making her purity acceptable.

I can imagine that by now the reader is starting to have his doubts. Is it really possible to make a perfect saint or a perfect villain acceptable to an audience? A drama is enacted among human beings and a human being is *eo ipso* morally imperfect. If it were otherwise, our theatres would remain empty: dramatic art exists by the grace of human frailty and ambiguity. And besides, one may raise a second question. How is it possible that in a work like *Otello*, which is generally recognized as a masterpiece of musical tragedy, two of the three principals seem unreal to such an extent that one suspects them to have been borrowed from the cast of some melodrama?

Verdi and Boito first considered calling the opera *Jago* instead of *Otello*. This idea especially appealed to Boito, who both as a poet and as a composer was always preoccupied with demonic figures, as is witnessed by his own operas, *Mefistofele* and *Nerone*. But ultimately it was agreed that the title should be the same as that of the Shakespearian play. And this clearly shows Verdi's and Boito's intention: the drama is fundamentally the tragedy of a single character, a tragedy enacted with the aid of two melodramatic agents.

To achieve such a task with purely verbal means would prove utterly impossible, at least in my opinion, and also in the form of a musical drama it would seem a true tour de force. Nevertheless Verdi succeeded in realizing *Otello* as a tragedy. I am intentionally saying 'Verdi' and not 'Boito and Verdi', since the drama essentially evolves within the music. However great the artistic merits of Boito may be, his creative role is restricted to the supply of verbal material, which by means of the music is raised to the level of tragedy.

How does Verdi set about it? In the first place he confers on Desdemona and Jago mutually contrasting physiognomies, underlining in this way their antithetical relationship. Jago's melodic language and the accompanying orchestra are characterized by chromaticism, octave leaps, trills, triple time rhythms or triplets, and a certain melodic motif, which by continuous connotation with his cunning persuasiveness gradually adopts an unequivocal meaning. Desdemona's musical idiom, on the other hand, is distinguished by diatonic melodies, rhythmic patterns in common time and strongly expressive harmonies.

For about one and a half acts Otello is still clearly under the influence of Desdemona; he borrows her melodic motifs and in the love duet the musical materials are equally spread over both parts. In the beginning of the second duet (act III) Otello and Desdemona also share melody and harmony; however, the meaning of this device is now completely different. Otello plays a role in a ritual and, because in the meantime his jealousy has been aroused, the ceremonial exchange of musical elements adopts a bitter-sarcastic tone. In this phase of the drama Otello's real idiom has considerably changed; all features of Desdemona have vanished. Instead we hear the increasing influence of Jago, and the way in which this influence is realized in the music forms an important structural determinant of the score. Jago keeps a few of his attributes, such as the octave leap and the trill, for himself. Others, however, gradually creep into the music of Otello, especially the chromaticism and the persuasion motif mentioned before. Boito's text gives a hint to this musical procedure; twice in the drama Jago says 'il mio velen lavora' (my poison works). Thus an essential factor in the action is dramatized by musical means. Forty years previously Verdi had already applied the same device in his *Macbeth*. There the witches' motifs are adopted by both Macbeth and his Lady. However in *Otello* the procedure proves much more effective. Not only the image of Otello himself but also Jago's function as the agent of Evil gains in cogency.

Of course Otello's role in the drama is not exclusively steered by Jago. This would mark the Moorish general as a flat character, which he is not. In the course of the action Otello several times alludes to his past. His life was a concatenation of sufferings, struggles and victories, not only on the military, but even more on the social level, and the crowning of these struggles was his marriage with Desdemona. Hence Otello considers his past as the very essence of his existence. In this instance, too, Boito does give us a clue, namely the word *gloria*, a concept which in this context has an extended meaning, as it signifies a *social* victory. Desdemona's alleged unfaithfulness now logically destroys the entire past of Otello and consequently the sense of his life: 'Questo è la fine del mio cammin ... Oh Gloria! Otello fù ...' (This is the end of my way ... Oh Glory! Otello has been). These words he sings standing by the lifeless corpse of his wife.

This element of glory also adopts an important structural function. Verdi translated it in the chords and sometimes even the keys of C and E, at first separately but in the course of the drama more and more coupled. The famous kiss motif, which occurs three times (in the love duet, just before the murder and after the denouement), is in the key of E with a turn to C, and the fact that the opera ends in E major is anything but fortuitous. Jago has driven Desdemona as well as Otello into death, but has failed to destroy their bond. Thus the music transcends the tragedy as a whole.[4]

These aspects of *Otello* and the more detailed analysis of the initial scene of *Le nozze di Figaro* clearly demonstrate that the composer is the true creator of musical drama. On the basis of this one would expect his function to be largely analogous to that of the creator of spoken drama, the playwright. This, however, is not quite the case; the role of the composer stretches farther. Strictly speaking the author of a play does not take part in the performance of his work, that is, he does not address the audience in a direct way. The composer, on the other hand, does have a medium at his disposal enabling him to pass over the heads of the characters on the stage and to communicate directly with the audience. And since the audience emotionally participates in the action, this kind of communication belongs to the dramatic process. The structure of Richard Wagner's operas is mainly based on this technique, but many composers before and after him have also used it in a most efficient way. The device is particularly to the purpose when it is applied as a means for dramatic irony. At a certain moment the musical language of a character appears to us to be in flat contradiction with his verbal text. Now who is speaking the truth, the librettist or the composer? In point of fact both: the words render the plot, the music the drama. Thus the tension between plot and drama becomes explicit.

The extended role of the composer implies a restriction of the stage director's freedom. It appears that the latter's task, with respect to the interpretation of the drama, is taken over by the composer; in other words, the enactment is already contained in the musical score. If the stage director chooses to ignore this score, then he will risk an unacceptable discrepancy between visual and audible action. When a few years ago, in an Amsterdam performance of *Le nozze di Figaro,* the director Goetz Friedrich made a nobleman, Count Almaviva, carry his own chair, this act clashed with the music given by Mozart to the count's role, music explicitly expressing the characteristics of the highest social class.

The obvious conclusion is that the present-day fashion of actualizing classical dramas turns out a disaster when it is applied to opera. Besides, it may be said that this fashion shows a gross underestimation of the public, who becomes the principal loser. Concern with the presentation of time-bound elements on the stage results in the loss of timeless values. The baby is thrown out with the bathwater and this is the more regrettable since in the case of *Le nozze di Figaro* this baby is almost two hundred years old. In the middle of the nineteenth century people had the doubtful enjoyment of the singer's dictatorship in opera. This was followed by the dictatorship of the conductor, and since the Second World War we suffer under the dictatorship of the stage director, who often appears to be musically deaf. I do not want to keep it a secret that I am eagerly looking forward to the end of the latter's rule.

It goes without saying that in opera, too, the stage director has a margin of freedom of interpretation. Like many different Hamlets, all of whom might be perfectly acceptable, we may have a great number of convincing Don Giovannis. These Dons should not depend on the homonomous, verbally dramatized characters from the plays of Tirso de Molina, Molière or Goldoni, let alone on nineteenth- or twentieth-century creations like those of Byron or Bernard Shaw, but solely on the conception of Mozart. The freedom of interpretation allowed by Mozart is not horizontal but vertical.

Operas based on plays are therefore independent dramas, irrespective of whether it concerns a comedy like Cimarosa's *Il matrimonio segreto* (based on *The Clandestine Marriage* by Colman and Garrick) or a tragedy like Alban Berg's *Wozzeck* (based on Büchner's play). The composer is the dramatist. He does not adapt, he creates.

NOTES

1. The play was written in 1778.
2. Set to music and performed at the *Burgtheater* of Vienna in the same year.
3. See M. R. Ridley in his introduction to the Arden edition of *Othello* (London: Methuen, 1968), pp. lx–lxv.
4. A detailed study of the relationship between structure and interpretation of *Otello* is included in the author's *The Signifier and The Signified: Studies in the Operas of Mozart and Verdi* (The Hague, 1977), pp. 130–70.

REVIEW SECTION

John Ford: baroque drama under control*

A review article by S. GORLEY PUTT

That John Ford (1586–1640) was something of a puzzle even to his contemporaries may be guessed from the surviving squib:

> Deep in a dumpe Iacke forde alone was gott
> Wth folded Armes and Melancholye hatt.[1]

That melancholy hat may remind us of Ben Jonson's fun at the expense of people so determined to follow the late Elizabethan and Jacobean fashion of sophisticated melancholy that they practised it, so to say, in the looking-glass. Like Master Stephen in *Every Man in His Humour*, they were so 'mightily given to melancholy' (III, i, 88) that they could seek to impress their friends by asking 'have you a stool there to be melancholy upon?' (III, i, 100). So far, so good; and the author of the squib was doubtless laughing at Ford whose dark broodings may well have lent him, in company, the outward appearance of a settled and predictable habit of mind.

Yet although in some of his work (especially in *The Lovers' Melancholy*) Ford does almost seem to be dramatising passages straight from Burton's *Anatomy of Melancholy*, a reading of his plays should nevertheless quickly reveal that to speak of a mere tendency to melancholy is, for almost obliquely different reasons, at once to understate and to overstate the case. Understating, of course, because the actual passions displayed by his major characters – through incest, murder, ecstatic suicide – go far beyond the state of pessimistic brooding. Overstating, because so often one senses, beneath the cool accuracy of his dramatic verse, a penetration to those negative areas of human psychology where, when strange lusts of abnegation or sacrificial zeal dictate our actions, the perverse results may to the afflicted person appear so natural, so wholesome, that any conscious notion of melancholy hardly seems relevant.

It is the contention of Ford's latest interpreter, Ronald Huebert,[2] that we shall understand him better if we think of him as wearing not so much a melancholy as a baroque hat. Freely admitting the 'risks involved in

---

* This article incorporates some paragraphs from the author's contributions to *English*, vol. XVIII, no. 101 and vol. XXVIII, no. 131.

adapting a term such as "baroque" to literary uses' and a generally healthy scepticism about 'transposing a concept from one discipline to another', he moves neatly to an unanswerable counter-attack: 'Terms borrowed from art history may never be purified of all ambiguities; but at least they are anchored in the broad cultural phases of Europe, not simply tied to the lives and deaths of the English kings and queens.' As Ford was alive during the reigns of Elizabeth, James I and Charles I, this point is specially valid in the case of a writer who does not comfortably fit any of the labels Elizabethan, Jacobean or Caroline. Indeed, most of his later admirers have thought him in advance of his times, none more so than Havelock Ellis who in the Mermaid edition of 1888 boldly claimed him for his own century:

> He was an analyst; he strained the limits of his art to the utmost; he foreboded new ways of expression. Thus he is less nearly related to the men who wrote *Othello*, and *A Woman Killed with Kindness*, and *Valentinian*, than to those poets and artists of the naked human soul, the writer of *Le Rouge et le Noir*, and the yet greater writer of *Madame Bovary*. (p. xvii)

For myself, I can sense in Ford's cool, sometimes icy, blank verse a medium for the expression of passion as individual (though in a very non-classical English way) as that of Racine himself. At other times I seem to feel him stretching out, quite unlike that great French advocate of the dramatic unities, towards the slower cumulative art of the psychological novel.

In Huebert's introductory chapter on the baroque in visual art, Bernini's *The Ecstasy of St Teresa* in the church of Santa Maria della Vittoria, Rome, is taken as marking 'a high point in the baroque preoccupation with the most emotional aspects of religious experience' (p.3), and from this and other works of painting, sculpture and architecture we are led to distinguish between 'renaissance composure and baroque dynamism'. Somewhere in between lies the style described as 'the fragmented vision of mannerism', which according to Huebert 'accounts for the unsettling artistic focus of plays like *The Revenger's Tragedy*, *Women Beware Women* and *The Changeling*', in which we are asked to see that 'Jacobean plays bitterly lament the past order of renaissance humanism in a tone of profound and disillusioned skepticism' (p. 17). Having myself claimed for Marston's *Antonio* plays the status of mannerist farce, a position ratified by Huebert's passing reference to the 'satiric world of mannerist comedy, best represented by Jonson and Marston' (p. 120), I am disposed to follow a further application of 'baroque' as a term similarly applicable and useful. There is, of course, one serious difficulty to overcome in that those three terms 'renaissance', 'mannerist' and 'baroque', when borrowed to elucidate English seventeenth-century drama, are packed so close together in that brief chronological flowering that one tends to be somewhat armed in advance against too rigid a definition in the case of works so rapidly following one another in time, so overlapping, so hazy at the edges.

'Baroque theatre, like baroque art, resolves the mannerist doubts through powerful emotional impulses.' Applied to ordinary life, this view may suggest that the best way to solve a problem is to give up thinking about it and just scream. Applied to drama, even this *reductio ad absurdum* formula can be effective enough, in the hands of a writer like Ford who does not lose his *own* control while demonstrating human beings in the toils of an over-mastering ('baroque', Huebert would say) passion. One could say the same, of course, of a Bernini not losing his *own* severe artistic control while demonstrating the literally superhuman raptures of his St Teresa. At a less exalted level, Huebert supports his main thesis by an impressive range of artistic-literary theories and examples, impossible to summarise in a review. One instance may be offered as a sample. After offering Botticelli and Rubens as illustrations of the linear and painterly styles (the former's figures 'given definite shape by clear and precise outline', the latter's 'slightly blurred'), Huebert moves to an analogy with the Elizabethan 'eloquently balanced Ciceronian prose style' and Jacobean prose 'often eccentrically out of focus, deliberately distorted'. In the one, 'logic is in full control of rhetoric'; whereas 'in baroque prose, rhetoric becomes the servant of psychology'. Some readers, of course, may feel that Huebert is blinding them, not by science, but by art history. It is true that a little of the sort of arguments illustrated above may go a long way. Such readers may be reconciled by the closing sentences of this chapter:

> The generalizations which I have sketched in outline will serve their purpose, however, if they develop into a fully realized picture through the process of practical criticism. It will be particularly helpful to approach Ford's plays through the lens of the baroque tradition in order to discover Ford the dramatic artist, rather than Ford the rebel, Ford the moralist, or Ford the psychologist. To study Ford as a baroque dramatist is at very least a reliable way of insisting that the artistic nature of the plays themselves should be the central concern of criticism. (p. 34)

The Lovers' Melancholy (there is no apostrophe on the title-page, and I agree with Huebert that the plot requires the plural) was performed in 1628 and printed the following year. It is the first of Ford's surviving plays. At first acquaintance it seems yet another courtly romance of the high-falutin' Beaumont and Fletcher type. Its plot could hardly be better summarised than in the following paragraph by Mark Stavig:

> At the beginning of *The Lover's Melancholy* we meet three lethargic but not rebellious victims of love-melancholy – Palador, Menaphon, and Amethus. Since each loves someone who is unmarried, the only problem is to produce the girls and gain their consent to marriage. The problems of Palador and Amethus are connected. Palador's love, Eroclea, has been forced to flee from Cyprus to avoid rape by Palador's father, who has since died. Eroclea's sister, Cleophila, is unavailable to Amethus since she must take care of the girls' father, Meleander, who has become melancholy because of Eroclea's absence

and his own disinheritance for not having agreed to the rape. Quite obviously what is needed to bring a happy ending is to produce Eroclea, thereby curing both Palador and Meleander and releasing Cleophila for Amethus. Since Eroclea is present in male disguise from almost the beginning of the play, there is no difficulty in bringing her forward at the proper time. When her true sex is revealed, the other love conflict in the play is also resolved. Thamasta, who has loved the disguised Eroclea, realizes her folly and returns to her faithful melancholic lover, Menaphon, thereby curing him as well. The plot is a conventional romantic one, but it serves as a framework for Ford's analysis of the causes and cures of melancholy.[3]

Indeed, the play might well be dismissed as little more than a dramatisation of some sections of Robert Burton's recently published *The Anatomy of Melancholy*, were it not for the manner in which Ford manages to draw the psychopathic inhibitions of his main characters, rather than any external impediments, into the centre of interest.

When young Menaphon returns from his travels, he finds like many a modern tourist that he has taken his disposition with him and brought it back unaltered:

> Such cure as sick men find in changing beds
> I found in change of airs: the fancy flattered
> My hopes with ease, as theirs do: but the grief
> Is still the same. (I, i)

He had set his heart on Thamasta, sister of his friend Amethus and, as cousin of the reigning Prince Palador, a cut above him socially. Yet it is the lady's general frigidity, rather than a dash of princely blood, that keeps him dangling in a state of melancholy, so bearable that he finds time to retell, in charming euphuistic phrases, the old legend of art's superiority over nature as exemplified by a nightingale, 'music's first martyr', who died of a broken heart after 'her warbling throat' had been surpassed by the 'quaking instrument' of a lutanist skilled enough to play

> So many voluntaries and so quick,
> That there was curiosity and cunning,
> Concord in discord, lines of differing method
> Meeting in one full centre of delight. (I, i)

The centre of delight for most of this play, whatever the 'lines of differing method', is a passive indulgence of self-abnegation, to which a curiously modern flavour of 'unisex' is added by a more than customary playing with the built-in transvestite theme by means of which Jacobean playwrights made virtue of the necessity of using boys to play female roles, by changing them back again into females dressed as boys.

For the returning Menaphon's 'page' Parthenophil is none other than Eroclea, Prince Palador's vanished love, disguised as a boy. With five acts to run, no audience would expect the prince to pierce the disguise until

further complications had been unravelled. Sure enough, the frigid
Thamasta, still distant to her suitor, becomes shamelessly infatuated with
his 'page'. 'He' has, indeed, a pretty turn of speech. Courtly enough to greet
the purblind prince with suitable hyperbole ('All the powers / That sentinel
just thrones double their guards / About your sacred excellence!'), 'he' is
also handsome enough to inflame the lusts of Thamasta's maid, and when
'he' has to reject maid as well as mistress, so much latent passion is aroused
that 'he' is compelled to reveal 'himself' as Eroclea, after receiving from
Thamasta an almost grovelling avowal of love:

> Parthenophil, in vain we strive to cross
> The destiny that guides us. My great heart
> Is stooped so much beneath that wonted pride
> That first disguised it, that I now prefer
> A miserable life with thee before
> All other earthly comforts.   (III, ii)

Menaphon is given yet another opportunity to revel in his own rejection and
squeeze a few more delights from the prevailing raptures of melancholy:

> Henceforth I will bury
> Unmanly passion in perpetual silence:
> I'll court mine own distraction, dote on folly,
> Creep to the mirth and madness of the age,
> Rather than be so slaved again to woman,
> Which in her best of constancy is steadiest
> In change and scorn.   (III, iii)

In the background to these strange chilly deceptions and perversions, a
more active form of melancholy is being played out by Eroclea's old father,
who, while his younger daughter is immolating herself in the combined role
of Cordelia and Florence Nightingale, is playing out the part of King Lear,
letting off under the cover of crazed grief a series of savage comments on the
world at large:

> But I'll outstare ye all: fools, desperate fools!
> You're cheated, grossly cheated; range, range on,
> And roll about the world to gather moss,
> The moss of honour, gay reports, gay clothes,
> Gay wives, huge empty buildings, whose proud roofs
> Shall with their pinnacles even reach the stars.
> Ye work and work like moles, blind in the paths
> That are bored through the crannies of the earth,
> To charge your hungry souls with such full surfeits
> As being gorged once, make ye learn with plenty;
> And when ye've skimmed the vomit of your riots,
> Ye're fat in no felicity but folly:
> Then your last sleeps seize on ye; then the troops
> Of worms crawl round and feast; good cheer, rich fare,
> Dainty, delicious!   (II, ii)

There is also, to be sure, a 'malcontent' character at court whose railings are licensed; but in spite of a full set of the usual mouthpieces for social and political commentary whose language is as vivid as that of Marston's or Webster's savage misanthropes, the play leaves us with a sensation neither of outrage nor (in spite of the conventional ending where every frustrated Jack gains his appropriate Jill) of relief and relaxation of tension.

Instead, there is a sense that just as the elaborate Masque of Melancholy in act III failed to account for the individual psychological quirks of the three sets of thwarted lovers, so their official nuptials in the final scene will merely bring together people whose tendency to withdrawal symptoms is not likely to be much diminished. For a tragi-comic romance, it has cut a little too near the quick of purely personal frustrations. The 'art' of these men and women, their 'curiosity and cunning', is too sophisticated, if negative, to be resolved by the 'nature' of a nightingale's song. In the words of another song designed to lull the crazed old Lear-like father,

> Though the eyes be overtaken,
> Yet the heart doth ever waken
> Thoughts, chained up in busy snares
> Of continual woes and cares:
> Loves and griefs are so exprest
> As they rather sigh than rest.   (v, i)

We have grasped by now that melancholy is an act of choice. It is, I feel, far too simple a reaction to say, with Mark Stavig, that Thamasta 'recognizes the sin of her earlier views' and 'finally sees that marriage and chaste love are positive virtues and must be sought diligently by the honorable' (p. 80). Indeed, by classifying as 'sin' this proud woman's reaction to 'the irresistible attraction that Parthenophil has for her', this critic has identified that very irruption of normal feeling through the disguises of decorum which could alone save all the major characters from their near-masochistic wallowing in melancholic *accidie*. It is sad when moralistic commentators get their morals wrong.

A more acceptable interpretation by Huebert points out that 'a scholarly reading of Burton is simply inadequate where the problems of mental anxiety and frustration press the human soul to the brink of madness and despair', and that 'the obstacles that now stand in the way of happiness are the various forms of delusion and imbalance in the lovers themselves'. There is a further clue to the deeper nature of this play, felt below the Jacobean stage conventions which Ford handles with more than adequate professional skill, in the observation that whereas the 'blocking characters of renaissance comedy are deceived or converted by a clever sleight of hand', the kind of unacknowledged love identified by the court doctor as 'the tyrant of the heart' may be recognised and satisfied only 'by degrees'. When Eroclea finally reveals herself to the prince, it is not simply a change of costume that focuses his long-averted eyes; it is rather the first sign of convalescence after a self-induced mental illness. In her plea for the healing effects of time, she seems also to be voicing Ford's own hankering after a medium for psychological fiction slower and more cumulative in organised development than is available in 'the two hours' traffic of our stage':

> Minutes are numbered by the fall of sands,
> As by an hourglass; the span of time
> Doth waste us to our graves, and we look on it:
> An age of pleasures, revelled out, comes home
> At last, and ends in sorrow; but the life,
> Weary of riot, numbers every sand,
> Waiting in sighs, until the last drop down;
> So to conclude calamity in rest.   (IV, iii)

It is beyond comprehension how an earlier generation of commentators could find Ford's verse and viewpoint 'decadent'. Lines such as these, from one of his least-regarded plays, not only bear witness to a splendidly controlled and confident originality of tone, they also point to an innovative, rather than wearily imitative mind. Just as Fulke Greville could come out with political insights which would not take active form until the days of the Tolpuddle Martyrs, so John Ford, a man of similar sinewy thought half-concealed under an acquiescence in current modes of expression, seems to be stretching out towards the full psychological amplitude of the nineteenth-century novel.

Ford's next surviving play, *Love's Sacrifice* (staged about 1632), has been tersely described as the action of

> strangely alienated, lunar characters, whose arbitrary motives and inexplicable principles derive from Ford's own unconventional conceptions of heroism combined with Burton's psychological theories, Sidney's idealized views of aristocratic conduct in his *Arcadia*, and Beaumont and Fletcher's quixotic and arcane portrayals of 'love and honour' in such plays as *Philaster*.[4]

At the same time, Huebert considers the play to be 'Ford's most consistent attempt to combine the intensity of erotic passion and the ecstasy of religious pathos'. How far this persuasive 'baroque' interpretation may be accepted can only be determined after a brief reminder of the activities of these 'alienated, lunar characters'.

We are introduced to yet another Italian city–state with an arbitrary Duke besotted by his recent wife Bianca and, though otherwise capricious, reposing a complete confidence in his courtly friend Fernando, for whom the Duke's sister Fiormonda nourishes an unrequited passion. Plagued by her attentions, he claims to have vowed himself to a life of celibacy. As contrast to the upright Fernando, we watch the shameless philandering of a more representative courtier, Ferrentes, a single-minded lecher much given to self-justification:

'Sfoot! I wonder about what time of the year I was begot; sure, it was when the
moon was in conjunction, and all the other planets drunk at a morris-dance: I
am haunted above patience; my mind is not as infinite to do as my occasions
are proffered of doing. Chastity! I am an eunuch if I think there be any such
thing; or if there be, 'tis amongst us men, for I never found it in a woman
thoroughly tempted yet.   (I, ii)

But a more ominous passion has been aroused in Fernando himself, who
though loyal to the Duke begins to own an infatuation with Bianca:

> Thus bodies walked unsouled! mine eyes but follow
> My heart entombed in yonder goodly shrine:
> Life without her is but death's subtle snares,
> And I am but a coffin to my cares. (I, ii)

All seems set for a hackneyed case of court adultery.

Not so. In language more befitting the chivalrous devotion of the old
conventions of courtly love, Fernando finds opportunity to lay before
Bianca's feet

> In lowest vassalage the bleeding heart
> That sighs the tender of a suit disdained.
> Great lady, pity me, my youth, my wounds;
> And do not think that I have culled this time
> From motion's swiftest measure to unclasp
> The book of lust: if purity of love
> Have residence in virtue's breast, lo here,
> Bent lower in my heart than on my knee,
> I beg compassion to a love as chaste
> As softness of desire can intimate. (II, iii)

The Iago-like secretary of the Duke, whose role it will be to inflame his
master's jealousy, spies on this old-fashioned scene with asides more fitting
to the morals of the court of Pavia:

> Not kissing yet? still on your knees? O, for a plump bed and clean sheets, to
> comfort the aching of his shins! We shall have 'em clip anon and lisp kisses;
> here's ceremony with a vengeance! (II, iii)

But with icy virtue the new duchess rejects even this harmless gallantry, so
that the audience is as surprised as the romantic lover himself when, the
same night, Bianca in night attire visits him in his bedroom, confessing that
'in my heart / You have been only king' (II, iv), that she has felt the tyranny
of 'A violence in love', and that 'if thou tempt'st / My bosom to thy
pleasures, I will yield'. This eager capitulation is followed in rapid succession by a reminder of her duty to the Duke, a passionate invitation 'here,
here, Fernando, / Be satisfied and ruin me', and an equally passionate
declaration that if he does so, she will instantly kill herself. To comment that
in modern parlance Bianca is a tease is only half the story. Repeatedly

kissing her lover, she nevertheless so mesmerises him with her devotion to chastity unto death that he babbles 'Heaven forbid that I / Should by a wanton appetite profane / This sacred temple!' – and with renewed kisses and withdrawals she glides from the second act, leaving him in a rapture of abnegation: 'I'll master passion, and triumph / In being conquered.' It is a scene swift, powerful, ambiguous and deliberate. With daring economy, Ford is displaying a knowledge of sexual behaviour that a later age would dub 'beyond the pleasure principle'. By the end of the play, this masochistic thrill will be all mixed up with a factitious religiosity which may indeed earn the description 'ecstasy', but an ecstasy so self-indulgently whipped up that martyrdom itself seems polluted by it. Once again, Ford's characters are testing themselves to and beyond the limit. But this is no 'decadence'. It is far too positive for that. It is more akin to the hungry death-wish that has defiled, and can still defile, some of our own sophisticated contemporaries as they extract the utmost in exhibitionism from their sick hysteria of rejection.

The third act relaxes this particular tension by reminding us of other court activities: as so often in plays acted out against a generalised setting of Continental corruption, half fascinating and half affronting to English audiences to whom 'Machiavel' was still another name for the Devil, we are somehow conditioned to accept as inevitable, or even at times admirable, the plight of passion-tossed figures whose problems are at least less squalid than the unheroic sin all around them. The Duke's malevolent secretary, Iago to his unheroic Othello, tells him that 'Fernando is your rival, has stolen your duchess' heart, murdered friendship, horns your head, and laughs at your horns'. While these lies fester away, the braggart lecher Ferrentes is stabbed to death at a court masque by three of his deceived wantons, acting in unaccustomed unison. One kind of illicit passion is seen to attract its just deserts – even though when the cheated ladies appear each with one of Ferrentes's bastards in her arms, we are less sorry for them than amazed that any errant courtier should ever be so reckless as to attend a masque, so lethal does this form of entertainment prove to so many characters in seventeenth-century drama.

The Othello-theme, with the Duke's frustrated sister adding her venom to that of the shadow Iago, is rescued from its Shakespearian echoes when the Duke, Bianca and Fernando find themselves gradually marshalled into such a tangle of broken vows, suspicions, disclaimers and agonies that all three become equal victims of an increasingly hysterical and competitive suffering. Duchess Bianca makes more verbal love to Fernando in her bedroom ('I had rather change my life / With any waiting-woman in the land / To purchase one night's rest with thee, Fernando') and they have reached the kissing stage when the Duke bursts in, waving his sword and threatening bloody murder. Like all Ford's heroines, Bianca is mistress of a chilly disdain: the pious lady who lured on the Duke's vowed friend now swiftly unmasks to address her husband in such terms as these:

Duke. Dost thou not shake?
Bianca.   For what? to see a weak,
         Faint, trembling arm advance a leaden blade?
         Alas, good man! Put up, put up; thine eyes
         Are likelier much to weep than arms to strike. (v, i)

This Desdemona is tougher than her local Othello, Iago and Cassio put together. This shrinking tease now speaks with all the shameless effrontery of Annabella of *'Tis Pity* taunting her husband with her besotted lust for her own brother:

         Can you imagine, sir, the name of duke
         Could make a crooked leg, a scambling foot,
         A tolerable face, a wearish hand,
         A bloodless lip, or such an untrimmed beard
         As yours, fit for a lady's pleasure? no:
         I wonder you could think 'twere possible,
         When I had once but looked on your Fernando,
         I ever could love you again. (v, i)

She clears Fernando by confessing how much she now regrets that he had *not* succeeded in seducing her. In a fit of self-righteousness worthy of Othello himself –

                              'tis not the tide
         Of trivial wantonness from youth to youth,
         But thy abusing of thy lawful bed,
         Thy husband's bed (v, i)

– the Duke stabs her to death.

The difference between Shakespeare's *Othello* and Ford's *Love's Sacrifice* (the difference, perhaps, between 1604 and 1632?) lies in the two short tense scenes after Bianca's murder. It is as if, before Othello had stabbed himself, he had first vied with Cassio in public tributes to Desdemona. After first threatening the captive Fernando ('I'll mix your souls together in your deaths, / As you did both your bodies in her life'), the Duke is convinced by his friend's plea of at least technical innocence – though any member of the audience who had seen or read *'Tis Pity* may well have raised an eyebrow at Fernando's choice of illustration of the unthinkable:

              If ever I unshrined
         The altar of her purity, or tasted
         More of her love than that without control
         Or blame a brother from a sister might,
         Rack me to atomies. (v, ii)

The bereaved husband and lover are reconciled in grief and remorse, the Duke tossing off one incidental proof of his murdered wife's fidelity in a false analogy which sounds very much like the simplistic black-and-white morality of Tourneur's *The Atheist's Tragedy*:

> Had not the fury of some hellish rage
> Blinded all reason's sight, I must have seen
> Her clearness in her confidence to die.

In competitive transports of post-mortal love and guilt, lover and husband alike prepare to follow Bianca beyond the grave. They meet at her tomb (where Fernando has already installed himself in a winding-sheet). When Fernando is threatened, he confesses his own death-wish ('Of death! – poor duke! / Why, that's the aim I shoot at') and swallows poison. Again moved by the fidelity of 'this unequalled friend', the Duke stabs himself and expires with similar relish:

> Sprightful flood,
> Run out in rivers! O, that these thick streams
> Could gather head, and make a standing pool ...
> So! I grow sweetly empty ... (v, iii)

As if to claim a post-mortem ban on straightforward sexuality after these ecstatic minglings of love and death, the Duke's lusty sister finds herself betrothed at last to yet another nobleman who swears eternal celibacy:

> henceforth I here dismiss
> The mutual comforts of our marriage-bed:
> Learn to new-live, my vows unmoved shall stand. (v, iii)

The play ends, as it began, with vows damming up the springs of life.

Of *'Tis Pity She's a Whore* (1633), Ford's most celebrated play, Macaulay wrote: 'it is painful to read and scarcely decent to name'.[5] The prudery of Macaulay is in amusing contrast with the attitude of Ford himself, who, dedicating 'these first fruits of my leisure' to the Earl of Peterborough, wrote: 'The gravity of the subject may easily excuse the lightness of the title.' In fact the play is a good deal more scarifying than its title, for it treats of the incestuous love of a brother and sister who, though they satisfy social morality by dying horrible deaths, are coolly conscious throughout the action of their immense physical and intellectual superiority to everybody else. They behave, the doomed Giovanni and Annabella, with a Pharaonic exclusiveness which Ford somehow makes attractive by a hundred small touches as the guilty but golden pair pursue their introverted passion as if oblivious of the seething intrigues of lesser mortals all round them.

The opening scenes are reminiscent of *Romeo and Juliet*. Ford's Parma is Shakespeare's Verona, with its brawling suitors, a babbling female tutor pretty clearly based on Juliet's nurse, and an inept friar-confessor quite overwhelmed by the passions confided to him. The poetry, too, consistently reminds us, by the beautifully modulated control of its blank verse paragraphs, that a man of rare literary sensibility and a strongly individual 'criticism of life' could, after Shakespeare's death and at the time of the so-called 'decadence' of dramatic art, produce work which reminds one of Shakespeare. One clue to Ford's mastery, present here as in *The Broken Heart*, is his ability to find a place for striking taciturnity of speech in the midst of great outpourings of emotion. Annabella's contemptuous words as her tutoress, a prattler like Juliet's nurse or Cressida's Pandarus, extols a suitor's qualities, are an index to that intellectual pride which more than anything else binds her to her brother: 'Sure the woman took her morning draught too soon.' The short scene (I, iii) of the declaration of mutual sexual love by the incestuous pair is notable for one or two chilly lines, embedded in the more conventional protestations of courtly love of which theirs is at once a parody and a transfiguration, arresting because of their tense quality of understatement:

> I have too long suppressed the hidden flames
> That almost have consumed me ...

says Giovanni, almost as if to himself. Equal to him in serenity, Annabella replies:

> Live; thou hast won
> The field, and never fought: what thou hast urged
> My captive heart had long ago resolved.

Even the subplot scene (II, ii), where Hippolita is railing against the philandering nobleman Soranzo who had won her adulterous love and now rejects her, glows at times with lines of simple psychological truth:

> I have a spirit doth as much distaste
> The slavery of fearing thee, as thou
> Dost loathe the memory of what has passed.

There is here a sick recognition of masochistic degradation long ante-dating the modern studies which have given such negative indulgences a name. And when the sated Soranzo turns her out with a self-righteous:

> Woman, come here no more;
> Learn to repent, and die; for, by my honour,
> I hate thee and thy lust: you've been too foul – (II, ii)

there is a repulsive superficial truth in what he is saying, over and above the braggart hypocrisy which causes his servant Vasques to speak a Ford-like aside as if to acknowledge the squeamishness of a modern reader: 'This part has been scurvily played.'

The same scene closes with the spurned Hippolita promising to give herself and her fortune to Vasques if only he will help her gain revenge by the murder of his master. Over and above the criminal intent, there is also a brutality in this breach of courtly class barriers, not unlike that of Beatrice and De Flores in Middleton's *The Changeling*. It has the same effect, in the general hot-house atmosphere of courtly love-and-honour posturings and bloody revenges, of sudden harsh psychological realism. A similar strange coincidence of conventional revenge and a purely personal psychological perversion may be observed, in a small character vignette easy to overlook in the major sequence of horrors, in the reactions of Hippolita's betrayed husband, Richardetto. Supposed dead on a journey, he has in fact returned to Parma disguised as a physician. He not only plots the death of Soranzo, his wife's seducer, at the hand of yet another of Annabella's dangling suitors; he also seems to take a more-than-natural pleasure in hugging his humiliation as an observer while his wife 'gives scope to her loose adultery'. They are mere subplot matters, these peculiar sidelights on the complex depravities of a Soranzo, a Hippolita, or a Richardetto; but they add, in their mixture of conventional theatricality and personal quirks, something of a parallel to the plight of Giovanni and Annabella themselves, whose own major sin is similarly made more personal and more credible by reason of their contributory faults of arrogant disregard for any law outside their own secret society of two.

There follows the significant short scene where Giovanni quotes back at the inept friar some of the old 'learning' about souls and bodies, the kind of argument which may lend an extra suggestion of thoughtfulness to a play like Chapman's *Bussy d'Ambois* but is here, in a play full of atheistic arrogance, merely reduced to the level of chop logic ridiculed when brought into juxtaposition with the grim reality of human passions:

> It is a principle which you have taught,
> When I was yet your scholar, that the frame
> And composition of the mind doth follow
> The frame and composition of the body:
> So, where the body's furniture is beauty,
> The mind's must needs be virtue; which allowed,
> Virtue itself is reason but refined,
> And love the quintessence of that: this proves,
> My sister's beauty being rarely fair
> Is rarely virtuous ... (II, v)

After which parodying speech, Giovanni returns to the superior taciturnity of:

> Then you will know what pity 'tis we two
> Should have been sundered from each other's arms.

If Giovanni is disrespectfully sarcastic, his elders can at times be tersely commonsensical in a surprisingly modern idiom, as when Annabella gently rejects the absurd suit of a poltroon, Bergetto, whereupon his uncle, who had been sponsoring the match, instead of feeling insulted, merely turns to the girl's father and remarks

> Why, here's plain dealing; I commend thee for't;
> And all the worst I wish thee is, Heaven bless thee!
> Your father yet and I will still be friends: –
> Shall we not, Signior Florio? (II, vi)

Her father's reply – 'Yes; why not?' – almost approaches the twentieth-century shrug-shoulder attitude of 'I couldn't care less'. It is certainly a sardonic and maturely amused flouting of the conventions of courtly love and the obligations of revenge which make up, in full flamboyant theatricality, the thoroughly and deliberately unrealistic atmosphere in which Ford's occasional laconic injections of truthfulness glow with a singular radiance. It is a play in which all the rules are broken, heaven's and the courtiers' alike. What the minor figures occasionally achieve, the incestuous young brother and sister consistently maintain in an astonishing display of self-possession, superiority, family pride sexually sealed, and a chilling unearthly nonchalance as they prepare, with a sick resolution matched by only the most advanced of our contemporary drop-outs, to face – and welcome – death and damnation.

We are soon embroiled again in the complicated plots of the highly 'Italianate' characters whose confused villainies almost make the young couple's sin noble in its detached privacy. Annabella, now pregnant by her brother, is affianced to Soranzo. The poltroon Bergetto is killed by mistake by the jealous Grimaldi with Richardetto's poisoned rapier, under the impression that he is his successful rival Soranzo. Just how successful that poor dupe actually was will soon appear. To complete the muddle, in act IV the adulterous Hippolita is poisoned by Vasques with the cup prepared for Soranzo, and dies in public, cursing the already 'damned' Annabella and her deluded 'husband'. There follows Soranzo's bewildered outburst against Annabella when he discovers the truth of her situation:

> Harlot, rare, notable harlot,
> That with thy brazen face maintain'st thy sin,
> Was there no man in Parma to be bawd
> To your loose cunning whoredom else but I?
> Must your hot itch and pleurisy of lust,
> The heyday of your luxury, be fed
> Up to a surfeit, and could none but I
> Be picked out to be cloak to your close tricks,
> Your belly sports? Now I must be the dad
> To all that gallimaufry that is stuffed
> In thy corrupted bastard-bearing womb!
> Say, must I? (IV, iii)

Her reply is contemptuously chilly: 'Beastly man! Why, 'tis thy fate.'

Yet even when she is taunting her gulled husband, the superior quality of her love for Giovanni breaks through:

This noble creature was in every part
So angel-like, so glorious, that a woman
Who had not been but human, as was I,
Would have kneeled to him, and have begged for love....
Let it suffice that you shall have the glory
To father what so brave a father got.

Goaded beyond endurance, the wretched Soranzo gives vent to the conventional Jacobean stage manifestations of jealous rage, dragging the 'lust-be-lepered body' of his sneering wife up and down the floor by her hair.[6] It is open violence of a kind only recently revived, in our own day, on the London and New York stage. What is 'modern' in Ford is not so much the violence, as the fact that these extravagances are immediately followed by a scene between Soranzo and his servant Vasques, who converses with his master with such man-to-man freedom that one is reminded this time not of Tudor brutality but rather of the impudent lowering of class barriers allowed by a later age in, say, the cheekiness of a Leporello to a Don Juan: 'Sir, you must be ruled by your reason, and not by your fury; that were unhuman and beastly.' But the *tour de force* of different behaviour from the same persons, in a matter of minutes, is not yet over. Left alone on the stage for the concluding moments of this powerful scene, Vasques manages to drag the secret of Giovanni's identity as the father of Annabella's child from the lips of the old go-between tutoress – whereupon violence returns with a sudden descent again into the 'Italianate' atmosphere, as Vasques sends the old crone off, gagged, with a band of cut-throats, to these almost routine instructions: 'Sirs, carry her closely into the coal-house, and put out her eyes instantly; if she roars, slit her nose: d'ye hear, be speedy and sure.' Already we begin to feel, even before Annabella and Giovanni come to confess and expiate their own crime, that they will – like Webster's Duchess of Malfi – be in any case quite literally better out of such a world.

Act v brings us in swift succession Annabella's formal repentance:

But they who sleep in lethargies of lust
Hug their confusion, making Heaven unjust; (v, i)

followed by Soranzo's plan for revenge, which Giovanni welcomes with desperate foolhardiness.

In a climax of introverted tenderness, Giovanni and Annabella, 'discovered lying on a bed', say their last farewells, sometimes with their customary arrogance, sometimes in the accents of the nursery, a kind of flash-back to the days when the young victims of a withdrawn, forbidden yet somehow proud and pure love first began to question, as children do, the meaning of things:

Giovanni.   The schoolmen teach that all this globe of earth
　　　　Shall be consumed to ashes in a minute.

Annabella.	So I have read too.
Giovanni.	But 'twere somewhat strange

To see the waters burn: could I believe
This might be true, I could believe as well
There might be Hell or Heaven.

Annabella.	That's most certain.
Giovanni.	A dream, a dream! else in this other world

We should know one another.

Annabella.	So we shall.
Giovanni.	Have you heard so?
Annabella.	For certain.
Giovanni.	But d'ye think

That I shall see you there? – You look on me. –
May we kiss one another, prate or laugh,
Or do as we do here?

Annabella.	I know not that. (v, v)

The mixture of sophistication and childishness is unbearably moving, bringing us with extraordinary economy to the heart of their presumptuous tragedy. Within minutes of this exchange Giovanni has stabbed and killed his sister:

> The hapless fruit
> That in her womb received its life from me
> Hath had from me a cradle and a grave.

He is now prepared, and eager, to die himself.

All is over, bar the shouting; but the shouting, in the form of Jacobean stage tricks, echoes of the mad scenes in *Hamlet*, and the winding-up of subplot issues, is still to be endured. After that quiet 'modern' scene of desolate love and ritual sacrifice, the sudden entry of Giovanni bearing his sister's heart upon his dagger is almost insupportable. Yet it is, one is forced to feel, the other side of the medal: the mad arrogance that could mate only by incest is now exhibiting itself in self-absorbed frenzy. One recalls Hamlet posturing at Ophelia's graveside: it is the exhibitionistic streak, the Byronic self-parading of the wounded heart, that offers another, hysterical, access to the tormented spirit within:

> The glory of my deed
> Darkened the mid-day sun, made noon as night.
> You came to feast, my lords, with dainty fare:
> I came to feast too; but I digged for food
> In a much richer mine than gold or stone
> Of any value balanced; 'tis a heart,
> A heart, my lords, in which is mine entombed ... (v, vi)

And so, in a final hugger-mugger of technical revenge and justice, Soranzo and Giovanni are slaughtered on stage after some spirited swordsmanship, the old father of the incestuous pair dies of a heart attack, Vasques is banished, the old bawd is sent

> Out of the city, for example's sake,
> There to be burnt to ashes.

Most anti-climactic of all, in the very last lines Richardetto throws off his disguise: as if anybody cared, by this time, who he had pretended to be, or even who he *was*. The squalid life of intrigue goes on. At the end of a thoughtful and intensely serious play we leave the theatre merely irritated by the follies and cruelties of Parma, but with the haunting farewell of the pitiful, pitiable Giovanni echoing in our minds:

> Death, thou'rt a guest long looked for . . .

A play so striking, so harrowing, has naturally called forth a wealth of commentary. Stavig and Huebert serve admirably as illustrators of the two chief, contrasting, critical approaches: the logical moralistic approach which argues the rights and wrongs of the 'problem' presented, and the dramatic approach which concedes a complete lack of rationality in the dramatist's presentation not of intellectual or moral 'problems' but the excesses of human emotion up to and beyond the boundaries of sanity. It will become apparent that I myself consider the second interpretation to be more helpful in explaining just what abnormal states of mind Ford, with amazing comprehension, was able to compass in a play which in other respects may be quite sensibly studied as yet another example – in the context of its structure, use of subplot, fidelity to orthodox sentiments, various stage devices and conventions, and so on – of Jacobean (strictly, Caroline) tragedy. But the first interpretation, with its inescapable set of mainly non-dramatic moral problems, does exist and deserves notice.

Stavig gives full weight to the evidence of Ford's earlier non-dramatic work, from which he concludes 'that Ford was a traditional and quite orthodox Christian who was deeply influenced by Classical ethics... Ambition, fame and pride are worthy if they are associated with honorable actions... Through reason man can achieve both the immortality of a worthy name and the immortality of heaven' (p. 35). So far, so good. Stavig also reminds us that

> we should not judge seventeenth-century plays by the platitudes of the age, but we should judge them by the best thought of their age, not our own; and we should beware of concluding that anything that now seems outdated was platitude then. It is at least more likely that their tragedies would reflect the prevailing intellectual atmosphere rather than express a new or original approach to life. (p. 58)

I cannot associate Ford with that last sentence. Nevertheless, *if* Ford's chief characters had been rational, they might well have given nodding assent to the claim that 'Most of the tragedies of the period are filled with stoical ideas, but the philosophy illustrated may be broadly stated as holding that a man must change what he can, endure what he cannot change, but, no

matter what happens, always remain virtuous'[3] (p. 61). Alas, those characters were *not* rational. The Stavig viewpoint fails to allow for human
inconsistencies as a legitimate field for dramatic treatment.

There is, too, in the Stavig approach a reluctance to face the truth, so
saddening for a moralist devoted to the provision of black-and-white
solutions for black-and-white problems, and yet so fruitful for a *dramatist*,
that 'good' people are often sadly insensitive and 'bad' people often devas-
tatingly attractive. For example, Stavig finds Friar Bonaventura at all times
a logical exponent of orthodox Christian doctrine. So he may be; but he is
also a temporising, cowardly and utterly ineffective butt, whose personal
inability to communicate with any authority the perfectly obvious truths of
his party line must have contributed not a little to the overweening intellectual pride of his young and cleverer pupil. Of course Giovanni is presumptuous and mistaken; that, after all, is the cause of his tragedy. Stavig rightly
points out 'that Giovanni is suffering from what Burton calls love-
melancholy and that Giovanni's illogical rationalizations are indications of
a mind twisted by passion' (p. 99). But even when that explanation is given
and accepted, it still remains true that some minds *are* twisted by passion.
Where I really disagree with this critic is in his reading of the passion
concerned. To my mind, the controlling passion of Giovanni (while he
remains sane) is not Lust. As the friar himself observes in a would-be
man-of-the-world aside, Lust could readily be quenched elsewhere: 'Leave
her, and take thy choice, 'tis much less sin.' The play is brimming with
instances of the permissive ways of the courtiers of Parma. Giovanni's fatal
passion is not so much Lust as Pride; a powerful combination of intellectual,
physical and family Pride.

In short, I believe that an over-moralistic treatment of this admittedly
highly moral tragedy does not even 'come out right' morally, still less
dramatically. One may flinch aesthetically when Ford brings on Giovanni
with his sister's torn-out heart held aloft on the point of his dagger, without
help from Stavig's extraordinarily prim comment that 'It should be apparent that none of Giovanni's feasting on Annabella has provided proper
sustenance.' One may wholly agree that 'Giovanni is a sick, confused, and
irrational sinner rather than a rational rebel', and still find him a proper –
and a sympathetic – subject for tragedy. Nor is one required to go to the
other extreme and admire him as a noble tragic hero. But the play will fail
altogether if one refuses to allow Giovanni the other side of the medal, so to
say, of his sin of Pride. It is in the quality of Ford's dramatic verse when he is
showing momentary sympathy with Giovanni that we detect the genuine
quality of response we are expected to recognise, at times, even in so
desperate a sinner.

Stavig has argued that 'When depicting worthy people, Ford avoids
elevated rhetoric and elaborate patterns of diction and imagery and concen-

trates instead on a direct and simple expression of their thoughts and feelings. Their speech could be described as natural, simple, rational, sensitive, and harmonious.' This is precisely where the dramatic poet surpassed the theoretical moralist: *he* is prepared, at certain key points in the play, to devote notable examples of 'natural, simple, rational, sensitive, and harmonious' speech not only to the 'worthy people' but also – and especially – to their unwitting victims. It is just at this point that Ford strikes 'a new or original approach to life' by accepting the existence of a golden human value in a protagonist who is quite severely enough judged, morally and in actual retribution, in the play itself, in strict accordance with the accepted standards of the seventeenth and twentieth centuries alike.

The Huebert approach, on the other hand, starts from a recognition that the kind of religion expressed by the doomed Giovanni and Annabella is not a religion of morals, but a desperately vulnerable adolescent religion of befuddled, arrogant and completely self-indulgent ecstasy. Morally speaking, they are even worse than the moralists imagine! Dramatically speaking, they are unforgettable. Whether or not one accepts the term 'baroque' for his excesses of feeling and behaviour, young Giovanni had 'committed himself to a fatal course of action that no meddling friar could possibly arrest'. Act I 'consummates a destructive impulse that is already overpowering when the play begins'. It is pointless to argue that 'the firm grip of reason would distinguish between the erotic urge and the religious instinct', because it is precisely the dramatic splendour and the human heart-wrenching of this play that 'Giovanni has passed the limits of reason'. What the Parmesan establishment, busy with its own more efficient depravities, can only consider immoral madness in this incestuous young murderer, *is* that very quality which he and his sister, in their adolescent irrational raptures, experience first as a 'ritual of adoration' leading to the 'warmth of erotic fulfilment', after which experience so absorbedly exclusive do they become, so completely anti-social in their 'obsessive, abnormal, overpowering love' that their blending of eros and death in 'histrionic martyrdom' is indeed the only *logical* – as it is in their surrender to unbridled sensation their final religious ecstatic – outcome. Thus, it can only be after a great effort of sympathetic imagination that a reader of the play may allow himself to wander, for a consenting moment, beyond the limits of disciplined morality and disciplined religious ritual, to grasp the dreadful truth that these poor deluded children (for their very obsessive exclusiveness has kept them in childish subjection to passions from which their obvious intelligence would otherwise have emancipated them) really do 'breathe the life of martyrdom into a private and chimerical mythology of love'. Only then, with the terror of pity, can we understand that Giovanni is not blaspheming but wholly, madly, serious when he tells his sister, as he is about 'To save thy fame, and kill thee in a Kiss',

Pray, Annabella, pray! Since we must part,
Go thou, white in thy soul, to fill a throne
Of innocence and sanctity in Heaven. (v, v)

Only then, if we have pity enough to see that 'Giovanni's flagrant piece of melodrama is the psychologically natural result of living in a world dominated by illusion', can we offer the poor youth a flicker of compassion as he uses 'words borrowed from the crucifixion story' to justify, within his madness, his finding what for him and Annabella was the only solution after they had indulged with vicious tenderness their last excess of passionate pride:

The glory of my deed
Darkened the mid-day sun, made noon as night. (v, vi)

The Broken Heart, like *'Tis Pity*, was printed in 1633; and, like *'Tis Pity*, was probably written a few years earlier. Like *'Tis Pity*, too, it has a leaning towards incestuous themes: two men have so jealous a love for their sisters that they demand the right to dictate or deny their marriage partners. The King's favourite, the laurel-crowned warrior Ithocles, has forced his sister Penthea to disregard a marriage contract with young Orgilus and marry instead an elderly buffoon named Bassanes; while Orgilus himself, who has turned into a court malcontent because of his grief at losing Penthea, demands that his own sister Euphranea should marry only a partner of his own choice – as if in revenge for his own loss of Penthea.[7] Yet although in one arresting scene Ithocles and the wronged Penthea come perilously near to declaring a mutual incestuous love, this theme is not developed to anything like the scale of *'Tis Pity*. Instead, Ford introduces two other chilling impediments to normal sexual gratification: for the Princess Calantha, a final scene verging on necrophilia when she 'marries' the dead Ithocles; and in the case of the doomed Penthea a deliberate suicide by self-starvation – the second full treatment on the Jacobean stage of self-starvation to death (the first being Heywood's *A Woman Killed with Kindness*). Yet to isolate these two horrifying themes is to give a false impression of sensational melodrama. In *The Broken Heart*, even more than in his other treatments of the hideous ramifications of thwarted or self-suppressed love, Ford exercises so masterly a control of the plot development, so terse a command of verse phrases encapsulating an icy passion, that in the context of the whole play these disasters seem to be inevitable, almost natural, and almost, indeed, welcome. Once again, it is a stunning achievement of dramatic poetry.

The play (set in ancient Sparta) opens with young Orgilus seeking his father's permission to take leave of absence to visit Athens. 'Why to Athens?' asks his father, a court counsellor. 'To kick against the world, turn cynic, stoic,/Or read the logic-lecture . . .' This, ironically enough, is a fairly good description of what Orgilus will in fact make of himself; but the cause for his withdrawal is quite other. Because of a family feud officially healed before the opening of the play, his affianced lover Penthea was forced by her brother Ithocles to marry another suitor, rich old Bassanes who is so pathologically suspicious of his young wife's fidelity that his fear of cuckoldry

> Begets a kind of monster-love, which love
> Is nurse unto a fear so strong and servile
> As brands all dotage with a jealousy... (I, i)

So Orgilus pretends to go into voluntary exile to avoid false accusations, having first made his sister Euphranea promise not to marry without his consent. Instead, he remains in Sparta, disguised as a poor young scholar of philosophy.

Meanwhile, Ithocles himself has returned as Sparta's victorious general, earning for himself a welcome as courtly as King Duncan's reception for Macbeth, and for his soldier-courtiers a reception by the ladies as ironical as that awarded by Beatrice in the opening scene of *Much Ado About Nothing*. Knowing, so far, only that he has cruelly wrecked his sister's hopes, we are introduced by the words of his friend Prophilus to the public, heroic, Ithocles:

> He, in this firmament of honour, stands
> Like a star fixed, not moved with any thunder
> Of popular applause or sudden lightning
> Of self-opinion... (I, ii)

His honourable nature is borne out by his own claims for his troops, much like the tender-hearted Perkin Warbeck in Ford's last play when to the amusement of King James of Scotland he spares a thought for the common people who suffer from wars and rebellions. With (as we shall recognise, later) stately hypocrisy, Ithocles disclaims the opinion of the populace

> Voicing the leader-on a demi-god;
> Whenas, indeed, each common soldier's blood
> Drops down as current coin in that hard purchase
> As his whose much more delicate condition
> Hath sucked the milk of ease... (I, ii)

The first two scenes, then, have presented us with a selection of wholly rational creatures. So it seems.

Orgilus, disguised in his student gear, has turned himself for the moment into a kind of emotional spy:

> Thus metamorphosed,
> I may without suspicion hearken after
> Penthea's usage and Euphranea's faith.
> Love, thou art full of mystery! the deities
> Themselves are not secure in searching out

> The secrets of those flames, which, hidden, waste
> A breast made tributary to the laws
> Of beauty: physic yet hath never found
> A remedy to cure a lover's wound. (I, iii)

It is a chilling role, that of an emotional *voyeur* determined that his sister
Euphranea shall not enjoy a freedom of choice denied to himself, and
watchful to see how his own love Penthea conducts herself as wife to
Bassanes. He spies balefully upon a budding romance between Euphranea
and Ithocles's friend Prophilus, with a negative relish equal to that of
Ithocles himself, whom he has just condemned (for Penthea's sake) as 'a
brother / More cruel than the grave.' These new sweethearts become
interested in the student stranger, who replies to their advances in glorious
phrases which should bring comfort to any present-day undergraduate with
an 'identity problem':

> *Euphranea.*   Are you a scholar, friend?
> *Orgilus.*   I am, gay creature,
> With pardon of your deities, a mushroom
> On whom the dew of heaven drops now and then;
> The sun shines on me too, I thank his beams!
> Sometime I feel their warmth; and eat and sleep. (I, iii)

The young lovers decide to employ Orgilus as an innocent go-between,
carrying boy-loves-girl messages for them. He, who is in his disguise as
scholar of philosophy has just babbled about the impossibility of reason
being able to 'hold fast in a net the sun's small atoms', quickly turns to
musing in his own person on morality, which 'Creeps on the dung of earth,
and cannot reach / The riddles which are purposed by the gods.' By the end
of the first act we have been given hints of various neurotic problems ahead
– but (and this is so essentially characteristic of Ford) always in narrative
blank verse of so marvellously spanking a pace as to equal (without imitating) Shakespeare's in its confident unrolling, yet with that lurking vein of
Ford irony surfacing, every now and then, with a chill rational accuracy
through all the convoluted plot.

Act II opens with a swift effective scene presenting Penthea's jealous
husband Bassanes. Alternately longing to display his wife in rich attire and
protect her from temptations of the public gaze, he is given some splendid
throw-away passages on the display of wealth which would have fitted
Jonson's Sir Epicure Mammon or Massinger's Sir Giles Overreach:

> We will to court, where, if it be thy pleasure,
> Thou shalt appear in such a ravishing lustre
> Of jewels above value, that the dames
> Who brave it there, in rage to be outshined,
> Shall hide them in their closets, and unseen
> Fret in their tears; whiles every wondering eye
> Shall crave none other brightness but thy presence. (II, i)

All this is met with icy pride by his frigid wife-of-convenience Penthea:

> Alas, my lord, this language to your hand-maid
> Sounds as would music to the deaf; I need
> No braveries nor cost of art to draw
> The whiteness of my name into offence:
> Let such, if any such there are, who covet
> A curiosity of admiration,
> By laying-out their plenty to full view,
> Appear in gaudy outsides; my attires
> Shall suit the inward fashion of my mind . . .

The next scene shows her brother Ithocles rehearsing his virtuous heroic role, disclaiming ambition in favour of morality which, when applied

> To timely practice, keeps the soul in tune,
> At whose sweet music all our actions dance:
> But this is formed of books and school-tradition;
> It physics not the sickness of a mind
> Broken with griefs: strong fevers are not eased
> With counsel, but with best receipts and means;
> Means, speedy means and certain; that's the cure. (II, ii)

We are re-hearing Giovanni's distrust, in *'Tis Pity*, of 'books and school-tradition'. We may also scent some kinly likeness between the rationalising Ithocles and the sister he has wronged. As for Bassanes, in his crazy jealousy the brother–sister likeness spells a danger more closely akin to *'Tis Pity*:

> . . . he's her brother.
> Brothers and sisters are but flesh and bood,
> And this same whoreson court-ease is temptation
> To a rebellion in the veins . . . (II, ii)

But it will not be incest, this time, that will cause the death or suicide of the main characters: other dread aberrations will bring the tragedy to its chilling end.

Ithocles's friend Prophilus confesses to Penthea that he is worried by her brother's loss of spirits, 'some kind of slackness'. Her anxiety is soon shelved, for Orgilus finds occasion to throw off his disguise and reveal himself. The separated lovers confess and formally re-swear their undying vows, but it is clear that Penthea (in this respect not unlike Duchess Bianca in *Love's Sacrifice*) will not countenance any adulterous thoughts, however much she may loathe her misalliance with Bassanes. She protests that her true love 'Abhors to think that Orgilus deserved / No better favours than a second bed' (II, iii). Given her situation, her case is logical enough. But her over-statement of the case is as suspect as Isabel Archer's determination to remain faithful to her abhorrent husband Gilbert Osmond in Henry James's *The Portrait of a Lady*: there is a more than necessary relish in her

rectitude, as the wallowing in her deprived state takes on a positive, rather
than simply resigned, note. She threatens even more distant withdrawal 'If,
of all men alive, thou shouldst but touch / My lip or hand again!' Like Isabel
Archer fending off Caspar Goodwood, there is more than a hint that she is
secretly glad to have an official excuse for her frigidity: 'My good genius
guide me, / That I may never see thee more! Go from me!' Called away to
nurse her sick brother, for the first time the young reluctant bride scents the
awful attraction of the ultimate withdrawal, death:

> In vain we labour in this course of life
> To piece our journey out at length, or crave
> Respite of breath: our home is in the grave. (ii, iii)

In act iii the painful sadistic–masochistic relationship between the
siblings Ithocles and Penthea is conveyed in a gripping scene in which the
invalid brother apologises for his cruel disposal of his sister to an unworthy
husband. It is wholly in the Ford manner that, instead of being relieved by
this confession and plea for forgiveness, we the audience find ourselves at
the end of the scene still more puzzled by the perverse motivations of both of
them. Almost like Giovanni of *'Tis Pity*, Ithocles opens the tense dialogue
with a scaring intimacy:

> Sit nearer, sister, to me; nearer yet:
> We had one father, in one womb took life,
> Were brought up twins together... (iii, ii)

Penthea makes the most of his repentance, finding in his contrition a chink
into which to insert, with maximum effect, her own treasured sense of
wrong:

> Here, Io, I breathe,
> A miserable creature, led to ruin
> By an unnatural brother!

Squeezing the last drop of negative longing from the situation, she even
invites her brother to kill her – and suggests that when she has revenged
herself on him by urging him to a fratricide which she herself would
welcome, 'Then will we join in friendship, be again / Brother and sister.' As
in *'Tis Pity*, the tendency to incest is inextricably tangled with a death wish,
as she, the victim of cruelty, now with her reproaches twists a knife in her
oppressor's guilty repentance, causing Ithocles to cry out:

> After my victories abroad, at home
> I meet despair; ingratitude of nature
> Hath made my actions monstrous: thou shalt stand
> A deity, my sister, and be worshipped
> For thy resolvèd martyrdom; wronged maids
> And married wives shall to thy hallowed shrine... (iii, ii)

In their revived intimacy, he reveals to his sister his desire for Calantha, Princess of Sparta and heiress to the throne. She immediately seizes the chance to point a parallel, taunting him yet again with the wrong he had done her and had now so recently repented:

> Suppose you were contracted to her, would it not
> Split even your very soul to see her father
> Snatch her out of your arms against her will,
> And force her on the Prince of Argos?

It is upon this tense scene of *odi et amo* family intimacy, brother and sister all but physically united as (in Penthea's words) 'but two branches / Of one stock' after their competitive sadistic exercises, that crazed old Bassanes rushes in with drawn sword, persuaded that they are already engaged in 'bestial incest'. They may indeed have come close to dangerous embraces, but the intemperate folly of Bassanes is quickly reversed, and the scene ends with the old man admitting 'Much wrong I did her, but her brother infinite...' He at least will strive to overcome his passion of jealousy. For Penthea to overcome *her* passion of self-mortification will be another matter. I have already called on a parallel from Henry James to suggest the degree to which earlier reproving, inhibiting, frustrating hands have already, by manipulating Penthea's pristine love for Orgilus, tampered with her very mainspring – adding James, it may be noted, to the list of other nineteenth-century novelists whom Havelock Ellis had already adduced as the nearest literary *confrères* of the astonishingly 'modern' John Ford, Jacobean adaptor of the old pattern of 'revenge tragedy', yet also John Ford the accomplished analyst of thwarted and peripheral erotic urges.

With brief efficiency a courtly scene presents the official engagement of Princess Calantha to the Prince of Argos and a public reconciliation between Ithocles and Orgilus, old feuds forgotten. But Orgilus soon discloses a sardonic discord with all this royal magnanimity; he has thrown off his scholar's 'mushroom' disguise but he still nurses the malcontent point of view of 'such undershrubs as subjects', angrily protesting to his father that

> Lordly Ithocles
> Hath graced my entertainment in abundance,
> Too humbly hath descended from that height
> Of arrogance and spleen which wrought the rape
> On grieved Penthea's purity; his scorn
> Of my untoward fortunes is reclaimed
> Unto a courtship, almost to a fawning:–
> I'll kiss his foot, since you will have it so. (III, iv)

His father is alarmed by this 'Infection of thy mind', and any audience to whom Ford's work was familiar would have been alerted to dangers ahead, when Orgilus makes occasion to swear, though 'A too unworthy worm', to respond to Ithocles's greeting of him as 'A fast friend'. Against this new uneasy peace, rivals reconciled and the princess betrothed, Penthea herself closes the act by informing Calantha of Ithocles's daring aspiration for her hand and love, and confessing that she herself, though 'on the stage / Of my mortality my youth hath acted / Some scenes of vanity', is now 'weary of a lingering life, / Who count the best a misery'. She asks the startled Calantha to be her executrix (not yet admitting her resolve to fast to death), leaving gnomic instructions for the bequeathing of her 'three poor jewels' – her youth, her fame 'By scandal yet untouched', and finally, since her own heart's love has died and 'Long have I lived without it', she leaves her last jewel, the very Ithocles who had blighted her troth to Orgilus, to the princess herself. It is clear that the last two acts, after these cool deliberate blueprints for negation in Ford's immaculate yet ice-charged blank verse, are doomed to end in calculated deaths – the only remaining question in an audience's mind being 'How many?'

As if to calm down our worst expectations, act IV opens with a piece of stage business when Calantha bestows a ring upon Ithocles to the anger of her official fiancé the Prince of Argos, plus a series of boring messages from the Delphic oracle alerting us to dire outcomes we had already scented. Then follows a scene in which Bassanes, quite credibly, repents of his 'humour' of jealousy, before the entrance of Penthea in an Ophelia-like scene, driven mad by melancholy and self-privation. A terrible, almost melodramatic scene, redeemed (as so often) by a few terse lines offering, in Ford's sudden chilling exactitude of simple phrases hitting the psychological bull's-eye, the truth beneath the horrific onstage revelations, when the 'mad' Penthea, prey to her own self-immolation, quietly remarks

> 'tis a fine deceit
> To pass away in a dream! indeed, I've slept
> With mine eyes open a great while. (IV, ii)

It is a scene calling for a high degree of acting: by the time an old courtier remarks 'The sight is full of terror', we have seen how Penthea's sleepless misery, 'ruined by those tyrants, / A cruel brother and a desperate dotage', has become the result of brooding on her wrongs as – in a daring image in which madness mirrors the paradoxical truth of her plight –

> a ravished wife
> Widowed by lawless marriage....

Her torments are now openly recognised in self-starvation, and the embarrassed courtiers, so recently fobbed off with betrothals and reconciliations, know that she soon will die. They learn that the King of Sparta, too, is mortally sick, and in the general state of shock the unlucky neutral visitor, the Prince of Argos, learning from 'Life-spent Penthea and unhappy Orgilus' how to be generous, publicly makes over to Ithocles his own claim on Princess Calantha. The dying king blesses the new betrothal of Calantha and Ithocles, but this rearrangement is swiftly blighted by the unforgiving venom of malcontent Orgilus who meets the re-offered friendship of Ithocles with a sour reference to the swiftly approaching time when

> We slip down in the common earth together,
> And there our beds are equal; save some monument
> To show which was the king, and which the subject. (IV, iii)

From the chamber of the dying Penthea comes a dirge which sums up, in its last line, the dreadful clue to this play and to so much else of Ford's work: 'Love's martyrs must be ever, ever dying'.

The brooding spirit of Jacobean revenge tragedy comes to the surface with a terrible blatancy when Ithocles and Orgilus visit Penthea's quarters to mourn her death: Orgilus has trapped Ithocles in a mechanical chair that pins him down helplessly while the malcontent, still mouthing the family wrongs –

> whiles Penthea's groans and tortures,
> Her agonies, her miseries, afflictions,
> Ne'er touched upon your thought: as for my injuries,
> Alas, they were beneath your royal pity;
> But yet they lived, thou proud man, to confound thee.
> Behold thy fate; this steel! (IV, iv)

– stabs him to death on full stage. The second victim to wounded pride has been sacrificed: but the 'broken heart' of the play's title has yet to be revealed. This is Calantha herself, twice-betrothed Princess of Sparta. She is presiding over, and taking part in, a state dance at the palace in honour of Euphranea's marriage to Prophilus and her own forthcoming marriage to Ithocles. The revels are in full swing, the stately dance proceeds through its allotted 'changes' as, one after another, messengers bring the news of the deaths of her father the King and the self-starved Penthea, and finally the bloody sacrifice of Ithocles himself, her husband-to-be. In one of the most famous scenes in all Ford's plays, the Princess earns her title to Spartan attributes by continuing the dance, and keeping the stunned court dancing, as if nothing amiss has happened. The King is dead: long live the Queen! She has become a monarch while dancing, accepting all three calamities with outward calm.[8] Her example steels lesser characters to lesser feats of masochism. Old Bassanes learns the unaccustomed art of resignation:

> But I have sealed a covenant with sadness...
>   ...mark me, nobles,
> I do not shed a tear, not for Penthea!
> Excellent misery! (V, ii)

We are to experience a new twist of the old revenge-tragedy knife, with innocent and guilty alike not only meeting dreadful ends, but with a resignation akin to welcome. Brushing aside the three deaths, the new Queen announces 'We'll suddenly prepare our coronation', and leaves the murderer Orgilus to choose his own method of public suicide. On the instant, he pierces himself and stands bleeding (as his lover has starved) to death in full courtly ceremony, with the enthusiastic support of old Bassanes, his official successful rival, who joins in a Spartan endurance test well beyond the bounds of simple stoicism. Like the Duke at the end of *Love's Sacrifice*, Bassanes admires the spectacle of flowing blood: 'It sparkles like a lusty wine new broached . . .' Orgilus himself makes the most of his final act: 'Welcome, thou ice, that sitt'st about my heart.' But in a splendid variety of elegaic lines, it is poor Bassanes who is given the best string of Ford's unforgettable monosyllables: 'He has shook hands with time.' (v, ii)

Nothing remains except to set the final stamp of Spartan royal approval on the prevailing necrophilia. The final scene enacts the elaborate ritual of Queen Calantha's ceremonial marriage to death: before an altar, in full royal splendour with all her courtiers about her, she places a wedding ring on the finger of Ithocles's corpse, admitting in her farewell speech that her rigid self-control when she refused to allow a triple death blow to interrupt her courtly dancing was all an 'antic gesture', pointing the moral that 'They are the silent griefs which cut the heart-strings; / Let me die smiling.' To the strain of a pre-arranged dirge, she dies simply by transfiguring her death-wish into a royal command, expiring to the last lines of the dirge:

> Love only reigns in death; though art
> Can find no comfort for a broken heart. (v, iii)

Ford's *Perkin Warbeck* (printed in 1634 as a 'chronicle history') looks, Janus-like, backwards and forwards in time. Backwards, because as the Prologue admits, 'Studies have of this nature been of late / So out of fashion, so unfollowed . . .' The author well knows that plays based on English history had disappeared from the stage since Shakespeare's (and Fletcher's?) already old-fashioned throw-back in *Henry VIII* (1613):

> He shows a history couched in a play;
> A history of noble mention, known,
> Famous and true; most noble, 'cause our own;
> Not forged from Italy, from France, from Spain,
> But chronicled at home . . .

Forwards, because in Ford's dedication to the Earl of Newcastle he boldly claims that his interest lies well below the surface records of even fairly recent history: 'Eminent titles may, indeed, inform *who* their owners are, not often *what*.' His own aim is not merely to act as chronicler, but to ask 'why?' as well as 'what?' –

> In other labours you may read actions of antiquity discoursed; in this abridgement find the actors themselves discoursing, in some kind practised as well *what* to speak as speaking *why* to do.

The play opens with a stately set scene giving the point of view of the reigning monarch, Henry VII, of the troublesome impostor Perkin Warbeck, claiming to be

> The new-revived York, Edward's second son,
> Murdered long since i' the Tower, – he lives again,
> And vows to be your king. (i, i)

From the very outset it is clear from Henry Tudor's mock-heroic description of Warbeck's claims that he considers him at worst a political nuisance:

> How closely we have hunted
> This cub, since he unlodged, from hole to hole,
> Your knowledge is our chronicle; first Ireland,
> The common stage of novelty, presented
> This gewgaw to oppose us...
>   ...Charles of France
> Thence called him into his protection,
> Dissembled him the lawful heir of England;
> Yet this was all but French dissimulation,
> Aiming at peace with us; which being granted
> On honourable terms on our part, suddenly
> This smoke of straw was packed from France again,
> T' infect some grosser air...

Even before the play gets going, in short, it is clear that whoever Warbeck is, or thinks he is, he will never topple Henry Tudor's crown. The mounting excitement of the play can never be 'What will happen?' – because the outcome is already known. It can only be: 'How did Warbeck conduct himself in his state of self-deception, and how did he affect other people?'

A similar state of mature reason prevails at the Scottish court, to which we are introduced before Warbeck's arrival there, in a brief 'modern' scene in which the Earl of Huntley, though welcoming Lord Dalyell as suitor for the hand of his daughter Lady Katherine, yet gladly leaves his daughter free to choose her own husband in her own time:

> *Katherine.*   For respects
> Of birth, degrees of title, and advancement,
> I nor admire nor slight them; all my studies
> Shall ever aim at this perfection only,
> To live and die so, that you may not blush
> In any course of mine to own me yours.
> *Huntley.* Kate, Kate, thou grow'st upon my heart like peace,
> Creating every other hour a jubilee. (i, ii)

We are back again, for an instant, in the company of the only two sensibly 'modern' courtiers of the Parma of *'Tis Pity*, Annabella's father Florio and the poltroon Bergetto's uncle Donato, who when the arranged match is opposed by Annabella very sensibly accept the girl's decision:

Donato. Your father yet and I will still be friends:
　　　Shall we not, Signor Florio?
Florio. 　Yes; why not? (*'Tis Pity*, ii, vi)

In beautifully controlled and competent blank verse, the first two scenes
have indicated, before the hero of the play puts in an appearance, that
though their medium of speech is highly stylised, his fate will be to follow
the logic of his own illusions against a background of mature realists –
whether antagonistic, in Henry Tudor's Westminster, or mainly sympathetic, at the Scottish court – who will judge each new situation as it arises.
This enveloping presence of an almost neutral rationality is suggested by
Ford with superb and elegant economy. His 'chronicle history' may be an
outmoded genre, but it is immediately apparent that he is bringing to it a
balance, a civil urbanity, quite new when set against the embattled partisans of Marlowe's *Edward II* or Shakespeare's *Richard II*, not to mention the
more 'heraldic' posturings of earlier Elizabethan history plays. As if to
prove this point, Ford closes act i with another swift scene at the English
court where Henry Tudor receives the latest news of Warbeck's growing
support from foreign backers and disaffected English noblemen. In the
midst of this hurried council meeting, the King feels secure enough to lapse
for a moment into irrelevant Marlovian magniloquence:

> We know all, Clifford, fully, since this meteor,
> This airy apparition first discradled
> From Tournay into Portugal, and thence
> Advanced his fiery blaze for adoration
> To the superstitious Irish; since the beard
> Of this wild comet, conjured into France,
> Sparkled in antic flames in Charles his court;
> But shrunk again from thence, and, hid in darkness,
> Stole into Flanders flourishing the rag
> Of painted power on the shore of Kent,
> Whence he was beaten back with shame and scorn,
> Contempt, and slaughter of some naked outlaws:
> But tell me what new course now shapes Duke Perkin? (i, iii)

It is splendid flamboyant stuff – but it is still, after all, a précis of intelligence
reports digested by a monarch whose cat-and-mouse power over Duke
Perkin is never in doubt.

In scenes alternating between London and Edinburgh, Ford bases his
historical account pretty closely on Bacon's *Life of Henry VII*. What is new in
the play is not any attempt to reinterpret accepted facts, but a sustained and
wonderfully successful effort to present Warbeck as an attractive young
pretender, so serene in his self-delusion that other men and women are
illogically charmed to his support. After hearing his measured account of
his claimed descent from the ousted Plantagenets, even an enthroned king is

beguiled into a 'willing suspension of disbelief', for James of Scotland himself speaks for the effect of Warbeck's eloquence on his court:

> He must be more than subject who can utter
> The language of a king, and such is thine. (II, i)

The audience knows well enough that the reaction of one Scottish nobleman, Crawford, is historically correct: 'this dukeling mushroom / Hath doubtless charmed the King.' It will be Ford's daring intention to persuade such an audience to give so much emotional assent to the pretender that they half believe his claims, just as he himself so graciously played the royal role that, so to say, his real face took on the actual lineaments of his mask. In the words of Huebert, Ford's dramatic skills are such that 'The most impressive instance of deception within the play is, of course, Perkin's ability to deceive himself.' His illusion is 'a starting victory for the world of artifice and deception' and it ends by being 'so compelling that it becomes almost impossible to distinguish appearance from reality'. In the mind of the audience, nature consents to imitate art.

We may well recognise that King James's recognition neatly fits the permanent Scottish policy of causing trouble south of the border, and yet yield full assent when he bestows Lady Katherine's hand on Warbeck as on a fellow monarch:

> How like a king he looks! Lords, but observe
> The confidence of his aspect; dross cannot
> Cleave to so pure a metal – royal youth!
> Plantagenet undoubted! (II, iii)

And even her affronted father, Huntley, though at first maddened by the 'Hotch-potch of Scotch and Irish twingle-twangles' of the nuptial celebrations, quickly switches his support from the disappointed suitor Dalyell:

> Thou dost not know the flexible condition
> Of my apt nature: I can laugh, laugh heartily,
> When the gout cramps my joints; let but the stone
> Stop in my bladder, I am straight a-singing...
> Come, thou'rt deceived in me: give me a blow,
> A sound blow on the face, I'll thank thee for't;
> I love my wrongs: still thou'rt deceived in me. (III, ii)

This is a far cry indeed from the theatre of Jonsonian Humour, when a character type-cast for the role of aggrieved father can become much more credible as an inconsistent quirky human being, swopping roles with erratic impulse, now railing at his impotence and now accepting the Divine Right of Kings –

> But kings are earthly gods, there is no meddling
> With their anointed bodies; for their actions
> They only are accountable to heaven –

now pleased to have his daughter achieve titular royalty, now dismissing her as 'a castaway, / And never child of mine more'. Whatever his mood may be, Warbeck and Katherine have fallen deeply in love, and the last two acts of the play will be irradiated by their mutual trust – one emotion in the whole chronicle which is quite devoid of pretence. The other genuine quality is Perkin's own bravery, more notable because it flowers from a sensibility touched to the quick by the barbarities of war, as he sets out on the doomed expedition to claim 'his' Kingdom of England. As the wordy challenges and ripostes are bandied between spokesmen of the two armies in passages where Ford's eloquent economy reaches a level of narrative verse far in advance of most of the chronicle plays 'so out of fashion' by the 1630s, Warbeck's own speeches have an effortless nobility, whether in asserting his claim or bewailing the cost in suffering:

> I had never sought
> The truth of mine inheritance with rapes
> Of women or of infants murdered, virgins
> Deflowered, old men butchered, dwellings fired,
> My land depopulated, and my people
> Afflicted with a Kingdom's devastation. (III, iv)

His temporary ally James, as prompt at first to strike at the old enemy, England, as he would be to desert Warbeck's cause when Henry Tudor proves too strong for him, is unused to such royal clemency: his own professional kingliness has a cruder language:

> You fool your piety
> Ridiculously careful of an interest
> Another man possesseth. Where's your faction? . . .
> No, not a villager hath yet appeared
> In your assistance: that should make ye whine,
> And not your country's sufferance, as you term it. (III, iv)

As the armed power of Henry Tudor closes in on the doomed cause, the same King James, acting like a responsible monarch, invites his now inconvenient guest to 'find an harbour elsewhere'. With grave courtesy Warbeck accepts the logic of the changed conditions, accepting James's chivalrous 'we will part good friends' with truly (if false!) royal magnanimity. His new wife Katherine is steadfastly loyal: 'I am your wife; / No human power can or shall divorce / My faith from duty.' Meanwhile at Westminster a less inspired but more established courtliness is deftly conveyed in Ford's impeccable blank verse as Henry Tudor expresses with complacent relish his own brand of frugal statesmanship:

> Such voluntary favours as our people
> In duty aid us with, we never scattered
> On cobweb parasites, or lavished out
> In riot or a needless hospitality:

No undeserving favourite doth boast
His issues from our treasury; our charge
Flows through all Europe, proving us but steward
Of every contribution which provides
Against the creeping canker of disturbance. (IV, iv)

Such unshakable self-approval can hardly spare time for the likes of Duke Perkin:

Thoughts busied in the sphere of royalty
Fix not on creeping worms without their stings,
Mere excrements of earth.

It is a formidable *tour de force* on Ford's part that against such a background and in the teeth of the known historical facts of the ignominious collapse of Warbeck's pathetic insurrection, he can still so endow the young pretender, on the very brink of disaster, with the valour of his illusions that an audience is for the moment beguiled into accepting the fantasy. Warbeck's feeling for his fantasy royalty is so much more compelling than Henry's masterly exposition of his own undoubted kingship that the playgoer's emotional assent is won by the illusory, the counterfeit. To achieve this switch from reason to illusion in a matter of minutes is a remarkable tribute to Ford's dramatic poetry as an instrument:

O divinity
Of royal birth! how it strikes dumb the tongues
Whose prodigality of breath is bribed
By trains to greatness! Princes are but men
Distinguished in the fineness of their frailty,
Yet not so gross in beauty of the mind;
For there's a fire more sacred purifies
The dross of mixture. Herein stand the odds,
Subjects are men on earth, kings men and gods. (IV, v)

Fineness of frailty is on the brink of the fineness of failure, but a failure which in the final act will be raised, by the nobility with which Ford invests his entirely created and unhistoric Perkin Warbeck and by the ecstatic quality of the love between Perkin and Katherine, to a sacramental passion well beyond the reach of Henry VII, reigning monarch.

Without this final sacrificial glow, the relentless crushing of the rebellion would be merely pathetic, not tragic. Even Henry cannot deny the attraction of the handsome young man who cherishes his illusion to the last as with moving eloquence he stubbornly argues his way to the executioner's block:

We observe no wonder: I behold, 'tis true,
An ornament of nature, fine and polished,
A handsome youth indeed, but not admire him.

To Warbeck, Henry is patronising and yet – for him – almost magnanimous:

> Turn now thine eyes,
> Young man, upon thyself and thy past actions;
> What revels in combustion through our kingdom
> A frenzy of aspiring youth hath danced,
> Till, wanting breath, thy feet of pride have slipt
> To break thy neck! (v, ii)

To Perkin's superb assurance of his own divine right, the king almost tolerantly comments:

> O, let him range:
> The player's on the stage still, 'tis his part;
> He does but act. (v, ii)

Reasonable, accurate, true. But true in essence *because* it has been Ford's intention, gradually and beautifully achieved, to bring us to accept a private truth in Warbeck's illusion and a complementary truth in his and Katherine's love unto death.

It is hardly surprising that in his study of Ford as a specifically baroque dramatist, Huebert finds *Perkin Warbeck* the most awkward play to fit into his persuasive presentation of Ford as an exponent of various forms of all-fusing baroque passion. His definition of the baroque is strained to the limit when he claims that Ford created 'a baroque history play' because of its 'one dominant motif' of deception. 'The deception of *Perkin Warbeck* is so compelling that it becomes almost impossible to distinguish appearance from reality.' True; but on the face of it, deception seems a pretty negative quality to figure in this embracing and transfiguring role. The critic admits that 'Perkin does not betray his pretence, but he certainly does not establish his authenticity either.' His claim is simply that 'the play becomes a miracle of deception, rather than a study in the givens of history'.

Where Huebert's baroque attribution does gain credence is in act v, when Warbeck and his Lady Katherine do indeed soar beyond reason, even the reason of an accepted pretence, to the private raptures of martyrdom:

> The joy of love, like the appeal of royalty, seems intensified to its highest pitch in the face of death. In fact Perkin does not die for love, but Ford manipulates the death scene in order to create the illusion that he too is one of love's martyrs. Again it is fair to observe that in glorifying Perkin's death, Ford is willing to sacrifice the records of Tudor history in order to reach a full emotional climax. (p. 56)

Here is the link with the 'baroque' excesses of *Love's Sacrifice* or *'Tis Pity* where the Huebert parallels from painting and statuary – Bernini's writhing ecstatic St Teresa and all – become relevant:

The pysychological movement begun by Perkin will not end arbitrarily. In a history play, of all places, one expects a social rebirth at the end of the action, and this indeed is what occurs in the typically closed form of the renaissance history play. But in *Perkin Warbeck*, martyrdom is an event with no political or social significance; like so many of Ford's lovers, Perkin and Katherine isolate themselves from society as they are remarried symbolically at the edge of the tomb. It is Perkin's unbroken spirit, and not the general good, that is reborn through suffering and death. (p. 106)

At this juncture, I am well content to leave with Huebert the last word on the last act, as Perkin assures his wife that she will 'Saint it in the Calendar of virtue', and the perceptive interpreter notes that 'the angelic tendency of the last parting of these lovers goes hand in hand with the erotic tendency of their first meeting'.

In general, however, I am at the same time equally (or more) struck by the evidences, in this play, of Ford's quite unbaroque qualities. Overall, the verse is beautifully cool and restrained, in keeping with the generally reasonable, even at times pedestrian, reactions of most of the characters even when caught up in chaotic circumstances. Their contributions, after all, make up most of the pattern of the play, bearing Ford's characteristic stamp of reticence, occasional dramatic taciturnity in the midst of strong emotion, plus vivid and telling glimpses, whether or not couched in 'baroque' language, of an unashamed and untheatrical common sense (a quality which, if I may indulge a private fantasy of my own, I like to attribute to his Devonshire origins).

NOTES

1. William Hemminge, *Elegy on Randolph's Finger*, ll. 81–2, ed. G. C. Moore Smith (Oxford: Blackwell, 1923), p. 24.
2. Ronald Huebert, *John Ford: Baroque English Dramatist* (Montreal and London: McGill–Queen's University Press, 1977).
3. Mark Stavig, *John Ford and the Traditional Moral Order* (Madison, Wisconsin: University of Wisconsin Press, 1968).
4. James E. Ruoff, *Crowell's Handbook of Elizabethan and Stuart Literature* (New York: Thomas Y. Crowell Co., 1975), p. 161.
5. Thomas Babington Macaulay, 'Burleigh and his Times' in T. B. Macaulay *Critical and Historical Essays*, 6 vols. (Boston and New York: Houghton Mifflin and Co., 1900), III, 88.
6. Behaviour of this kind had been alleged (and vigorously denied) in the very highest circles a century earlier, in the days of the morality-based Interludes. The Duke of Norfolk, father of the gentle Earl of Surrey, refused to see his wife because she had, he wrote, falsely accused that 'when she had be In chyld-bed ij nyghts and a day of my doghter of richmond I shuld draw her out of her bed by the here of the hed abouts the howse and w^t my dagar geue her a wonde In

the hed'. (Cited by Edwin Casady in his *Henry Howard, Earl of Surrey*, New York: M.L.A., 1938, p. 19.)

7. An earlier view that Orgilus was based on Sir Philip Sidney, the first suitor of Penelope Devereux (his 'Stella') who later became Lady Rich, is challenged by Katherine Duncan-Jones (*Review of English Studies*, November 1978) who identifies Orgilus with Charles Blount, Earl of Devonshire, who married Penelope, when widowed, after she had been his mistress for fifteen years. Duncan-Jones argues that Ford, using the parallel case in his play, accepted Blount's betrothal to Penelope, before her enforced marriage to Lord Rich, as a pre-contract. She also suggests that hints of incestuous feelings between Penelope and her brother the Earl of Essex ('the remarkable Devereux siblings') may have been in Ford's mind when he created Giovanni and Annabella of *'Tis Pity She's a Whore*.

8. Katherine Duncan-Jones, in the article cited in the previous note, sees in Calantha's regal behaviour an echo of Queen Elizabeth's splendidly sustaining 'the appearances of office, including dancing', after the execution of her favourite, the Earl of Essex.

Restoration drama criticism: revisions and orthodoxies

A *review article by* LAURA BROWN

The most recent major studies of Restoration drama, Peter Holland's *Ornament of Action* and Robert D. Hume's *Development of English Drama*,[1] are both presented as revisionist works – correcting, modifying, and even overturning current assumptions about the plays and the period. Holland's revision is in his insistence that an awareness of contemporary theatrical practice and an appreciation of the techniques and details of performance will produce a more complete and more accurate interpretation of the plays: 'If we are to understand the full complexity of the experience of watching a play, one in particular or any play at all, we *must* look at the actors and their careers, at the shape of the theatres, at the use of scenery and at a host of other matters in detail' (p. xii). Hume's corrective is more encompassing: 'My aim in this book is to bring a new perspective to the study of "Restoration" drama' (p. vii). This includes a new system of dramatic categories, a new definition of the 'development' of the genre, and a new assessment of the merit of the plays themselves.

Dissension and revision have a venerable tradition in this field. In fact, the study of Restoration drama can be characterized as a series of critical reversals, from Steele's early moralistic attack (1711) on *The Man of Mode*,[2] through Lamb's attempted recanonization of the comedy of manners as amoral fantasy (1828),[3] to L. C. Knights's blunt dismissal: 'trivial, gross, and dull' (1937).[4] Perhaps this tangle of interpretive reversals itself contains a clue to the special nature of Restoration drama, to the stable underlying shape which each of the various irreconcilable assessments of the plays partially reflects. Certainly Restoration drama criticism has a development of its own; its history is as discernible as that of the plays it seeks to describe. Indeed, the continuities and reversals in this critical tradition are as significant as any of the specific interpretations advanced by individual critics within it. In examining these two recent contributions to the study of Restoration drama, then, this paper will consider the development of the critical tradition, its coherences and discontinuities, its orthodoxies and revisions. Holland's and Hume's books demand our attention not only as important individual critical works, but also as historical documents whose meaning for the study of the drama transcends their surface significance.

Describing the scholarship which precedes his own, Hume mentions Allardyce Nicoll's *History of Restoration Drama* (p. vii).[5] In fact, despite the intervention of half a century, Nicoll's work is the closest major, full-length approximation to Hume's encyclopedic approach to the subject of Restoration drama, 'examining a large number of plays with special attention to chronological sequence' (Hume, p. vii). In the development of drama criticism, Nicoll's books, with their exhaustive description and their commitment to classification, represent the culmination of an empiricist critical tradition, a tradition commonly associated with nineteenth-century philosophical positivism and best represented, in Restoration drama studies, by the pioneering work of John Genest. In this tradition the recording of literary phenomena, the amassing of sources, analogues, and backgrounds, is an end in itself and is assumed to possess its own explanatory significance. The individual work rarely becomes the object of close analytical scrutiny, and the task of the critic is simply the accumulation and arrangement of evidence.

In the twentieth century, Restoration drama criticism has followed the main trends in Anglo-American literary studies. Concerns with development and evolution have largely given way to the specific explication of major texts. John Palmer's early defense of Restoration comedy (1913) is the first example of this modern critical approach.[6] For Palmer, it is the play's transformation of the immoral 'manners' of its age into the material of art that matters, both in his argument on the literary value of the drama and also in his interpretations of the works themselves. Readings of the plays have changed since 1913, and the critical assessment of this drama has moved beyond Palmer's emphasis upon the amorality of art, but the tendency to examine the artistry of the major works by means of an analysis of theme, character, language, and literary motif has remained a constant. Critical studies of this field in the mid-twentieth century have been remarkably consistent in their format. Palmer discusses, in separate chapters, Etherege, Wycherley, Congreve, Vanbrugh, and Farquhar, and subsequent books on the comedy only deviate from his practice in the direction of greater selectivity. Thomas Fujimura restricts his analysis to Etherege, Wycherley, and Congreve, as do Norman Holland and Virginia Birdsall. Dale Underwood writes on Etherege's three plays, W. H. Van Voris on Congreve's five, and Paul and Miriam Mueschke on *The Way of the World*.[7] These works, though they implicitly accept the major categories of positivist literary history, are essentially ahistorical in their premises: their aim is the explication of particular texts, or at most of related major texts and playwrights, their method is a kind of formal analysis derived from the close readings of the New Critics, and their emphasis is upon artistry, wit, and – most specifically and recently – ambiguity, irony, and self-consciousness. Even the serious drama, which has received less critical attention than the comedy of manners, is viewed from this modernist perspective: several recent studies of Dryden argue that his most extravagant heroic plays are self-consciously parodic or satiric.[8] This is the immediate context of Hume's and Holland's critical revisions – the tradition from which they dissociate themselves and also the one to which they most intimately belong.

The first, fundamental assertion of Hume's *Development of English Drama* is that the plays exhibit a 'radical diversity' (p. 62). Hume argues that the dramatic works of this period 'seem altogether lacking in uniformity' (p. 11), that 'not even the most capacious of pigeon-holes will accommodate more than a limited selection' (p. 62) of the comedies, and that tragic theory of the seventeenth century offers 'an almost infinite variety of emphases and combinations [of emotional effect] which add up in practice to several very disparate sorts of serious drama' (p. 185). Hume's book elaborates the implications of this initial premise. The kind of diversity which he posits makes classification perilous or impossible and reduces 'development' to the documentation of 'trends in a large number of plays over fairly short spans of time' (p. 18). For Hume, 'any statement about progression tends to be rash' (p. 14) and 'the usual notions of "development" are simplistic nonsense' (p. 15). Seeking to avoid hypotheses or 'assumptions' about the history of the drama, he proceeds to set up a system of 'common types' or 'dramatic modes' based upon 'similarities or disparities' (p. 18) in plot, style, characterization, setting, and tone, and to apply these types to a chronological description of the genre.

The two parts of the book correspond to these two aspects of Hume's procedure: part I outlines the major dramatic types, part II provides an historical narrative from 1660 to 1710. Hume discusses eight 'cases' of comedy: Spanish romance (*The Adventures of Five Hours*), reform comedy (*The Squire of Alsatia*), wit comedy (*The Man of Mode*), sex comedy (*The Country-Wife*), sentiment-tinged romance (*Love for Love*), city intrigue comedy (*The Committee*), Augustan intrigue comedy (*The Busie Body*), and 'French' farce (*The Citizen Turn'd Gentleman*). The serious drama is likewise described under eight categories: the 'heroic' play, horror tragedy, 'high' tragedy, 'English' opera, split plot and mixed plot tragicomedy, the 'pattern' tragicomedy, pathetic tragedy, and 'parallel' plays. Hume's premise of diversity keeps these categories loose and makes their application provisional. Because the 'types' are defined as empirical gatherings of works whose similarities outweigh their differences, they often overlap. The 'pattern' tragicomedy and the split plot and mixed plot tragicomedy, for instance, are almost wholly coterminous: 'most split plot and mixed tragicomedies could be partially defined' as 'pattern' tragicomedies (p. 213).

In this kind of system, 'whether a play like Durfey's *The Injured Princess*, with its slight comedy part and heavy emphasis on near-catastrophe, is better called mixed or pattern is an aimless question' (p. 213).

In his discussion of the comedy, Hume further complicates his typology by providing a list of additional criteria separate from the eight 'cases' by means of which he initially addresses the problem. These include a list of four common plot formulas, twelve common male characters, and ten common female characters. The possible permutations among these criteria are then elaborated by a general discussion which cites other 'almost innumerable' (p. 139) variables, including the setting, the attitude evoked toward the characters, and the method or combination of methods stressed. The result is a typology informed by the premise of diversity, one which starts 'by accepting the idea of a wide-ranging and untidy genre' (p. 128) and which reproduces that kaleidoscopic variety in an equally kaleidoscopic profusion of kinds, numbers, and levels of distinctions. Unlike Northrop Frye's multiple categories, then, which ultimately cohere in a larger systematic structure, Hume's classifications simply coexist.

In applying this typology in a chronological narrative, part II suggests five main historical phases from 1660 to 1710. First, 'the establishment of Carolean Drama' in the 1660s, a period of strong continuities with the preceding Caroline theatre, but also of gradual innovation. Hume sees the 1670s as the peak of Carolean drama, characterized by sex, horror, and spectacle, and the 1680s as a watershed in which the character of the theatre, in a period of relative inactivity, undergoes a gradual but drastic alteration. The 'muddled' 1690s demonstrate the difficulty of documenting generic change. In this period of the dilution of Carolean drama, two traditions compete: the old sex comedy and the new pure or exemplary comedy. Backward-looking modes of serious drama stage a resurgence, along with the newer classical tragedies, but ultimately moral pressures exerted by the changing tastes of the audience lead to the 'dilution of the Carolean tradition' and to the emergence, between 1697 and 1710, of Augustan drama, a product of theatrical retrenchment and reform characterized by the collapse of tragedy and by a tendency toward humane, genteel, moral, or exemplary comedy.

Though this narrative describes a change in the drama, it is notable for its avoidance of 'easy dichotomies' and 'reductive formulas' (p. 482). In almost every segment of his history, Hume finds more divergence than similarity, more variety than direction, and the transition which he finally acknowledges is, in the local discussion of the multiplicity of the genre, barely perceptible. His conclusion, however, makes an unambiguous assertion of 'profound change' in dramatic types, in theatrical vitality, in audience preference, and in 'the whole philosophy reflected in the plays' (p. 493): 'Translating such particulars into broadly ideological terms, one may say that we have seen what is, philosophically speaking, an aristocratic Tory drama give way to one which is increasingly bourgeois and Whig' (p. 494).

Hume's book – in its format of chronological survey, its comprehensive treatment of the material, and its premise of diversity – is strikingly different from the other major twentieth-century studies of Restoration drama. Its 'new perspective' is formulated in explicit opposition to the 'pernicious' modern tendency to provide a close reading of a small number of plays, to assume that these major works or dramatists represent the 'quintessence' of the age, and to accept implicitly and without question the broad and untenable categories: 'Restoration drama', 'comedy of manners', and 'sentimental drama'.

Hume's purpose, then, is to revise both the materials and the methods of Restoration drama criticism. But the critical ideology of his revisionism is surprisingly similar to that of his predecessors. Like the earlier studies by Fujimura, Underwood, Norman Holland, Birdsall, Harriett Hawkins, Ian Donaldson, Arthur Kirsch, Bruce King, Anne Barbeau, and others,[9] Hume's *Development of English Drama* conceives and represents its subject as a series of discrete and unrelated aesthetic objects. Its preference for diversity over similarity, its notion of an uncodifiable profusion of evidence, and its rejection of evolution or progression have the same consequence as the previous critics' emphasis upon explication: the subordination of process to specificity and the alienation of the individual work from the history of the drama. *The Development of English Drama* expounds a new kind of ahistoricism, based not on the isolation of a few plays but on the inclusion of all.

In this respect, Hume's book is the product of its past. It combines the ideology of modernism with the methodology of positivism: it sees the plays as a series of isolated, unrelated texts, but it seeks to describe the 'development' of the drama. Its revisionist stance is derived from the marriage of these two critical modes. Like Nicoll, Hume defines the task of criticism as exhaustive documentation, and thus he rejects not only selectivity, but also the 'pernicious and misguided' 'demand for profundity' (p. 145) and the search for aesthetic value; he gives no priority to 'major' works and he argues that ' "Restoration" plays ... almost without exception ... aim more at entertainment than at deep meaning' (p. 30). As a modernist, however, Hume rejects positivist notions of progress and development, and even of relationship (pp. 14–15). Thus he expresses explicit opposition both to the New Critical preoccupation with meaning and value in isolated 'major' works and also to historical argumentation. Hume's position, then, in all its strengths and limitations, can be understood as the consequence of a unique amalgam of analytical modes, which results in a recapitulation of the entire recent critical tradition in this field.

Peter Holland is the first critic of Restoration drama to demonstrate the full relevance of performance to an understanding of the plays. As he observes in his preface: 'It is now customary for critics writing on Restoration drama to genuflect in the direction of the theatre and mention, in a passing footnote, some piece of casting' (p. xii). These passing mentions have invariably taken the form of discrete and local extrinsic confirmations of an independent intrinsic argument: for instance, Harriett Hawkins finds substantiation for her description of the moral ambiguity of Congreve's *Way of the World* in the casting of Thomas Betterton as the villain Fainall,[10] and Eric Rothstein discusses the role of the actress pair Elizabeth Barry and Anne Bracegirdle in creating the 'rival queens' formula of Restoration tragedy.[11] Holland's approach is not only quantitatively but also qualitatively distinct from these earlier tangential references to performance. *The Ornament of Action* argues that 'the physical shape of the theatres, the use of scenery, the casting of the actors and other such details of playhouse activities are the basis from which a concept of a larger "text", a text that has performance as part of its own meaning, rather than as a necessary evil, can be understood' (p. x). The material of performance is, in Holland's view, not a source of extrinsic evidence for intrinsic explication; he rejects such a dichotomy in principle. The whole theatrical event is Holland's 'text', and his critical enterprise is to define the series of sign systems of which it is made and to reveal their meanings. Such meanings are both integral to the whole 'dramatic *gestalt*' and also multiple and distinguishable from it. In regard to scenery, for example, 'a semiotics of scenery would allow the double attraction of scenery to text, not only pulled towards the moment but also towards its own separable system, embodying a meaning that could be contrary to the information offered by the other codes of the text' (p. 19).

Holland's first four chapters establish the nature of the theatrical material under the categories of audience, staging, acting, and publication of the printed work. These discussions include examples of how the sign systems of performance are to be read. The analysis of theatres and scenery, for instance, reveals a substantial and significant distinction in staging between the serious and the comic drama. In both the Dorset Garden and Bridges Street theatres, heroic plays made consistent use of the scenic stage – the deep upstage 'discovery' area – for acting. In the comedy, on the other hand, downstage acting predominates, and even when scenes begin with an upstage discovery, the action moves immediately onto the forestage. This distinction in staging reveals broader differences in 'the theory of acting, the intentions of the dramatist, [and] the relation of actor to audience' (p. 36). Holland suggests that the high proportion of upstage acting in the serious drama is 'equivalent to a stronger divorce from reality and a weakening of the claim on the audience to see the actors as individuals similar to themselves' (p. 36).

In the examples he gives of the relevance of casting for interpretation, Holland argues that Farquhar's problematic moralistic comedy *The Twin Rivals* contains a consistent, ironic juxtaposition between the actors' customary roles and their parts in this particular play. Robert Wilks, ordinarily the witty gentleman, here plays the Elder Wou'dbe, a sober and sentimental hero 'rather dull, foolishly impetuous and socially inept' (p. 95). In this case, the casting conveys a message as significant as any discoverable in the language of the drama: it 'conjures up the generic expectations of comedy, only in order to overturn them' (p. 87).

The last three chapters of *The Ornament of Action* apply the materials of theatrical production to particular explication: the comedies of the 1691/92 and 1692/93 seasons, William Wycherley's *Plain-Dealer*, and Congreve's four comic dramas. The first enables Holland to describe continuities and coherences in the casting and scenery of a body of contemporary plays, and to document the establishment of conventions which, once violated or manipulated, transmit a special message to the audience. The discussion of *The Plain-Dealer* brings Holland's method and materials to bear on the interpretation of a single, notoriously difficult, Restoration play. And Congreve is chosen as a final example because of the special nature of his comic practice, observable in the 'tension between the audience's presuppositions and the events of the plays themselves, the tension between the predictions founded on the casting and the action of the plays as seen in the scenic structure, in the fictional event and the theatrical movement' (p. 206).

Holland's is a pioneering book in the history of Restoration drama criticism. Not only does it open up the virgin territory of theatrical production for future scholarly settlers, it also provides a model for the application of that new material to an interpretation of the plays. In fact, it is Holland's conceptualization of the mutually dependent but potentially contradictory multiple sign systems of the complete dramatic 'text' – including scenery, staging, and acting lines as well as verbal content – which gives his insistence upon the relevance of contemporary performance its potency. In these respects, despite the modesty of his revisionist claims, Holland stands in blatant opposition to the main tendencies of recent criticism in the field. But, like Hume, he also propounds them.

The ultimate aim of Holland's critical endeavor is an understanding of the larger 'text' of the play in performance. His goal, in short, is a more complete kind of explication of individual works. But these interpretations, though they are based largely upon previously neglected material, reproduce the familiar modernist motifs: the best plays of the Restoration are characterized by irony, ambiguity, and self-reference – their primary subject is their own use of dramatic convention, their own creation. In the casting of Farquhar's *Twin Rivals*, for instance, Holland sees a dramatic tension, in which comic convention undercuts the moral claims of the action: 'Demanding that the play should be recognized as play, [Farquhar] disrupts the audience's comfortable preconceptions, both dramatic and moral, through the focus of the casting' (p. 98). In *The Wives Excuse* Lovemore's failure to seduce Mrs Friendall is a disruption of conventional casting ('Betterton [who played Lovemore] somehow stood for successful rakishness', p. 142), signalled earlier by a self-referential scene in which the characters discuss the honesty of a beset wife in a play of the same name: 'The scene calls attention to the play's own plot while calling into doubt the conventions according to which the play thus far appeared to have been written: the play becomes open-ended' (p. 142). Holland goes on to discover in the final scenes of *The Wives Excuse* a merging of stage and world in which 'the reality of the theatre pushes the play towards the audience. They are implicated in the play's actions, in its analysis of society; they are both analyser and analysed' (p. 169). *The Plain-Dealer* ends in a similar pregnant ambiguity: 'The epilogue carries the play out again to the world. Acting on stage – doing and pretending to do – is no more ambiguous than acting in society. Social perception has been revealed to be governed by the ability to use pre-existent definitions, ones that place Hart [who played Manly] as hero or rake. In removing the comforts of expectation, Wycherley disturbed the neat lines of separation on which society claims to depend: rake and hero, doing and pretending, actor and author and character are merged' (p. 202). And finally, Congreve's drama seems to represent the epitome of this self-conscious modernist mode. *The Way of the World*, 'like reality, poses itself as an enigma to evaluation and perception' (p. 236). The tension between dramatic convention and the formal pattern of the play enforces an acceptance of 'the imprecision of perception' (p. 238). In the end, 'the traditions of the comedy, the reliance on action as the essence of its form, are again overturned by Congreve.... The experience of watching the play has brought the various apparently irreconcilable strands together; the fragments of disrupted conventions are brought back into a harmony stronger than before. The performance, the experience of the flux in the theatre, in itself becomes the end of the text' (p. 243).

This last sentence is Holland's coda, and except for its reference to performance, it accurately voices a modern interpretive consensus. Harriett Hawkins, too, describes *The Way of the World* as a self-conscious commentary on comic convention which duplicates the uncertainty and ambiguity of life itself, 'defining its own form as that of a typical Restoration comedy, and then proceeding to escape from its own definition'.[12] Norman Holland concludes that *The Way of the World* is 'in part at least, about playwriting', and he exemplifies this interpretation with a self-referential citation in which 'Congreve simply picks up the play and drops it in his audience's lap'.[13] Critics of *The Man of Mode* have commonly praised its self-conscious and lifelike ambiguity.[14] Ian Donaldson emphasizes both the irony and the self-consciousness of *The Plain-Dealer*, 'which treats ... the problem of the hazards which beset a satirist'.[15] And Gerald Weales discovers a similar ambiguity in Wycherley's *Country-Wife:* 'It is this uncertainty about how we are to react that gives the character [of Horner], the play, and Wycherley's dramatic work as a whole its peculiar richness.'[16]

Thus, the revisionist perspective of *The Ornament of Action* reproduces in the end an interpretive orthodoxy: the book discovers and celebrates precisely the qualities hallowed in modernist critical ideology. These qualities constitute an aesthetic ideal, characterized by Holland as the 'controlled fragmentation of the dramatic illusion' (p. 57). The best drama, Holland suggests, achieves a kind of 'realism' through its consistent undermining of theatrical illusion, through its disruption of the idealistic division between the real world and the stage. Such a disruption is foreign to the plays of the mid-nineteenth century and to the sentimental drama of the eighteenth, but characteristic of English Renaissance drama and of Restoration comedy. It produces a more moral and a more socially responsible kind of art, because it maintains the intimacy of actor and audience, the proximity of play and reality, and thus the applicability of the drama to the real world.

In *The Ornament of Action*, then, just as in *The Development of English Drama*, revision and orthodoxy coexist. Holland's allegiance to the modernist dramatic ideal of self-referentiality turns his critical innovation to the service of contemporary consensus, and as a result his argument itself is fractured and incomplete. His stated goal is to incorporate 'the force of historical circumstance' (p. xi) into his explication of the drama, but that 'force' is in practice reduced to the conventions of staging and casting. Not only does Holland actually neglect any fuller treatment of 'historical circumstance', but the opening chapter on the audience, which argues for its relative heterogeneity, is strictly irrelevant to the book that follows. All Holland needs to show is that 'the real audience was "informed", made up of regular visitors to the playhouse, an audience that would recognize the changes that the playwright might make in an established mode' (p. 18). In this respect, the substance of the discussion of the audience – its careful refutation of Nicoll's notion of an aristocratic coterie, its definition of class constituency, its documentation of the limited role of anti-theatricalism – is put to no purpose in the later chapters: here Holland accumulates material which his own premises seem to require, but which his argument largely fails to incorporate. This faint fissure, separating premises from conclusions, reveals the tensions in Holland's own critical ideology.

The Development of English Drama contains a parallel and equivalent fragmentation. Hume's combination of positivism and modernism enables him to identify the inadequacies of both ideologies: the facile progressivism of positivist literary history, and the predisposition of modernist critics to find complexity and profundity everywhere. But the result is a critical double negative, an absence of argument that turns his revisionist claims back upon themselves. Hume has no answers, he offers no interpretations, he draws no conclusions. His 'primary aim is to show *how* the drama changed, rather than *why*', and thus his 'concern is with relatively factual matters' (p. 19). *The Development of English Drama* is not a new beginning; it is not even a 'historical prolegomenon to future critical studies' (p. viii). It leaves us to begin again, and this, perhaps, is the best evidence of its revisionism. Among their numerous other conscious contributions to the study of Restoration drama, Hume and Holland also teach a more abstract, less intentional, and ultimately more enduring lesson – the lesson of critical history.

Such lessons are always difficult to decipher. In general, they serve to sharpen our awareness of the critical traditions in which we inevitably participate; they make us self-conscious. In this particular case, the pattern of revisions in the history of Restoration drama criticism suggests a certain elusiveness on the part of the critical object. The fact that each major interpretation can cast itself as a reversal of the previous reading reveals a crucial absence of common ground; the only shared assumptions in this field are the largely unconscious ones of critical ideology. That absence begins to define the nature of the problem presented by this drama. It is critically unmoored. The early moralistic attacks of the eighteenth century, the ahistorical perspective of the modern period, and even the positivist literary histories have consistently detached the interpretation of these plays, their significance, and their evolution from a comprehensive account of their historical circumstances. Contexts and backgrounds, of course, are often mentioned. Themes and sources have been fertile concerns. But the dynamic relationships between theatre and history, between form and ideology, between generic evolution and the larger processes of cultural change, have been largely unexplored. This absence may point to the special difficulties of perceiving and defining such relationships for Restoration drama. But these difficulties themselves reveal the necessity of just such an enterprise.

NOTES

1 Peter Holland, *The Ornament of Action: Text and Performance in Restoration Comedy* (Cambridge University Press, 1979). Robert D. Hume, *The Development of English Drama in the Late Seventeenth Century* (Oxford: Clarendon Press, 1976). Subsequent page references to these two books will be noted in the text.

2. Sir Richard Steele, *Spectator*, LXV (15 May 1711).

3. Charles Lamb, 'On the Artificial Comedy of the Last Century' (1828).

4. 'Restoration Comedy: The Reality and the Myth', *Scrutiny*, VI (1937), 122–43.

5. *A History of Restoration Drama 1660–1700* (Cambridge University Press, 1923), later included as vol. 1 in *A History of English Drama 1669–1900*, 4th edn (Cambridge University Press, 1952).

6. *The Comedy of Manners* (New York: Russell and Russell, 1913).

7. Thomas H. Fujimura, *The Restoration Comedy of Wit* (Princeton University Press, 1952); Norman Holland, *The First Modern Comedies: The Significance of Etherege, Wycherley, and Congreve* (Cambridge, Mass.: Harvard University Press, 1959); Virginia Ogden Birdsall, *Wild Civility: The English Comic Spirit on the Restoration Stage* (Bloomington: Indiana University Press, 1970); Dale Underwood, *Etherege and the Seventeenth-Century Comedy of Manners* (New Haven: Yale University Press, 1957); W. H. Van Voris, *The Cultivated Stance: The Designs of Congreve's Plays* (Dublin: Dolmen Press, 1965); Paul and Miriam Mueschke, *A New View of Congreve's 'Way of the World'*, University of Michigan Contributions in Modern Philology, no. 23 (Ann Arbor: University of Michigan Press, 1958).

8. See D. W. Jefferson, 'Aspects of Dryden's Imagery', *Essays in Criticism*, 4 (1954), 20–41, and '"All, all of a piece throughout": Thoughts on Dryden's Dramatic Poetry', in *Restoration Theatre*, ed. John Russell Brown and Bernard Harris, Stratford-Upon-Avon Studies, 6 (London: Edward Arnold, 1966), pp. 159–76; Bruce King, *Dryden's Major Plays* (London: Oliver and Boyd, 1966), p. 2; and Robert S. Newman, 'Irony and the Problem of Tone in Dryden's *Aureng-Zebe*', *Studies in English Literature, 1500–1900*, 10 (1970), 439–58.

9. Harriett Hawkins, *Likenesses of Truth in Elizabethan and Restoration Drama* (Oxford University Press, 1972); Ian Donaldson, *The World Upside-Down: Comedy from Jonson to Fielding* (Oxford University Press, 1970); Arthur C. Kirsch, *Dryden's Heroic Drama* (Princeton University Press, 1965); Anne T. Barbeau, *The Intellectual Design of John Dryden's Heroic Plays* (New Haven: Yale University Press, 1970)

10. *Likenesses of Truth*, p. 130, n. 9.

11. *Restoration Tragedy: Form and the Process of Change* (Madison: University of Wisconsin Press, 1967), pp. 141–4.

12. *Likenesses of Truth*, pp. 127–8.

13. *The First Modern Comedies*, p. 197.

14. See Underwood, *Etherege*, pp. 91–3; Holland, *The First Modern Comedies*, pp. 94–5; and Jocelyn Powell, 'George Etherege and the Form of a Comedy', in *Restoration Theatre*, ed. Brown and Harris, pp. 43–70.

15. *The World Upside-Down*, p. 116.

16. Introduction to his edition of *The Complete Plays of William Wycherley* (New York University Press, 1966), p. xiii.

W. B. Yeats's dramatic imagination

A review article by WARWICK GOULD

Once a number of Icelandic peasantry found a very thick skull in the cemetery where the poet Egil was buried. Its great thickness made them feel certain it was the skull of a great man, doubtless of Egil himself. To be doubly sure they put it on a wall and hit it hard blows with a hammer. It got white where the blows fell, but did not break, and they were convinced that it was in truth the skull of the poet, and worthy of every honour ... In some of our mountainous and barren places, and in our seaboard villages, we still test each other in much the same way the Icelanders tested the head of Egil.[1]

Yeats, then, endorses a rigorous, vigorous criticism of dead poets. 'Good strong blows', he thought, 'are delights to the mind.' There are two reasons why he need not anticipate such a hammering, at least at present. The first is that he applied such procedures in a rigorous self-criticism. The burden is familiar enough – 'Hammer your thoughts into unity', 'follow to its source / Every event in action or in thought, / Measure the lot'[2] or more startlingly

Test art, morality, custom, thought, by Thermopylae; make rich and poor act so to one another that they can stand together there. Love war because of its horror, that belief may be changed, civilisation renewed. We desire belief and lack it. Belief comes from shock and is not desired ... Belief is renewed continually in the ordeal of death.[3]

The second reason is that if one may judge by Andrew Parkin's *The Dramatic Imagination of W. B. Yeats* and *A Critical Edition of W. B. Yeats's* A Vision *(1925)*, edited by George Mills Harper and Walter Kelly Hood,[4] even if the scholars are disinterring Yeats's thought, the critics have not yet swung the hammer at it.

A Vision (1925) ends its discourse with an eloquent plea:

That we may believe that all men possess the supernatural faculties I would restore to the philosopher his mythology. (p. 252)

From this familiar imperative we turn to 'All Souls' Night', a poem which establishes three of his friends, Horton, Florence Emery and Macgregor Mathers as figures in the mythology of modern culture. *A Vision,* which elaborates myth on a crabbed skeleton of astrological geometry, is the more disturbing for having been cobbled together from the recondite odds and ends of his reading and from personal friends who are obscure to us. That imperative connection between the necessity *of* philosophy and the necessity *to* philosophy of myth is one of the more constant of Yeats's intellectual obsessions. And from 'The Autumn of the Body' (1898):

> Man has wooed and won the world, and has fallen weary ... He grew weary when he said, 'These things that I touch and see and hear are alone real', for he saw them without illusion at last, and found them but air and dust and moisture. And now he must be philosophical about everything, even about the arts, for he can only return the way he came, and so escape from weariness, by philosophy. The arts are, I believe, about to take upon their shoulders the burdens that have fallen from the shoulders of priests, and to lead us back upon our journey[5]

to a more wonderful articulation of the idea in 'Discoveries' (1908):

> All art is dream, and what the day is done with is dreaming-ripe, and what art has moulded religion accepts, and in the end all is in the wine-cup, all is in the drunken fantasy, and the grapes begin to stammer (*Essays and Introductions*, p. 285) ·

to *A Vision*, and onward to the Old Man who belongs 'to Mythology' in 'The Death of Cuchulain', the supernatural faculties have had their spokesman in Yeats, and all for a significantly under-discussed imperative: revelation, or even, revealed religion. In his dedication to Moina Mathers, Yeats summed up the staple belief of himself and his fellow-students, while thinking of Horton and those 'traditional experiences of a saint' which the latter felt he had gained through the 'trampling of the grapes of life' (p. x):

> We all ... differed from ordinary students of philosophy or religion through our belief that truth cannot be discovered but may be revealed, and that if a man do not lose faith, and if he go through certain preparations, revelation will find him at the fitting moment. (p. x)

For Yeats, poets are not merely unacknowledged legislators, and the place of art, dream and mythology in his religion would require a very special kind of critical scholarship of his poetry as an integral part of its approach: the converse is also true, and critics of his work have frequently undervalued the study of his thought.

What is the relation of 'All Soul's Night' to the rest of *A Vision*? Can it stand alone as a poem? What is the significance of séance to the art of the lyric? What are we to make of that poem's studied carelessness, following as it does 'mind's wandering', while it 'holds tight' its 'mummy truths'? How does one respond to the teasing, relaxed poet who refuses to provide on demand those truths mocked by 'none but the living'? Consider its elegant ramble, its dismissal of that personality it has sought and caught in reverie over the dead:

But names are nothing. What matter who it be,
So that his elements have grown so fine
The fume and muscatel
Can give his sharpened palate ecstasy
No living man can drink from the whole wine.

This reversal of attitude from the earlier thought:

His element is so fine
Being sharpened by his death,
To drink from the wine-breath
While our gross palates drink from the whole wine

is perhaps an admission of fellowship with the living, by the poet, but the
wine has become spiritual, the wine of the Ephesian topers, the wine from
the stammering grapes, to be taken in ceremony – even sacrament – with
the bread baked from 'mummy wheat'. Our living poet recognises the
dangers of solipsism in recording the lives of Mathers and Horton, 'driven
crazed' by 'loneliness':

For meditations upon unknown thought
Make human intercourse grow less and less;

yet approves the chosen isolation of Florence Emery and revels in it himself:

Such thought – such thought have I that hold it tight
Till meditation master all its parts,
Nothing can stay my glance
Until that glance run in the world's despite
To where the damned have howled away their hearts,
And where the blessed dance;
Such thought, that in it bound
I need no other thing,
Wound in mind's wandering,
As mummies in the mummy-cloth are wound.

Howsoever occasional (and the whole question of what constitutes the
'occasional' in Yeats's poetry requires analysis), this 'secret, exultant',
contradictory poem opens up all of the critical questions a study of his thought
demands. When all in it has been glossed, one well-nigh imponderable
question remains: is it a good poem, and to what extent does its quality
depend upon its author's handling of his heterodox beliefs? After all,
'murmuring name upon name' he has *performed* his beliefs in a poem which
embodies them rather than comprehends them.

Most undergraduates ask of their tutors the question none can answer:
'What did Yeats believe?'. This is a *critical* question, and the only true
answer seems unhelpful. One can gesture towards that statement quoted
from the dedication above about revealed truth and connect it to Yeats's
last letter where at least he formulated the problem: 'When I try to put all

into a phrase I say, "Man can embody truth but he cannot know it"'.[6] This
is Yeats's reformulation of a comment of Goethe's quoted in *A Vision* (p. 80)
– though the editors do not refer us to it in the context. It is a pity, for a
moment's study of Goethe's version: 'Man knows himself by action only, by
thought never' shows us at once the *dramatic* perspective Yeats brings to the
formulation of philosophical thought.

Yet there is a sense in which we can formulate Yeats's *beliefs* (for his
lifelong concern was with multitudinousness) and their relation to his work
more satisfactorily than ever before. A real achievement of Mr Harper's
refusal, in his writings upon Yeats's occult interests, to provide easy
answers, is that now we have in front of us a quantity of evidence which
compels the provisional assessment that it is 'something of great constancy,
but howsoever strange, and admirable'. Now with the republication of the
1925 version of *A Vision*, Mr Harper gives us a dense account of the gestation
of that work which compels a fresh look at the critical problems. The more
of such material that emerges, the less is it possible, as critics must have
thought it possible once, to formulate critical questions without thinking
too much about it all. Those critics of the past (such as Henn or Melchiori[7])
who chose the *via philosophia*, rather than the *via biocritica*, have endured the
challenge of such new discoveries best.

The critical problem of belief and its relation to poetry and drama is one
which calls for scholar–critics, 'schoolmates' in mystical thought who yet
preserve a commitment to 'human intercourse', for solipsism is inimical to
criticism (*pace* Harold Bloom for whom 'criticism is the discourse of the deep
tautology'[8]). The interdependence of scholarly and critical labours is essential: however much the editors and annotators pile up in front of us by way
of occult writings, we cannot delay critical activity until every last horo-
scope has been stuffed and mounted. The reason for this urgency is vivid: so
much of Yeats's religious thought is based by analogy – the method of the
Smaragdine Tablets, of Swedenborg – upon his poetic that the scholars
have much to learn from the critics.

Mr Parkin writes as a critic, while Mr Harper and Mr Hood try to induce a
little scholarly order in their author, as Frank Pearce Sturm once tried.[9] Mr
Parkin is to be congratulated, for books on Yeats's plays almost always start
with a xenophobic defence of his theatre against popular ignorance,
whereas Mr Parkin begins, as his title indicates, with a different subject,
and a good one. Further, he begins by tackling his author's theory of
imagination. At least then, the skull is dusted off.

If Yeats is a 'subtle-souled psychologist' as *A Vision* would suggest, then
the account of daimonic man at phase 17 is probably a pregnant piece of
self-analysis. There we read that 'the *Will*, when true to phase, assumes, in
assuming the *Mask*, an intensity, which is never *dramatic* [my italics] but

always lyrical and personal, and this intensity, though always a deliberate assumption, is to others the charm of the being' (p. 76).

That word 'dramatic' needs some sort of interpretation. Does it mean 'rhetorical' in the pejorative sense of *Anima Hominis* meditation V, where rhetoric is seen as the opposite of poetry and the result of the 'quarrel with others' (*Mythologies*, p. 331)? Mr Parkin unyieldingly asserts that Yeats's imagination is 'neither epic nor even wholly lyric, but essentially dramatic' (p. 2). His evidence is impressive. Indeed, the book is so wholly evidential that the case lacks development and the argument lacks definition. 'Dramatic' seems an easy word to use when discussing Yeats's ideas, and familiar passages might indicate that his usage of it is uncontentious. For example, Mr Parkin (and most other commentators on Yeats) quote 'I have tried to make my work convincing with a speech so natural and dramatic that the hearer would feel the presence of a man thinking and feeling' (*Letters*, p. 583). Nothing could seem less contentious than to take at face value that splendid sentence from the correspondence with John Butler Yeats, that 'first seminary' of so many of Yeats's ruling ideas. But all is not so simple, for here is the full context:

> I thought your letter about 'portraiture' being 'pain' most beautiful and profound. All our art is but the putting our faith ... into words or forms and our faith is in ecstasy. Of recent years instead of 'vision', meaning by vision the intense realization of a state of ecstatic emotion symbolized in a definite imagined region, I have tried for more self-portraiture. I have tried to make my work convincing with a speech so natural and dramatic that the hearer would feel the presence of a man thinking and feeling. There are always two types of poetry – Keats the type of vision, Burns a very obvious type of the other, too obvious indeed. It is in dramatic expression that English poetry is most lacking as compared with French poetry. Villon always and Ronsard at times create a marvellous drama out of their own lives. (*Ibid.*)

At the back of this excerpt is a continuing debate about portraiture, art and drama which one can partially assemble, with the help of Hone's edition of J. B. Yeats's *Letters*, and Finneran, Harper and Murphy's *Letters to Yeats*. The train of thought culminates in that central meditation V of *Per Amica Silentia Lunae*. But when Mr Parkin discusses that crucial sentence he ignores the hinterland of Yeats's thought though he pays lip service to Yeats's notion that his writings 'germinate out of each other' (p. 32). Accepting the sentence at face value he draws a firm but essentially artificial distinction between the 'lyric of vision' and the 'lyric of self-portraiture'. While such a distinction might have some preliminary appeal, when one proposes any serious analysis it is quite useless, since the latter category does not repudiate the former. When poem or play dramatises the man 'thinking and feeling' one is forced to ask what *kinds* of thinking and feeling are involved, and when the poem is one of self-portraiture the answer is very often 'vision', or reverie about 'ecstasy'. These questions involve issues in poetics: Mr Parkin is not inclined to see the intractibility of these issues, and the homely tone of his discussion of them is likely to dismay readers who have thus far approved his project.

> Historians of the lyric assert that it is difficult to define because so many different kinds of poem have accrued in the tradition, been bundled together and labelled lyrics. Our habit of calling the words to a piece of music 'the lyrics' suggests the musical origin of lyric poetry as song in the ancient world. By Renaissance times a lyric had come to mean any poem for a singer. The proliferation of printed poetry soon meant that lyrics were more often written to be read than set to music and sung. The lyric, though, tugs back towards its dramatic and theatrical origins in the songs, dances and rituals of worship. It is a relatively modern fallacy that 'lyric' and 'dramatic' are necessarily distinct, or opposing tendencies. Towards the end of the sixteenth century in Italy, the madrigal, especially in Monteverdi, became overtly dramatic; influenced by secular drama, it developed marked affinities with the *Commedia dell'Arte.* (p. 35)

Thus far, the infuriating, accommodating tone of the lecture, historically and philosophically indulgent, and highly unsatisfactory to readers at all thoughtful in a variety of related disciplines, but the real failure of critical nerve is only fully apparent in the succeeding paragraph.

> It therefore seems best to acknowledge the close links between lyric and dramatic poetry, making the distinction, when necessary, depend on context: the lyric poem establishes its own clearly circumscribed context in itself, and more rarely in a sequence, as in the case of some sonnets; speeches and songs in plays, however lyrical in form, feeling or performance, find their context, when their use is truly dramatic, not in themselves but in the structure, characterisation, themes or conflicts of the play in which they appear. A lyric which pre-exists [*sic*] the play which later uses it, if it is given the right context, becomes dramatic. Lyrics are part of the poetry of performance, closely associated with an oral tradition linked with song and even dance. Thus Yeats's dramatic imagination could go far indeed to express its dramatic view of life in lyrical terms. (*Ibid.*)

Perhaps Mr Parkin felt it high time that a spokesman for Yeats's plays took brutish revenge for the dramatic criticism of those commentators who, in the past, have been inclined to be either brusque or apologetic about the plays while seeing Yeats (as, it must be admitted, he saw himself) as primarily a poet. But these two paragraphs have a slippery logic and syntax, which avoid serious issues, obliterate profound distinctions, and thereby make the reader uneasy about the seriousness with which Mr Parkin can be said to examine the plays. One turns this page, with its slack grasp of theoretical issues, expecting to find the usual paraphrase of Yeats's own writings on his imaginative processes, and one is correct. However the speed with which such passages earn his unquestioning endorsement is surprising, and quite breathtaking is the pace at which he essays to cover Yeats's poems before tackling the plays. The comments are rather random, and it is an enduring difficulty of his whole enterprise that the discussion refuses to comprehend the thought of previous critics, or to develop his new perspective as a thesis. But the pressure to be novel leads him to include whatever new perceptions he may have, and the result is a prose of vacillating critical pressure which at times falters to a windy halt.

> From the early manifestoes through the curt, aphoristic renunciation of the early style in 'A Coat' and the elaborate, pivotal declaration of faith in imagination and spirit which is 'The Tower', to the last poetic testament of 'Under Ben Bulben', Yeats is acutely aware of what he is doing. (p. 39)

One wonders whether Mr Parkin really wanted to write a book on the plays from a new angle and was trapped by his title into perfunctory chapters on the poems? I wish I thought so. But the book proceeds from theory to literature, from an introductory survey of Yeats's thinking, via a meagre but opportunistic account of the issues such thinking sustains in the speculative prose, with heavy concentration upon the failed novel, *The Speckled Bird* – more perhaps because little has been written on it than because it is vital to his thesis. Mr Parkin has an eye for good quotations, such as 'The most fundamental of divisions is that between the intellect which can only do its work by saying continually "Thou fool" and the religious genius which makes all equal' (*Autobiographies*, p. 467),[10] but he then does little with them save squander the reader's interest on the obvious. Of 'The Bounty of Sweden', for instance, he makes the point that Yeats spoke in Stockholm as a dramatic poet, more dramatist than lyricist, as though that were one in the eye for some partisans of a lyric, rather than dramatic, Yeats; this ignores the nationalistic use Yeats made of the Nobel ceremony to gesture towards his fellow dramatists of the Abbey.

But it is not that the opposition between lyric and dramatic is merely misconceived and then used or not as the occasion seems to demand. There has just not been enough thinking about the nature of drama and poetry, and the result is a hint of the *rechauffé* lecture such as in:

> 'Byzantium' is a subtle, allusive, intricate lyric; it also excites us with its dramatic energy, and that spectacular dance of ghosts. It could only have been written by a poet who was also a masterly dramatist.
>   Yeats's dramatic imagination demanded strength of syntax, characterisation or embodiment, and vigorous enactment of meaning to achieve its true expression. It is because of this that on the whole in Yeats's poetry, at least, things do *not* fall apart, and mere anarchy is *not* loosed upon his readers. (p. 49)

This passage concludes a strained analogy between poem and dance play which remains exterior to the poem as well as remote from any engagement with the notion of 'a man thinking and feeling'. Perhaps most disturbing of all, however, is the convenience Mr Parkin finds in referring to poems such as 'News for the Delphic Oracle' and 'The Municipal Gallery Revisited' as

'dramatic phantasmagoria'. The overwhelming tautology of this description betrays a real indifference to the exactitude with which Yeats used this
word, as an analogy in his poetics and as an analogy of that analogy in *A
Vision*.

In writing on the poems Mr Parkin is grappling with the cliché that
Yeats's best lyrics are dramatic as his best plays are lyric. And if he declines
to discuss 'dramatic', then he also contents himself with neither examining
the way in which that quality is incarnated in 'a written speech', nor with
defining the faculty which produces it with any precision or depth. Imagination, he tells us, is 'our way of thinking in images and symbols to interpret
the physical and psychic *environment* [my italics] and our life in it' (p. 3).

I dwell upon these early chapters because, if Mr Parkin retreats from
writing the book about Yeats's imagination the title might have led us to
expect, he does in them try to establish a critical focus for the discussion of
Yeats's plays about imagination, to which two-thirds of his book is devoted.
So it is necessary to say why he does not succeed in this secondary but
extremely important task. He moves too briskly and unreflectingly over
intractable if pregnant material from Yeats's theoretical writings. 'Magic'
is the point at which he retreats from the coalface. Having summed up some
of its argument by writing

> Thus the imagination is capable of projecting involuntary symbolic visions of
> our crucial, inner and often hidden moods, visions which may be compelling
> enough to exist in several minds (p. 7)

Mr Parkin might have followed Allen Grossman[11] into some account of
'The Moods' and what they meant to his author, or he could have ignored
sources and explicated these difficult matters in terms of Romantic aesthe-
tics. At the least, he might have examined the analogies with Yeats's
theories of the drama which constitute the harmonies between Yeats's
religious thinking and literary criticism.

But instead, Mr Parkin shrinks into a petulant *da capo – 'Whatever the precise
mechanism* [my italics], Yeats took such visions as proof of "the supremacy of
the imagination"' (p. 7). Those precise mechanisms are worthy of study
because the process of composition is the scene of instruction for most
Romantic and Symbolist poets, and because this is especially true of Yeats,
since in his case the 'precise mechanisms' of the imagination are so intimately associated with the subject-matter of his work, reverie, and the
articulation of it in 'the presence of a man thinking and feeling'. 'Precise
mechanisms', such is the syncretic and symbolical nature of Yeats's philosophy, are profound and profoundly *dramatic* analogies for the critic of texts.
As Owen Aherne remarks 'nothing is unimportant in belief' (*Mythologies*,
p. 298).

Yet for Mr Parkin, 'Magic' and its opening tenets are 'now notorious' (whatever that may mean) and he quotes only so much of the sentence which follows them – 'I often think I would put this belief in magic from me if I could . . .' – as will support his comfortable contention that if Yeats's 'soul soared, his reason could not but scratch the sceptical itch' (p. 9). But the rest of the sentence is disturbing, because it suggests more the threat of religious despair than the challenge of reason:

> for I have come to see or to imagine, in men and women, in houses, in handicrafts, in nearly all sights and sounds, a certain evil, a certain ugliness, that comes from the slow perishing through the centuries of a quality of mind that made this belief and its evidences common over the world. (*Essays and Introductions*, p. 28)

We recall the rhetorical (or perhaps real) question of *The Symbolism of Poetry*:

> How can the arts overcome the slow dying of men's hearts that we call the progress of the world, and lay their hands upon men's heartstrings again, without becoming the garment of religion as in old times? (*Ibid.*, pp. 162–3)

and are reminded that the holistic nature of Yeats's thought, that hard skull, resists easy answers.

When Mr Parkin turns to the second part of the cliché, the lyric nature of the plays themselves, he opens with a brisk reply to O'Casey's comment 'His poems are more dramatic than his plays, and his plays are really poems' (quoted, p. 51). This comment seems worth serious consideration, but Mr Parkin spurns inquiry:

> There is no doubt about the dramatic force of Yeats's poetry, but O'Casey was wrong about the plays. The vast majority of them go beyond dramatic poetry and exist as intense one-act poetic dramas. If the poems are highly dramatic, the plays are highly lyrical; it is as if the principle of conflict in Yeats urged his dramatic imagination to find its mask in lyricism, while all the time gazing through religious eyes, alive with myth and ritual. (p. 51)

Despite the curvetting fantasia upon Yeats's thought here, and the ambiguous syntax of the last sentence, Mr Parkin has a point which he reiterates throughout the next two chapters. The one-act play, he insists with some success, is a useful 'context' in which to examine Yeats's development as a playwright and in which to come to some critical estimate of his plays. So while the account of, say, *The Land of Heart's Desire* seems to be written for undergraduates who have gained little from a first reading, and while his account of the history of the one-act play is too hastily sketched in, the point remains. But there is another kind of historical context which does not get established here, and nor does it emerge from the chronological discussion of Yeats's plays from *The Island of Statues* onwards. That context is the relationship between dramatic poetry and poetic drama in the mind of an author who is feeling his way not just towards the successful use of the stage for the revival of a discredited genre, but also for the expression of some of his ultimate concerns. Never does Mr Parkin come to terms with this problem, even in the lengthy discussion of *The Shadowy Waters*, which exists in several states as both dramatic poem and poetic drama.

In his general avoidance of literary theory such matters are not discussed, but nevertheless the 'highly lyrical' nature of 'intense one-act dramas' should bring us back to lyric. Mr Parkin is adroit:

> To describe the lyric elements in Yeats's plays is a straightforward task. He achieved the lyric qualities through both traditional and original songs, dances and music, and verse passages of varying lyrical intensity in both dialogue and monologue. For Yeats, lyric drama meant these musical elements together with the revelation of a character's spiritual life at a moment of poetic intensity. This could be achieved relatively quickly, and so the lyric play, like the lyric poem, had to be short, as short as was compatible with establishing character and situation enough to make the crisis significant and impressive, and with allowing Yeats to pattern his events. (pp. 51–2)

And that according to Mr Parkin, is that. For when he returns to the matter he does not develop and test the idea, but rather tilts, not at imaginary giants, but at imaginary windmills, for who would seriously advance the notion against which he turns his unnecessary indignation?

> To complain that such lyricism and literary reference [he writes of *The Land of Heart's Desire* and *Cathleen ni Houlihan*] is undramatic is to make a critical axiom out of ignorance preferred, and to subscribe to a parochial definition of drama which hobbles criticism with a single set of conventions – those of twentieth-century realism. (p. 65)

Gallant, but not pertinent, for although in these chapters the plays are brought into some sort of focus (and out of that xenophobic theatrical breathlessness which plagues current criticism of Yeats's plays), he misses the issues of lyricism in drama, which could have been faced with the help of Susanne Langer, for example, in a discussion of the lyric of contemplated feeling, or that of Donald Davie in some consideration of 'written speech'. Yeats himself could have helped here. There are many statements about the purpose of rhythm to prolong contemplation in the essays, and there is the renowned critique of moments of lyric ecstasy in Shakespeare, which could have provided a focus for a critical discussion of the relationship of lyric to drama. In such a focus, with the realities of speech uttered, in a playing of the piece, kept firmly in mind, O'Casey's remark has a curious truth. It is the sort of truth we recognise in the statement that *Antony and Cleopatra* is an extended lyric. Yeats was himself penetrating and convincing on this point.

> The heroes of Shakespeare convey to us through their looks, or through the metaphorical patterns of their speech, the sudden enlargement of their vision, their ecstasy at the approach of death ... all must be cold; no actress has ever sobbed when she played Cleopatra, even the shallow brain of a producer has

never thought of such a thing. The supernatural is present, cold winds blow across our hands, upon our faces, the thermometer falls, and because of that cold we are hated by journalists and groundlings ... the rhythm is old and familiar, imagination must dance, must be carried beyond feeling into the aboriginal ice. (*Essays and Introductions*, p. 52–3)

Of course this comment is familiar, more so perhaps than the comment which follows it about the variation of lyric metres and blank verse in the plays. But its truths, if tested against the texts, offer fruitful ways of examining the lyric intensity of the plays in the context of a discussion of his development from dramatic poet to poetic dramatist.

When one considers, for instance:

> *Forgael.*　　　　　　　　　　　　　　　All comes to an end.
> 　　The harvest's in; the granary doors are shut;
> 　　The topmost blossom on the boughs of Time
> 　　Has blossomed, and I grow old as Time,
> 　　For I have all his garden wisdom (*Variorum Poems*, pp. 55–6)

while bearing in mind lines such as

> *Cleopatra.*　　　　　　　　　　　　...My lord!
> 　　O! wither'd is the garland of the war,
> 　　The soldier s pole is fall'n, young boys and girls
> 　　Are level now with men; the odds is gone,
> 　　And there is nothing left remarkable
> 　　Beneath the visiting moon (IV, xv, 63–8)

with due allowance for the different occasions of them, one can see how important to any discussion of lyric in drama is Yeats's study of rhythm and its relation to and evocation of 'vision', 'ecstasy' and the 'presence of the supernatural'. And why did Yeats scotch these lines from the dramatic poem after it had been tried out on the boards of the Abbey? Was it, one wonders, a compromise with actors incapable of making 'imagination dance', of 'lifting tragedy out of history with timeless pattern' (*Essays and Introductions*, p. 523), incapable, in short, of uttering the lines with the holding down of feeling he required? Frank Fay wrote touchingly:

> There will be the *hats* or *helmets* to consider and if Forgail wears a helmet or hat, do you wish him to remove it at the lines commencing 'The harvest's in, the granary doors are shut', which I take to be the entrance of Love. Am *I right* as to the interpretation of that speech.[12]

There is a lack of critical focus in the discussion of *Calvary* which suggests that this book might have had its centre in a consideration of Yeats's thought, and its development. Mr Parkin somewhat jejunely suggests that Yeats depends heavily upon an assumption which gives the text great economy: that this audience will be Christian and orthodox. An interesting comparison is made with *Christ's Ministry*, but Yeats had an enduring interest in the morality play – he once thought of collaborating with

Katherine Tynan in writing some but her achievements as single author in the genre suggest that he was wiser to concentrate upon writing his own *The Adoration of the Magi* – and this interest over a long period deserves consideration. Then there is his account of the 'terrible beauty' (yes, *his* description) of Wilde's parable of Lazarus – 'Lord, I was dead, and You raised me into life, what else can I do but weep?' (*Autobiographies*, p. 287). For Yeats, the interest in the morality play and parable was an interest in appropriate form and speech: regretting that when Wilde published the parable he did so not in the unadorned speech of the dinner table but 'spoiled with the verbal decoration of his epoch', Yeats judged Wilde 'a comedian ... in the hands of those dramatists who understand nothing but tragedy'.

In discussions of *Calvary*, *The King of the Great Clock Tower* and *A Full Moon in March* there is no attempt even to gesture at Yeats's early thinking, and while in the consideration of these plays some account of 'The Binding of the Hair' or of Wilde's parable would not take us very far, even the briefest consideration of such sources would have helped the reader towards an appreciation of the syncretic unity of Yeats's thought. It is not possible to examine *Calvary* or *The Only Jealousy of Emer* without some consideration of *A Vision* (1925). Mr Parkin examines no play which does not pursue themes central to a discussion of Yeats's imagination (so regrettably *The Herne's Egg* is ignored) but does not face squarely up to the way in which some of the dramas grew out of the occult centre of his thought and experience. Mr Parkin gives three perfunctory pages to *The Words upon the Window Pane*. A piece of 'twentieth-century realism', it suffers more than the dance plays from amateur desecration, because it suffers more often, yet it is as subtle an experiment in the juxtaposition of styles of speech as is *The Herne's Egg*, *Purgatory*, or *The Dreaming of the Bones*.

> Swift haunts me; he is always just round the next corner [says Yeats in the notes to the play], sometimes I remember something hard or harsh in O'Leary or in Taylor, or in the public speech of our statesmen, that reminds me by its style of his verse or prose. Did he not speak, perhaps, with just such an intonation? *This instinct for what is near and yet hidden is in reality a return to the sources of our power, and therefore a claim made upon the future* – [my italics]. Thought seems more true, emotion more deep, spoken by someone who touches my pride, who seems to claim me of his kindred, who seems to make me a part of some national mythology, nor is mythology mere ostentation, mere vanity if it draws me onward to the unknown; another turn of the gyre and myth is wisdom, pride, discipline. I remember the shudder in my spine when Mrs Patrick Campbell said, speaking the words Hofmannsthal put into the mouth of Electra, 'I too am of that ancient race'. (*Variorum Plays*, p. 958)[13]

This is a remarkable comment, by any standards, but its transparent quality to a critic of the plays is the dimension it brings to the study of speech. 'No character upon the stage spoke my thoughts', says Yeats and the 'motley' of the séance room is capable of being thrown away or vividly held in focus as a Dublin which rots and rots, depending on the players. But what of the characters not on the stage? If 'mediumship is dramatisation' as Yeats avers, then the reverse is also true, and illuminatingly so, and no student of imagination, as Mr Parkin is, should let slip this chance to draw what conclusions can be drawn from this play's speech, even if ostensibly it is in prose.

> Five great ministers that were my friends are gone, ten great ministers that were my friends are gone. I have not fingers enough to count the great ministers that were my friends and that are gone. (*Ibid.*, p. 956)

Although at his most successful in an account of *Purgatory*, there is no fully realised account of a play which fully engages the texture of speech, the skill in dramaturgy and the holistic thinking out of which the plays are shaped. One wonders why Mr Parkin would wish to hasten so unrememberingly over great speech.

When one turns to Yeats's own writings, even to the abstruse pages of *A Vision (A)*, one finds in the very fabric of argument statements about the nature of drama which raise profound questions

> The world is a drama where person follows person, and though the dialogue prepares for all the entrances, that preparation is not the person's proof, nor is Polonius disproved when Hamlet seems to kill him. Once the philosophy, nation or movement has clearly shown its face, we know that its chief characteristic has not arisen out of any proof, or even out of all the past, or out of the present tension of the drama, or out of any visible cause whatever, but is unique, life in itself. There can be neither cause nor effect when all things are co-eternal. (pp. 171–2)

How do we read this text? What kinds of relevance does it have to the reader of the plays? Now one can see why Yeats demands of those who would test his thought and work, that they be scholar-critics who are 'schoolmates', philosophers, cabbalists as well as 'tavern comrades'. And when we turn to the simplest of his analogies, we need to pause for thought in an identical way. 'We begin to live' said Yeats, 'when we have conceived life as tragedy' (*Autobiographies*, p. 189). This dramatic perspective is the 'vision of reality' denied to rhetoricians and sentimentalists. It is the preserve, in fact, of those who have 'found life out', 'who have awakened from the common dream', 'whose passion is reality'. Whenever Yeats talks about his ultimate concerns, the metaphors are drawn from drama, illusion, pageant, and it is a vexed question whether in the last analysis the discourse is metaphorical or not, so do the substance and the analogy interpenetrate each other. Of the later version of *A Vision* he wrote:

> Some will ask whether I believe in the actual existence of my circuits of sun and moon... To such a question I can but answer that if sometimes, overwhelmed by miracle as all men must be when in the midst of it, I have taken

such periods literally, my reason has soon recovered; and now that the system stands out clearly in my imagination I regard them as stylistic arrangements of experience comparable to the cubes in the drawing of Wyndham Lewis and to the ovoids in the sculpture of Brancusi. They have helped me to hold in a single thought reality and justice. (*A Vision* [1937], p. 25)

Reality and Justice: A Vision is Yeats's *Summa*, and that which enables him to hold two such opposed structures of thought 'in a single thought' is, must be, a metaphor. That it is drawn from the drama is the ultimate develop-ment of aestheticism, yet the book is no product of *fin de siècle* modishness, but rather a work of mythography, late antique or medieval, born out of phase. In it, we perceive that for Yeats, all belief rests upon a cosmology vivid in its dramaturgy. The Mask and the Body of Fate, the Phantas-magoria and the Dreaming Back (a form of soliliquy), the *commedia dell'arte* and the Dance, the Dramatisation which is Mediumship – all these theatri-cal concepts are pondered and tested by belief in Yeats's mind: there can be no shirking of this issue. The question penetrates each aspect of his life's thought, be it his use of earlier literature and its forms, or his discovery of 'gradual time's last gift, a written speech / Wrought of high laughter, loveli-ness and ease' (*Variorum Poems*, p. 264).

So it is a pleasure to welcome *A Vision (A)* back into print after fifty-four years, even though it must be said at once of this *Critical Edition* edited by George Harper and Walter Hood that Kusta ben Luka's letter remains hidden, perhaps hidden even deeper, in the great treatise of Parmenides.

For if 'nothing is unimportant in belief', its editors had set themselves a Herculean task. Mr Harper presents a long and valuable history of the automatic script, card file, dialogues, sleeps and meditations, foul papers and fouler smells, Controls and Frustrators which went into the seven-year making of this book. The monumental labour imposed on Yeats and his passive medium is summarised by Mr Harper who followed that labour, reading and transcribing the papers left from 450 sessions of automatic writing, involving 8672 questions and 3627 pages of surviving script, and 270 pages surviving from a further 164 'sleeps' and meditations. The introduction traces the growth of the system from an automatic script shown to Yeats by Lady Lyttleton in 1913 or 1914 and the complementary use of its principal symbol in a manuscript of W. T. Horton until, in the words of the rejected dedication to Vestigia Mathers, 'something that has troubled my life for years has *been folded up & smoothed out & laid away*' (p. xlvii).

Mr Harper contents himself with recording what facts can be gleaned from a study of the surviving archive and refrains from any kind of comment or interpretation at all. On this basis, there is little to question, since the editors alone have had extensive access to these materials. However, Mr Harper asserts that the title of Yeats's Judwali bible was concocted by the marriage of the titles of two books well known to Yeats, W. T. Horton's *The Way of the Soul: a legend in line and verse*[14] and Cecil French's book of poems and woodcuts dedicated to Yeats and entitled *Between Sun and Moon*.[15] Mr Harper tells us that in a rejected draft the book is entitled simply *The Way of the Soul* and concludes that *Between Sun and Moon* was added to the title sometime after 1922 when Yeats had received his copy of French's volume.

Now I have no further evidence to adduce to matters already published here and elsewhere in Mr Harper's studies, but this conclusion sounds alien to Yeats's thought. Horton's 'legend in line and verse' is the way of the soul towards spiritual completion and perfection, which is seen as a union with a beloved and a reconciliation of all opposites which will be instantly recognisable, even in Horton's lamentably bad verses, to any who have puzzled over Yeats's 'There':

> The Sun and Moon in Her do meet
> And blend as One in rapture sweet. (*The Way of the Soul*, p. 145)

This idea is repeated here and there in Yeats's thought, and in Horton's verses, and of Horton's book itself it is very hard to say who influenced whom. On p. 119 of Horton's *Way*, for example, is a bad drawing of what must be W. B. Yeats surfacing in some celestial pool, and looking like a pearly-eyed demon after a sea change. He depends for his buoyancy upon some invisible, sub-aqueous support from an immense female life-saver of faintly Egyptian and singularly repellent aspect with a third eye in what appears to be her headpiece. Behind her shines a radiant sun all set about with roses.

But in Mr Harper's co-edition *Letters to Yeats* there is a much earlier document, which goes unnoticed in *A Vision (A)*, but which points precisely to the symbolism of *The Way of the Soul between the Sun and the Moon*, the fictive sacred book of the equally fictive Judwalis, from whose spurious tradition the supreme fiction of *A Vision* receives its necessary authority and from whose sacred dance we gain just some meagre clue to what kind of reading *A Vision* needs.

> I am walking with two angels, one of Power, Strength, Sadness, Mystery; the other Clearness, Warmth, Joy & Rest. One is the Moon, the other the Sun. I see them both as glorious Woman shapes ... One thing they have in common, they bid me to leave earthly things. (*Letters to Yeats*, i, p. 59–60)

Now given Yeats's relationship to Horton (and we await Mr Harper's book on that relationship with interest) there seems to be no need to assume that Yeats was stumped for a fictitious title which would gesture towards but not plagiarise Horton's *The Way of the Soul*, until the 'flea' Cecil French dedicated *Between Sun and Moon* to him. Yeats's mind was not a shunting engine and, to judge by French's epigraph which tells us that the book was finished before 1914, his title may itself signal some community of interest with

Horton's symbolism, as displayed in the letter quoted above. French, of course (*Letters to Yeats*, II, p. 424), recalls 'Woburn Nights' and his poems are the classic tributes of the flea to the dog – 'The Nets of Song', 'The Way of Peace', 'Make-Believe' (which purloins the rhythm of 'The Cap and Bells') and 'The Wood of Laragh' which is a sort of eighth wood to those who know well the first seven woods – but in 'Beyond' occur the lines:

> To blow as in the blessed fields
> Beyond the Sun and Moon and Death (p. 13)

which hint at that celestial *topos* of Horton. Of course the whole question of the influence of admiring poetasters on Yeats needs examination, for even French has a line Yeats probably recalled. The refrain of his 'Avalon Remembered' varies the burden of

> Mayhap we trod the Lawns of Avalon.

and the superiority of Yeats's handling of rhythm shows up in his later poem 'The Statesman's Holiday'

> *Tall dames go walking in grass-green Avalon.* (*Variorum Poems*, p. 627)

But as the origin of *A Vision* is in Horton's script concerning the black and white horses of Plato's *Phaedrus*, where the soul is seen as trifurcated into hapless charioteer, good, and unruly horses, the congruence between the symbolism of that script and Horton's letter of eleven years before needed a note at least.

It is at this point in Mr Harper's introduction that the reader who had hoped to find in *A Critical Edition* a key to all mythologies of *A Vision* will experience a sinking feeling as he wonders if Mr Harper cannot see the wood for the trees. And yet minute particulars themselves are ignored. The automatic script of Lady Lyttleton and the enigmatic scrap of paper of Horton's which set Yeats thinking yielded three oracular phrases, so far as he was concerned. Lady Lyttleton's phrases included

> Yeats is a prince with an evil counsellor.
> Zoroaster and the planets. If this is not understood
> tell him to think of the double-harness – of Phaeton
> the adverse principle
> The hard rings on the surf
> Despair is the child of folly
> If the invidious suggestion is not quelled there may
> be trouble. (p. xiii)

She interpreted all this not a whit, and communicated to him another message which of course echoes the Book of Common Prayer

> In the midst of death we are in life – the inversion is
> what I mean (p. xiv)

(though for Yeats its Heraclitean suggestions may have been more luminous). The editors, who have had access to letters of Yeats which they may not print, are silent upon these sources, and, although they do provide evidence that Yeats interpreted the Zoroaster reference as applying to Nietzsche's work rather than to Zoroastrian texts such as *The Chaldean Oracles* (easily available in a Golden Dawn tract, edited by Sapere Aude, i.e. Wynn Westcott, and in Yeats's library), they do not trace for us the 'Miltonic' reference he apparently saw in Lady Lyttleton's broken sentences. Even if it is a loose thought about that 'evil counsellor' one feels that the editors might have intervened between the documents they adduce as of vital importance to the study of *A Vision* and the reader. *A Vision* is that 'wise man's discourse' of which Socrates says it 'is able to defend itself, and knows before whom to speak and before whom to be silent'.[16] But the editors seem to be both guarding the mysteries and in some respects adding to them. For in no sense is this a *critical* edition. It is, rather, an annotated reprint with an introductory essay on the genesis of the book. It is a photolithographic reprint of copy 513 of T. Werner Laurie's privately printed, subscribed edition of 1925. Errors in the text have not been emended, and there is no indication that the copy-text was collated with any other copies of the first edition. Line numbers have been added to aid reference to the textual notes, and there are indices and a bibliography. The paper and binding are not up to the standard of the original; the woodcuts have been printed on white paper and not the United Service Bond of the original. The upper cone of the gyre diagram on p. 177 and its annotations have been printed in black and not red. These economies are slight and are noticed. The editors apologise that their notes have been truncated because of cost, 'prohibitive to the audience for whom it was intended'. (Though who that audience is we are not told.)

The conjectural *histoire du texte* of the introduction is the indispensable basis for a critical edition. One's dissatisfaction is not with what is there but with what is not there. The edition is not true to label, and some critical imperatives for such an edition might include consideration of the status of the book as a work of art in its own right, of its importance for the student of the poet and playwright, of its relation to contemporary thinking in historiography and psychology, of its relation to astrology as practised by Yeats and of its relation in the development of his thought to its precursor, *Per Amica Silentia Lunæ*, and its successor, *A Vision* (1937).

All through Yeats's life there are examples of writings which, like the Aherne/Robartes poems, are 'texts for exposition'. This is true of 'The Tables of the Law', *Ideas of Good and Evil*, *Discoveries*, *Leo Africanus*, and the three texts of which *A Vision* (1925) represents the central exfoliation. Yeats himself avers that his instructors had developed their tale from *Per Amica*, and this is surely as true as is the notion that the text 'grew' in the spiritualist investigations of 'The Poet and the Actress', 'Swedenborg, Mediums and the Desolate Places' and *Leo Africanus.*

The editors are also discreet about the problems the book raises with respect to its successor, *A Vision* (1937). There is no discussion here of the embarrassing description of the 1925 edition to be found in the later text.

> The first version of this book . . . except the section on the twenty-eight phases, and that called 'Dove or Swan' . . . fills me with shame. I had misinterpreted the geometry, and in my ignorance of philosophy failed to understand distinctions upon which the coherence of the whole depended. (*A Vision* [1937], p. 19)

The notes generously reward the student of strategies of allusion in Yeats's self-referential writings, but do not open up the critical questions they should, for it is the responsibility of the editors of a central abstruse text, which appears to have been the poet's 'supreme fiction', to convince readers of both plays and poems of the relevance of that work to their reading. In the case of plays such as *The Only Jealousy of Emer* written, as Professor Harper tells us, out of the automatic scripts, this is a particularly urgent task. Helen Vendler's book *Yeats's 'Vision' and the Later Plays*[17] is valuable but has been out now for seventeen years.

It may seem that I ask the editors for too much and, close to this material as they are, they might well reply that I seek a big book on Yeats's religion. This is not so, for there is a crisis in the criticism of Yeats's poetry and drama which is too immediate and too perennial to be satisfied by a large study of his religion. This constant crisis is one of reading, of relating thought to imaginative writing. *A Vision* is not just a mythography out of phase; it is a philosophical drama. Unlike Hardy's *Dynasts*, it exists in what one can only call an 'exploded view'. Its chronicle is all history, its plot is all character in opposition. In reconciling 'reality and justice' it is both a comedy and a tragedy. Its psychology is a geometry, its fable a modern annex upon the many-pavilioned *Arabian Nights*. It studies the metaphor that all the world is a stage, and a stage in eternity, and the results of that study are plays which bring to the boards presences summoned by mediumship. Above all, its *dramatis personae* are the presences of his thought, his reading and his life, lifted into myth, and set to dance in some of his finest prose and comic fantasy. Though Yeats wrote of the future study of *A Vision*

> thought is nothing without action, but if [my fellow-students] will master what is most abstract and make it the foundation of their visions, the curtain may ring up on a new drama (p. xii)

we still 'crack our wits and never find the meaning'. We do not know how to read *A Vision*, and while we remain so, in Drumcliff churchyard there sleeps an untested skull.

1. *Mythologies* (London: Macmillan, 1959), p. 95.
2. *Explorations* (London: Macmillan, 1962), p. 263; *The Variorum Edition of the Poems* (New York: Macmillan, 1957), p. 479.
3. *A Vision* (1937), reissued with corrections (London: Macmillan, 1962), pp. 52–3.
4. Andrew Parkin, *The Dramatic Imagination of W. B. Yeats* (Dublin: Gill & Macmillan, 1978; New York: Barnes & Noble Books, 1978), pp. vi, 208; George Mills Harper and Walter K. Hood (eds.), *A Critical Edition of Yeats's* A Vision *(1925)* (London: Macmillan, 1978), pp. 1, 256, 108.
5. *Essays and Introductions* (London: Macmillan, 1961), pp. 192–3.
6. *The Letters of W. B. Yeats*, ed. Allan Wade (London: Hart-Davis, 1954), p. 922.
7. See T. R. Henn, *The Lonely Tower* (London: Methuen, 1950, second edn 1965) and Giorgio Melchiori, *The Whole Mystery of Art* (London: Routledge, 1960).
8. Harold Bloom, *The Anxiety of Influence* (New York: OUP., 1973), p. 96.
9. Sturm's patient attempts to footnote *A Vision* can best be followed in Richard Taylor's *Frank Pearce Sturm: His Life, Letters, and Collected Work* (Urbana, Chicago, London: University of Illinois Press, 1969).
10. *Autobiographies* (London: Macmillan, 1955), p. 467.
11. Allen R. Grossman, *Poetic Knowledge in the Early Yeats: a study of 'The Wind among the Reeds'* (Charlottesville: University of Virginia Press, 1969), esp. ch. iv.
12. Richard J. Finneran, George Mills Harper and William M. Murphy (eds.), *Letters to Yeats*, 2 vols. (London: Macmillan, 1977), I, 122.
13. *The Variorum Edition of the Plays of W. B. Yeats*, ed. Russell K. Alspach, with the assistance of Catharine C. Alspach (New York: Macmillan, 1966).
14. W. T. Horton, *The Way of the Soul: a legend in line and verse* (London: George Redway, 1910).
15. Cecil French, *Between Sun and Moon: Poems and Woodcuts* (London: Favil, 1922).
16. *Phaedrus*, para. 276. The translation is that of J. Wright, first published in 1848, and to be found in Plato, *Five Dialogues*, edited and with an introduction by A. D. Lindsay (London: Dent, 1910), p. 273.
17. Helen Hennessey Vendler, *Yeats's Vision and the Later Plays* (Cambridge, Mass.: Harvard University Press, 1963).

FORUM

Mimesis and the language of drama: a reply to Michael Anderson

ANDREW KENNEDY

In his article 'Word and image: aspects of mimesis in contemporary British theatre' (*Themes in Drama volume 2, Drama and Mimesis*, pp. 139–53) Michael Anderson makes so many points about dramatic language that indicate positions that he and I share (quite apart from his generous references to my work) that it is tempting to use this space merely to define and expand areas of agreement. However, as my main interest now is dramatic dialogue as verbal interaction in the full sense – a dialectical opposition of voices even where there is affinity – it may seem appropriate that my response should move from 'yes, *but*' to outlining a different approach.

Early on in his article, Anderson declares: 'language is of the essence of theatre . . . and attempts to displace it result in a coarsening of the dramatic effect and our response to it'. This statement, with its almost manifesto-like confidence, would probably gain assent from *most* writers, directors, actors and critics in and of the theatre. However, Anderson's follow-up argument seems to contain some uncertainties. For one thing, he gives far too much space to the modish, and almost exclusively trivial, 'Happenings' movement of the 1960s. I would argue that the *anti*-verbal movement has proved to be no more than an episode in the history of entertainment, to be chronicled with bear-baiting and performing fleas; by contrast, *non*-verbal theatre is an authentic and permanent dimension of dramatic art. By non-verbal theatre I mean, among other things, the great tradition of mime, still best exemplified by Marcel Marceau (the whole tension of role-acting epitomised in 'the mask-maker' who cannot tear off the mask from his skin) and the type of post-Dada, but profoundly humanist, theatre seen, for example, in the work of the Polish director Józef Szajna, who in a collage called *Replika* makes us feel our 'extreme condition' since Auschwitz (as in the opening scene where mannikin-like people, dressed in grey sacks, slowly crawl out from under a vast mound of refuse). Moreover, some of the most radical experimenters in physical theatre have made use of words: the Living Theatre used the Hölderlin/Brecht *Antigone* as a text for one of its word-chant-movement collages; Grotowski values his encounter with the text; and Robert Wilson has recently been reported to be using a kind of

dialogue in his far-reaching experiments in the theatre[1] (everyday conversation pointing towards the 'marvellous'). In short, non-verbal theatricality, as distinct from the rather puerile post-Artaud attacks on language
itself, deserves the constant attention of those concerned with dramatic
dialogue.

I would go further: there is, or need be, no 'quarrel' (only a creative
tension, an attunement of modes) between what Anderson calls language *in*
the theatre (words) and language *of* the theatre (image). These terms, by
the way, although neat and memorable, make me a little uneasy; I consider
that words are distinct from all other *signs* (visual/auditive) in the theatre =
distinct through being simultaneously precise and multiple in meaning,
with a grammar and vocabulary inseparable from the 'common language',
and a unique potential for interaction. If we had a clearing house of critical
terms I would propose that the word 'language' should never be used
outside (verbal) language – and if used it should be recognised as metaphorical, with compulsory scare quotes: the 'language' of movement, of scenery,
of music, etc. Having said that, I would reaffirm that the dramatist in
working on a play, and the audience in experiencing the performance of the
play, *relate* 'word' and 'image' at every level. There is a fusion or counterpoint between the verbal and visual (i) in the central metaphors of a play,
like Mother Courage's cart (which Anderson mentions among the few most
enduring images in the theatre); (ii) in the gesture that is written into the
text as counterpart to the verbal encounter (as in Cordelia's reconciliation
with Lear, where the pathos of her kneeling is inseparable from the pathos
of her speech); (iii) in the gesture dictated by the stage direction as the
counterpart, or, as in my example, the counterpoint, of an utterance (Let us
go. [*They do not move.*]). These and other levels of verbal/visual *Gesamtkunst*
should be in the foreground of our attention all the time in the study of the
dialogue in a playtext. Perhaps the director's extra-textual stage business
(interpretation through a new performance or gimmick) is not strictly our
business; but even a deliberately distortive re-creation of the text (the
Marowitz Shakespeare or *Hedda*) will teach us something, and I would
generally favour attending to variations in performance before, during, or
after close reading of any playtext.

It will be noticed that my paragraph speaks of the indissoluble unity of
word and image for the dramatist and the audience – not the critic. This
does not mean that I consider the critic to be less capable of wholeness in
vision; but criticism, like any analytic discourse printed in consecutive
sentences in an inexorable linear sequence, is not *like* the multi-dimensional
theatre experience. And some of the best criticism comes from a conscious
fencing off of the playground of discussion, a particular approach and focus,
a concern with this or that element of drama, with as precise terms as one
can manage. One would hope, therefore, that it is justifiable – morally,

intellectually, aesthetically – to concentrate on language, verbal expressiveness, provided that (i) one keeps trying to 'see the play whole' and (ii) one keeps a certain trust in the co-operative possibilities of criticism. I would put some money on a concerted attempt to understand the system of signs in the theatre, pioneered forty years ago by certain members of the Prague School of semiotics, Mukařovský, Honzl, and Veltruský.[2] In our own time and nearer home, John Russell Brown (mentioned by Anderson) has illuminated the connection between text and subtext; and J. L. Styan has, in several studies,[3] deepened our understanding of the playtext as translatable into a kind of para-language of tones, gestures, images and sounds, precariously dependent on the subjectivity of actor, director and audience. My strongest interest remains verbal interaction in dialogue. What values, what changes are being exchanged in this or that dramatic encounter? What is the structure for and the texture of a particular encounter – say an intimate duologue? Does a new dramatic convention extend or restrict the 'sayable': what speech taboos are broken and what is left unsaid when a new style of utterance is created by a dramatist? These are some of the questions I intend to work on in a longer study.

It was, then, particularly interesting to see Anderson begin his article with two passages of naturalistic dialogue, which he proceeded to discuss in terms of both interpersonal meaning and language. That is a valid form of criticism, much needed in the often far too high-toned study of dramatic language. The 'crisis of language' thesis, to which Anderson returns, is an example of the latter. I may have contributed my share to the 'argument from crisis' in *Six Dramatists*,[4] but then it was a hypothesis (not a thesis), a guiding question: what happens to language in drama when it is written under almost intolerable pressures of language-consciousness? The conclusion, or part of it, was that the 'crisis of language' had itself become a condition of creativity; and I am pleased that Anderson has selected for quotation: 'the idea of the failure of language has served Beckett as a myth *for* creation'. To understand the 'fall of language' myth we need a complex understanding of our whole cultural history, as well as of the proponents of the myth from Vico to Hofmannsthal, Eliot, Beckett, and George Steiner; and we need a very precise grasp of what to read as signs of strain in the language of a particular text. For me the most problematic dramatic language is still what I call the new *mannerism*, as in late Pinter.[5] The prevalence of what Lloyd Evans calls the 'vernacular', as distinct from a 'literary', idiom worries me much less; and I do not think that a wholesale decline of contemporary drama can be deduced from a fear of the demotic.[6] What we need is clear and, as far as possible, shared criteria for understanding the difference between the 'stuff' and the 'shaping' of language. The 'stuff' – whether demotic or hieratic – is not our principal concern; what matters is whether and how the linguistic raw material is shaped into a dramatic language, distinct voices and rhythms for a precise vision of interacting persons.

With this interest in 'shaping' in mind, I would like to add a few pages based on a paper on dramatic dialogue[7] which asks a general question: how does 'speech' come to be 'writing' in the finished playtext? Underlying that question is a still wider one: how does *mimesis* in dramatic dialogue differ from reproduction (the tape-recorded transcript) of ordinary language, and from any narrow view of representation?

Dramatic dialogue is a unique mode of verbal expression, fusing what we often think of as opposites, the spoken and the written language. (That opposition was also stressed by Roland Barthes in his essay on style.[8]) I shall call the total dialogue of a playtext *the play-language* to distinguish it both from the spoken (everyday) language and from the major modes of written/literary language (including the dialogue sequences in an unperformed novel or poem). The play-language is fictive and fixed, coming between the fluid speech (1) spoken in our lived world and the precarious fixed/fluid speech (2) spoken by the actors in performance. The play-language is not just written but it has the tension between speech (1) and speech (2) written into its text, thus:

SPEECH (1)	PLAY-LANGUAGE	SPEECH (2)
spoken/actual	written/fictive	spoken/fictive
half-formed	formed	performed
fluid	fixed	fixed/fluid

My present concern is with the first arrow, the way writing uses, selects and transforms portions of 'raw' speech, rather than with the second arrow, the significant speech-act that occurs when the dialogue spoken by the actors is overheard by the audience.

Not long ago a television production of an Ibsen play in Norwegian brought home to me the fact that the general public tends to assume a virtual identity between the play-language and speech (1). The text of *John Gabriel Borkman* had been changed by the producer to bring the dialogue up to date. I became particularly interested in just one small change: the colloquial *du* (you familiar) was substituted for the formal, and no longer spoken, personal pronoun *eder* in the great final scene of the play where the materially and spiritually bankrupt Borkman turns from his loving companion, Ella, and declares his love, not to her, but to the normally less intimate spirits of the mines. What Ibsen had written seemed doubly significant: for the style-shift in the personal pronoun underlined the shift from personal dialogue to an almost solipsistic monologue, from intimate encounter to an ego-centred death-wish. The producer's change in the text weakened the significance. (Small beer, compared with giving Rebecca in the television *Rosmersholm* a low-cut dressing gown and sensual look to suggest there was no sex-taboo between Rebecca and Rosmer – a total change in the conception of Ibsen's play.) However, the small verbal change in the text of *Borkman* was enough for me to see it as an advertisement of the *conversational fallacy*: the view that the play-language is made up of ordinary conversations, and if it is not, it ought to be, for the greater enlightenment of the television audience. I admit that this occasion revived in me a certain awe for what *is written* – note the biblical undertone.

The naturalistic play-language from Ibsen on provides, I think, a direct point of entry into studying the speech/writing relationship. For Ibsen was the first dramatist to practise, in a conscious poetics, 'the very much more difficult art of *writing* the genuine, plain language *spoken* in real life'. In the present context the word 'writing' – or rather the tension in the phrase 'writing ... the language spoken in real life' – seems to stand out as never before. Ibsen did not pretend that he was going to invest in an early phonograph, and reproduce the structures and sequences of conversation recorded. On the contrary, he wrote a colloquially-based but highly-shaped dialogue, at once severely logical and imagistic. The conversational fallacy, which considered Ibsen and post-Ibsen dialogue as a kind of replica of speech (1), was launched by the critics – roundheads, like William Archer, celebrating 'pure imitation', and the cavalier critics, like Eliot and Raymond Williams, deploring the same. (Eliot once said that Ibsen characters 'do not even talk prose, but merely make human noises'.[9]) In our own time, Pinter has been praised for his 'tape-recording ear', despite all the evidence that his main interest is, precisely, in *shaping* dialogue, often with a mannerist dislocation and word-consciousness. And it is worth noting how often reviewers say something like this about the dialogue of a play: 'conversation so naturalistic that it seems to have been taped'.[10] True, in this instance the reviewer, Irving Wardle of *The Times*, went on to say that this effect is an illusion – I would say it is a deliberate illusion in any play-language.

Before going on to demonstrate this, I should like to reflect briefly on the peculiar status of the naturalistic playtext. For a start, we may place it between the fully literary text and the scenario. Purged, from all the most palpable features of the *literary* text – the metric of verse, the lyrical and rhetorical conventions of speech, tropes and figures, the broadly epic or choric modes of narration, the set speech, the soliloquy, and so on – the reduced writing wishes to exhibit itself as 'mere' speech. It may even be said that the single most significant discovery of naturalistic drama – in its poetics as distinct from its politics – is the discovery of ordinary speech. The almost inexhaustible wells of raw speech – all that speech-oil – would supply the energy needs of drama for a century or so. It would supply an immense range and variety of individual speech: slang, jargon, dialect, idiolect, every sort of idiomatic and even idiotic idiosyncrasy of speech. It would use what could be heard and overheard: from Gaev in *The Cherry Orchard* muttering 'I pot into the corner pocket' to the tense quarrel over the phrase 'light the kettle' in Pinter's *The Dumb Waiter*. As the written text shrinks, the subtext increases in significance: unpoetic words, syllables, 'oh', 'ah', 'on', may decide destinies. A principle of 'less is more' is written into the naturalistic playtext: less writing means more implied text; less words for speech means more unspoken speech. I may add, parenthetically, that this new significance of ordinary speech opened up the way not only to later documentary or film and television naturalism but also, as a conscious reaction against 'talk', to the post-Artaud physical theatre. So, on the one hand, we have the minimal speech of the scenario; on the other, something like the wholly invented collage-lingo of *Orghast at Persepolis* (directed by Peter Brook and wrought, hardly written, by Ted Hughes), or the radiophonic thriller without dialogue, made up of sounds alone, using 'the naturalistic recording techniques of the binaural stereo'.[11]

Just because the naturalistic and ultra-naturalistic playtext *seems*, for the first time in the history of drama, to use ordinary speech – speech (1) – directly, it can serve to show that even such a reduced play-language is not 'raw' but 'cooked' to a high degree. Speech (1) is controlled and transformed (i) by the structures of interaction, the interplay of what is said by characters within precise formal and emotional limits; (ii) by verbal and rhythmic *shaping*; (iii) by what I shall call *counter-speech*; (iv) by complexity of speech texture. The first and last of these, the structure of interaction and complexity of texture, are, respectively, too large in scale and too intricate in detail to be dealt with in a short paper. (Complexity of speech texture can be seen in almost any dialogue sequence in Beckett's *Endgame* or Pinter's *The Homecoming*.) Here I am concerned only with shaping and counter-speech.

The shaping of speech into a play-language can be read and heard in some of the simplest, most directly colloquial and mimetic texts. Take this exchange from one of Pinter's revue sketches, *The Black and White*, where we are, as it were, overhearing the conversation of two old women in an all-night café:

Second woman. Yes, there's not too much noise.
First woman. There's always a bit of noise.
Second woman. Yes, there's always a bit of life.

Here the rhythmic pattern seems to emerge from within the données of a casual exchange, from its banal repetition of words and phrases: 'Too much noise' – 'a bit of noise' – 'a bit of life'. I say *seems*, for the shaping is there in the writing. Or consider this brief group dialogue of four youths from Edward Bond's *Saved* (1965) (which still tends to be remembered for the cruel stoning of a baby in a pram):

Mike. Wass 'e doing?
Colin. Pullin' its 'air.
Fred. 'E'll 'ave its 'ol woman after 'im.
Mike. Poor sod.
Barry. 'E's showin' off.
Colin. 'E wants the coroner's medal.
Mike [*comes to the pram*]. Less see yer do it. (Scene 6)

Clearly, the exchanges here build up in a crescendo pattern, and have a degree of compression that springs from the shaping. A stylistic description in the manner of Roman Jacobson would yield pages, perhaps, on the rhyme-like effect created by the repetition of 'e'; a chorus of voices pointing to the fifth boy, Pete, who is the first to torture that baby. Further, the dialogue is not only compressed, it is also coherent: it articulates, to a degree, the inarticulacy of the hooligans' speech. Not only does the design of the group dialogue make the sequence of speeches cohere, but the individual speech, the *patois* of the tough youths, is also rounded out, in, for example, the black wit of a line like: ' 'E wants the coroner's medal.' In their actual speech we would find more noise, hesitation, muttering, cross-talk, repetition, irrelevance, in short, verbal waste. Apart from trusting our own ears, we can turn to the description of tape-recorded conversations, made by David Crystal and Derek Davy in *Investigating English Style* (1969).[12] That study confirms that ordinary conversation is highly inarticulate: the jumbled-up syntax, the fumbling for words, the gaps, overlaps, useless repetitions, blurs, nonsense, and so on. So, the linguistic evidence supports what we can see and hear: the extent of shaping undergone by speech (1) even in its seemingly close imitation in a play-language.

I turn now to *counter-speech*: the simple yet subtle juxtaposition of different modes of speech written into the play-language. We can see this, first of all, in the shifting speech-styles of traditional poetic drama. Shakespeare remains our supreme example. In the opening scenes of *Macbeth* we find, in rapid succession: the witches' spell with their four-beat couplets, the martial rhetoric of the Captain as Messenger, the oracular speech of the witches' prophecy to Macbeth, the first intimate duologue (between Macbeth and Banquo, leading to an imagistic soliloquy), then broadly public or forensic speech as King Duncan enters, the prose text of the letter to be read aloud, Lady Macbeth's incantatory or magical speech, 'Come you spirits' – all within the same play-language, and still only a section of the total play-language. No doubt other dramatists, Racine among them, are more univocal (to use Fergusson's old term). But speech modes are opposed even in Racine: Phèdre and Hyppolite, for instance, seem alien to each other in their speech which reflects alien visions of the world.

In naturalistic drama, counter-speech is of a different order. As it can no longer display a rich tapestry of speech woven out of different *conventions* of speech style, it displays a gallery of speech *types*. Panoramic plays, like Hauptmann's *The Weavers*, Gorky's *The Lower Depths*, O'Neill's *The Iceman Cometh*, fill their precise local worlds with a mass of speakers (each limited in his or her own type of speech) to portray the varieties of social and personal ethos. But the dramatist controls them all, connecting and counterpointing. A play by Chekhov, we briefly recall, gains much of its verbal power from the harmonies written out of – and into – so many contrasted and 'peculiar' ways of speaking. Above and across the individual speech of this or that character, all the time we can hear the interplay of speech types in a subtle form of super-speech, written into the play-language.

In contemporary drama, especially in Beckett and Pinter, counter-speech is again significant: think only of the sudden entrance of Lucky in *Waiting for Godot*. How powerful is the collision between the music-hall based repartee of the two *clochards* and Lucky's aphasiac speech (metaphysical ruins no longer propped up by grammar). In the present context, Lucky's speech may be linked with two points already made. As counter-speech it has the violent poetic incoherence of Poor Tom in *King Lear*, when he bursts into a natural dialogue with: 'Frateretto calls me, and tells me Nero is an angler in the Lake of Darkness' (III, vi). And though never heard before – that is, never heard as speech (1) – Lucky's speech is at once accepted as an integral part of Beckett's play-language. As pathological speech (comparable to Poor Tom's speech) it offers an extreme example of the character imprisoned in his own type of speech. Beyond that particular and terrible fixity of individual speech, there is no speech, no counter-speech, for him. But then, even Hamlet, linguistic genius and chameleon poet as he is, has limitations clearly marked: he can, for example, hardly speak the plain language that comes so naturally to Horatio. Hamlet could not have written the play *Hamlet* any more than Lucky could have written *Waiting for Godot*. The opposite of the character condemned to a fixity, a perpetual mimesis of his own speech scale, is the dramatist whose multivocal play-language counterpoints a vast variety of individual speech.

NOTES

1. Jerzy Grotowski, *Towards a Poor Theatre* (London: Eyre Methuen, 1976), pp. 56–7; Roger Planchon, 'Wilson at the TNP: poet of the otherworld', reprinted from *Le Monde* in *The Guardian Weekly*, 25 November 1979, p. 13.
2. Some of the key articles by these critics are included in Ladislav Matejka and Irwin R. Titunik (eds.), *Semiotics of Art, Prague School Contributions* (Cambridge, Mass., and London: MIT Press, 1976).
3. J. L. Styan, *The Elements of Drama* (Cambridge University Press, 1960), and *Drama, Stage and Audience* (Cambridge University Press, 1975).

4. *Six Dramatists in Search of a Language* (Cambridge University Press, 1975).

5. See Andrew Kennedy, 'Natural, Mannered and Parodic Dialogue' in *The Yearbook of English Studies, Theatrical Literature Special Number*, ed. G. K. Hunter and C. J. Rawson, 9 (1979), 28–54, esp. 45–9.

6. Gareth Lloyd Evans, *The Language of Modern Drama* (London: J. M. Dent & Sons, 1977) (also discussed in Michael Anderson's article). For my review see *The Yearbook of English Studies*, 9, 351–2.

7. 'Writing v. Speech in Dramatic Dialogue', read, in a somewhat different form, at the xivth FILLM Congress, Aix-en-Provence, 31 August 1978.

8. Roland Barthes, 'Style and its Image', in *Literary Style, a Symposium*, ed. Seymour Chapman (London and New York: OUP, 1971). Barthes writes: 'the opposition of speech and writing has never been completely clarified' (p. 7). He sees this opposition inherent both in philosophy (different ontologies of speech and writing) and in linguistics (it has a lot to say about sentences, but little about 'subsentence' language).

9. T. S. Eliot, 'The Need for Poetic Drama', *The Listener*, 25 November 1936, p. 995. William Archer's views are well known and can be seen in summary form in *The Old Drama and the New* (London, 1923), pp. 24–5. Raymond Williams's anti-naturalism was most marked in the first version of *Drama from Ibsen to Eliot* (London: Chatto & Windus, 1952).

10. *The Times*, 29 July 1978.

11. See: *Radio Times*, 31 July 1978, introducing *The Revenge* by Andrew Sachs.

12. David Crystal and Derek Davy, *Investigating English Style* (London: Longman, 1976), part ii, ch. 4. See also my *Six Dramatists in Search of a Language*, p. xii and p. 168, n. 8.

A note on mimesis:
Stanislavski's and Brecht's street scenes

GERALDINE COUSIN

The fundamental aim of our art is the creation of [the] inner life of a human spirit, and its expression in an artistic form. (Stanislavski[1])

The Philosopher: What interests me about your theatre is the fact that you apply your art and your whole apparatus to imitating incidents that take place between people, with the result that one feels one is in the presence of real life. As I'm interested in the way people live together I'm interested in your imitation of it too. (Brecht[2])

In 'Culture', the first of the 'Clare Poems', Edward Bond defines art as 'whatever looks closely / In the human face'.[3] In a very obvious way theatre draws its inspiration from observing the human face, but the observation can be carried out in a variety of ways. The playwright and the actor may look closely only into the face they will imitate, or they may focus also on elements of the environment which underline the reasons for the face's expression. Two incidents, one from Stanislavski's *An Actor Prepares* (pp. 161–2), the other from Brecht's poem, 'On Everyday Theatre',[4] serve as a useful focus for considering the ways in which these two theatre practitioners observed the human face and consequently the kinds of imitation of human experience they produced.

The Stanislavski incident is taken from chapter 9, 'Emotion Memory'. Kostya, the young student, is returning home when he sees a large group of people. He pushes his way to the front, and finds that he is a witness of the results of a street accident. The victim, an old man, has been killed by a tram. Stanislavski depicts the scene with a grim physicality:

At my feet lay an old man, poorly dressed, his jaw crushed, both arms cut off. His face was ghastly; his old yellow teeth stuck out through his bloody mustache. A street car towered over its victim . . . Not far away some children were playing. One of them came across a bit of bone from the man's hand. Not knowing how to dispose of it he threw it in an ash can. (p. 161)

The horrifying images are what first impress themselves upon the mind of the reader. Kostya describes the event as a 'street scene', but its effect is rather that of a tableau. Neither Kostya nor the reader learns anything of the events leading up to the accident. 'The conductor was fussing with the machinery to show what was wrong with it, and why he was not to blame.' The crowd, with the exception of one weeping woman, look on 'with indifference and curiosity'. The scene, largely isolated from past and future, lacking cause and effect, is sharply delineated, frozen, focused on the present moment.

   The chapter of *An Actor Prepares* from which the incident is taken explores the phenomenon of emotion memory and its usefulness to the actor. Emotion memory is 'that type of memory which makes you relive the sensations you once felt...' (p. 158). Through the use of emotion memory the actor attempts to discover within himself feelings that are analogous to those experienced by the character the actor is playing. It is a means of helping the actor to build up the inner life of the character. Stanislavski refers to it as archive material, which the actor can use as a spur to imagination. In *An Actor Prepares*, Stanislavski, through the medium of Kostya, uses the event of the street accident in an attempt to understand more fully the workings of emotion memory. Kostya wakes during the night following the accident, and finds 'the visual memory' of what he has seen 'even more terrifying than the sight of the accident itself had been' (p. 161). He ascribes this intensification of the initial experience to the 'emotion memory and its power to deepen impressions' (*ibid.*). As the days pass the incident grows remote, an excuse for philosophising. A week later Kostya once again passes the scene of the accident, but the blood and the ampu-tated limbs have been replaced by snow, and Kostya speculates on the nature of life and death, and of eternity. The brutal immediacy of the initial experience has been dissipated, but there is a rider to the event – two in fact. Eventually, the street car comes to dominate Kostya's memory of the accident, but, strangely, it is not the actual vehicle, but one taken from an earlier memory. More important, I think, is the fact that, when Kostya thinks back to one aspect of the accident:

> A man in a white uniform, with his overcoat thrown over his shoulders, was listlessly dabbing the dead man's nostrils with a bit of cotton on which he poured something out of a bottle. (*Ibid.*)

another image, again from an earlier, but different memory, is transposed upon it:

> It was long ago – I came upon an Italian, leaning over a dead monkey on the sidewalk. He was weeping and trying to push a bit of orange rind into the animal's mouth. (p. 162)

Kostya finds to his surprise that it is this earlier and seemingly less terrible incident that is more deeply impressed upon his memory, and that, if he were required to re-enact the scene of the accident, it is in this earlier event that he would search for emotional inspiration 'rather than in the tragedy itself' (p. 163).

The incident of the Italian and the monkey highlights a problem which Stanislavski was to tackle firmly later in his career, the fact that emotion memory is not directly accessible to conscious control. It also serves to illustrate the way in which the emotion memory frequently retains single, sharply focused cameos, rather than broad, panoramic visual memories of the entire event. The incident of the accident and that of the weeping Italian are in essence emotion memories. They remain in the mind of the reader clearly delineated, yet curiously unattached. As with personal emotion memories, what is retained is the individual detail – the children playing with the dead hand, the Italian trying to put the rind into the dead animal's mouth. The straightforward imitation of the details of these events would not constitute a piece of theatre, but they do serve as a source of inspiration for those who make theatre. Stanislavski, as Brecht himself pointed out,[5] was first and foremost an actor when he directed just as Brecht was first and foremost a playwright, and it is Stanislavski, the actor, who looks at the street accident and the weeping Italian and wonders how they can be used.

Brecht also looks carefully at the event to be imitated to see how best it can be used, but his definition of usefulness is different from Stanislavski's. Part of his poem, 'On Everyday Theatre', is also concerned with a street accident: 'Take that man on the corner: he is showing how / An accident took place',[6] he writes, and immediately demonstrates a characteristic way of looking at events. Kostya concentrated on physical images of horror and speculations as to the nature of fate, but in Brecht's poem there is no severed hand, no bleeding torso. Instead a bystander gets up in front of the crowd and re-enacts the event. He shows what took place, how the driver held the wheel, how the victim moved; and he does these things for a clear and definite purpose, to demonstrate clearly to the crowd the cause of the accident. The spectators cannot look on 'curious and indifferent' as in the incident from *An Actor Prepares*. They must pass judgement on the event, understand not only what happened but why, and how it might have been prevented.

In 'On Everyday Theatre', Brecht presents the actor with various models for imitation: he shows that acting is, in itself, nothing special. Every day men and women re-enact events, and they do so, like the witness of the accident, for specific reasons. It is this purposefulness, this utility of theatre that Brecht asks the actor to search out. The bystander demonstrating the accident is exemplary. In a variety of ways he teaches the usefulness of imitation: he shows the ways in which theatre can look constructively in the human face.

'Everyday Theatre' is first and foremost not a theatre of empathy. The actor is concerned that what he shows should be believable, and so he imitates the event with care, but he only shows as much as is necessary so that the event will be clearly understood. So the victim is only 'apparently'[7] an old man. It is not important that the spectators should be shown a fully delineated character; only those qualities in him that contributed to the accident are of importance. The demonstrator knows nothing of the characters he is imitating except their actions: he demonstrates these actions 'and so allows conclusions to be drawn about them'.[8] The accident need not have happened. Both driver and victim could have behaved differently, and the street actor goes on to show how the accident could have been avoided. Stanislavski does not consider the possibility of avoidance. He speaks fatalistically of the towering street car which moves unstoppably, like eternity. Worked on by Kostya's emotion memory, the street car takes on the menacing, unconnected quality of a dream object, its threat assignable to no obvious cause. When Kostya returns to the scene of the accident after a few days have elapsed, the ground is covered with snow which obliterates all traces of the accident. Street car and snow are both strongly tinged with a fatalistic view of life, but for Brecht 'the snowstorms have hats on',[9] the street car has a driver and man is his own fate.

> Have you really
> Not yet heard it is now common knowledge
> That this net was knotted and cast by men?[10]

Brecht's street actor does not show actions as deriving unavoidably from the characters who perform them. The character is for him of secondary importance to the action. In this way the actor questions the cause of action.

Not only does the street actor focus on the action rather than the character, but his performance is 'essentially repetitive',[11] he shows the incident as one which has already happened. His action is a replay, and it is offered as such. In this way he presents not the incident itself, but a demonstration of it. Theatre for Brecht must follow the example of the street actor and admit its essential artificiality. It then becomes possible to define the purpose of the imitation of 'the incidents that take place between people'. The imitation is of value only in so far as it furthers the spectator's understanding of the event which is being imitated. In order to help the spectator to consider critically what is being presented to him, Brecht turns the lights full on: he stresses the artificiality of the theatre. Stanislavski devoted a lifetime to the search for a means of focusing the actors' attention away from what he thinks of as the black hole of the auditorium. The basis of his continual struggle to develop a systematic method of training for actors was the fact that inspiration cannot be relied upon, and the consequent necessity of a structure which the actor can fall back on. A good deal of his work was devoted to exercises to help the actors to focus attention on the 'I am' of their roles, and the concomitant part of this was the focusing away from the auditorium. The spectators assist the theatrical event, but they do so silently and anonymously. Essentially they are passive. It is perhaps not too fanciful to see in the still, indifferent crowd around Kostya an embodiment of those aspects of an audience which actors fear, and which Stanislavski worked to give actors a means of coping with during those performances when inspiration is lacking. Brecht is concerned primarily with the illumination of the spectator's understanding rather than with the actor's sources of inspiration, and for this reason he turns on the lights in the theatre, considering that theatre should be a place of enlightenment rather than a 'home of dreams'.[12]

Stanislavski's concentration on the 'I am' of a part, and the fact that actors and spectators tacitly agree to disregard the fact that they are sitting in a theatre does not mean that the present moment in the theatre is cut off from a past and future. I have stressed the separate, isolated quality of the street accident in *An Actor Prepares* and examples of emotion memory in general, but emotion memory is simply one tool of the actor. It is a means of helping the actor to understand more fully from his own experience the character he is playing, but by the time the play reaches performance these aids will have been removed like scaffolding once the building is complete. The actor, if he has been successful, will have understood the logic of the sequence of actions, and through this, the superobjective of the play. Although the actor is always focused on the 'I am', this contains all the past moments and possible future ones of his role, and this, together with experience of the superobjective, gives the play dimensionality.[13]

Brecht's stressing of the need for the actor to demonstrate the fact that he repeats an event which has already taken place[14] is different in emphasis from Stanislavski's notion that all past and possible future moments of the role are contained in the actor's 'I am'. In 'Portrayal of Past and Present in One', the first of 'Four Theatre Poems', Brecht amplifies the concept of showing, of acting in the third person. The actor must always perform as though what he portrays were 'Happening now and just the once'.[15] That is taken for granted, but it is not sufficient:

> To act in this way
> Is habitual with you, and now I am advising you
> To ally this habit with yet another: that is, that your acting should
> At the same time express the fact that this instant
> On your stage is often repeated; only yesterday
> You were acting it, and tomorrow too
> Given spectators, there will be a further performance.
> Nor should you let the Now blot out the
> Previously and Afterwards, nor for that matter whatever
> Is even now happening outside the theatre and is similar in kind
> Nor even things that have nothing to do with it all – none of this
> Should you allow entirely to be forgotten.[16]

Brecht stresses always the relatedness of the theatrical event to events taking place around it. The present moment of stage action is shown to be part of a sequence of moments within the play and also part of the world beyond the play. In this way the spectator comes to understand the present moment more fully, and to question it in the light of his own experience.

The street actor in 'On Everyday Theatre' 'repeats' his performance but he does so with great care and precision. He has observed the accident carefully and he re-enacts it thoughtfully. Sometimes he will stop, and repeat what he has just done. If he is unsure of the course of events, he will ask the advice of another witness of the accident. Observation is the art that Brecht requires actors to master before all others.[17] From this comes the capability of seeing each event afresh, and of comparing what happened with what might have happened.

The constant ability to see things anew is also vital to Stanislavski, but it is used differently. In *An Actor Prepares*, Tortsov praises Kostya for his powers of observation and recall of the accident. The Stanislavskian actor uses his powers of observation to build up a series of images which, along with examples of emotion memory, become part of the archive material on which he can draw to create a role. Brecht's street demonstrator shows his re-enactment of the accident to spectators who may not have seen the incident, or who, if they have seen it, may not agree with the depiction of events. What is important is that the actor demonstrates the driver and the victim in such a way that the spectators can form an opinion of the incident. The Stanislavskian actor uses his powers of observation primarily for himself as an aid in building his character. The Brechtian actor observes incidents with astonishment, and depicts them in such a way that the spectator also sees them as new and astounding. Seen in this light, the world becomes capable of change. Brecht's street actor has observed and shows with care because his performance will have real and tangible results. It may decide where blame is to be affixed, or affect the amount of compensation the victim receives. Brecht advises actors to strive for a theatre which, likewise, can intervene in the world. Stanislavski, too, mentions compensation, the probably inadequate amount that the victim's family will receive, but he mentions it fatalistically. It is part of a course of events which, like the unstoppable street car, is predetermined.

Brecht asks actors to observe particularly one very important thing about the street demonstrator, the fact that:

> this imitator
> Never loses himself in his imitation. He never entirely
> Transforms himself into the man he is imitating.[18]

The demonstrator '*repeats* a real-life incident', and 'he *quotes* his lines'.[19] He acts in the third person, and by eschewing complete transformation into his role he further aids the critical response of the spectator. He does not encourage the audience to feel what the character he is showing feels:

> (It can feel anger where the character feels joy, and so on. It is free, and sometimes even encouraged, to imagine a different course of events or to try and find one, and so forth.)[20]

The problem of the degree to which an actor transforms himself into his role is a difficult one, chiefly, I think, because the actor while performing is to a greater or lesser degree in a heightened emotional state, and so to describe the sensation of performing clearly is difficult. For this reason confusion has arisen as the terms used are imprecise. Stanislavski did not advise an actor to transform himself totally into his role. Indeed he warned of the dangers of this:

> *Never lose yourself on the stage. Always act in your own person, as an artist. You can never get away from yourself. The moment you lose yourself on the stage marks the departure from truly living your part and the beginning of exaggerated false acting.*[21]

However great the actor's understanding of and sympathy with the part, his feelings remain his own. They are analogous with the part, but they belong not to the part but to the actor. He employs the magic 'if':

> Throughout the performance we see a man, *not who becomes Hamlet, but who places himself in Hamlet's situation* ...[22]

Brecht himself understood that Stanislavski did not advocate the complete transformation of the actor into his part, and acknowledged the fact that epic theatre is 'not interested in the *complete* exclusion of identification'.[23] It is a matter of the degree of identification. Stanislavski stresses the dangers of losing oneself in a part. The actor must remain conscious of his actual surroundings and identity whilst giving form to the inner and outward vision of the play, but actor and audience agree to abide by the magic 'if'. Once that is established, all else follows, and the audience accept the man who places himself in Hamlet's situation as Hamlet for the duration of the play. The actor remains within his role. That is the nature of the contract which is established between actor and audience. The epic actor exploits the discrepancy between himself and his role. In this he learns from the street actor who will halt his performance to establish that he is demonstrating correctly and to answer a question put by one of the spectators. He doesn't cast a spell over his audience: he remains 'not the subject, but the demonstrator'.[24] Though the spectator may sympathise with the subject, the demonstrative nature of the performance discourages empathy and encourages the spectator to take a critical attitude to what is being shown.

The vexed problem of transformation is further elucidated by the attitudes of Brecht and Stanislavski to the use of masks. In chapter 1 of *Building a Character*, Tortsov proposes that the class at their next lesson hold a masquerade: 'Each student will prepare an external characterization and mask himself in it' (p. 10).[25] Kostya finds an old morning coat of an unusual material and colour which attracts his attention. He feels that if he adds a hat, gloves, make-up and wig, '... in the same colour and tones as the material – all greyish, yellowish, greenish, faded and shadowy, one would get a sinister, yet somehow familiar effect' (p. 11). However, exactly what this effect will be he cannot discover, and when the make-up man covers his face with a conventional make-up he despairs of ever discovering the secret. Realising the pointlessness of continuing the search, he reaches for the greenish removal cream and begins to smear it over his face; and, as he does so, his face becomes a similar colour to that of his costume, his features blur and become indistinct, and he discovers the character for whom he has been searching. It is the critic who lives within himself, a peevish, carping figure; and, hidden behind the mask of his role, Kostya can say and do things which in his own personality would be impossible for him. For Stanislavski, '... a characterization is the mask which hides the actor-individual. Protected by it-he can lay bare his soul down to the last intimate detail' (p. 30).

Brecht, on the other hand, draws attention to the mask as a mask. Actors, as he points out, are not the only people who use masks. Street hawkers also mask themselves when showing their wares. One will try on a hat, fix on a moustache, demonstrate the use of a cane in order to present a man of the world, but he does not become the character he demonstrates. He refers to him all the time in the third person. In this way he shows his own face side by side with the mask. He does not create hidden behind the mask; instead he, as it were, holds the mask in his hand and demonstrates the discrepancy between the face he re-enacts and his own face.

Thus, Brecht's actor observes the everyday life of the street and learns the purpose of the imitation he engages in nightly. He may perform with greater skill than the street actor. His mask may be 'grandly conceived',[26] far beyond the scope of the street hawker and his wares, but, if his theatre has less meaning and utility than that of the street, it fails. If the actor retains the model of everyday theatre always before him, then constantly his 'playacting / Harks back to practical matters'.[27]

Theatre in Brecht's terms concerns itself most successfully with practical matters when it is focused firmly on the action, the thing done. The characters derive from the action, not vice versa. The event is not used as the excuse to further enlighten the audience as to the motives of the characters; instead, the characters have shape and solidity only in so far as this is necessary for the understanding of the event. Brecht himself has highlighted the similarities between his own focus on 'the plot, the event' and the method of physical action[28] which Stanislavski developed late in his career, and which is outlined in *Creating a Role*.[29] Throughout his entire career Stanislavski sought to balance the outward image of the play and its inner life. As a director he had a love of, and a gift for the spectacular, and his early productions were outwardly brilliant, inventive, packed full of imaginative detail. Increasingly, however, he felt them to be hollow, lacking in true expression of the inner content of the author's work. As an actor he felt the same over-reliance on the external in his work. In *My Life in Art*, he formulates the problem for himself in the following way:

> What do you feel? The physically outward image or the fundamental spiritual feeling of the role? The idea for the sake of which the poet wrote the play?[30]

Stanislavski devoted the rest of his life to the constant search for a system which would provide actors with a concrete base from which to explore the author's intentions, and to bring to life his artistic creation. In the early stages of his work, reacting against what he considered to be too great a concentration on the outward, physical aspects of production, Stanislavski used all his ingenuity to develop exercises to build up the actors' psychotechnique and in this way to help them to understand the inner essence of their roles. Towards the end of his life, however, Stanislavski advised beginning not with the emotional, inner life of the character, but with the actions of the character, the plot of the play. This reversal of his former ideas is more apparent than real. It comes from the perception that emotions and feelings are not separable from physical actions. Stanislavski came to view the physical and psychological natures of man as indivisible, and to believe that it was simpler and more effective to begin with the physical objectives of a role. Through the performing of these in a variety of proposed circumstances the actor gradually builds up a simultaneous understanding of the inner and outer action of the play.

> The bond between the body and the soul is indivisible. The life of the one engenders the life of the other, either way around. In every *physical action*, unless it is purely mechanical, there is concealed some *inner action*, some feelings.[31]

Through work on the separate physical actions of his role the actor builds up 'the *line of physical being*',[32] and it is this understanding of the logic of the play's action which leads to his realisation of the superobjective.

An understanding of the unity of the physical and the psychological in a role is apparent in Stanislavski's earlier writing although it is not stressed. For example, in *An Actor Prepares*, he tells a story of two men marooned on a rock (p. 157). Afterwards they remember the event from opposing view-points: one remembers only what he did, the other what he felt. At the time of writing, Stanislavski prizes the example of the second man over that of the first. It is he that in Stanislavski's terms possesses a developed emotion memory, and, in his persona of Tortsov, Stanislavski holds up this man as a model worthy of imitation. However, if the students' emotion memories are insufficiently developed to enable them to recall events with this kind of emotional clarity, then Stanislavski advises them to play the physical scheme of the action hoping that in this way they will release the emotional content of the event. The emphasis is different from the method of physical action: Stanislavski still considers the outward image as being of less value than the inner, and fails to grasp what he later came to see as the psychophysical nature of performance.

Another, and slightly earlier example from *An Actor Prepares* (pp. 142–7), reveals a greater dependence on the physical aspect of a role. Dasha, one of the students, is asked to play a scene from *Brand* in which a young woman finds an abandoned child, and decides to keep it, only to watch it die in her arms. Her performance of the sequence is so truthful that the other students who are watching are moved to tears. Unbeknown to everyone except Kostya, Dasha has herself previously given birth to an illegitimate child, which died, and it is this painful personal experience which has given her the understanding necessary to play the role with such fervour. However, when Dasha attempts to repeat the performance she is unable to do so. She considers the units and objectives of the piece, builds up a sequence of 'imaginative inventions' (p. 144), but all to no purpose. Her playing is lifeless. Stanislavski then takes her back not to what she felt during the first performance, but to what she did. When the physical scheme is clear, he reintroduces Dasha to the emotions which informed her playing the first time. This time Dasha performs well, but without her initial fervour. Then accidentally, Stanislavski hits on Dasha's own early history. 'If you had a child which died, how would you feel?' he asks; and this time Dasha's portrayal of the scene is even better than her first attempt. Kostya questions the value of this. Isn't it the case that Dasha's performance was the result of Stanislavski's suggestion, which happened to coincide with the truth of her own life, rather than the technical means by which Stanislavski had helped her to recreate her original performance through a 'scheme of physical actions' (p. 146). Tortsov agrees with this, but explains the necessity of introducing the correct imaginative stimulus at the moment of maximum impact. Work on the physical actions of the role prepares the actor and helps him to be receptive to stimulus when it offers itself.

In the method which he elaborates in *Creating a Role*, Tortsov–Stanislavski uses physical actions as a key to the understanding of the role and the play. The point, as he explains, 'does not lie in these small, realistic actions but in the whole creative sequence which is put into effect thanks to the impulse given by these physical actions' (p. 238). Kostya queries Tortsov's request that he begin with the plot rather than with an attempt to understand his character's motivation:

> You say convey the plot and the simplest physical actions, ... But the plot is conveyed by itself as the play unfolds. The plot was made by the author.

Tortsov replies:

> Yes, by him and not by you. Let his plot remain. What is needed is your attitude toward it. (p. 215)

It is hardly surprising that Brecht seizes on the overriding concern with physical action as the point at which his method and Stanislavski's come closest. Brecht himself begins rehearsals with 'the plot, the event'. He requires his actors not only to have an attitude to the plot, but to reveal it through the way they perform.

The nature of the performer is, as Brecht states, a double one. He is, at the same time, 'both actor and character and this contradiction takes precedence in his consciousness'.[33] Brecht stresses the importance of the superobjective in Stanislavski's theory. The actor in realising the superobjective retains his social function: 'If the actor understands the superobjective he is representing society and stands outside of his character to that extent.'[34] The method of physical action can be seen as a means of concentrating the actor's attention on the superobjective from the start of rehearsals. Through the playing of small, outward actions, he gradually builds up at one and the same time the unbroken line of the inner and outward action.

Brecht does not rule out empathy completely. He accepts it at a certain point of rehearsals. He begins, however, from the assumption that actors are able to create 'rounded, contradictory, real human beings',[35] and then goes on to exploit the discrepancy between the character created and the one who creates. He uses physical action not simply 'to build up a role realistically', but 'to become the chief focus of the role's orientation, mainly in the form of a plot'.[36] Brecht stipulates:

> I need an actor who can completely empathize and absolutely transform himself into the character. This, indeed, is what Stanislavski holds to be the first goal of his System. But at the same time and before all else I need an actor who can stand away from his character and criticize it as a representative of society.[37]

The performer has a double nature: it is a matter of balance between them. Brecht's actor retains his own face, as did the witness demonstrating the accident, and holds up beside it the mask of his role. It is a mask which can be picked up and put down as the exigencies of the plot dictate. Stanislavski never asks his actor to erase his own face when depicting that of his character. This is impossible and to attempt it is to violate the actor's nature. He does not become the character; he remains himself, but assembles those parts of himself that most resemble the character. The face remains his own, but gives expression to the joys and fears of the face the author has looked closely into.

NOTES

1. C. Stanislavski, *An Actor Prepares*, trans. E. R. Hapgood (New York: Theatre Arts, 1936), p. 14.
2. Bertolt Brecht, *The Messingkauf Dialogues*, trans. John Willett (London: Eyre Methuen, 1965), pp. 11–12.
3. Edward Bond, *The Fool and We Come to the River* (London: Eyre Methuen, 1976), p. 73.
4. John Willett and Ralph Manheim (eds), *Brecht Poems* (London: Eyre Methuen, 1976), part two, pp. 176–9. See also 'The Street Scene: A Basic Model for an Epic Theatre', *Brecht on Theatre*, ed. and trans. John Willett (London: Eyre Methuen, 1964), pp. 121–9.
5. Bertolt Brecht, 'Notes on Stanislavski', *Tulane Drama Review*, 9, 2 (Winter 1964), 165. (This material is taken from volume 7 of Brecht's *Schriften zum Theater*, Frankfurt, 1963–4, pp. 187–219.)
6. *Brecht Poems*, part two, p. 177.
7. *Ibid.*
8. Willett (ed.), *Brecht on Theatre*, p. 124.
9. 'The Playwright's Song', *Brecht Poems*, part two, p. 258.
10. 'Speech to Danish Working-Class Actors on the Art of Observation', *Brecht Poems*, part two, p. 234.
11. Willett (ed.), *Brecht on Theatre*, p. 122.
12. 'The Theatre, Home of Dreams', *Brecht Poems*, part three, p. 340.
13. Stanislavski deals in detail with the actor's sense of 'I am' in a role and 'the present tense of the play' in *Creating a Role*, trans. E. R. Hapgood (London: Geoffrey Bles, 1963), ch. 1.
14. See *Brecht on Theatre*, p. 129 and p. 137, for the acting exercise, 'memorizing first impressions of a part'. The retention of first impressions helps the actor to perform in such a way 'that his acting allows the other possibilities to be inferred and only represents one of the possible variants'. See also 'Notes on Stanislavski', p. 159 for looking for the contradictions in a character.
15. 'Portrayal of Past and Present in One', *Brecht Poems*, part two, p. 307.
16. *Ibid.*
17. See 'Speech to Danish Working-Class Actors on the Art of Observation', *Brecht Poems*, part two, p. 235.
18. 'On Everyday Theatre', *Brecht Poems*, part two, p. 177.
19. *The Messingkauf Dialogues*, p. 104.
20. *Ibid.*
21. *An Actor Prepares*, p. 167.
22. P. V. Simonov, 'The Method of K. S. Stanislavski and the Physiology of Emotions', *Stanislavski Today*, comp., ed. and trans. S. Moore (New York: American Center for Stanislavski Theatre Art, 1973), p. 42.
23. 'Notes on Stanislavski', p. 158.
24. *Brecht on Theatre*, p. 125.

25. C. Stanislavski, *Building a Character*, trans. E. R. Hapgood (London: Methuen, 1968).

26. 'On Everyday Theatre', *Brecht Poems*, part two, p. 179.

27. *Ibid.*

28. 'Notes on Stanislavski', p. 160.

29. See particularly *Creating a Role*, ch. 8.

30. C. Stanislavski, *My Life in Art*, trans. J. J. Robbins (New York: Theatre Arts, 1956), p. 333.

31. *Creating a Role*, pp. 227–8. For further information on the method of physical action see *Stanislavski Today*.

32. *Creating a Role*, p. 227.

33. 'Notes on Stanislavski', p. 164.

34. *Ibid.*

35. *Ibid.*

36. *Ibid.*, p. 165.

37. *Ibid.*, p. 166.

Index

.C2